SINGER'S CIRCLE

Jeff Houlahan

SINGER'S CIRCLE

HISTRIA
FICTION

Histria Fiction

Las Vegas ◊ Chicago ◊ Palm Beach

Published in the United States of America by
Histria Books
7181 N. Hualapai Way, Ste. 130-86
Las Vegas, NV 89166 USA
HistriaBooks.com

Histria Fiction is an imprint of Histria Books. Titles published under the imprints of Histria Books are distributed worldwide. We appreciate your support of copyright by purchasing an authorized edition of this book and for respecting intellectual property laws by not reproducing, scanning, or otherwise distributing any part of it by any means without permission. You are supporting authors and enabling Histria Books to continue publishing books for everyone.

Certain characters in this work are historical figures, and certain events portrayed did take place. However, this is a work of fiction. Names, characters, places, and incidents are either the product of the author's imagination or are used fictitiously. Any resemblance to actual persons, living or dead, is entirely coincidental.

First Edition

Library of Congress Control Number: 2024948859

ISBN 978-1-59211-562-4 (softbound)
ISBN 978-1-59211-569-3 (eBook)

This book is dedicated to the real Peter Singer.

The Peter Singer character in Singer's Circle grapples with the moral problem

that the real Peter Singer raised. If you want to know more about Peter Singer's

*work read Famine, Affluence and Morality or go to **www.thelifeyoucansave.org**.*

and

To Kim, always.

BOOK 1

Chapter 1

Singer never forgot the moment the first message arrived in the last year that he received emails.

Pete Singer could tell by the rhythm of the approaching footsteps that something was wrong. The usual cadence was even and deliberate, but this was faster, erratic, long urgent strides punctuated by several running steps that landed like open-faced slaps on the pebbled concrete.

Singer let his eyes drift closed and took a long breath before turning as one of his guys appeared around the corner. His workstation pinged and it stopped him just long enough to see the subject line on the incoming message—*The Living List*—before Singer turned back to the man jogging towards him.

"Pete? We got a problem in seventeen! The new guy got himself all locked up."

Singer reached behind without looking, grabbed his vest, slipped it on and flattened the Velcro across his chest with a single sweep of one hand. He gestured at the other man's vest, dangling open.

"Tighten up, Eggo. Martin sees that and you'll make the list. What section again?"

The other man flushed and flattened the Velcro edges in an uneven fold across his belly.

"Sorry, Pete. It gets hot back there…he's in seventeen."

"Shit. Appliances? What's he doing in appliances!? Wasn't today his first day?"

Singer shook his head and stepped from his station into the wide central aisle that bisected the massive warehouse. Both men paused to let two of the orange, floor-level robots glide by, then stepped into the pedestrian lane. The corridor rolled out to the back of the warehouse and the shelves extended to the fifty-foot-high ceiling of corrugated metal panels. A package slid by on rollers, clattered in two spots then shuddered where something needed to be oiled or balanced. Singer avoided looking down to the end of the warehouse. It always left him slightly unnerved. The shelves on opposite sides of the warehouse aisle appeared to rise from the floor in the distance, a merged strand of latticed grey metal, annealing as they spooled from the far wall as if the harsh, brittle overhead fluorescent lighting was required to break the bonds linking one shelf to another so that the rolling filament of mass-produced aluminum could part, allowing space for the countercurrent flow of conveyor belts, orange floor-robots and self-driving forklifts; all directed by a vast network of barcode synapses ensuring that every single essential element was stored, packaged and moved as intended.

And him. The space that was left for Singer and the other 'associates' was an afterthought.

Singer slowed a little so Diego 'Eggo' Valdez could find the right sub-artery off the main corridor and then trailed him into a slightly dimmer aisle between two high shelves before falling in step beside him. The driver had stepped down from his seat and was standing with another man looking at the lift as if inspecting a dead animal at the side of the road.

Singer took a couple of long strides ahead of Valdez to the front of the 'lift' for a better look. One of the forks had punched through the refrigerator crate and was buried to what would have been the first knuckle if it was a finger rather than a hard metal alloy already scraped nearly paint-bare. Singer could see what had happened. The driver had wedged himself into a spot with almost no room to move forward or backward and then made a panic move—jumping the lift forward, thinking he would shove the refrigerator to the side. But with no room to move, the left fork had driven through the outer packing and almost certainly damaged the product beneath. Singer turned back to the other men, looking at Valdez first.

"Thanks, Eggo, I'm good now. You better get back. Lisa will be wondering what happened to you."

Singer turned to the other two without waiting for a response. He didn't recognize the man slouched beside the driver but nodded at him.

"Picker or packer?"

The man, short but muscled beneath his safety vest, grinned without straightening from where he leaned against a shelf frame.

"Picker, boss man."

Singer allowed himself an answering smile.

"You better get back to it too."

The guy took a moment, looking at Singer the whole while before he pushed off and turned to the driver, cadaverous, with long, light, almost blonde hair straggling out from beneath a stained, misshapen Atlanta Braves ball cap.

"Come see me later, R-man."

He nodded at the forklift.

"Tough luck."

He looked at Singer again before he walked by. Singer shuffled a little to one side to avoid brushing shoulders. He watched the man walk away then turned back to the driver.

"What happened?"

The driver looked up from the floor and Singer noticed again the faint network of red lines scalpelled into the whites of his eyes and the pocked scars tracing his chin and cheeks, clearly visible beneath the patchwork of moustache and goatee that hung somewhere between deliberate and indifferent.

The man kicked at the machine with a work boot.

"This thing's fucked. I put it in reverse, touched the gas and it jumped forward like something bit it."

Singer paused, keeping his face still.

"Ray. It's Ray, right?"

The other man shook his head.

"Raymond."

"Okay, Raymond. I told you this morning…if you run into something that you're not sure about…just give me a call. I'll come and give you a hand. It's your fi…"

The other man kicked at the machine again.

"It wasn't a tight spot. I knew exactly what the fuck I was doing. I've done this a hundred times. I'm telling you it's the fucking machine. It's fucked up."

Singer nodded, looked away annoyed, his gaze rolling across the expanse of stacked cardboard—stoves, refrigerators, washer/dryers, freezers - before coming back to the other man's face, reasonably certain that he wasn't letting it show on his face.

"You didn't hear the buzzer?"

The other man reddened, and his eyes narrowed slightly.

"What buzzer?"

"All the lifts are equipped with pressure sensors, specifically designed to avoid this kind of incident. Lets you know if you're going to puncture a package."

Raymond shook his head.

"There was no buzzer. Wouldn't need a buzzer if this machine wasn't fucked."

"Raymond. It's possible there was a malfunction…and we'll have a look at that. But these machines are pretty reliable."

Singer stepped away, walked around the forklift, then crouched to get a better view of the way the wheels were angled and where the forks had collided with the appliance. He came back around the vehicle, stopped in front of the driver, then tilted his head to look directly at him. The other man stared down, challenging.

"Look, Raymond, I'm not trying to drop you in it, but it's pretty clear to me what happened here. You got yourself in a tight spot, got locked up, couldn't get out and you panicked a little; went a little heavy when you needed to feather. It happens. It's happened to all of us. But the key is you need to be able to ask for help…

Raymond's face flushed, the damaged skin beneath his beard showing purple, and he reached past Singer, striking at the machine, shifting at the last second to punch the padded leather seat rather than the hard metal side.

"It's the fucking machine—it's fucked!"

Singer held up his hands as if showing they were empty.

"Okay Raymond, we'll check the lift for problems—we always do after an incident. But…and I'm not even talking about this now…if you get yourself in a spot and you're not sure, just give a shout. I don't need you guys to be perfect, but I do need you to know your limits. Okay?"

When he spoke, the driver's voice was low and deliberate, each syllable rising and falling along a serrated edge between clenched teeth.

"I didn't – get – in – a – spot."

Singer looked from the man's face down to his fists clenched like stones, then back up to his face, narrow, pinched, his eyes pulled in tight around the beveled bridge of his nose as if whatever had turned his hands from supple flesh to coiled bone had flowed down from his face and skull then turned hard and obdurate when it had travelled as far as it could. Singer felt something tighten and catch in his lower back and slid his right foot back a little, settling his weight over his hips.

"Raymond? Ray? I think it's probably a good time for a break. We can talk about this later. You head to the break room, grab a water or something. Alright?"

There was a moment when Singer wasn't sure what would happen, whether the tell at the corner of the driver's eye and above one side of his mouth would give and whatever was resting right at the lip, pushing up hard against the nasal and the lacrimal and the palatine, would split his skull wide open and spill out all over the concrete floor and metal shelving. But somehow the man pulled it back, sucked things back into some interior space, the skin around his eyes and mouth loosening so that each molecule no longer strained against every holding bond and his face relaxed into recognizable curves and folds. But the nod was forced, the nerves connecting thoughts to physical action still taut and erratic.

"Sure."

He spun on his heel and walked away, the movement of his arms and legs still unsynchronized as if under-rehearsed for the performance.

Singer stepped around to where the fork had entered the package, crouched down and closed his eyes, running his hand along the cold metal sheath of iron until he stopped up against the shredded cardboard. Once, twice and a third time, then he opened his eyes. It was there. How the fork had entered and how it would come out.

It reminded him of the summer he had worked as an undergraduate field assistant for a Ph.D. student doing work on the feeding ecology of songbirds. Their days had started well before the sun came up, threading the mist nets into place over the anchored wooden poles, the mesh fine like spun mercury so that in the full light of day it was only visible as a variegated spark and sizzle and in the dim light of dawn was not visible at all. The birds would spin in, sensing the net at the last moment, but only able to tilt and veer so that when they collided with the net, they became even more tangled and enmeshed than if they had flown in perpendicular to the mesh. It had been his job to remove the birds from the net and place them in soft cloth bags to be weighed and tagged.

There had been three of them, research assistants. On the first day, the graduate student had them stand with their hands outstretched so she could inspect them. When she had seen Singer's thick, blunt fingers, the pinky on his left hand standing out at an odd angle where he had caught it in a running back's facemask during a tackle, she had assigned him a spot away from the net, weighing the bags and filling in the data forms. She hadn't explained, but he understood. His hands were too thick and clumsy for the delicate work of removing the tiny birds from the net—sparrows, savannah, swamp and field, wrens, winter and house and most often of all, chickadees. Birds died in the net. Not often, but sometimes. Either because they injured themselves in the collision or were injured in the attempt to remove them. Or because it took so long to work them free that they died from the sheer stress of the experience. And Singer didn't have the artist's hands required for the job.

But there was a morning when he was the only research assistant. He never found out why the others had missed that day, whether it had been arranged or unexpected, but there had been no choice except to put him on the net. He and the graduate student had been required to do all the tasks: remove the birds, bag them, tag them, weigh them, record the data and release them. It had been unexpected and revelatory.

Singer had been able to tell as he approached the net, even in the dimmest light of dawn, how the bird had entered. The speed and the angle. He could see how the collision had bent and refracted its flight as water contorts light, the subtle pivot as first one covert then another caught and broke loose, the half or quarter revolution in deceleration and the final stuttering bourree as the bird shuddered to a stop. The path was etched in his mind like the streaked lines on a sunlit window after being wiped with a moist cloth. When he reached in and grasped the struggling bird, it would calm in his hand and the flight path would rise in stark relief. As if, in holding the bird, the residual muscle memory of its last moments of flight was conveyed to Singer and he could backtrack along the entry path with two or three deft hand motions so that the bird came free like a berry from a bush. To an observer, it appeared that Singer did little more than wave his hand over the net and the bird lay free in his palm. Singer had been the 'net man' for the rest of the summer.

It was the same with the machines, even though inanimate. He could see and sense how the machine had arrived where it was and what he needed to do to release it. He took a few seconds to examine the wheels and the angle of the lift, slipped up into the seat, pressed the starter button and waited for the motor to settle. The first grind as the fork released from the package told Singer that the damage would not be minor, the refrigerator was likely a write-off. Then with two easy, smooth motions on the wheel, a quick gear change and a last subtle spin of the wheel, the lift was no longer wedged in the aisle. Only then, Singer noticed that Raymond was still standing at the end of the aisle, but he stepped away as Singer motored out to the end of the aisle, shut down the lift and jumped down from the seat.

Singer reached up to fiddle with something on the dashboard of the lift, stalling so that Raymond could get well ahead of him and they wouldn't have to walk together. But he needn't have worried; the other man strode, hard and fast towards the far end of the hanger-style warehouse.

Even from a couple of hundred yards away, Singer recognized the easy bounce and slouch of his friend coming the other way. Brian Ferris paused as he passed the driver, turning to watch him before he continued towards Singer. The two men slowed and stopped. Ferris held out a fist that Singer bumped.

"How things going, buddy?"

Ferris tossed his thumb behind without looking.

"What was that all about?"

Singer shrugged.

"New guy. Shish kebabbed a fridge in seventeen."

"A fridge? He couldn't start with a pallet of Corn Flakes? Got to go right to the big stuff? Fuckin' newbies."

Singer nodded and made a face.

"And the lift was the problem."

Ferris threw his hands up in the air, the motion lifted one side of his safety vest off his shoulder so that he had to grab it to keep it on.

"Not one of those fucking guys. Can't we just fire him now?"

Singer pointed at his friend's vest.

"You're worse than any of them—anybody needs to get fired…"

Ferris stepped back as if he had been pushed.

"Hey! Hey! Hey! Just 'cause you got the milky white skin that the bossman love, don't mean you the boss a' me."

Singer rolled his eyes and shook his head.

"How did you get this job? No way a friggin' cement-head like you gets this kind of work without a leg up."

Ferris raised his finger.

"Don't you talk to me about dumb, Tin Man. It ain't me that's got a machine sitting idle and a guy sulking in the break room."

"Scarecrow, dumbass. Tin Man needed a heart."

Ferris laughed and tapped Singer on the cheek.

"Brain, heart, whatever—you didn't get a full share buddy. If I wasn't watching out for you, you'd be pickin' and packin'. All I know is that my belts are running smooth as cream. And you? You're trying to keep some asshole from bringing the roof down."

It was true. Brian had put a good word in for him eleven years ago, just after Cheryl had got pregnant. It had worked out for him, moving up from low-level picking to heavy machine supervisor. Brian had followed a similar path and now supervised the conveyor belt day shift. Ferris pulled out his phone took a quick look then tapped him on the shoulder.

"I better get moving, two more minutes and they'll be talking about docking pay."

They bumped fists again and started away in different directions, but Singer stopped at his friend's voice.

"Tin Man! You gonna be there tonight?"

Singer shouted over his shoulder.

"Wouldn't miss it."

Chapter 2

Singer sat on the top step of the deck watching the boys play in the backyard. The early morning chill was already starting to fade, shouldered out by the sun two fingers above the eastern horizon. Tommie, only six but already almost as tall as Dougie, struggled frantically to squirm out of his older brother's grasp and gave a final lunge that tumbled both boys to the ground. Dougie let go so he could use both arms to break his fall. Laughing, Tommie scrambled to his feet and darted to the base of the old maple growing almost in the center of their lawn then sidled around to keep the trunk between him and his older brother.

He would need to rake soon. The first few leaves were already dappling the yard, untethered, unmoored. But the tree was already almost bare—the leaves in the branches, even at the peak of spring, were as sparse and scattered as a pinch of salt tossed for luck. Singer felt his wife's hands on his shoulders and reached up to place his right hand over hers without looking back.

"Aren't you supposed to be sleeping in, ninja girl?"

"I tried. But once World War III broke out in our backyard, I decided I might as well get up."

The pressure on his shoulders increased then released as she nestled herself in behind him, both of her legs edging out around his, her arms stretched over his shoulders and draped across his chest, her cheek tucked in alongside his neck so that he could feel her breath on his ear. Even now, after eleven years, the warm pressure of her belly and breasts against his bare back could work on him. She reached down, tapped him with one finger and laughed.

"I knew it. That's all it takes? Settle down, big boy, now is not the time."

Singer slapped her leg.

"Hey, I was just sitting here minding my own business. I am not to blame on this one."

She chuckled in his ear.

"You getting tired of minding your own business, Petey? Want your girl Cheryl to mind a little of it?"

Singer reached behind with both hands, grabbed her butt and jerked her forward so that she was wedged in tight against him and held her there for a moment. She made a quiet sound deep in her throat and squeezed with both arms, her palms flat against his chest. Singer let go.

"Really? That's all it takes, ninja girl?"

She slapped him lightly on his shoulder and leaned into his ear.

"Let's find a little time tonight once the boys are in bed."

He nodded without looking around.

"Look at them… Another year, maybe two, Tommie's going to be taller than Dougie."

"Would you stop calling him Dougie."

Singer shook his head.

"Sorry, Cher, I'm not calling him Douglas. There are a lot of things that can get you beat up in a schoolyard, and calling yourself Douglas is definitely one of them."

"Stop being a jerk about this, hon. What's the point of naming him Douglas if everybody's going to call him Dougie."

Singer shrugged.

"Hey, look. I wanted to call him Jack. Douglas was your idea."

She mumbled something that he couldn't hear and he leaned forward so that her mouth wasn't muffled up against his neck.

"What?"

"I said, just be glad that Mahatma Gandhi wasn't my hero."

Singer shook his head.

"There are lines in the sand, girl. There is no chance in the world that I was ever going to be at a ballgame shouting 'Good eye, Mahatma, good eye!' Don't kid yourself."

She reached down and flicked him again with one finger.

"Don't YOU kid yourself. You'd have named him Jesus Hitler if I'd asked you right."

Singer shook his head and let his chin drop to his chest.

"Really? You have so little respect. You think I'm that easily manipulated?"

He could feel her smiling against the back of his neck. He cocked his head to the right as if thinking.

"Although…I guess if we pronounced Jesus the way the Mexicans do and spelled Hitler with a 'J'…"

She tapped him on the shoulder and pointed across the yard.

"You see what your crazy kids are doing?"

Both boys had managed to scramble up to the first branch above the ground and were pulling themselves higher into the tree, Tommie already two branches ahead of Dougie.

Singer shook his head in wonder.

"How did they get up there? They couldn't even reach the branch when we moved in?"

She slapped him lightly on top of his head.

"That was a year ago, dummy! Haven't you been paying attention? They both eat like they're about to hibernate."

She pushed off his shoulders to her feet.

"You want a coffee?"

He nodded, still watching his boys.

"Sure."

His wife looked over her shoulder as she pulled the screen door open.

"Petey? Get them down out of the tree now, okay? It's not safe."

They seemed almost perfectly synchronized so that Singer could never be sure which sound had contributed which note to the chord—the thin squeal of the door hinges still hanging in the air above the snapped clap of door against frame, the sharp crack of the branch as Tommie gripped it and released his weight from the branch beneath on which he stood, and the pinched yelp that Dougie made before his throat clutched shut around the air in his chest.

The only sound from Tommie was created when his body collided with the ground, air crushed and compressed as the space between Tommie's skin, blood, bone, viscera and the ground—packed hard and tight by the weight of a trillion air molecules stacked one upon the other for 10,000 meters into the sky - diminished to nothing and the air that had sat in that space, unsuspecting, dormant, resting, was expelled and hurtled across the yard in a single, brittle wave. But even as the wave struck Singer's ear and then rolled by and beyond, a faint ringing lingered like the sound of a distant struck bell.

Tommie's face was pale but peaceful, as if all the force of the impact had been absorbed and contained by the sound, leaving no residual effect in the colliding bodies—Tommie's or the ground. Cheryl pushed Singer aside and knelt beside her son, looking back to point up into the tree before turning back to their son.

"Get Dougie down."

Singer looked up. His eldest son was still hugging the trunk at the place he had been when Tommie fell past. He had pulled himself tight against the tree and clung to it now, his cheek pressed up hard against the rough bark and his eyes closed.

"Dougie?"

Singer had meant to speak softly, but it had come out sharp, harder than he had intended. He tried again, this time getting it right. But there was no response from his son other than a string of choked mewling noises. Singer pulled himself into the tree and clambered higher until he was able to find a spot just beneath where his son stood. Singer reached out, but Dougie flinched at the contact and clutched the tree more closely. Singer edged up higher onto a thick stub, once a branch but now trimmed or broken, and was able to pull in tight against his son's body then whisper in his ear.

"It's okay, buddy. You're alright. But it's time to come down. We have to climb down."

For the first time, his son acknowledged his father, but Singer couldn't tell if he shook or nodded his head.

"Okay Dougie, you're going to let go of the tree a little. Just enough so you can move. Then you're going to step down onto the branch just below you. I'm going to have a hold on you. Don't worry, buddy. I won't let go."

Singer felt his son's grip loosen on the tree, then shifted his weight so he could lower himself to the next branch. Together, they inched down the tree, one slow step at a time—Singer holding his son's arms and shoulders at each step, the boy's body rippling like water in a struck cup - until they reached the lowest branch and Singer could lower Dougie to the ground.

His wife was still crouched over Tommie.

"How is he?"

She shook her head.

"He's breathing but unconscious. There's a knot on his head, it's swelling."

Singer turned to his son.

"You stay with Mommy, I'm calling an ambulance."

His wife looked up at him, already shaking her head.

'No, it's Saturday morning. They'll be short-staffed—it could take a while. And Vern's on Saturday mornings—I don't want Dougie riding with Vern."

She turned back to her youngest son, touching a spot behind his ear then made a noise that trailed out through her nose.

"It's bigger. Take Dougie over to Mrs. Carmichael's, she'll watch him while we're at the hospital, then get my blue sweatpants and a sweater. I'll meet you at the car.

"What sweater…"

She turned on him, her eyes narrowed.

"Just get me a fucking sweater, Pete. Any fucking sweater."

***

"Take Churchill, Petey, there'll be less traffic this morning."

The words came out in two or three segments as if she had to catch her breath between phrases. In the rearview, Singer could see that she had pulled the green sweatshirt over the plain white T that she had worn to bed—his—and was trying to wriggle the sweatpants up over her hips without removing Tommie's head from her lap.

"How's he doing?"

He knew she was aware he was watching her in the rearview, but she didn't look up to meet his eye, wrenching at the waistband with one hand while she steadied her son's head with the other.

"He's breathing."

Singer had a powerful urge to pull over and close his eyes, as if with eyes closed he would be able to speak directly to God in a way that he couldn't as he peered out through the windshield and navigated each bump, turn, traffic sign and signal. But he spoke to him even with his eyes open.

"Anything, God. Whatever you need. I don't know what it is that you need but whatever it is, you tell me. Please tell me, God. Don't make me guess. Just tell me. I can't guess. Please, God."

As they turned into the hospital complex Cheryl pointed over the seat.

"Up there. Take that lane between those two buildings, it'll bring us out right beside the emergency entrance."

Singer pulled up over the NO STOPPING painted on the asphalt in front of the sliding doors, threw the car into park and jumped out. Cheryl had immediately swung her door open, eased her son's head off her lap onto the seat and scrambled out. She was already almost at the door.

"You bring Tommie. I'll make sure we get things going."

He looked at his son, stretched out on the back seat as if placed for viewing, his eyes closed, lids pale, almost translucent, a single blue vein bisecting each, like an accidental scribbling, no sign of damage except for a subtle asynchrony where his left ear tilted away from his head, Singer closed his eyes for a moment trying to create an image, something real that he could speak to but nothing came and he settled for *Please God*. Please, please, please. Then he bent, scooped his son up, one arm beneath his knees and the other cradling his shoulders, feeling the flutter of his son's heart against his own chest, as vague and ephemeral as a whispered prayer.

***

The young doctor held back her blonde ponytail while she leaned over Tommie on the padded table.

"Keep your eyes open, Tommie, I just want to have a look."

She leaned in close then stood up, turned to where they stood but ignored Singer.

"I don't see any sign that anything is happening in his brain, Cheryl. They're a little dilated but he just fell out of a tree—that would make anybody's pupils pop a little. I don't see any asymmetry. Have a look."

The doctor stepped back so Singer's wife could step in. Cheryl leaned over her son, pushing his hair back from his forehead, though there was no need, before she looked into his eyes.

"How are you feeling, buddy?"

"Can we go home, Mommy?"

Cheryl didn't speak for a second, staring down into her son's eyes before she straightened.

"It won't be long, Tommie, we just have to talk to Doctor Merrithew for a minute. Okay?"

His jaw set stubbornly

"I want to go home."

But Cheryl had already turned to the doctor.

"I don't see anything either."

The doctor nodded, stepped back slightly so she could look at both of them as she spoke.

"I'm not seeing any warning signs. He seems bright, no signs of drowsiness. He's not saying he has any ringing. He's not even complaining about a headache. His pupils look fine, no sign that there's any brain swelling."

She paused but then shrugged.

"But you know better than anybody, Cheryl…that doesn't mean Tommie hasn't had a concussion. In fact, he almost certainly has—he was unconscious for thirty-five minutes. But it might be mild and have no lingering effects…or you could start to see signs of something more serious. You'll want to keep an eye on him."

Merrithew paused for a moment, glanced at Singer then held Cheryl's eye.

"I don't need to tell you, Cheryl, you've given this speech a hundred times. If he seems unusually drowsy, if he complains about being dizzy, if he feels nauseated or starts to mention ringing in his ears, bring him back in. On the bright side, it's early in the day. If you don't see any signs between now and Tommie's bedtime, I don't think it will be necessary to wake him during the night to make sure he's okay."

When she was done, she stepped in close and the two women hugged for several seconds. When Cheryl stepped back her eyes were moist.

"Thanks so much, Judy. You don't know how much this means to me. To us."

The doctor waved her hand and turned to Tommie.

"You can go now, young man. But stay out of tall trees."

Tommie looked at her, frowned and shook his head before he slipped off the table and moved over beside his dad. Merrithew grinned and looked at Cheryl, then Singer, and shrugged.

"He's your problem now."

The doctor started to turn away.

"My next shift's Tuesday evening, Cheryl. You on?"

Singer's wife nodded.

"I'm evenings all week, Judy. See you then."

They drove home, saying little, Singer driving single-handed so he could hold his wife's hand across the seat.

***

When Singer came into their bedroom she was sitting on the edge of their bed, her feet flat on the floor, staring straight ahead at the window looking out over the backyard and the big old maple. The tears rolled down her face in two parallel streams, coursing past the hollows on both sides of her nose, past the corners of her mouth, some following the curve of her chin and throat to gather in the faint lines of her neck, and others collecting in the cleft before falling to darken the front of her shirt. Her face bent and shaped by what she was feeling so that her tears followed a strange and contorted topography.

It had startled Singer the first time he had seen his wife cry, the way the planes of her face and the plates beneath slid, shifted and held, like the motion was tectonic rather than muscular, but also the stillness, how once the shift occurred, she remained motionless, her limbs, her body, her face, her eyes, as if, once contorted, she was spasm-frozen unable to move out from under the emotion that held her in place. All that moved were the tears—emerging, flowing, gathering and falling…over and over again.

Singer sat beside her on the bed, the mattress giving slightly so that her body had to lean into his and she let it. He put his arm around her.

"He's okay. He's going to be fine."

He expected her voice to be choked or thick when she spoke but it wasn't.

"Jennifer's husband runs a tree removal business. He's coming over tomorrow morning to take it down."

"Tomorrow? Tomorrow's Sunday."

"It'll cost an extra two hundred dollars but I told him it wasn't a problem."

Singer hesitated then nodded.

"Okay."

She spoke to him without turning to face him.

"Peter, can we make love?"

She turned to him then.

"I don't want to use my diaphragm."

He cocked his head and looked at her.

"Are you sure?"

She nodded.

***

She didn't always come but she had this time. Though he had felt her tears on his shoulders in the moments before. Afterward, they lay together holding each other for several minutes. Then she smiled, kissed him on the forehead and turned away to set her alarm.

"I'm going to wake Tommie at 1 AM. Will you be alright? I can sleep downstairs."

He smiled and shook his head.

"I'll come with you."

***

Cheryl fell asleep quickly and Singer lay beside her in the gloom, not quite full dark, staring at the ceiling, still able to make out the swirls and curlicued stucco that had been applied by the previous owners. Finally, convinced that he wouldn't sleep, he slipped off his side of the bed, crept to the door and walked down the hall to the boy's room. In a couple of years, they would need their own rooms but for now they preferred to share. He stood looking in at them, their smooth, steady breathing almost synchronized but not quite—Tommie's deeper and a little faster, Dougie's steady and even, so that they slipped further and further out of sync before starting to close back in and then, for just a second, there was the sound of only one boy as if each was breathing for the other. Then Tommie edged out in front again and began to pull away. He listened for several cycles before he turned away and padded downstairs.

The den was dark but there was enough light from the street that he could pick his way across the room to his laptop. His Gmail was open and Singer noticed that the top message wasn't greyed—was new.

The Living List—it was an odd subject line and an odd font—all lowercase except for the first letter of each word, but thick and blocky. Now there was a second email, *The Passed List*, same odd font, also flagged urgent, separated from the first by a reminder from Brian of Sunday night's pick-up hockey and an update on the football pool standings. The second had arrived while Singer had been at the hospital with Tommie—his phone must have 'buzzed' him, but he hadn't noticed. The time stamp on *The Passed List* email was exactly twenty-four hours after the time stamp on *The Living List*.

Singer selected *The Living List* and his finger hovered over the delete button for several seconds before sliding away to open the email. It was a list of names, nothing more, black on white as stark and exposed as peppered flour.

The memory came to Singer unbidden, the door of the screened-in porch that hung from the front of his grandfather's farmhouse creaking closed behind him before slamming shut, the first hard clack echoed twice by softer collisions as the door bounced to a stop. Two metal wash basins filled almost to the brim with cold well water, chilled by an eighty-foot descent into clenched dark soil and stone and hauled up by hand before the sun had done more than grey the eastern horizon. An aluminum hand ladle floated in the nearby basin, just beneath the surface of the water so that the tip of the handle broke the surface as if reaching for air. Tacked to the ceiling directly in front of him and falling almost to eye-level, the yellowed coil of flypaper speckled with a spray of black bodies, most inert, still as letters on a page, but a few rasping to life to hum and burr against the close summer air before giving in to the gummed mucilage that bound them tight as any spike to wood.

He stared at the list, two or three dozen names, one set exactly beneath the other like rungs on a ladder, perfectly aligned as if the first letter of each name wedged up tight against an invisible side rail on one side and the last letter of the last name stopped against the other, and each rung captured the same eighteen-character span. But the last name on the page was partially obscured so Singer knew that the names extended beyond what he could see. He swiped down through the list and there were hundreds of names, maybe several thousand. It was dizzying to scroll through them, the letters blurring into a single grey column that rushed past as if the names had gathered then poured across a hard edge and tumbled from the sky in an ordered, even flow so that Singer expected, as he approached the bottom of the message, that the names would splash and puddle, accumulate in a scrambled stack of snapped and shattered letters - serifed pieces, broken beaks and bowls, splintered spurs, shoulder separated from tail and crossbar so shapes that held sound and meaning would be left as unbound and inchoate as blown ash. But the names simply slammed to a halt—constrained by an alphabet that ended at Z.

Innocent Zziwa

Singer scrolled back to the top

Aisha Amari

Kaikara Asiimwe

Bisan Atiyeh

Grace Bakakrishnan

There were at least ten more rows. Each of the names was underlined and blued, linked to something more. Singer again poised over the first name on the list then pulled away. He scrolled to the bottom, and again, he held for several seconds before pulling away. Then he closed the email, hit delete and did the same to the email titled *The Passed List*. He closed the lid on his laptop and went back to bed.

***

The next email arrived on Sunday afternoon while Singer was tracking his fantasy league players. *The Living List*. The list was as long, although he didn't recognize the names. Surely, some could have been the same, he wouldn't have known for sure—there were too many names—but he was almost certain that the first few names were different…and Innocent Zziwe was gone. He closed and deleted but something about doing it unsettled him, left him wanting to drag it back into his mailbox. But he didn't.

The Passed List arrived twenty-four hours later while he was standing at his workstation but as with the first, he deleted it unopened.

***

The third *Living List* email arrived Tuesday evening. He felt it against his leg, paused to lean the rake against his shoulder, pulled his phone from his pocket, saw the subject line and dismissed the notification. Singer stood for a moment looking across the lawn, the spots where the leaves had been scraped clean exposing the grass beneath, still mostly green but beginning to brown. He looked over to where Cheryl knelt, examining a rose bush in the far corner of her garden. She pulled at first one branch, then another, her brow furrowed in concentration, until she found the one she wanted, clipped then tossed it onto a small but growing pile beside her. She sensed him watching and looked over. He pushed the phone back into his pocket and nodded at the bush.

"How's it going?"

Cheryl nodded.

"I think I'm getting the hang of this."

"Whatever you did last year worked."

Cheryl nodded again.

"Yeah. But I'm not sure exactly what I did."

She looked down at her watch.

"It's a school night, Dougie should be home by now. Do you mind tracking him down?"

"Sure, babe, give me five minutes to get this last little piece done, then I'll haul him back."

***

Singer sat staring at the subject line. *The Living List.* He heard Cheryl come to the door and could tell she was looking in at him, but he didn't look away from the screen.

"The boys are down, Pete. But they want a story, and I won't do."

Singer made a noncommittal noise in his throat but kept looking at the screen. His wife took a step into the room.

"What is it, hon?"

He shook his head.

"I don't know, Cher, I keep getting these emails. Strange. Just a list of names."

He tapped a key, opened the email and shifted his chair back a little so she could stand beside him.

"Look. Just one name after the other."

His wife put a hand on his shoulder and leaned in to see the screen before pulling back.

"Don't click on a name—who knows what you'll be opening?"

"I know, Cheryl. Any more email tips for me? I'm really not familiar with the whole concept of sending messages through a wire."

"Don't get pissed, Pete, I was just saying…"

Singer sighed and sat back in his chair so that his head rested against her belly, not as flat and hard as when they had first met but it still felt good. He reached behind without looking and linked his fingers behind her back, pulling her in a little closer.

"I know, Cher…it's just bugging me. They keep coming. And it doesn't feel like they're going to stop."

"What do you mean?"

He shrugged against her.

"I don't even really know what I mean. I'm not sure why I even said that…except that it feels like they aren't going to stop."

His wife leaned down so her cheek was next to his and her chin was resting on his shoulder.

"You could always open one somewhere else—work? Or the library?"

Singer chuckled.

"Aren't you the good neighbor—screw up somebody else's machine."

His wife tapped his cheek.

"You know what I mean. Those places like your work, they have protection against viruses, they'd be able to handle this."

Singer nodded.

"Yeah. Mostly what they do is prevent you from accessing any of those kinds of links. It probably wouldn't even let me open the link at work."

Cheryl stood up.

"You're probably right. But right now, your boys need a story."

***

Singer sat in the blue glow of the computer screen looking at the list of names.

Their love life had always been pretty good. He knew from a few of the things that the guys said at work that after eleven years it wasn't always like this. Okay, it wasn't like the first year, when all it took was a shared look and a deserted place. But it was still pretty good.

This was something different.

Once Cheryl got it in her head that she wanted another baby, everything ramped up—it had been the same when she had decided that she didn't want Dougie to be an only child. It wasn't as if she turned into a woman on a mission, just mechanically getting the job done. Again, Singer had overheard guys talking about thermometers and calendars and schedules and times of day, but that wasn't Cheryl. With her, there was always something primitive, something that reached back to a time when everything—your life, the lives of your children, the lives of their children—might have depended on this, this moment that brought you together, bound you together, reminded you that you needed each other, that the world was harsh and relentless and alone you would succumb, but together you might be able to eke out the moments that made life worthwhile. Afterward, she slept, spent, emptied, exhausted. Singer usually did, too. But not tonight.

Singer stared at the first name.

Mercy Adan

The cursor poised over the M then clicked. The screen opened and the video took a moment to begin. But he couldn't tell exactly when because at first the picture appeared motionless, resting on the face of the child filling the screen. It was only when he noticed the barely perceptible expansion and contraction of the saliva bubble at one corner of the child's mouth that Singer realized it wasn't a still. The child was too young for Singer to be sure whether it was a boy or a girl. Then the camera pulled away to reveal a ragged grey tunic and a flower woven into her close-cropped hair.

The child's forehead was smooth and dark, rounding in a gentle even curve to the place where her hairline began. Her eyes were closed but one twitched as a fly landed, scuttled a few steps towards the place where moisture gathered at the corner of one eye, then flew away as a hand came into view and brushed it away. The hand, long slim fingers topped incongruously by ragged nails marred by toil or tension, rested for a moment on the child's cheek then traced the shallow curve of the orbital ridge, the gap between skin and bone reduced to a filament by fatigue and hunger. Her face was symmetrical but misaligned somehow. It was the way her skin strained to contain the bones of cheek and chin and eye, the flesh that separated skin from bone, long ago drawn back to the viscera where what was left to fuel the girl's body was most needed.

The camera lens moved like a drawn curtain, away from the child's face to pan the room in which she lay. Two women, one much older than the other, and a man crouched around the child's pallet. Each looked away from the child for a moment as the camera passed, their faces carved from the same stone, eyes large, gleaming at the edges, yellowed by hunger and deprivation, dark, infected and buried at the center, set in faces too meager and shrunken to contain them so that they appeared to bulge beyond the natural boundaries, trying to pull free, escape what they had seen and what they had yet to see. They turned back to watch the child.

The room was dim but not completely dark because the sun leaked through gaps where the scraps of wood and metal didn't meet and Singer could see that the room had no flooring. The dirt was worn bare and brown except where a scrap of rug lay holding three cracked plastic plates, a chipped ceramic mug and a small plastic cup. An overturned crate rested against the back wall, a few feet behind where the three were gathered around the girl. The faint buzz of dissolute flies rose and fell as they resonated alone or in unison.

The camera rested for a moment on the younger of the two women, crouched on her heels, probably the child's mother. A second fly landed on the woman's lower lip and her arm, narrow and fleshless, twitched but then settled, too weak or enervated to respond. The camera panned to the second woman, cross-legged in the dirt, her eyes closed, the forefinger of her left hand scratching repeatedly at a spot on her knee. The camera panned back to the man, also hunkered on his heels, tapping with one finger at a length of dried grass clutched beneath his teeth. Though spare, he carried more flesh than either the child or the two women. Unlike the two women, when the camera panned to him he turned to look, his eyes bleak and angry, the shadows beneath seemed to rise, dark and malignant, formed from something burnt and braziered, something that should have been left as ash and bondless carbon but that managed, by rage and boundless terror, to adhere and creep towards the surface—not to find the light but to smother it. He stared beyond the lens for several seconds to whoever held the camera, held them, pinned them. The image tilted then righted itself as if the person holding the camera had forgotten what they were doing and then recovered. The man stood up suddenly, stepped over the child's body, leaned to push apart the curtains covering the entrance and ducked from the room.

The camera spun 180 degrees to show a woman of indeterminate age holding the phone, her skin worn and lined but it could have been by sun and worry as much as time. Each line was coated in dust and grime and her hair was pulled up beneath a battered ballcap so that only scattered strands pulled free. Her voice sounded harsh and unexpected in the darkened room, though neither of the two women gave notice.

"Peter. Twenty-five dollars can save Mercy's life. Follow the instructions at the end of the video."

The sound of his own name hit like a slap. The camera held for a moment on the woman's face then tilted as she searched for the 'stop recording' button. The screen went dark for several seconds before the screen lit again and three short sentences describing how money could be transferred scrolled by. The instructions scrolled past four times before disappearing. Singer sat bathed in the mix of blue and white light, staring at the names hanging on his screen. Singer deleted the message, shut down the computer and sat in the dark for a long while before heading up to bed.

Chapter 3

Singer hadn't noticed her at first, forfeited to his own thoughts, unable to shake the series of emails that had been arriving each day. First *The Living List*, each with as many names as the last, followed by *The Passed List* on the day following. Without fail. First the one and then the other. For the last three weeks. And since watching the video, he had deleted them all. The first few, as he discovered them, but then waiting for them because they always arrived at the same time—right around 4 PM. In the hour before one arrived he was barely able to concentrate, checking his phone every few minutes, always hoping that this would be the day they stopped. But they didn't stop.

So, he hadn't noticed the woman at first.

She was dark-skinned, middle-aged or maybe older, her hair drawn into long Jamaican braids tinged with grey, her narrow, planed face punctuated by wide round eyes. The woman was unlined in the forehead and cheeks but webbed where her upper and lower lids met and faintly around her mouth. When Singer finally became aware and looked up, she didn't look away, made no pretense of not staring at him, holding his gaze for several long seconds before she rose from her seat, gathered up her coffee and walked over to his table. She pointed at the seat across from him.

"May I?"

Growing up on the prairies, Singer had watched storms roll in. The threat of a gathering storm filled his throat like leavened dread. Singer wanted to refuse her request, but nodded at the chair and she pulled it back to sit across from him.

"My name is Angella, Mr. Singer. It's a pleasure to meet you."

The fingers of the hand she extended across the table were long and slender, though on the back, where the tendons stretched taut against her skin, there were faint white scars as ordered and even as a furrowed field—they looked like they had been made with design and purpose. Her palm was warm and dry. As he returned his hand to his lap, his sleeve caught the coffee cup beside the last scraps of his sandwich and he moved quickly to stop the cup from spilling. The woman's eyes never left his face.

"Do I know you?"

She smiled and shook her head.

"No. As I said, we've never met."

Singer held her gaze for a long moment then let his eyes move around the Tim Horton's, taking in the other patrons, the few scattered around the seated area and the growing line at the counter. Nobody seemed to be watching them.

"Then how do you know my name?"

For the first time since the woman had arrived at Singer's table, she looked away from his face. Not because she was distracted by something else but as if needing a moment with just herself to decide something. She took a breath and looked at him again.

"We've been sending you emails."

"We?"

She tilted her head, puzzled, waiting.

"You said we. Who's we?"

She waved her hand, dismissing the question.

"Fine. I've been sending you emails."

He nodded.

"Okay?"

Singer looked around again but it didn't seem that anybody was observing them. He turned back to the woman but didn't speak and they sat in silence for several seconds before the woman spoke.

"Do you want to know why?"

He shook his head.

She looked puzzled again.

"No?"

Singer shrugged.

"It seems obvious. You want money from me."

The woman looked away again and took a deep breath before answering.

"Well…yes. But are you curious about why? Why you?"

Singer shrugged again.

"I'm guessing that there are lots of people like me, that you send out thousands of these and if you can get a few hits, it's all worth it—you make your money back plus a lot more."

The woman was shaking her head, but Singer pushed away from the table and began to stand. He was already on his feet by the time she had his hand in hers. To reach him, she had been forced to stand and reach across the table, holding herself up with one arm braced against the table so she could grab his hand with the other. His first intention was to pull away, but there was something about the way she held him, barely cradled in her palm, so that there was nothing to pull against, no intent to hold him in place, no will to prevent him from leaving if he really wanted to leave. Her fingers rested lightly against the side of his hand, warm and dry but also extending a faint tremor from her fingers to his, allowing him to feel her fear, her apprehension, her concern. It held him still. Singer took his seat again. He put both hands on the table and the woman allowed both of her hands to rest across his.

"I belong to an organization. W…"

"What organization?"

The woman paused again but this time looked at the ceiling as if searching for an answer in the tiles. She let her eyes come back down and rest on his face.

"How many people do you think die of starvation each year?"

He wanted to shrug but there was something in her face, pulled drawstring-tight, stretching her skin taut across chin, cheek and nose as if grief could pull the water from your body, leaving you wasted, drawn, each layer of skin held together by bonds as fragile as those that cohere a child's blown soap bubble, that wouldn't allow him to dismiss the question. Though he was sure if he had, she would have stood, left and he would never have seen her again.

"I'm not sure."

She nodded, without speaking, at his phone lying face down on the table. He picked it up and tapped out the question before looking up.

"Nine million?"

He looked down again then back up.

"More than three million of them are children."

She made a face.

"Really?"

He nodded at her and turned the screen towards her so she could see the number and she made the face again.

"It's not wrong but they include people who die of 'hunger-related' problems. People who succumb to diseases they would have survived if they weren't suffering so badly from malnutrition. I'm talking about people who die because they have not received enough energy for their bodies to continue to function, people who, when their body reached for another molecule of ATP to power the next contraction of their heart or the next compression of their lungs, it was not there and so, oxygenated blood no longer ran through their arteries and they died, not because they have been weakened by malnutrition and cannot survive a measles infection or a bout of malaria or covid-19 infection. They die because they have been unable to obtain enough food to survive another hour, another minute, another second and they are gone, before our eyes, dusted like seed heads in the breeze."

The words tumbled from her mouth as if they were gravity-impelled, as if she was unable to stop them and that it was only towards the end that the ground levelled out and she was able to bring them to a halt so that they lay scattered and hard on the table between them. She shook her head as if annoyed with herself.

"I'm sorry. That wasn't necessary."

She took a breath and started again, this time slower more measured.

"That number is much smaller than nine million. We don't know how many. But our best estimate is that one to two percent of those deaths are 'true' starvations."

She held Singer's gaze as she spoke.

"All we would need to save that life is to provide enough food to sustain their body. Nothing more. No complex medical procedures, no ongoing service or treatment. Simply, provide the calories required for them to continue to breathe. If we put an apple or a bowl of soup to their mouth, they have another day. So, every day somewhere between two hundred fifty and five hundred people die for the lack of an apple or a bowl of soup."

She paused again, waiting but Singer wasn't sure for what. When he said nothing, she spoke again.

"Any idea how much money it would take to keep them alive?"

Singer shook his head and she nodded.

"As you might guess, deaths by 'true' starvation occur mostly in southeast Asia and Africa. In those places, food is scarce—but by our standards, also cheap. Less than a dollar per day would do it. Say, twenty-five dollars a month."

She paused again, but Singer only continued to look at her.

"Our organization…my organization, seeks out those people, those near death, those for whom death is imminent, a minute, an hour, a day, perhaps a few days away. And we film them in those seconds and minutes and hours and we show those videos to people like you, Peter. And we ask you to save that life. To give what is needed to keep the person, the wife, the mother, the daughter, the brother, the son in the video, alive for another month. There is no uncertainty. If you transfer the money upon receipt of the email, there will be food for that person within hours. That's what we do. But if you don't, they will die. Without question. Because we can do no more than that."

Singer looked at the table then back up at the woman, his green-grey eyes set wide around the bridge of his nose, narrowed and angry.

"This isn't right. Sitting down here and telling me this."

He waved his arm around the room his voice rising so that the woman at the next table looked over at him then away.

"Look at this! I'm just some schmuck sitting in Timmie's having a sandwich and you want to tell me I'm responsible for hundreds of people dead every day? What the fuck is that? I make sixty-two thousand dollars a year and out of that we try a save a little, so our boys will be able to go to college and maybe take a week in the summer so they can swim in a lake."

More people were looking over now and he paused, closed his eyes and took several deep breaths. The woman sat, hands folded on the table in front of her, her face calm, unperturbed, waiting.

"Look, Angella. You seem like a nice woman. I'm sure you're trying to do something good here. But there are people out there who could save every one of those lives without blinking, without even moving the decimal place on their bank account. Why me? What I can do will be a drop in the bucket. What if I could save one or two or even five lives every month, they're still going to pile up like leaves in the fall. I'm not who you should be talking to."

Singer stood now but this time the woman remained seated. He had intended to stand and leave on his last words but something in the way she held herself stopped him; she had more to say and he was unable to turn away without allowing her to speak. She looked down at her hands, pulling the sleeves of her sweater up to her elbows, revealing her narrow wrists and forearms, picking at a loose thread on one cuff absently before noticing herself and letting go as if she has been admonished.

"We don't only seek out those who are taking their last breaths. We look for those who hold it in their hearts to help."

Her gaze had changed, no longer gentle, patient, concerned, now intent, unyielding holding him where he stood.

"We have a large network of people who identify potential candidates, each year we receive hundreds of suggestions. And from those we identify around one hundred people for further investigation, discreetly talking to people, observing the candidates, their everyday lives and interactions."

"You've been following me!?"

"Save it, Peter. You can be offended on your own time. I'm not interested in your discomfort."

She paused.

"We've been doing this a long time. And we have very smart people working on this. We know the tells. They're subtle but they are there. And each year we select a handful of people who will receive the emails and who I will contact, if necessary…this year, you were one of eleven."

She raised one eyebrow.

"Not surprisingly, they are rarely wealthy. Few people become wealthy by mistake. Wealth is always acquired through happenstance and good fortune but it's retained with intent. So, I'm rarely sitting across from somebody with the means to do more than their small share."

She paused again.

"And we are never able to recruit everybody. We are asking you to do something very difficult and you will be met with resistance by those you love and who love you. And even though all the people we contact have this rare quality, something that compels them to help, they live every day in a world that blunts, deflects, and discourages their finest instincts—and they are unable to resist the world in which they live."

The woman glanced at Singers fists clenched against his thighs, looked as if she might speak again but then stopped. He stood for a short moment.

"This isn't fair."

Then he turned away.

"Peter?"

He turned expecting her to say more but she only nodded at his tray still sitting on the table. He stepped to the table, gathered it up without looking at the woman, paused at the garbage container beside the door and watched the last fragments of his sandwich and the half-empty cup of coffee slide off the tray. The swinging entrance to the mouth of the container was prevented from falling cleanly back into place by the accumulation of wrappers and discarded food.

***

Singer sat in the muted blue light of his computer staring at the screen. He reached out to type in his username and password then stopped, stood and padded upstairs. He paused to listen to the sound of his boys syncopated breathing, then at the door to his room. For now, there was just the steady sibilant bur as air entered and left her body, but he knew if he waited long enough she would begin to make the muted sighs and moans that would continue through the night at irregular intervals once she was deep asleep. He considered getting back in bed, but turned and went back to his office instead.

Singer felt silly sitting in the dark with his fingers poised over the keyboard unwilling to login as if something loathsome and dangerous lurked just beyond the password text box. But it was the same old screensaver, Bobby Orr in mid-air having just scored the goal that would win his Boston Bruins the 1970 Stanley Cup, the joy on his face as naked and unadorned as age and time would allow. Singer hesitated again. He had not opened a *The Living List* email for several weeks now. But he had never opened a *The Passed List* email. He had little doubt what he would find, but after his conversation with the woman at lunch, the compulsion to see what was there had been one he couldn't shake. He had come back to the message over and over again during the evening, like a tongue to the moist fleshy depression left behind after a molar is removed. But had never taken the final steps of clicking on a name. Now, here in the dark with his family asleep, he was finally able.

It was the same small child as he had known it would be because he had chosen her name—Mercy Adan. The scene appeared almost identical, so Singer had no indication of how much time had passed. Except that, where light had seeped in between cracks in the walls to provide dim illumination of the shelter in the earlier video, now the only light was being supplied by a single candle, little more than mounded wax on a crockery shard. Several times, the flame almost failed before it sputtered back to life as if there was a temporary timing fault in the laws of physics and chemistry. The flame held for the three minutes and thirty-seven seconds of the film. There was nothing in the video that allowed Singer to be certain that it was the same person filming this video but there was something about the technique that suggested to Singer that it was the same person.

As it began, the camera was focused on those sitting around the pallet, the child's mother, her grandmother, chin on her chest but the glint of corneal viscera caught by the lens, and Mercy's father crouched on his heels and separated from the women by his daughter's body. Only the father looked into the camera when it rested on him, but the rage he had emanated hours before had been replaced by a weighted fatigue that that had worn flesh from his body so that he seemed a much smaller man than the one who had stalked away in the earlier video. The camera walked slowly from face to face for the first two minutes and twelve seconds of the video but then shifted to the child's face as if prompted by something or someone.

She looked the same except that something had been muted in her as well, like the light that had been drawn from the room as night had fallen had taken some of her with it. It was also obvious in the first seconds that the pause between breaths was much longer than it had been. The child's head, neck and shoulders filled the frame and after each exhalation, Mercy's mother's forehead would edge into the frame as she leaned towards her child. When Mercy took the next sharp inhale, her mother's profile would recede from the frame as if she could rest for a moment. But with each exhalation additional light drained from the child's face so that her skin, which had glowed like an obsidian diamond in the earlier video faded to the dullness of ash. The last pause extended for fourteen seconds, but then the girl's face flared, bright and shimmering as if formed and nurtured under a brilliant gentle sun, before taking three harsh gasping breaths and falling empty. The camera held on her face and chest, motionless—for ten, then fifteen, then thirty seconds before the screen went black. Singer sat in the dark until he heard Tommie cry out from his bed. He stood then and went to see what had frightened his son in his sleep.

Chapter 4

Singer's wife came into the dining room carrying the potatoes and the gravy and stood for a moment trying to find a space on the table that would hold them. Singer leaned across the table to slide Dougie's plate a little closer to him and to push the dressing towards the center of the table and his wife wedged potatoes and gravy into place before sitting down.

"Thanks, Petey."

Cheryl's mother, a tiny woman with hair the faded blonde color adopted by older women in an attempt to convince people that it's natural, smiled across the table at their youngest son.

"So, he's been fine?"

Her husband interrupted.

"Jesus H. Bev, I think I fell out of a tree twice a day until I was fifteen. Nowadays, you scrape your knee and they're firing up the MRI. The boy's fine."

Earl looked across at his youngest grandson.

"Eh, T-man? No harm, no foul, right?"

Tommie nodded at his grandfather, beaming.

"Didn't even hurt, Grandpa."

Earl stuck a couple of thick pieces of turkey with the serving fork and dragged them onto his plate while he looked around the table.

"See that, the kid's tough as nails. Must skip a generation, eh Pete?"

Earl winked and grinned at his son-in-law. Singer folded his napkin in his lap and glanced at his older son, who stared down at his hands before answering.

"Sure, Earl. But then I don't make any claims to have spent most of my childhood falling out of trees onto my head."

Earl's brow furrowed slightly and the smile dimmed, but Singer was already looking away, reaching over to rub Dougie's shoulder.

"You wanna handle grace, Dougie?"

His older son nodded and looked up at the table. As he drew a breath, Earl raised his hand.

"Wait a minute, now. Shouldn't the wounded warrior get the honors?"

He winked at Tommie again, who beamed back then looked over at his father then to his mom. Singer smiled at his youngest before shaking his head.

"Sorry, Grandpa, it's Dougie's turn today."

The other man began to reply but felt his wife's hand on his arm and stopped. Dougie had paused to watch the exchange and Singer nodded at him to begin. The boy looked at his father and then to his mom, who nodded, before he bowed his head, closed his eyes and began.

"Bless us, oh Lord, and these thy gifts which we are about to receive from thy bounty through Christ our Lord, Amen."

His younger brother made a face.

"I could have done that."

Singer reached across to ruffle his hair.

"Relax, wild child, you'll get your chance."

***

The boys had already escaped the table for the basement and it was just the adults around the table. Singer's father-in-law leaned forward.

"Peter, you got any of that Glenfiddich left…the stuff we gave you for Christmas? Nothing like a little snort to settle the pie."

His wife touched his arm.

"You sure, honey? You know how you have trouble sleeping."

He waved her off without looking.

"I'll be fine, only had a couple of glasses of wine. What do you say, Peter?"

Singer nodded and stood up.

"Sure, Earl. Ice?"

"Why not? I like the sound."

Singer looked at his wife and her mother.

"You ladies want anything?"

Both declined and Singer went to the kitchen to get the ice and came out with a thick tumbler holding a couple of ice cubes and a couple of narrow fingers of scotch.

Earl held the glass up to the light and squinted.

"You saving it for somebody you like better?"

Singer glanced at his wife, allowed a small smile, shaking his head.

"Not sure who that would be, Earl. There's always more where that came from."

His mother-in-law had caught the exchange between Singer and his wife and looked away, down at her lap. The older man looked across at Peter and gestured.

"You not having one, Peter?"

Earl glanced over at his daughter and grinned.

"My daughter got you on a short leash?"

Singer shook his head.

"Nah, Earl. Got a game early tomorrow. Ice time's hard to get."

His father-in-law nodded.

"Right. Still playing, eh?"

He patted his belly and glanced at his wife.

"Sometimes I wish I had kept playing. But things just got busy—couldn't do everything, eh hon?"

Earl didn't wait for a response.

"How are things going at work, Peter? They moved you upstairs yet?"

Cheryl blew air out through her lips.

"Dad."

Her father looked over with his hands raised off his lap, palms up, his eyebrows raised in surprise.

"What? I'm just asking. We both know he's smarter than most of those guys up on the top floor."

He turned back to his son-in-law.

"Right, Peter? You understand what I'm saying?"

Singer allowed another half-smile.

"Sure, Earl. I understand. But I like it on the floor."

"Right. Right. But you can't stay there forever. And you'll never make real money in the warehouse."

Singer felt the first spark of irritation.

"I don't know, Earl. It seems real."

Singer nodded at the table.

"Loblaw's let us use it to buy the turkey."

Earl waved him away.

"You know what I mean."

He paused and then continued.

"And you know what the problem is. If you had stuck it out and got that piece of paper, you'd already be up a couple of floors."

Cheryl started to stand up to gather the dessert plates, but Singer was ahead of her.

"Let me get that. You relax."

She knew him well enough to let him.

***

They stood at the sink, shoulders touching while he rubbed a plate dry and placed it in the cupboard to his left. Cheryl leaned forward to scrub at the roasting pan and they broke contact, but when she straightened again he felt the warm skin of her shoulder through her shirt and his.

"Sorry about Dad."

"Don't worry about it, Cher, I'm used to it by now."

"He doesn't mean anything by it."

Singer swiveled to look at his wife.

"Oh, I'm pretty sure he means something."

He gave her a gentle push, so she teetered away from the sink before rocking back.

"And he means…get a better job."

His wife pulled her hands from the sink, raising them dripping and covered in soap bubbles.

"Really? You're going to lay hands on me?'

Singer turned to face her, grinning.

"Are you threatening me? Because, you know? I fear no man. Or woman."

She held her hands in the air for a long second then slapped them on his chest before pulling them away to reveal two large wet handprints on his shirt. Singer looked down then back up as if stunned.

"I can't believe you did that. After how good I was tonight."

Cheryl leaned forward to wipe the backs of her hands on his shirt.

"You weren't that good…"

His wife relaxed her face so that she completely captured her husband's deadpan expression at the table earlier in the evening.

"I don't know. Loblaw's let me use it to buy the turkey."

Singer laughed.

"I didn't say 'me' I said 'us'."

His wife's eyes widened and she slapped his chest again.

"Even worse. Dragging me into it."

She turned back to the roasting pan.

"Speaking of money. There were four twenty-five-dollar charges on the credit card that I don't recognize. Does that ring a bell with you?"

Singer froze. He had been expecting this but also hoped that the charges would slip by unnoticed. His first impulse was just to feign ignorance, pretend that he was as confused as his wife. But the subsequent events spooled out in his head, Cheryl contacting the credit card company, denying the charges, the credit company investigating, discovering that the charges originated from a phone owned by Singer, accusing Cheryl of attempting to defraud the company, and Singer having to ultimately reveal what he had done under threat of criminal charges. He shook his head.

"Honey?"

"Yeah, Cher. A couple of guys at work were involved in some fundraising stuff. Actually, their kids."

Singer looked to the ceiling as if trying to remember the details.

"I think one was a walkathon for diabetes. Another one was some kind of raffle, and I'm not sure what the last two were about."

His wife glanced at him, puzzled.

"All of them exactly twenty-five dollars? Are you sure you're not getting pranked?"

Singer forced a chuckle.

"Yeah, Cheryl. The guys are all conspiring to get a hundred bucks from me."

She smiled at him over her shoulder.

"I've met some of those guys, not much would surprise me."

Singer chuckled again but didn't reply. His wife, finally finished with scrubbing the roasting pan clean, placed it upside down on the drain rack then turned to face him.

"Look, Petey. I know it's tough to turn them down when they come to you with their stories…and it's a good cause, and it's their kid's school—I know it's hard to say no. But we've got a charity budget and we've decided what we give money to. And we can't afford to just decide to give another hundred dollars whenever we want. If you want to set aside money for this kind of thing in next year's budget, we can, but the money will have to come from one of the places that we're already donating to. Okay?"

Singer nodded.

"You're right, Cher. I didn't mean to screw things up."

She leaned into him, her face against his shoulder, letting her wet arms drape around his shoulders and back, leaving dark streaks across his shirt.

"I know Petey. You're just too nice of a guy. It's why I picked you."

Chapter 5

The video was filmed in the same spot. The cast was also the same, a girl, maybe even a young woman, and a woman of indeterminate age who Singer assumed was her mother but who could plausibly have been her older sister, both of them brown-skinned and dark-haired. But the scene was very different. The earlier video had shown the young girl lying on the ground. The older woman sat with her back against one wall of what might have been their shelter or simply the place where they had stopped to rest with the young girl's head in her lap. It was little more than scraps of abandoned plywood arranged so that the edges leaned against each other to hold them erect, then topped with a slab of corrugated metal gapped and torn where the metal had been pierced by something, leaving the edges ripped and splayed and rust-red like attack wounds. The women were surrounded by trash, mostly plastic and paper but occasional scraps of fabric so small as to be of no use for cover or comfort, which had either been left where they lay or scattered and blown. The young girl had been asleep. At first Singer had thought she was dead, that she must be, because it was impossible for somebody composed of such meager flesh, with such a narrow whisper of meat between skin and bone to still be capable of drawing breath, but then she had shifted in the other woman's lap and made a small noise as if that tiny movement alone had caused pain and drawn from her almost all she had. The older girl had not looked away from the camera when her sister? daughter? had moved. But her right hand, which had been resting on the child's cheek, rose to her own forehead and brushed away the tangle of hair that had blown across her eye, before returning to its place along the child's throat and cheek. They wore the same kind of sleeveless garment, a shift more than a dress, little more than a dirty sheet with holes for head and arms. The rags were a slightly different shade, whether because the material had once been different colors or because they had been soiled at different times or by different substances, Singer couldn't tell. The dress might have fallen below the knee if they were standing, but lying and sitting it had shrugged to a spot just above their knees. The young woman staring into the camera was not as drawn and sparse as the girl in her lap, but her eyes dominated her face as if they had been transplanted from someplace untouched, unmarred by time and decay to a landscape blighted by every possible misfortune. They shone unblinking and unwavering despite the fading light.

At one point during the filming, the camera had shifted and turned as if the person holding the camera had moved from one vantage point to another while trying to keep the camera trained on the girls. There was a flash of sandal-covered feet but Singer couldn't tell if they were the feet of the person holding the camera or of somebody passing by. The young woman's expression remained unchanged and her eyes never left the camera lens as if she was past the point where the world included anything but the girl in her lap, her heart beating in her chest and the camera that captured these moments. And then the screen went to black.

The new video showed the two girls in the same spot but now standing. It was clear to Singer now that the age difference was too small for them to be anything but sisters or maybe cousins. But the resemblance was so close that he was fairly certain they were sisters. There was almost no difference in height, but he couldn't tell how tall they were because there was little around them to provide perspective. But one was clearly older than the other, aging present in the way that time and worry tugged at every angle and edge, fine lines cut by months as sharp as diamond radiating from the corner of both eyes towards her temples, her brow, eyelid and nose tip poised to slip, not yet showing but something in the way the skin gave and held, anticipating the sag and fall of tomorrow or the day after that. But none of that mattered on this day as they stood smiling into the camera, one arm of each girl around the waist of the other. The younger of the two removed her circling arm to brush at something in front of her face before holding her sister again; it was as the girls were bound by nerve, tendon and muscle, because as her arm pulled away, the smile on her sister's face flattened until her expression shifted from solemn to empty but the smile re-emerged like an unfolding flower when her sister held her again.

There was a moment where the older girl spoke to somebody off-camera and waved them away with both arms. Her face stern and angry as she did it but in the seconds that they were separated the younger girl didn't show the same shadow; she continued to gaze happily into the camera as if unaware that she had lost contact with her sister, as if there was still something out there beyond the two of them that could bring her joy.

Singer didn't know how much time separated the two videos but he thought it must be several days or longer, because life had been inhaled by the younger girl, the skin at her cheek and chin rising off the bone so that her features appeared shaped and kneaded from something soft and malleable rather than cut, cast or hewn from granite or timber aged as hard as stone. There was something in her features, even in what he could see of her arms, legs and hands that reminded him of a watered plant. Her eyes still appeared unfamiliar in size, shape and succulence from the rest of her features, but no longer expatriate as if imported from some foreign land. And the difference seemed exotic rather than ominous, no longer signaling something dark and desperate lurking beneath the skin. The girls wore the same worn dirty dresses, and there was something in the way the younger of the two moved that suggested lingering effects. It was as if it was difficult to coordinate the flexion of complementary muscles, as if the synapses and neurons that connected and synchronized all the necessary pieces had lain dormant for too long and had to refamiliarize themselves with their form and function. This lack of coordination and subtle spasticity was completely absent from her face where each emotion—joy, tenderness and an ineffable sadness that suffused her features when she looked at her sister—was etched, shaded and filled by genius, unimpeded by physical laws or limitations.

Singer would not have believed that such a transition was possible, would not have believed that the corruption and damage inflicted upon a human body by want, by the withholding and expropriation of the most basic of needs, could be shed in a way that left her unscarred except in ways that were almost undetectable to the human eye. In the last few frames of the video, both girls raised their hands to wave at the camera and a disembodied voice, clearly discernible above the background noise of traffic and construction that Singer couldn't see, spoke.

"Thank you, Peter."

The screen went blank. Peter watched another four videos from *The Living List* and contributed twenty-five dollars to each one.

Chapter 6

Singer sat across from Brian, his coffee untouched in front of him, hair still damp from the postgame shower. His friend gestured at the table in front of them.

"Here?"

"Yep. This table."

Singer gestured across the room.

"She started out sitting over there but then came over and sat with me."

"And black? Like me?"

"Like you? You're barely black. You're Canadian black. She was civil rights black, fighting the revolution black. Not Bruno Mars 'how do I look in my new chapeau?' black."

Brian rocked back in his chair.

"You telling me I'm not black enough for you—pasty white motherfucker like yourself?"

Singer made a face.

"Don't go all street on me. When was the last time you even dropped an mf-bomb?"

His friend grinned at him.

"It's been a long time, I admit. But the timing seemed right. And I still got it, don't I? That sounded pretty legit to me."

"Yeah, you're down—no doubt."

"Don't you try it, Pete. You try any of this stuff on?… You always look like you're trying to stuff your head through the armhole."

Singer rolled his eyes and shook his head.

"Fine, Fine. But what about the story?"

"It's the usual bullshit, buddy. It's one step up from the Nigerian prince scam."

Singer shook his head.

"Nah. It's not a scam, Bri. If you'd met her you wouldn't say that. She was…"

Singer looked away from his friend, letting his eyes wander around the room, watching a father pointing at the display case waiting for his daughter to decide what she wanted, but not really seeing them.

"Authentic…"

Singer shook his head.

"But that's not exactly what I mean…"

He reddened a little.

"Don't friggin' laugh, okay? The only word I can think of that really fits is…"

Singer was still looking away, but cut his eyes towards his friend without moving his head.

"Sanctified."

He shrugged, registering his friend's unspoken skepticism.

"Like she had some greater responsibility…"

Singer gestured around the room and then at the two of them.

"Bigger than this. Than selling stuff. Than killing time on a Sunday morning. Than doing something as small as trying to wheedle a few bucks out of some sucker's pocket."

Brian leaned forward.

"Pete. Buddy. How do you think they pull this shit off? It's because they're so good at it. They're not like you and me. We wouldn't be able to avoid a tell— you'd be able to see it on our faces. But these people, it's like they step into a new skin. Maybe they even believe their own story while they're telling it. If they were easy to spot, they'd never make any money. What do you think everybody that's ever been conned says when they're describing it? 'Well, y'know, I thought he was a little fishy but…'"

Brian stared at Singer, waiting.

"Of course not! They all say the same thing, 'But he was so sincere, he seemed so honest'."

Singer shook his head again.

"You weren't there. You don't get it. Plus the videos. There's no way they're fake."

His friend crooked his head at him then held out his hand.

"Show me a video."

Singer had been shifting his phone around on the table with his little finger without really being aware of it, but now he picked it up and swiped into his mailbox, tapped in a quick search message then stopped, staring across the table at his friend.

"Brian, don't…"

Brian held out his hand as if to take the phone, but Singer pulled back.

"Don't…"

"C'mon, Pete, don't what?"

Singer looked down at his phone at the cursor sitting on the underlined blue name, then rubbed at the corner of his eye with one finger before looking directly at his friend.

"You may not… You don't have to bel…"

Singer paused again, stuck, spinning in his own words, trying to find purchase.

"Whatever you think about this. Whatever you believe… It's not funny. It's not a joke."

Singer had pulled his phone close to his chest as if sheltering it, protecting it.

"I'm telling you, Bri… If you… I won't…"

It was as if the oxygen, nitrogen and carbon dioxide that had gathered in his lungs had expanded - just at the spot in his trachea where muscles constricted to begin manipulating the bolus of air into the molded exhalation that would carry meaning and intent. The words no longer slid smooth and unimpeded but hung and caught leaving Singer mute except for slivers of air that broke free and rose, sibilant and inchoate from his lips. His friend reached across the table and laid his fingertips on the back of Singer's hand.

"It's okay, Pete. Just let me see."

Singer felt things loosen in his chest, nodded and held the phone out.

"Just click on the file."

He watched his friend's face as the video played. Singer didn't need to see it, he had watched it so many times that he could almost see what Brian saw as he watched. The dimness of the tiny room, the muted glow of the child's face in the light of the puddled candlewax…and those bearing witness, the stranger holding the camera and the ones who loved her in her last minute and beyond, as their faces, hers and then theirs, emptied, and those who remained had to take their next breath.

His friend's expression as he took the phone had been patient but resigned, sure of what he would see, but it had softened, slackened as the minutes passed and when the video was complete he continued to stare at the screen as if trying to place what he had just seen into a context he could understand and then, finding it. He looked up at Singer then handed the phone across the table.

"Wow, Pete. That's heavy."

Singer leaned across the table.

"I know, right? I tried to tell you…"

Brian had raised his hand and was waving his fore and middle finger back and forth.

"Just a second, Pete. It's true. That's pretty powerful stuff. But they're getting good at this."

Singer sat back as if he had been pushed.

"They're getting…? Who's they?"

Brian gestured at Singer's phone.

"These people. The people who do this kind of stuff."

Singer held up his phone, showing the evidence.

"This stuff? Children dying?"

Brian managed to nod and shake his head almost at the same time.

"I get it, Pete. It looked real. But have you seen the shit they can do now? I bet we could go on there right now and find a video that would convince you that Jesus Christ himself was back and working at a Wendy's in Scarborough."

Singer had already dropped his phone into the inside pocket of his jacket and started to gather up the nearly empty cup of coffee in front of him. Brian reached out and grabbed his arm.

"Pete! Petey! Slow down. Okay. Let's say it's real."

His friend held his gaze and his arm, so that to stand Singer would have had to jerk his arm free. He settled back in his seat.

"And I'll grant you. It's pretty convincing. But what are you going to do? How many names are on the list?"

"Two hundred and forty-three."

"Two hundred and forty-three names?"

Singer nodded.

"That's just today."

"The list changes all the time. Names come off. New ones go on."

His friend looked uncertain. Singer just looked at him. Then tucked his chin down at where his phone rested inside his jacket.

"Her name wasn't on the list after that. What would be the point?"

"So, it's a new list every day?"

"Not completely new. I guess sometimes they hang around for a day or two longer than expected. But it looks like no more than five to ten percent repeats."

Brian threw up his arms.

"You're making my point for me. So, what can you do? Let's say you helped two percent. Two percent? That's nothing! It would cost you one hundred and twenty-five dollars a day. Almost four grand a month."

"You think I haven't done the math, Brian? Do you really think I haven't done the math? I get it. But look at this!"

Singer gestured around the room, his voice rising. He stood up so he could see better.

"Look there! The three old g…"

Brian grabbed his arm and pulled Singer back down into his chair.

"Would you sit down, fer Chrissake! You don't have to talk to the whole room!"

Singer shook him off but stayed seated.

"Fine. But you see those three guys? Two extra-large double-doubles, an iced cap, and three breakfast sandwiches—how much? Twenty bucks easy. That's almost enough to take one off the list. Look over there—blonde buzzed on the sides, probably a student…broke."

Singer made air quotes with the fingers of both hands.

"But she's got enough for her morning double-double every day. Guy in the suit with the take-out? Coffee, sandwich and a donut, close to ten bucks."

Singer pointed across at Brian's cup and crumpled sandwich wrapper, then at his own cup.

"Eight bucks. Just here, just this minute…easy hundred bucks in the room. Four names off the list. And what would we be giving up? A coffee and a few calories we don't need."

Brian leaned forward again.

"Would you keep it down, Pete, I can hear you. You don't need the whole place in on it."

Singer looked up and several faces shifted back to their own tables. He flushed.

"Fine. But it wouldn't hurt them to hear it. And that's just here. Now."

Singer gestured out the window.

"How many Tim Horton's in the country?"

"I don't know, Pete. I don't know how many Timmy's there are, but that's not the point…"

"Forty-three hundred and sixty-two—as of last month. Might be more now."

Singer reached across, gathered up his friend's wrapper, tossed it into his own cup then placed his cup inside his friend's without slowing down.

"And if everybody at every location just skipped one coffee this morning, one friggin' coffee! And maybe a sandwich! It's what? Five hundred thousand dollars! Twenty thousand names off the list. That means almost three months without me getting a single name. Three months, Brian! And what's the cost? One frickin' coffee this morning!"

He paused now and his friend just looked at him. Singer waited to see if he was going to respond and when he didn't, he started to speak again, but then Brian raised his hand and for the first time his face was impatient.

"I get it, buddy. But do you think you're the first guy to figure this out? You think you're on to something new. Ohhh, look! The world's unfair. There are poor people. But what do you do about it? You think you're going to fix this, Pete? What can we do? You and me? Two regular schmucks trying to pay the rent and save a little money for our kids to go to college. Fuck all. That's what we can do. Just so you know—Pete Singer ain't fixing this."

Singer stood up, eyes averted and picked up the stacked cups.

"Thanks Brian. I gotta go."

Brian reached across and grabbed his arm again, but this time Singer shook free.

"Cheryl's expecting me. I'll see you at work."

"Hang on, Pete. I'll walk you out."

But his friend had already turned. Nobody watched him leave except Brian.

Chapter 7

Singer scrolled up and down the list several times, the names flashing by in a blur, a streak of blue that barely hinted at the names beneath. Names of people, each alive and breathing somewhere in the world. On his phone, he could do this—turn the names into something else, something almost beautiful, something that if he scrolled fast enough, moved beyond the sensation of motion to a blue as still and settled as a summer sky. Like the rotation of a spoked wheel, starting with easy, lazy revolutions but accelerating so that it appeared the speed and force would shake the wheel loose, send it whirling into the sky, torn free from what bound it the bike…until, despite the rising pitch as the wheel completed each rotation with greater frequency, the rotations of the wheel appeared to slow, then appeared to stop and then gradually seemed to reverse direction as if the wheel was returning to the place it had started, even as it accelerated headlong towards the distant horizon. But this was different, because even when his screen was awash in a single slash of blue, Singer knew that just beneath the cobalt smear, letters and words, each forming a name, jostled past as relentlessly as scrap before an atomic wind.

"What are you doing, Petey?"

The house was dark and she was little more than a shadow in the doorway. As his eyes began to adjust, he could make out the wet gleam of her eyes and the way his t-shirt fell to just above her knee so that the shade of grey shifted where cotton met flesh.

"Cher. How long have you been standing there?"

"Petey? What are you doing?"

Singer slid the phone onto his desk beside the computer face down.

"Is it porn?"

"What?"

"Porn, Petey? Or gambling? Is it gambling, Pete?"

There was something in her voice as she discovered the second option that sounded like hope.

"What are you talking about, Cheryl?"

But he knew what she was talking about.

"Seven hundred and fifty dollars. This isn't somebody's kid fundraising. What's going on, Pete?"

Singer closed his eyes. He didn't know if she could see it or not, but he thought she probably could. She had been standing in the dark not staring at a lit screen, so her eyes were probably well adjusted to the darkness. It felt as if there was no right move, safe move, nothing he could say that would allow him to move back to where he had been two weeks ago. He opened his eyes and moved over to make room on the chair.

"Come on over, Cher. I want to show you something."

She stood in the doorway and he could hear her breathing. He wasn't sure if he hadn't noticed before or whether her breathing had changed. He patted the empty space beside him.

"Come on, hon."

It took a second, but then she stepped into the room and came over to where he was but she didn't sit down, standing just to the side of the chair.

"Sit down, Cher."

"I'm fine."

"Come on, Cheryl, just sit down."

She hesitated but then relented. The warmth of her hip against his, through his t-shirt made him feel that maybe it would be alright. They would be able to understand together.

"Do you remember those emails I was telling you about?"

He felt her nod beside him.

"I opened one. There wasn't a virus."

Singer looked straight ahead at his computer, his Gmail account. There were three unopened emails. One titled *The Living List*.

"What were they?"

Singer opened the email and the list of names popped up on the screen. He scrolled down. The most recent list had contained two hundred and seventy-four names, but this one looked a little longer. He scrolled back to the top of the email and settled the cursor over the top name.

Concepcion Flores

Just sitting with the arrow over her name changed him, his breathing, his heart rate, the way his eyes moved in their sockets as if everything around him was moving at the same speed but his body had slowed, his movements more deliberate, considered.

"Peter. What is it? You're scaring me."

She had moved away so their hips no longer touched.

"Watch."

She turned to look at him.

"Watch what!"

Singer's voice was serrated, harsher than he intended.

"Would you just watch, Cheryl?"

She stared at the side of his face for several seconds but when he didn't shift towards her, she looked back at the screen. The video had already started. It was different in the details but like all of the others. This was not a child. She was older, in her teens. But tiny, wasted. The couple sitting with her looked too old to be her parents, but Singer had begun to realize that what he knew of aging, he had learned where people had enough food and water—and so he was unsure.

Cheryl didn't speak until the video was over and then she stood up and walked to the window. She pulled back the curtain so she could see out into the street, as if needing to be sure that there was another world than the one she had just witnessed, a world with street lamps and new model vehicles parked outside of modest but well-kept homes. A world where nobody would raise their lids to reveal eyes so exposed by receding flesh that the inner curve of the sclera was visible. We rarely if ever saw enough of a blinking eye to make explicit its full shape and substance.

"Why did you show me that?"

"What do you mean?"

"Why did you show me that? What's it got to do with anything?"

"What's it got…? That's where the money's going, Cher. That's where I'm spending the money."

Her voice trembled when she answered.

"Why do you want those videos, Peter? Why in the world…?"

He had recognized every word, had understood each piece but now tried to pull them together, see if by examining them together he could discover what meaning they held, because they seemed as disconnected and incoherent as shards of a broken bottle.

"Why do I w…!?"

It came to him like watching an old film running backwards, rewinding so that the pieces of the bottle reversed motion, splashed away from the wall, tumbling towards the concrete poured a long time in the past so that the surface was now cracked and filled with gravel and debris and the coarse stems of whatever was able to push up from below, the shattered glass drawing back together so that in the moment just before it struck, it was whole and glaucous green, the curlicued uppercase C sliding into the lowercase o but the rest lost in the whirl and spin.

"You think I buy these videos? You think I want to watch these videos?"

He felt something give where he had been tethered, moored to a world he understood. When he spoke it was not quite a whisper.

"The money is to save them, Cheryl. I send them money. For whatever they need to breathe for one more day or one more week."

She turned away from the window, the curtain falling back into place and came to him, placing her arms around his shoulders from behind.

"I'm sorry, honey. I'm sorry. I was confused, upset. I didn't know. I w…"

He took her hands in his, unlinked her fingers, pushed her arms to the side so he could stand and went up the stairs to bed.

***

She was only a few minutes behind him and got into bed, edging over towards him before realizing that he was lying on top of the sheets and blankets so there was no way to get next to him. Singer stared up at the ceiling, his fingers laced behind his head, waiting for her.

"I'm sorry, Pete."

Singer could imagine the ceiling but it was too dark to see the swirls the previous tenants had added. He had never understood the effort invested in making the ceiling appear rough-textured and unfinished, as if they lived in a house fashioned from mud and rainwater.

"I should have known better."

Singer was tired suddenly, wanted to turn over, tuck his arms under the pillow, close his eyes and fall asleep but waited.

"I should have known that you were using the money to try and do something good."

Singer tried to bring up the image of the ceiling, the raised edges coiled from the ceiling fan out to every corner of the room, but when he closed his eyes tight, lights flared and sparked behind his lids. When he opened them again the light remained, glowing phosphene blue waiting to be tapped to life, before fading like a receding phosphorescent wave. He squeezed his eyes shut again and when he opened them the same effect reappeared, held then faded.

"It's why I married you, Pete. It's why I wanted you to be the father of our children. Because you're good and kind and you don't just think about yourself— you care about other people. I wouldn't want you to be any other way.

Singer had to resist the compulsion to get up, go back downstairs, click the name at the top of the list, watch the video, then send the money. Even as he lay in his bed listening to his wife, one passed. Then another. Then another. But it faded, and he could feel himself settle back into the bed, the tension draining and with it the urge to stand.

"But we can't afford for you to do this. We don't have that kind of money. We just can't do this. Honey?"

He nodded in the dark not knowing if she could sense it.

"I know, Cher. I know."

She reached over, found him and rubbed his chest through his t-shirt.

"We just don't have that kind of extra money, Pete. We have to watch our pennies just to have a couple of hundred bucks a month to put aside for the boy's education. You know?"

He put his hand over hers, stilling the circular motion.

"You're right. It's just sad."

She shifted towards him.

"I know, hon. Let's take some time on the weekend and work through the books. I can show you where the money's going and maybe we can find an extra twenty-five, find something we can cut back on."

He nodded again in the dark.

"You're right, Cher. I know. I'm not sure what I was thinking. I just wasn't looking at the big picture. Just…while I was doing it, it seemed like the right thing. It seemed like the thing I had to do. You know?"

His voice splintered.

She pulled her hand from beneath his so that she could reach across and lean in to kiss him on the cheek and then gently on the mouth before drawing back.

"I know, Petey. You meant well."

She turned on her side and Singer listened until her breathing settled into an even rhythm before rising from the bed and going down to his computer. He sat in the dark with his hands clasped tightly in his lap until the rising sun beggared the first wan gap between earth and sky, then returned to bed and fell asleep.

Chapter 8

Dougie tilted the box carefully so that the cereal poured out in an even kaleidoscope of tiny round circles, stopping when his bowl was half full. Tommie grabbed the box from his brother's hands before it had settled on the table and spilled cereal into his bowl until cereal scattered onto the table and down into his lap. Distracted, Tommie began plucking pieces from the folds of his pajamas, dropping the box onto the table without looking so that Singer had to reach out and steady it before it fell over, splashing cereal everywhere.

"Whoa! Whoa! Whoa! Buddy, none of it's going to run away. Take your time. It's not eat or be eaten for heaven's sake!"

Tommie continued to search around in his pajamas for any missing pieces as if he hadn't heard his father. Singer glanced at his older son, who was watching him over a spoonful of cereal paused just below his lower lip. Singer shrugged as if to say "What can you do?" and Dougie allowed himself a small smile. Singer reached across the table, grabbed the lip of his younger son's cereal bowl and shuffled the bowl so that the cereal, which had been mounded up against one edge, settled into an even pile that almost filled the bowl. Tommie noticed just as his father was pulling his hand away…

"Hey!"

…and clutched at the bowl as if to protect it from thieves but caught the edge so that several pieces flew out onto the table.

"Relax T-man, just straightening it out."

Singer picked up the pieces scattered on the table, tossed a couple in his mouth and dropped the rest back into his son's bowl.

"Hey, those were mine!"

Singer intercepted his son's hand, already reaching for the box to replace the ones his father had eaten.

"Eat what you've got—if you're still hungry, we'll worry about it then."

His youngest made a sour face but then pointed at the milk. Singer brought the container close and paused.

"See that, Tommie, you've got to leave a little room. There's almost no room for the milk."

His son pushed a small pressed metal version of a Lamborghini back and forth on the table beside the bowl, making small whirring noises deep in his throat, then nodded though Singer was sure he hadn't heard. He tilted the milk container, slid a thin stream of milk in at the edge of the bowl and stopped as the cereal quickly rose to the upper edge. Cheryl looked over her shoulder from the counter where she was preparing lunches.

"Get that off the table, Tommie. How many times do I have to tell you?"

Tommie didn't acknowledge his mother except to let go of the car, grab up his spoon, scoop up a mound of cereal and stuff it into his mouth so that he had to use his other hand to force pieces of cereal that tried to squeeze out at the corners back into his mouth, but he still tried to say something that got lost before getting past his lips. Tommie's spoon came up short against the back of Singer's hand, shielding his son's bowl and he tried twice to get around it at the cereal but Singer shifted his hand to block him each time.

"Finish what you have in your mouth, then speak, then take another bite."

Singer shared a glance with Dougie, who this time gave an almost perfect imitation of his father's shrug, his mouth rippled slightly at one corner and one eyebrow raised.

"So, what were you saying, Tommie?"

His son glanced up as if he had forgotten his question then dug into the cereal again, speaking as he raised the spoon to his lips.

"Where were you going?"

"What?"

Tommie started to answer, but his mouth was full of cereal again and Singer raised his finger. Tommie paused and chewed. Singer hoped he would lose track of his thought but he didn't.

"Where were you going? You walked by our room when it was really dark and you didn't turn on the light."

Singer looked over at his wife's back and saw Dougie catch him looking, then turned back to his son.

"I must have been going to the bathroom."

But Tommie was already shaking his head before his father finished.

"No. I can tell when you go to the bathroom. I can hear you. It's loud."

He giggled and looked at his brother, expecting a smile in return but Dougie was looking down into his cereal.

"Well, I…"

But Tommie had lost interest already, shoveling another spoonful of cereal into his mouth and moving the Lamborghini lightly on the table so his mother couldn't hear. Only his wife, who was standing straight at the counter, her back to the table, but her hands now flat on the counter and his oldest son, still staring down into his cereal bowl as if there was something frightening there, waited for an answer. Singer left it hanging and after several seconds, they both went back to what they were doing.

***

"Do they always do this?"

The kids had tumbled out the door, barely making it to the stop as the bus pulled up, leaving Singer and Cheryl alone in the kitchen.

"Do what?"

Singer gestured at the cereal bowls, Dougie's empty of cereal but with milk covering the bottom quarter of the bowl and Tommie's still half full of soggy pieces.

Cheryl shrugged.

"Yeah, I guess. I'm usually pouring stuff down the sink or tossing it in the garbage."

Singer rubbed at his face, already tired.

"Well, it's a friggin' waste."

Cheryl drained the last of her coffee and pushed off the counter.

"I've got to get dressed."

Singer, clearing the table, paused.

"Did you hear me?"

His wife stopped in the middle of the kitchen.

"What do you want me to do, Peter? Shove it down their throats? I can do that. You hold their arms, and I'll pry their mouths open and we can force it into them. We could use a funnel and a sharp stick. You let me know."

Singer listened to his wife climb the stairs. She had always been good at the grand exit. He had never been able to get the timing quite right.

He poured Dougie's milk down the drain, scraped Tommie's cereal into the garbage under the sink and fit the dishes into the dishwasher rack. He heard his wife stop on the landing at the top of the stairs, hurried to the door, slipped into his shoes, shrugged on his thick canvas coat, settled the ball cap on his head and opened the door. It was starting to get cold in the morning, cold enough that pearled strands of frost streaked the storm door window but not cold enough for winter boots yet. Cheryl's voice trailed down from the top of the stairs.

"Where were you going last night, Pete?"

Singer closed the inside door behind him, let the storm door fall shut and walked down the steps to his car.

***

Brian was already coming down the walkway as Singer pulled up. His girlfriend, a small Asian woman, who Singer had only chatted with once at the annual Christmas party, stood in the doorway watching. She smiled and nodded at Singer and blew a kiss to her boyfriend. Brian blew one back then slid into the passenger seat.

"Cute"

His friend craned his neck to look back at his girlfriend still standing in the doorway as Singer pulled out from the curb.

"Hey, don't blame me if the heat's gone from your relationship, Petey. It's the little things. Guys like you just never learn."

Singer tapped the brakes hard so that his friend had to put out his hand to avoid getting thrown forward into the dash.

"Guys like me?"

"You heard me! And that's exactly what I meant. White guys. You take it all for granted. You just don't appreciate a good woman. Now, me. A proud black man. I understand that a fine woman waiting at home is the difference between a life well-lived and an empty hollow existence filled only with late night pizza deliveries, Sports Centre at two in the morning and whatever amount of porn you can stand before self-loathing sends you off the nearest overpass into rush hour traffic."

"Where were you? I thought you said you were going to be there?"

Singer raised a finger.

"Hold on. I just have to digest taking advice about women from a man whose longest relationship lasted eighteen months and who is already looking a bit antsy in month sixteen. And by the way, it's a very bad sign when you measure the length of your relationships in months."

Brian started to speak but Singer stopped him again with a raised forefinger, making a show of gathering saliva in his mouth before leaning into a deep swallow making a loud gulping sound then hammering at his diaphragm twice with his fist before settling back into his seat.

"'There. I think I got it down. What was the question?"

"Where were you?"

"Something came up. Were you short guys?"

Brian shrugged.

"Two lines and three D. Would have been good to have the extra body. You going to be there Friday night?"

Singer shrugged.

"I'll have to see."

His friend turned to him.

"Have to see? What are you talking about?"

Singer shrugged again.

"Money's getting tight."

"Eleven bucks a week for ice-time? Are you kidding me?"

Singer accelerated to find a gap where he could get over into the right lane and onto the freeway.

"Single guy like you, eleven bucks seems like nothing. When you're trying to save for your kids, eleven bucks is a big deal."

Brian was silent for several seconds.

"Is this about those emails?"

He looked over at Singer.

"Oh for Chrissake, it is!"

Brian slapped the dash with both hands.

"You're getting played, Petey. It's a scam. I didn't mind at first, as long as it was just affecting your marriage. But…getting in the way of hockey night—this has to stop."

Singer didn't answer and Brian stared at the side of his face.

"Too much on the marriage?"

"Maybe a little."

"Okay, so forget I said that. But really? You're going to quit hockey to save eleven dollars a week. I'll give it to you, buddy. If it's that big of a deal."

Singer shook his head.

"Why not?"

Singer put on his blinker and slid the car right onto the off ramp.

"It wouldn't work. Look, if you want to help out, that's great. I'll take whatever money you're willing to give. But not to pay for my hockey."

They didn't speak for the rest of the drive or the walk into the building, bumping fists where the aisles split towards their respective work areas.

***

Singer scraped his chair back and stood up. The noise wasn't enough to get everybody's attention, so he cleared his throat and that was enough to get everybody turned his way.

There were just under six hundred floor workers in the warehouse and about a dozen break rooms, equipped with tables, hard plastic chairs and machines dispensing pre-packaged food and drink. Singer had only been in a couple of them, but as far as he could tell they were identical. The rooms were equipped to hold, at most, about twenty people at a time so, breaks and lunches were on a rotation. Some workers took their breaks in the parking lot, mostly the smokers and the functioning alcoholics. Singer had a couple of guys who he knew were almost always drunk or high, but it didn't seem to affect their work so he let it slide. So there were about a dozen people in the room. One of them was Brian. They had managed to get their breaks and lunches scheduled for the same time. Brian was assigned to a different room but nobody really seemed to care. Singer's had the reputation as a 'good' room—no cliques, no fights, the assholes kept in line.

Singer shuffled his feet, trying to sort out how to start. He knew his friend was staring at him. The others, including the new guy who had pranged the fridge, looked almost as puzzled. Singer reddened a little.

"I never do this kind of thing…"

He let it hang, trying to figure out where to go next.

"Not even when my kid has some kind of fundraiser at the school…"

Ronny Smithson flushed a little and looked away.

"No. Nah. There's nothing wrong with… That's what I'm saying…"

Singer stopped and looked at the other man.

"That wasn't my point, Ronny. I think it's great that you were helping your daughter. I was just saying that I've never asked before…"

The new guy grinned, enjoying the discomfort, folded his arms across his chest and leaned back in his chair so only the back legs were on the ground. Singer looked away from him to the rest of the room.

"I don't know how many of you are aware, but there are people dying every day because they can't get enough to eat. Kids mostly. Some adults but mostly kids. And all if would take is a few dollars to save them."

The new guy interrupted.

"I think I heard this same speech this morning on TV, I forget what I was watching—CNN, Fox News, one of those. Who are those guys…?"

Singer stared at him for several seconds then looked around the room.

"As I was saying. Kids are dying every day. And I was thinking that maybe we could start a little fund here, enough to raise…I don't know…maybe fifty bucks a week. That would be enough to save two people. Two people every week."

Now the only people looking at him were Brian and the new guy, the rest had looked away.

"UNICEF! That's it. UNICEF. You working for UNICEF now, Petey? How do the big bosses feel about moonlighting? They okay with that?"

Singer didn't even look over this time.

"I don't want to put anybody on the spot, I know you've all got your own thing, but…"

"Or are you freelancing on this, Petey?"

The new guy was grinning even wider, tilting his chair further back until he had to put one hand behind him against the wall to steady himself.

"Are you our very own Mother Teresa? Is that it, Petey? Are you our Mother T?"

Singer could see that a couple of the other guys and one of the young women were trying not to smile or covering it with a hand. He knew he had lost them but he pushed to the finish.

"So, if it's something you're willing to help out with, just come talk to me or drop me a text or email. Okay? There's no pressure…"

The new guy was looking around the room now.

"And you ever notice that right after they're asking us to feed the Africans, there's usually one for saving the dogs? Every time I see that, I always think— there's the answer right there! It's right in front of us! We got all these fucked-up dogs and all these starving kids? Feed one to the other—your call."

This actually drew a couple of snickers from down the table and Singer let the last words go.

"What's your name, asshole!"

Brian was still sitting but had turned until he was almost facing the guy.

"Who the fuck wants to know?"

Brian just nodded.

"Don't need to know - asshole will do fine. So, shut the fuck up, asshole. And learn how to drive a fucking fork before you get up in the big boy seat."

Brian had hooked his foot around one of the front legs of the chair while he was talking and as he finished, he stood, pulled hard and the chair went out from under the guy, sending him crashing to the floor, the back of his head slamming hard into the concrete floor. Singer's friend stood over him for a second.

"And maybe figure out how to work a fucking chair."

Then he turned and walked from the room. The guy scrambled to his feet as the door closed, and a couple of guys grabbed his arm to stop him as he lunged for the door. But they didn't have to try hard.

***

Singer sat at the kitchen table, staring over his sons' heads out the door that led onto the deck. The first dusting of snow had arrived overnight and the wind had picked up so it skirled around the deck in fits and starts, settling for a moment before being torn loose and tossed again.

"Tommie!"

The sound of Dougie's voice brought him back, his youngest's bowl filled past the brim so that cereal was scattered across the table. It hit Singer as if it had been waiting just below the surface, looking for a shadow to pass overhead, a signal to strike, closer to rage than annoyance. He reached across the table and snatched the cereal box out of his youngest son's hand.

"What the hell are you doing, Tommie! Are you stupid? It's the same every f…friggin' morning! And then half of it just sits soaking in the bowl while you trot off to school!"

The look on his son's face should have stopped him, white, frozen, as if his son was seeing him for the first time. But it only made him angrier.

"Don't you get it! The food you leave behind every morning would keep some other kid alive, for Chrissakes! Some kid who's not nearly as lucky as you would give anything to have the food that we toss in the garbage every day! Do you get that, Tommie!?"

His wife had been stopped by the force of it, but only for a second. She was across the room now and had gathered Tommie into her arms, holding his head against her chest. The air that had been caught in his chest unable to work its way free finally leaving his body in deep heaving sobs.

"What…? What is wrong with you! My God…"

She picked him up from his chair, cradled him in her arms and left the kitchen. Singer listened as she made soothing noises in his ear in the living room. When Singer looked at his other son, Dogie was staring at him, his mouth agape, his eyes pulled wide as if what he was watching was more than he could capture. Singer blinked twice then gestured at his son's bowl, speaking quietly.

"Eat your breakfast, Dougie."

Dougie continued to look at him for several seconds, closed his mouth, set his spoon down in his cereal, stood up and went in the other room.

***

Singer sat on the edge of their bed, looking at his wife's back. She stood facing the window that looked down onto the street in front of their house. The street didn't get past the end of the block running up against a dozen acres of forest that developers had been trying to pry out of Old Man Leary's hands for a decade. He would sell eventually and another development would go in, and they'd extend Wallace Street into the new neighborhood and the volume of traffic would pick up on their street.

He could hear the boys through the closed window, the clatter and scrape of sticks, the skid of sneakers on still-bare asphalt. The forecast said first snow by tomorrow and almost six weeks since Halloween. Singer could remember years when he had worn a parka over his Spiderman costume—had to leave the zipper down so people could see the red and blue polyester. This year, one of the kids had worn a ballerina costume, bare legs and arms except for a thin layer of nylon.

"What was that about this morning?"

Singer shrugged and shook his head.

"I know, hon. I just... I don't know."

When she turned away from the window to sit beside him on the bed, Singer knew that she had decided not to be mad.

"Look Petey, I know those emails have been bothering you... They bothered me too."

Singer could feel that she had swiveled to look at him.

"But you can't just decide to give money out without talking to me. And especially to somebody on the Internet. Who knows what's going on? You know it's probably a scam?"

Singer looked over at his wife.

"Did it look like a scam to you?"

Cheryl shook her head, but Singer could tell she was placating him.

"No. It looked real, Pete. But they've gotten very good at this. The technology keeps improving and I'm sure there's a lot of money to be made if they can foo—persuade enough people."

Something clicked in his jaw and he drew a deep breath as if it might be a lubricant, but nothing loosened.

"That's some serious acting, Cheryl, real character stuff. But you can't act thin. You either are or you're not. You saw her. She looked shrink-wrapped, skin on bone. You think they faked that?"

Singer no longer looked at his wife but he felt her shrug. She was silent for a moment before trying a different tack.

"You may be right, Pete. But we don't know anything about who's getting the money. Do they have a name?"

Singer shook his head.

"See! You're sending money out into the ozone and you have no idea who's getting it! Does that seem smart to you, Pete? What legitimate charity doesn't say who they are?"

Singer thought of the woman sitting across from him in Tim Horton's. The way her fingers had worried at the edges of her sleeves, the sorrow that had soaked her so that she had to force herself straight against the curl of the weight.

"I know it seems weird, hon. But I'm sure they're legitimate."

She exhaled her impatience in a thin stream.

"But even if they are legitimate, Peter. Look what it's doing to you. Tommie was terrified."

Singer nodded. He could still see his son's face. The moment when it had seemed like it might hold, but then, as if hinged in a thousand places, it collapsed at once. And then the opposite happening to Dougie, any flex or bend in his oldest son's face setting in hard lines as he stood and left the kitchen. His wife's voice drew him back.

"Are they doing it right? Is the money getting to who needs to get it? I've heard about how it goes in these countries. Most of the time the money never even gets to the people who need it—it gets stolen."

Singer nodded.

"It's just hard… Hard to look at those faces and…"

When she turned to him this time, Singer shifted to face her and let her put her arms around him and pulled him in close so she was speaking almost in his ear.

"I know, sweetie. But we can't fix everything. We're already doing as much as we can, we talked about this. We're sponsoring Osuna in Chile, there's the spina bifida foundation and the Boys and Girls Club. We just can't afford any more. Especially with Christmas coming. But we can talk about this in January, maybe drop one of the charities and shift a few dollars to this. Or maybe we can even find a few extra dollars."

Singer nodded against her shoulder.

"You're right, hon. I know you're right. I just got carried away."

Singer pulled back so he could look into his wife's face.

"You saw one. They're hard to ignore."

His wife nodded and reached up to touch his cheek.

"I know, sweetie. And maybe someday we'll be able to do more. You know that when we can, we will."

Singer nodded.

"I know, Cher."

His wife nodded back then let go of him and stood up, smiling.

"I better go get the boys, it's bath night."

Singer smiled at her and watched her leave. He sat on the edge of the bed and listened to her calling to Dougie and Tommie and listened to their complaints and requests for more time.

***

Singer's wife's breathing was slow and even, but broken at irregular intervals by indecipherable muttering. Singer slid out from underneath the sheet and comforter and sat with his feet flat on the floor before pushing himself up and padding downstairs to his computer screen.

***

The boy was eight or nine, laughing as he chased a plastic bag stuffed with something that provided a little weight but that gave beneath the arch of their foot when it was kicked and sent tumbling across the dry-baked ground. Singer couldn't tell whether it was a laneway or a yard or maybe a school playground because it was just hardpack with the occasional tuft of dried brown vegetation. But the boy was alive and happy as he chased the makeshift 'ball' amongst a pack of other children around his own age. Singer could still see the effects—he was a little slower than the other children and rarely made it to bag first. And when he did, he had to pause and find his balance so that kicking the ball didn't send him off balance to the ground.

In the earlier video, the boy had been curled on his side as if, even asleep, hunger pangs drew his legs up into his body. But Singer knew that it was an illusion. That by this late stage of starvation there were no longer hunger pangs, attempts to remind the body it needed food had been discarded in favor of autonomous physiological responses designed to ensure that the precious little energy still deposited in meager strands of muscles strung from and between his bones was used as efficiently as possible. Twenty-five dollars had moved Amoru from what little remained on the hard wooden pallet covered in cloth rags to the boy playing in the yard. Singer watched the video of the children playing several times before walking back up the stairs to bed. He paused only to send one more twenty-five-dollar donation. This would be the last. As Singer pushed the 'Send' button, he felt the tension give. It had built as he had readied for bed, as if every movement he made caused an almost imperceptible ratcheting rotation, stretching the ends of each muscle fiber slightly further apart so that by the time he lay down beside his wife he was sure that she would sense the vibration, the kinetic energy building beside her. But she hadn't, falling asleep as she almost always did, as if leaping from a cliff, one moment awake, even speaking and in the next, gone, buried in sleep. But Singer lay beside her, every breath turning an internal crank, drawing him tighter until he felt that strands must snap. Cheryl would understand.

Chapter 9

There was one person between Singer and the only teller—a heavyset woman of about sixty who had turned and smiled when she felt Singer step behind her before turning back to face the counter. The woman deposited money and appeared to be done quickly, but as she was about to turn away asked another question, which had led to the teller making a computer enquiry that led to several more questions and several more computer queries before the teller finally wrote several notes on a large Post-it note and handed it to the woman. She looked at it for a few seconds, folded the paper, placed it carefully in her wallet, which she then placed in her purse before nodding at the teller and turning away from the counter. So, it was fifteen minutes before Singer stepped to the window.

"I'm sorry for the wait, sir. What can I help you with?"

"I'd like to open an account."

The teller smiled. She was young and pretty except for the scar from the top right side of her lip that ran almost to her right nostril where her cleft palate had been repaired.

"Do you currently have an account with us or have you ever banked with us?"

Singer shook his head.

"No."

The teller smiled again, but as she did she covered her lip for a moment with two fingers.

"If you don't mind me asking, sir. Where do you currently do most of your banking, because we have a special off…"

Singer felt a quick surge of annoyance but forced himself to smile back.

"No, I'm happy with my current bank, but Christmas is coming and my wife always manages to figure out what I'm getting her just by tracking where I'm making my purchases. This way she won't have a clue."

The teller smiled once more.

"I know what you mean, my boyfriend is always trying to guess what I'm getting him, but luckily, he doesn't get to see my bank statements. Have you got some

ID, sir—driver's license, passport. I'll also need your SIN number and proof of address."

Singer slid the paperwork across the counter along with an envelope containing four hundred dollars.

***

"I'll take an arm's length."

Singer looked at his wife and then at the young mom holding the thick roll of tickets to her shoulder and stretching the loose end to the tip of her fingers.

"Really?"

Cheryl held out the five-dollar bill and waited for the woman to tear off the long string of tickets.

"Relax, cheapskate, it's for a good cause."

Singer continued to look at her.

"A good cause? The locker rooms are fine. And even if they're not, shouldn't taxes cover it?"

Cheryl exchanged the money for the tickets then glanced over at her husband.

"It's five bucks, Petey. Settle down."

Singer continued to look at her, but she had already returned her attention to the ice where both Dougie and Tommie had come off the bench. Tommie had gone over the boards and hit the ice with both legs churning and was already several strides ahead of Dougie, chasing the puck into the corner.

Tommie was still supposed to be in 'initiation', for kids under seven, but Cheryl had petitioned the league to allow him to play up with Dougie and the other eight-year-olds so they wouldn't have to shuttle them around to two different ice times. Tommie wasn't as skilled or fast as many of the eight-year-olds and Singer had been concerned that he wouldn't be able to keep up, but he had made up for it with determination and a reckless disregard for his own physical wellbeing.

A couple of players had arrived before Tommie, but overskated the puck and he barreled in, gathered it off the boards, swerved hard to the net, misjudged the angle and ran right into the near goalpost hard enough to bang his helmet off the corner and tumble to the ice, his stick coming loose and sliding into the corner.

Dougie always more thoughtful and considered watched the play develop, saw what was coming, coasted to the top of the circle to the left of the net and now when the puck drifted loose in front of the net as Tommie went down, he stepped in and directed the puck toward the far corner, but the goalie moved across and tipped it wide.

Singer and his wife were on their feet, neither of them watching the puck, eyes only for their youngest son on the ice, but he was already scrambling after his stick on all fours. He used it to push himself to his feet before chasing the puck into the far corner, kicking it loose falling to the ice and batting the puck with his glove towards a teammate. The whistle blew as Nicky, one of three girls on the team, touched the puck.

Singer sat back down, shaking his head.

"Kid's going to be the death of me."

His wife put her hand on his arm.

"Think we should go down and have a look at him?"

Singer looked over.

"He's fine. You see him get back in there? Leave him be."

Cheryl was looking down at the bench trying to pick her son out of the line of red helmets.

"It's only been a few weeks. The doctor said he had to be careful."

"Seven weeks, hon. And he's fine."

She nodded but still watched the bench intently. It was as if her oldest somehow felt it, looking up into the stands at his mother. She smiled and waved, and he nodded at her before looking away.

***

Singer and his wife sat alone in the stands. The buzzer had gone. Dougie and Tommie's team had lost 6-3 but both the boys had scored a goal, Dougie's on a rebound into an open net and Tommie's on a scramble in front that he might have kicked in but nobody saw. The other parents had already left the stands for the area outside the dressing rooms. But Cheryl hadn't stood up yet.

"What was the four hundred dollars for?"

Singer watched the doors at the far end of the rink open and the Zamboni rumble out of the dim recesses of the arena onto the ice. Singer loved watching the shiny, slick band grow as the Zamboni circled the arena, filling and smoothing every tear, crack and crevice until the ice had been restored to a single gleaming sheet, unscarred and unmarred as if newly created rather than restored. He watched a complete revolution, until both ends of the first ring were connected before answering.

"That's how it's going to go now? You watching every penny?"

Cheryl turned to him but he didn't return her gaze.

"Come on, Pete. Four hundred dollars?"

He looked at her now.

"You really want to know? It's near Christmas and I have some shopping to do. And I don't want you to know where I'm doing it."

Her eyes widened but she smiled.

"I thought we agreed no more than a hundred and fifty. You're going to make me look bad."

Singer leaned forward and kissed her forehead.

"You deserve something nice, hon. We can splurge once in a while."

She smiled at him again, took his face in both hands, kissed him on the tip of the nose and then on the lips, holding it for several seconds before leaning back.

"Okay. But don't go too crazy."

***

Singer sat in the blue glow of his computer screen, looking at the list of names before glancing up at the open window. The coming sun was little more than a whisper, light seeping echo-faint as if from a basin cracked so thin that the spreading stain barely changed the shade of sky. In another hour, the morning would break like the world beyond what Singer could see was on fire. He had watched thirty-three videos, one after the other. He could only choose ten. He couldn't spend the entire four hundred dollars there had to be presents under the tree. But if he could find something used or on sale, she might believe four hundred dollars.

Finally, he simply took the first ten names. As the last of the donations was confirmed, the tension drained from his body. He would be able to sleep now, but there was no time. He would have to wait for tonight.

Chapter 10

The email had been sitting in his inbox when Singer arrived at his workstation.

Pete – drop by and see me when you're done.

Singer had talked with Steve Watson twice since Watson had started two and a half years ago. Once at a Christmas party and a few weeks later when they had recognized each other in the parking lot. He had seen him several times at meetings when Watson spoke to all the delivery station managers. But there wasn't much need or opportunity for delivery station managers to talk to operations managers. It didn't seem like a good thing to be called to his office.

Singer held up his lanyard ID and the security guard buzzed the door to let him into the mezzanine level. Singer approached the guard's desk.

"Who you looking for?"

"Mr. Watson?"

The guard pointed to his left.

"End of the hall, take a left and he's room 263, I think it's the fourth door on your right."

Singer nodded, but the guard was already looking back down at his magazine.

The only marking on the door was the number, not even a name plate. Singer knocked and heard a muffled sound from inside, but nothing he could distinguish so he knocked again. This time the voice spoke louder. Singer opened the door but the man behind the desk was on the phone, talking and scrolling through something on the screen. He glanced up at Singer, raised a finger, pointed at the phone then gestured for Singer to wait. He stood in the doorway, unsure whether to step in or to back out and close the door. So, he stood where he was. The man behind the desk—sandy-haired and athletic looking in a polo shirt and khakis that Singer could see because the guy had both feet up on his desk, looked up after a few seconds—saw Singer was still standing in the doorway, gave a quick smile and waved at a chair against the wall. When Singer didn't move immediately, he impatiently waved at it again. Singer went to the chair and started to sit down, realized he had left the door ajar, went back, closed it tight and then sat down. When he looked at the desk, the man was off the phone and waiting for him to sit down. Then he stood up, came around the desk, with his hand extended and Singer stood so they could shake hands.

"Hi Pete. Good to see you again. It's been a while, eh?"

Watson stepped back to his desk but just to lean against it, still standing, then waved at Singer's chair.

"Go ahead. Take a load off, Pete."

Watson reached behind himself to shuffle a few papers out of the way so he could half sit on the edge of the desk.

"How many years have you been here, Pete? Seven?"

Singer nodded.

"Seven years. That's a long time. And we're really happy you've stayed with us. You've been a great employee."

Singer nodded again.

"Yessir."

Watson made a face and waved his hand.

"Steve, Pete. None of that Sir or Mr. Watson shit. Not our style here at Amazon. Jeff doesn't go much for formalities."

Singer nodded again. There didn't seem much else to do.

"So, like I was saying. You've done good work for us. But…"

Singer waited.

"We've had a complaint."

Singer waited.

"That you've been asking some of your guys—and I use the term 'guys' in a non-gendered way—so, some of your 'people'…"

Watson made air quotes around the word people.

"…to donate to one of your charities. You know what I'm talking about, Pete?"

"Yes, Mr. W—Steve. Yes, I do."

Watson waited for Singer to continue but filled the silence when he realized Singer was done.

"Look, Pete. Amazon is a big believer in giving back to the community. It's one of the pillars of the Amazon philosophy. I'm not sure there's anybody who contributes more than Jeff to local communities…maybe Bill Gates. But it can't be something that makes people feel uncomfortable, pressured."

"I understand, Steve. My intention wasn't to…"

Watson raised his hand.

"I know, I know, Pete, you weren't trying to create a problem. But it has created a bit of a problem so I'm going to have to ask you not to mention this to your g—people again. Is that going to be a problem, Pete?"

Singer shook his head.

"No sir, it was never my intention to make anybody feel like they were obligated. I…"

"Good enough, Pete. That's all I needed. As long as we understand each other."

Watson smiled, clearly satisfied that things had been sorted out.

"But, while you're here, Pete. Anything we should chat about, ways for the floor to run better, improvements we could make? We don't get a chance to talk one-on-one like this very often."

Singer shook his head again.

"I don't think so, sir. Things are running fine."

Singer's phone pinged in his pocket and they both paused almost imperceptibly, then Watson clapped his hands together and pushed off the desk.

"That's great, Pete. Well, in that case, I should get back to work and I'm sure you're ready to get home."

Singer nodded and turned away but stopped with his hand on the door and turned back.

"Well, Steve…"

Watson had already moved behind his desk and sat down and had to look up at Singer's voice.

"…you mentioned the large charitable donations that Amazon makes. Is there any opportunity to make suggestions to Mr. Bezos or his team—organizations that are particularly needy?"

Watson was already shaking his head and managed a smile around the grimace that had emerged first.

"I don't think so, Pete. Jeff is pretty strategic about charitable donations. He has a team devoted only to that, ensuring that the good works that Amazon does for communities fits the brand, aligns with the Amazon corporate vision. It's amazing how wrong charitable donations can go if they aren't thought through carefully."

Singer nodded, turned and left.

***

Brian caught up to him in the parking lot and stepped in beside him, matching him stride for stride as if they had been together since leaving the building.

"So, what was that all about?"

Singer looked over.

"You got nothing better to do?"

"Than spend time with my good buddy, Pete? Are you kidding me? So, you get the promotion?"

"They aren't happy with me asking the guys to help out with money to feed the kids."

His friend nodded.

"Figured that might be it. They don't like anything that might disturb the Force."

"I wonder who complained?"

They paused on one of the lanes between rows of cars. Singer gestured around.

"Where are you?"

Brian pointed off to a spot in the distance across the spill of cars stretching out to where they could just make out the edge of the parking lot.

"Northwest corner."

Singer looked off to his right.

"I'm the other way. You get here late?"

His friend grinned.

"You know how it is, some mornings it's hard to get out of bed."

Singer forced a grin but couldn't stick the landing.

"I've heard about such a thing."

"Yeah, stop your bitching. You've got a hottie."

They stood for a moment.

"Maybe nobody complained."

Singer looked over.

"What do you mean?"

"You know they've got cameras in the main warehouse. They don't even try to hide them. But I bet they have them in the break rooms too. They may know without anybody ratting."

"Probably the new guy who pranged the fridge."

Brian shrugged.

"Sproul? First, he's been here three months now—he ain't the new guy. Second, you could be right but I'm telling you it wouldn't have to be anybody."

They stood for a second.

"You sure you're not coming tonight, buddy? I've been able to get the boys to hold off bringing in a new guy but the bench is getting short."

Singer shook his head.

"I told you, Bri. I'm done. I won't be coming back. Bring in whoever you want."

Singer started to walk away but Brian grabbed his arm and spun him back around.

"Look, Pete, this isn't funny anymore. It's fucked up."

Singer stood with his hands thrust deep into his pockets like they held something he didn't want his friend to see and looked down at his feet, pushing a piece of frozen slush around with one toe. His friend used three fingers to push on his shoulder so that Singer had to take one step back to catch his balance.

"What are you doing, Pete? This doesn't make sense. People are dying in Africa so you have to be miserable? People are always going to be starving, Pete, and you're not going to be able to save them all. This is just the way it has always been and you can't change that."

Singer shook his head.

"You don't understand. You haven't seen them."

Brian made a snorting sound.

"We all see the commercials, Pete. And fine, foster a kid, send a few bucks a month. But this? How much have you sent already?"

Singer didn't answer but looked up from the ground towards his friend. The late afternoon sun was low in the sky, and he had to pull a hand free to shade his eyes so that Brian was more than an indistinct silhouette against the glare.

"I got one while I was in talking to Watson—he's asking me if things are going alright on the floor but he just wants me out of the office. His big problem for the day has been sorted out. I won't be bothering the pickers anymore."

Singer used the hand shading his eyes to dig into the inside pocket of his jacket and pull his phone out.

"And there's a hundred more names in my inbox. Maybe, one-fifty."

Singer held his phone between his thumb and forefinger and waggled it a couple of times.

"Right here, Brian. You want to watch?"

His friend took a step back and held up his arms.

"I don't need to see them, Pete, I believe you. I don't think you're making this up. I'm just saying you can't carry this. You've got a life too."

He waved at the phone.

"This shouldn't mean you can't enjoy your life."

Singer looked at his friend for several long seconds, finally smiled but it didn't catch and hold.

"Two ice times. Two. What do you think? Should I go? I'll tell you what — let's look at a video right now. Or let's look at a few. And then you tell me which one is the one who dies so I get to play a little shinny. You pick. Alright?"

Singer swiped at his phone, tapped pause then tapped again before turning the phone to his friend. Brian took a step back but Singer followed him.

"There! You pick. We'll have a look."

Singed flipped the phone around so he could glance at it then turned it back to his friend.

"Grace Okinibye. The top one. That's easy. Just have a look at Grace. No?"

Singer flipped the phone back around for a second again so he could glance at it then turned it back to Brian.

"What about, Asif? Or Winxi? Or Honore? Or Roberto? I'm sure that you'll be able to find one that isn't worth a couple of hours of ice-time for me. Come on, Brian! Take the phone. Have a look. Just pick one. I promise you—you pick one and I'll come. Easy as that. But you have to watch the whole video and then pick one for me. I can't. But you know what? I'm all fucked up. I just need a little help."

A woman crossing the narrow lane a couple of aisles down glanced over at the sound of Singer's voice but then kept walking. Singer had stepped in close, holding the phone up to his friend so that he had to draw his head back to avoid being touched by the screen.

"I'm serious, Brian. I'm not bullshitting you, here. I can't choose. You choose. That's all. You choose and I'll come. Tonight."

His friend backed off a step as Singer stepped closer, holding up his hands to ward Singer off.

"What the f… Cut it out, Pete. What are you doing? Get your fucking phone out of my face."

Singer stopped where he stood, staring at the arm holding the phone still outstretched towards his friend as if it belonged to somebody else, before letting it drop to his side. When he spoke again, it was at the ground, his voice flat and quiet, pitched low and barely audible.

"Sorry, Brian. I want to play. I really do. I just can't pick."

Singer looked up at his friend, his eyes pleading, the hand holding the phone flexing as if to move but remaining at his side.

"If y…?"

Brian looked at Singer as if stricken and some recognition dawned on Singer and he nodded.

"I know. I know."

And turned away to walk to his car. He wound his way through several aisles before stopping beside the 2014 Corolla,88 the only new car they had ever owned, and stared off across the expanse of parked cars that stretched almost to the edge of the darkening sky. His arms sagged like drenched cotton towels from his shoulders. Finally he searched in his pockets, found his keys, got in his car and pulled away.

***

Singer stood in line waiting for a teller to come free. He was third in line but there were two tellers so it shouldn't take long. He checked his watch. Singer was already running more than an hour late after his meeting with Watson and talking with Brian in the parking lot. The line shuffled forward and then again as both customers moved away from the teller windows so that it was just Singer waiting for a teller.

He wondered how much cash the bank was holding. It was so hard to know now, when money spent most of its time as charged particles, electrons or ions, racing up and down bundled wires, existing in a shared imagination rather than as something that could be packed into a briefcase and exchanged for gold or diamonds or somebody's freedom.

In the old heist movies, it always seemed that some days were better than others, the beginning of the week, or the end of the week, and there was always an explanation somehow related to paydays or deposits but Singer had never followed the logic. But he suspected that it no longer mattered, that cash on hand was as random and transient as the dimples created in a stream surface by emerging mayflies in June or July. That it was always in motion, all spin and angular momentum around the infinite mass of human wants and desires, so rarely still, that to even attempt to capture it in those resting moments was as futile as trying to hold a single moment, pure and inviolate, untouched by the second that preceded it or the one that followed. It no longer made sense to take money from where it settled, it only made sense to divert the flow so that it passed through you before moving to a neighboring node.

"Sir?"

Singer looked up, and the teller at the left-hand window smiled and gestured for him to come forward. Singer stepped to the window and dug around in his pocket, found what he wanted, pulled it out and laid his debit card on the table.

"I want to set up an automatic withdrawal to one of our other accounts."

"Did the account originate at another branch, Mr. Singer?"

Singer shook his head.

"It's another bank."

The woman allowed herself a small frown.

"It's a long story. But I just want to set up an automatic withdrawal from our savings account with you, to this other account. Is that going to be a problem?"

The young woman smiled again and pushed a small portable debit machine across to him.

"No problem. Just sign in. How often do you want the withdrawal?"

"Once a month."

She nodded.

"And on what date?"

Singer considered that for a moment.

"When do most of our automatic withdrawals come out?"

The teller tapped several keys and then scrolled through the screen.

"Well, you get paid every two weeks, Mr. Singer, and most of your withdrawals come out on your paydays, but the second pay of the month is where you have more withdrawals."

Singer nodded.

"Okay. Let's put it there."

The teller looked at him.

"We generally advise people to space withdrawals out over a few days—they're a little easier to monitor if they aren't occurring on the same day. Would you like me to just make this for the day after your second pay of the month?"

Singer shook his head.

"No. Same day. We'll be fine."

The woman shrugged and smiled.

"No problem, Mr. Singer. Same day."

She turned to her screen, tapped a few keys then turned back to him.

"And how much?"

Singer closed his eyes, thinking.

"What are our current withdrawals?"

The woman frowned.

"Excuse me, Mr. Singer?"

Singer forced himself to meet her eyes.

"What are our current withdrawals?"

She looked to the screen, still frowning, scrolling up and down a couple of times.

"Well, there's your mortgage—it's six hundred fifty dollars every two weeks, water is one hundred, two hundred for hydro and two hundred to pay a student loan."

Singer nodded then paused as if he was thinking, and used the fingers of one hand to count on the other before looking up.

"Let's make it two hundred."

The teller tapped at her keyboard several times, glanced up at the screen several times, paused once to run her finger under a line on the screen before entering the command. When she was done, she took a small step away from her screen and smiled at him.

"There you go, Mr. Singer. Anything else we can do for you?"

Singer looked down at his card then back up at the teller, noticing the nameplate on her sweater.

"Actually, Sylvie. Could I transfer one hundred over right now? I just want to make sure it's all working the way it should."

"No need to worry, Mr. Singer. These things are foolproof. I couldn't screw it up even if I tried."

Singer smiled at her.

"I'm sure you're right, Sylvie, but I'd just feel better…"

The young woman smiled and held up her hand.

"No problem, Mr. Singer. Let's do it."

She looked over the top of the computer.

"Is your card still in? Yes, it is. Okay."

It only took a few seconds.

"There you are—good to go."

Singer nodded, pulled his card from the machine and turned to leave, but then leaned back into the window before the next client arrived.

"Sylvie, just out of curiosity how much money would you guys keep on hand these days?"

Her eyes widened and she smiled but it was uncertain. Singer shook his head.

"Never mind. I was just curious."

It had begun to snow again but not enough that he had to brush the windshield.

***

Singer sat in the wash of the computer screen light. It was always the same now, like frayed exposed nerves were connected and coated, charges that had been sparking and flaring, bridging neuronal clefts at random so that unrelated muscle fibers flexed and relaxed at unexpected intervals now fell into place, found order and direction, returned a sense of fluidity and self-control; stimuli, sounds, smells, visual cues that had seemed to arrive without buffer or barrier like shrapnel from a chain and nail bomb now retained shape and sense revealing a world that was once again recognizable.

He had only watched the first four videos because spending more than one hundred dollars would almost certainly lead to questions. A young father surrounded by three children and a woman who had appeared to be the grandmother of the children, although Singer couldn't be sure, one approaching teen years and the other two, infants not more than a year or two old. As always, the spoken message was the same. The relief had grown with each donation.

Irhaa stood leaning against the sheet of corrugated metal that served as one half of the front wall of her family's hut, watching four boys kick a bundle of rags up and down the bare patch of ground separating the rows of huts facing each other and stretching in both directions almost as far as you could see. Singer had only been able to see that because the person holding the camera had done a slow panorama before returning to Irhaa's face. The camera occasionally panned to the boys playing and Singer recognized one of the boys as Irhaa's brother, who had been sitting beside his sister on the first video, occasionally wetting a cloth and placing it to her lips. He was lost in play, but in one moment he flicked the makeshift ball to one side with his right foot, caught it in midair, tipped it left around a bigger, older boy and kicked the rags between two mud clods serving as goalposts. He had turned to his sister, his arms raised in triumph, then pointing at her as if she had somehow played a role in what he had done. The camera panned back to her and it was as if she was lit from within, like a sun rose and set for her alone, her face radiant with a vitality as real as a new dawned day. Then she raised her arms in imitation of her brother, angled her face to the sky, closed her eyes and the screen went blank. Singer played it over and over again, until he could close his eyes and see her face tilted to the sky, accepting every benediction the sun and whispering breeze could offer with grace and gratitude as if they were an unexpected and unwarranted gift.

Singer rose and climbed the stairs to his bed, sure that he would find a few hours sleep.

Chapter 11

Steve Watson looked at Singer across the desk.

"I thought we talked about this, Peter."

Singer nodded, but a muscle clenched and set in his jaw.

"I didn't say anything, Mr. Watson. I just put up a little notice in the break room letting them know where they could donate."

Watson sighed, used both hands on his desk to push himself up and came around the desk and leaned against it as he had in the first meeting, looking down at Singer in the chair in front of him.

"C'mon, Pete, are you telling me that you thought the sign was okay? Really?"

Singer shrugged.

"I don't know, Mr. Watson. It didn't seem like a big deal. All kinds of notices end up on the walls and half the guys don't even read them. I didn't think there would be any harm. And it's important. This is important."

Watson blinked twice before speaking.

"I don't want to have this meeting again, Peter. I didn't think we would have to have it twice, but I definitely don't want a third one. You understand?"

Singer nodded.

"Yessir."

"Good then. Let's both get back to work."

***

Singer's youngest stood up on his chair to reach across the table for another slice but his dad grabbed his hand.

"Not yet, Tommie. Finish your first slice."

Tommie looked down at his plate and scowled.

"I don't like the crust."

"It's all pizza, Tommie. Eat up."

Cheryl reached across, grabbed a slice and placed it on her son's plate, grabbed the remnants of his first piece and ate them in two quick bites.

"Would you relax, Petey. What's the big deal—he doesn't like crust."

The anger flared quick and surprised him. He tamped it down before speaking.

"That crust would be a meal for some people, Cheryl. Do you realize that? That piece that we toss in the garbage would be all the food somebody might have for a day."

Cheryl grinned at him.

"C'mon grumpy. Relax a little. And we didn't throw it in the garbage. I ate it."

Singer didn't look at her.

"Do you realize that, Tommie? That there are kids who aren't as lucky as you? Kids who don't get enough food?"

Tommie had already worked his way through the slice almost to the crust and looked up at his dad over what was left and then over at his brother, already losing interest in the conversation.

"Why doesn't somebody get some for them?"

Singer looked at his wife and threw his hands up.

"Have I made my point?"

His wife made a face.

"What do you expect? He's six."

She turned to her son.

"Daddy's just saying that we have to think about other people sometimes. That everybody's not as lucky as we are."

Tommie had fashioned the crust into a miniature hockey stick and was batting a fragment of pepperoni around on his plate. He nodded without looking up.

"Okay."

But then, as if reminded of something, he looked up at his mother.

"But some people are luckier. Jason's sister has a horse."

Cheryl looked across at her husband, raised her eyebrows and shrugged.

"Mouths of babes and all that."

Singer's eyebrows furrowed into a deep V.

"Really? You buy that?"

She held his eyes for several seconds then cut her eyes to their youngest son, who had stopped playing with his food and was looking back and forth between the two of them. Singer glanced at Dougie, whose head was down as if there was something fascinating on his plate, but the tips of his ears glowed red the way they did when he was angry or upset. Singer let the air out between his teeth in a long, thin stream before he reached across the table to tap Dougie's arm.

"Another piece, D-man?"

His oldest, still looking down, shook his head. Singer looked at his wife, raised his eyebrows and shrugged then turned back to his son.

"It's okay, Dougie. I didn't mean we shouldn't be eating pizza. It's just easy to forget how lucky we are. C'mon, there's still a couple of pieces left."

Dougie shook his head again before looking up at Singer then across at his mother.

"May I be excused?"

Cheryl nodded.

"Sure, honey."

"Me too!"

Tommie had already dropped the pizza crust, jumped down from the table and was out the kitchen door ahead of his brother. Singer and his wife listened as the boys went up the stairs, Dougie muttering something he couldn't hear and Tommie shouting 'leave me alone!' Singer pushed the hair back off his forehead, running his fingers straight back across his scalp, curling his fingers around a clump at the crown and tugging as if trying to pull it free before letting go and placing one hand across his mouth and chin.

"I just don't want them taking this for granted, forgetting about other people."

Cheryl nodded.

"They're kids."

Singer's jaw set.

"Sure. But this is where it starts. This is where they learn how not to see, not to think about it, not to care. If we don't show them, how will they know?"

His wife waved towards the stairs.

"How's it going so far?"

Singer ran his hands over his face.

"I know. I know. But what do we do?"

Singer looked at his wife for the first time since the kids had left the room. He waved around the room, taking in the stove and microwave above it, the dishwasher, the cupboards, full so that they had to line the cereal boxes up along the top of the fridge.

"Look at Tommie! He's got all of this and all he can say is 'Jason's sister has a horse'."

Cheryl made a face.

"Peter, he's six! What do you want from him? He's just a little boy! Give him some time."

Singer had been leaning forward, both arms on the table but now he pushed back, throwing his arms out.

"Some time to do what? He's no different from anybody else! Nobody gives a shit, Cheryl! Nothing changes! They start out thinking like Tommie and they're still thinking like that now. Pissed off because Jason's sister has a horse! While kids die because they can't afford enough food to stay alive!"

Cheryl had started at her husband's first quick motion but then she leaned forward as if trying to draw him back, bring him closer, turning her hands palms up.

"I know, Petey. I know. But we can teach them. Help them understand. We can do that. It's our job."

Singer nodded but he wasn't looking at her or when he did, he looked quickly away around the room.

"Sure. Sure. But how? How do they learn?"

He looked at her then, closely.

"Should we show them the videos? Let them see what it's really like."

His wife closed her hands into fists, opened them again to slap down on the table and thrust herself to her feet.

"The videos! Show them the videos! Have you lost your mind, Peter!?"

Singer had pushed back further in his chair, struck by the force of his wife's reaction.

"But h—"

"Did you see Dougie's face? That kid takes in every word you say like it's oxygen. All he knows right now is that he doesn't care enough! That he's not good enough! But he doesn't even know why. And you think the best thing to do is show him a video of a little kid dying right in front of his eyes? How fucked up do you want him to be? He's got to live in this world, Peter! Do you understand that?"

She was almost standing over him now.

"Those videos! Those fucking videos!"

She slumped back in her chair, the anger draining away from her like something had cracked, like how she felt was just one more thing she couldn't hold on to.

"All you had to do was delete them. That's all."

She sat forward, both hands covering her face so that her voice was muffled as she spoke.

"I want to find them. Whoever is sending these videos. They shouldn't be allowed to do this to people. It's wrong. Somebody should find them and stop them."

She dropped her hands. He had thought there might be tears, but her eyes were cold and flat.

"It's just another scam. Just another way to separate suckers from their money."

It was like she had slapped him. He straightened in the chair.

"Suckers, eh?"

He pushed the cardboard box holding the last slices of pizza across the table towards her.

"How much was this? How much?"

He stood up and went across the kitchen counter where the paper bag his wife had pulled it from still lay. He flipped the bag over to get at the receipt.

"Twenty-seven dollars! For some dough, sauce and cheese!"

Singer walked over to the floor-to-ceiling cupboards and pulled the doors open, revealing rows of canned, bagged and boxed food.

"Couldn't find any food?"

He slammed the doors shut and pulled the fridge door open hard enough that one of the cereal boxes fell to the floor, spilling Cheerios in every direction.

"Couldn't find anything for us to eat in here!? But I'm the sucker!?"

Singer strode back to the counter, Cheerios crunching beneath his feet, ripping the bag apart.

"There's got to be a coupon in here somewhere. Ten percent off for the next time! And that will be worth it. Twenty-four dollars and thirty cents so that you don't have to heat up soup on the stove. Sounds like a fair trade to me!"

He turned on her, each breath coming in a harsh burst as if it caught for a moment at the place where larynx and throat converged before being catapulted forward and forced from his nose and mouth.

"But the emails are the problem! The fucking emails are the problem!"

She looked at him, dry-eyed for several seconds then stood and left the room. Singer listened to her footsteps on the stairs leading to the upper floor and the bedroom door close behind her.

***

"Read some more, Daddy."

Singer smiled at his youngest son.

"One chapter, Tommie."

Singer tapped him on the butt.

"Get up to your bunk, buddy."

Tommie giggled and squirmed away.

"Just one more. You won't need to read one tomorrow night."

Dougie snorted.

"If Dad said he wasn't going to read to you tomorrow, you'd cry like a little baby."

"Would not!"

"Would so!"

Singer swung his legs off the lower bunk, gathered his youngest son into his arms, still giggling, stood up and tossed him onto the top bunk. Tommie crawled over to the edge and hung his head and shoulders over the edge so he could look down at his older brother.

"Would not!"

Singer tousled his hair and pulled him back up into the bed.

"Lie down and stop bugging your brother."

Singer stepped up onto the edge of the lower bunk so he could lean into the upper and kissed the top of his son's head, then crouched beside the lower bunk and kissed Dougie on the forehead.

"Sleep good, buddy."

"Dad?"

Singer had been rising to his feet but let himself settle back in beside his son.

"What's up, Dougie?"

"What videos?"

Singer paused, looking at his son, waiting for him to look up from his hands but he didn't.

"What do you mean?"

"What videos was Mommy talking about?"

Singer felt the strain in his thighs and shifted out of his crouch onto the lower bunk, pushing back with both hands so the wall was at his back. He saw Tommie's head hanging down again but pretended not to notice.

"You were listening?"

Dougie shrugged.

"Couldn't help it."

"He sat at the top of the stairs!"

Dougie grabbed a rolled-up sock, threw it at his brother and missed. Tommie ducked away but was back in seconds.

Singer reached out, touched his son's cheek then chucked his chin.

"It's okay."

Both boys waited. Singer drew a long breath then let it escape in a thin audible sizzle.

"Y'know I was telling you about kids who aren't as lucky as you?"

He looked at both of them for a response, but they just looked back.

"Well, I get videos of those kids."

"Can I see?"

"Shut up, Tommie."

"Dad! Dougie said shut up."

Singer waved a hand to quiet his youngest then waited. It took several seconds.

"Who are they from?"

Singer shook his head.

"I don't really know."

Dougie was looking at him now.

"Why are they sending them to you?"

Singer shook his head again.

"I don't know, son."

"What are they doing?"

"The kids?"

Dougie nodded.

Singer closed his eyes and let his head fall back against the wall behind him. He remained like that for several seconds before pushing away from the wall to the edge of the bunk and standing up. He kissed the tips of his fingers then held them to Tommie's forehead before kissing them again and bending over to place them against his oldest son's head.

"You guys sleep good."

Singer paused at the door to flip the overhead light switch. The dresser and the table under the window were fronted by a red plastic chair and the bunk beds and the scatter of toys and clothes on the carpeted floor. They had stood out clear and sharp-edged under the glare of the overhead light but became vague ill-formed shapes just at the edges of the dim wash from the night light plugged low into the wall beside the door.

"Dad?"

Singer edged the door shut behind him, leaving the crack that Tommie had insisted on since he was old enough to point.

***

Singer had thought Cheryl was asleep when he finally came to bed but she curled up against him, her belly soft and yielding through her nightie against the spot just above the curve of his butt at the base of his spine, her left arm coming across his shoulder to drape across his chest, her lips close to his ear.

"I'm sorry, Petey."

Singer turned so he was facing her.

"I'm sorry too, Cher. I just don't kn—"

"Shhh. Shhh."

She ran her hand down his side and slipped it under the waistband of his briefs, catching the edge with her thumb to slide them down his hip. He raised himself off the bed so they could slide down his legs to his ankles.

***

They made love. Singer waited until her breathing had evened and settled except for the irregular mutterings before slipping out of bed and down to his computer.

It was Friday morning and the transfer would have come in.

He sat watching videos and making decisions until a streak of cloud lit from below by the circling sun braised the eastern horizon. Then he rose from his desk and went upstairs to dress for work.

Chapter 12

Singer spotted Ray Sproul and two of his buddies coming across the parking lot and slowed so they wouldn't get to the door at the same time. Any interaction with Raymond Sproul was always unpleasant…and when he had an audience it was usually worse.

***

Lights flashed on his screen. Three jobs that were running more than thirty minutes behind time—packages that should have already made it to the loading dock but hadn't been scanned yet. They had all been assigned to the same picker—employee number G67291. He looked them up—Hannah Clermont. He couldn't put a face to the name but that wasn't surprising, she had only been with them for six months.

Singer texted her.

Hannah, you alright?

Singer stood at his workstation flipping through the job log. It was one of those mornings—a weak crew. Jennifer had called in sick, and Bobby and Vijay had booked time and their replacements just couldn't move product the same way. But only Hannah was getting flagged. The rest had figured out how to move just fast enough to be left alone.

Singer stepped away, pausing before entering the main aisle to make sure nothing was coming. He peered towards the back of the warehouse, able to see the back wall of the building as faint shaded grey in the distance. Singer shaded his eyes against the hard fluorescent lights, feeling the ache starting to build at the base of his neck but shaking it off. There were a couple of tiny figures walking towards him and he watched them, unable to tell their gender, but then one ducked into a side aisle and the other stepped up onto a parked forklift at the end of an aisle and spun away towards the back of the building.

Singer stepped back to his workstation. Seven more orders for his section had come in. He looked at the picker queue. Nobody was free but there were several that would be in the next few minutes. He let the automatic assignments stand but when Clermont's name popped up, he overrode the automatic assignment and passed it along to one of his veterans, Anne Shirley. Not fast, but steady.

Singer's phone pinged and he took a quick look at the text.

"WHEN YOU BREAKIN?"

Singer checked the time then responded.

"TEN MINUTES. SOUTH END."

"SEE YOU THEN."

***

Brian Ferris was already sipping a coffee when Singer arrived, he pulled back a chair with his foot so Singer could sit down then pointed at a second coffee on the table.

"That one's for you, figured you'd need it."

Singer nodded his thanks and sat down. Singer raised his voice over the scrape of chairs as the pickers from the early break gathered themselves to leave.

"How was the game?"

"Not bad. We won and I got a couple. But they moved Thibodeau up onto the wing and that guy couldn't take a pass if we velcroed his stick. Somebody should tell him it's not a ping pong paddle."

Singer took a long sip.

"He'll come around."

"Sure he will. Because rec league players always get better at forty."

Brian looked over.

"We miss you, buddy. Not just on the ice. Dressing room's not so much fun either."

Singer took another sip but didn't answer. Ferris waved his hand.

"Alright. Alright. I'll leave it alone."

Singer looked over.

"You worked with a picker named Clermont? Hannah?"

His friend looked up at the ceiling, thinking.

"Short. Kinda skinny? Maybe twenty-four, twenty-five?"

Singer shrugged.

"I'm not sure. I don't know if I've ever met her. She's filling in but she's been flagged three times this morning already."

Ferris frowned and tilted his head.

"If it's the girl I'm thinking of, never had a problem. She's not a star but she was always fine. I don't remember her getting flagged at all. Maybe on the first day but not after that."

Singer nodded.

"Funny. I'll have to check her out."

He pulled his phone out to take a look but she hadn't responded. Ferris nodded at the phone.

"Nothing?"

Singer shook his head and his friend frowned again.

"Strange."

"Yeah."

They sat for a moment without talking, surrounded by the smash of voices caroming off the hard concrete walls and floor as the break crew talked at angles across and around the table and shouted to each other as they entered and left. Brian leaned in to be heard.

"How are things going with the emails?"

Singer nodded.

"I've got things sorted out."

Ferris nodded back.

"Good. You've talked to Cheryl?"

"Sure."

"She's on board?"

Singer looked at his phone and stood up.

"I'm going to head back and check on Clermont before I have to be on the station."

Ferris watched his friend leave and shouted after him.

"Pete! Pete!"

Singer didn't turn around, though Ferris was pretty sure he had heard him.

***

Singer found Clermont on one of the outside loading docks sitting with her back against the brick wall, the heels of her work boots tucked up tight against her butt, surrounded by four or five cigarette butts smoked to the filter. He would have missed her if he hadn't caught a glimpse of her toes just beyond the edge of a concrete wall pillar that must have supported the overhang protecting the stacked packages in bad weather. The dock had been shut down for maintenance so they were alone.

He caught a glimpse of her arm moving up to her face as he approached the pillar, and when he was in front of her he could see where her thumb or heel of her palm had smeared a thin streak of mascara across her cheek.

"Clermont?"

Nothing.

"Hannah?"

She didn't look up until he used her first name. She looked vaguely familiar although enough of a type that it was possible I recognized her from a dozen other women I had met—fine brown hair that fell along the side of her face and down her forehead, limp and insubstantial as if made of something less than anchored keratin. She had small features but not fine or delicate, as if somehow exposure to unnamed elements had left her weathered, abraded, like a fine china doll abandoned in the late fall and left through a hard, cold winter so that what was left had lost any subtlety of shading, texture, edge and curve.

She held his eyes now but without intent, simply waiting. Singer let himself down beside her, the cold of the concrete loading dock seeping through his pants as soon as he settled.

"What's up, Hannah?"

She shrugged without looking over. Singer nodded.

"You don't have to tell me anything, Hannah. But you can't just sit out here. Another hour and they'll slap a label on you, load you on a truck and who knows where you'd end up."

Clermont said something he couldn't make out. Singer tapped her knee.

"What's that?"

"Have to be better than here."

Singer shrugged.

"I don't know…ever been to upstate New York?"

She shook her head and might have smiled, but Singer couldn't tell because she held her hand to her mouth.

"Mostly rust and torn tarpaper. We have to pay drivers double to deliver there."

"Do not."

Singer made a face.

"Damn. I knew it was too much as soon as I said it. No way you were going to believe the bosses would pay double on anything."

They sat for a few seconds.

"We have to go back in, Hannah. I took you out of the queue so you won't have any more flags but if you don't get back on the line, I'm going to have to book you off for the day. And if I book you off, you'll need a doctor's note."

She leaned so that her forehead rested on her knees and her hair slumped forward, obscuring her face. Then she placed her palms flat on the concrete surface and pushed herself up in a quick smooth motion with a fluidity and grace that caught Singer by surprise. He braced himself against the wall and pushed himself to his feet beside her. Now that they were standing, he saw how short she was—the top of her head coming to barely his shoulder—and slight, her shoulders, arms and torso lost beneath the blue cotton shirt and worn jean jacket. He stepped in beside her.

"Anything you can tell me before we get back in."

She shrugged.

"Sproul…"

Singer thought she might keep going, but the name just hung there while they walked.

Singer pulled the heavy metal door open and held it for Clermont. He followed her through and it was like stepping into another world, the ceiling telescoping away so that he was struck by the way that physical dimensions had changed, the way that they were dominated and diminished by the boxes and packages slotted and shelved in racks and scaffolding that towered to the ceiling coiled above them, curling to the tiered and buttressed metal walls, the ribbed vaulting interrupted by angled metal trusses and shadowed just beyond the lines of industrial strength fluorescent lighting dangling from heavy chains; as if each hanging unit had dropped through a trap door in the roof and been jerked to a sudden halt at the end of a short fall. The air Singer inhaled as he stepped into the warehouse was different from what he had just exhaled on the loading dock, like the mix of nitrogen, oxygen, argon, CO_2 and water vapor had changed, creating something less fluid, less supple, rougher textured, malleable but hinting at brittle. Under different atmospheric pressure or colder temperatures the warehouse air would shatter into edged shards. It tasted stale. It was as if the renewal created by the breaking and reformation of chemical bonds had slowed so that what linked nitrogen molecules, oxygen to hydrogen and carbon to oxygen and each of the those to the other, were the same tired strands that hand linked them yesterday and the day before and they had begun to stretch and fray as the condensed energy dissipated, degraded, leaving behind the faint flavor of quantum decay. The cool wash of muted light that had bathed the loading dock beneath the overcast sky was replaced by the stone-hard glare of the warehouse lighting, designed to pry and invade every shadowed curve and angle.

The young woman paused to look back at him and he saw the blemish at the corner of her mouth, raw and red, scabbing at the far corner where she had peeled away skin. But it extended right to where her upper and lower lip met and perhaps beyond into her mouth. One front tooth was broken but not recently because the jagged burs of the fresh break had been smoothed and scalloped. She followed his eyes and turned quickly away, raising her hand to her mouth before dropping it again. Singer had fallen several steps behind and had to hurry to fall in step beside her.

"What about Sproul?"

She shook her head. Singer felt a surge of irritation.

"Hannah! I can't help if I don't know what's going on!"

Clermont raised her hand to pull her hair behind her ear but then paused and let it fall back across her cheek.

"I didn't ask you to help."

Singer took a moment to let the next surge ebb.

"I know you didn't, Hannah. But you can't spend your day sitting out on the loading dock. You've already been flagged three times."

Singer looked over at her, then away.

"You know how it works here, they'll just find somebody else."

He glanced over again and saw the moisture accumulate at the corner of her eye and gather until the narrow ledge formed by the lacrimal canal could no longer contain it, allowing a tear to spill down her cheek. The irritation left like air from a popped balloon. Singer stopped and waited while Clermont took a couple more steps then also stopped. It took a while before she decided but then turned, peering at him through the hanging strands of hair. Singer spoke softly.

"It's okay, Hannah. You can tell me what's going on."

The young woman smiled, touched two fingers to her lips then looked to her right at the aisle beside her.

"This is my station. I should get back to work."

Singer was unable to think of what to say next. The young woman smiled through her fingers again.

"I'll be fine."

She turned away and walked down the aisle. Singer looked down the main aisle to the front of the building where a few miniature figures milled around. They appeared from aisles, holding packages to be labelled and placed on the conveyor belts or the roving floor-level robots then disappeared again. A forklift sat idling at the end of an aisle, a picker standing up on the lower step to lean in and talk to the driver, but from this distance Singer couldn't make out either of them. Singer broke into a jog—he had been away from his station for too long and would still be a few minutes getting back.

Lost in thought, Singer hadn't noticed the forklift, still idling in the same spot, until he was almost upon it. The driver and the picker, Sproul and one of his buddies. They had stopped talking to watch him, the picker down from the step and using the lift to lean against, one foot propped on the vehicle. Sproul, heavy-lidded and grinning, tipped two fingers to his brow in a mock salute and his friend did the same, as if they had discussed and rehearsed it. Singer felt the fuse flush and catch. He slowed to a walk and angled over to where the forklift idled. He looked directly at Ray Sproul, ignoring his partner except to include him in the comment.

"You boy's got nothing to do?"

Sproul's eyes dropped a little further and his grin widened as if his eyelids and the corners of his lips were connected on a swivel. Sproul gestured at the other man, but Singer didn't look away.

"Me and Henry were just strategizing, figuring the most efficient way to get the job done. You don't have to worry about us, bossman. We're staying on schedule."

Singer knew that they were. They had figured out exactly how fast to move without getting flagged. He felt the fuse flare hotter but kept his face still.

"I know you are, Sproul. Your kind usually do. But eventually you cut the corner just a little too fine."

Sproul's eyes sagged a little further down to two narrow glints of black between the upper and lower lid. Singer raised his head a little and sniffed the air.

"You alright, Sproul? That weed I smell?"

He took a quick glance at the second man, who looked startled, but Sproul's expression didn't change.

"'Because you know—don't you, boys—that high on the job is a firing offence?"

He looked at the other man again and then back to Sproul.

"You've explained that to your friend, right?"

Sproul opened his eyes a little wider, narrowing his grin and leaned forward a little out of the cab.

"You don't have to worry about us, boss. We're always straight on the job. Wouldn't want to be called into the office and set straight. Right, Henry?"

Sproul let his eyes stray to look away over Singer's shoulder to the back of the warehouse.

"But you might want to talk to your little gal back there. Sometimes her head don't seem like it's right in the game."

Sproul had let his eyes fall almost shut again but the big grin was belied by a stroked edge to his voice.

"I guess I see the attraction, kind of like one of those little strays show up at your backdoor, beat-up, a little ragged, but there's something kind of cute about just how lost they is. I get it—makes you want to just hold 'em close and make 'em feel safe—"

The wick sparked, burnt and hit powder.

Singer had Sproul by the front of his jacket and half out of the cab before he could grab for purchase, his hips beyond the narrow metal rail protecting the floor of the cab, so that the only thing between Sproul and falling face-first to the concrete was the grip Singer had on his front. Singer leaned in close, his lips up against the other man's ear.

"If I hear you've bothered her again, Sproul, you'll be gone."

The other man's eyes flared for a moment, his lips drawn back from his teeth in a grimace but then dropped quickly back into place, the grin spreading across his face again, holding Singer's eyes for several seconds before letting his eyes drift to a spot high over Singer's shoulder before silently mouthing the words.

"You getting all this?"

Singer let his eyes drop closed for a moment, exhaled, then pushed Sproul back up into his seat. The other man adjusted his ball cap, which had been knocked askew, looked at his friend then back at Singer.

"You should watch that temper. It's going to get you in trouble."

Sproul put the forklift into gear, swung around Singer almost brushing him with a front tong and drove to the next aisle. Singer stood for a long moment then headed back to his station, walking now.

***

The child lay on a ragged blanket beneath a strange tree with a straight, bone-white trunk that broke into several rotating stems about five feet above the ground to create a swirl of stems, skirling into an oval canopy that let sun through in a spackled kaleidoscope. The arms and legs of the child, still too young to walk, waved in the air and he grinned and made gurgling noises at the person holding the camera. The distended belly, grey-tinged skin and hollows around the mouth and eyes were gone. It was as if he had burned to the last ember and then been re-ignited. Singer shut down his computer and returned to bed, certain that he would be able to sleep.

Chapter 13

"Pete, c'mon! The boys have to be there early! Let's go!"

Singer trotted from the bedroom, stopping to scoop up his youngest who was waiting for him at the bottom of the stairs, tousling his hair with a free hand. He heard the door close behind his wife as she went out to start the car.

"What are they going to do, eh Tommie? Can't start the show without the stars."

Tommie laughed, pushed off from his Dad and squirmed down.

"We're not the stars. The grade sixers are the stars."

Singer followed his son into the kitchen, grabbed his jacket off the wall and shrugged into it. Then he grabbed Tommie's jacket from the wall and crouched down to help him put it on. He looked over at his oldest, already standing at the door dressed in jacket, toque and mitts.

"C'mon Dougie. Tell him who the stars are."

Dougie rolled his eyes.

"Dad!"

Singer stopped for a second to put his hands up in surrender.

"Alright. Alright. If I'm the only one who knows who the stars are, that's fine. The world will find out soon enough."

Singer stood up and held the door open so both boys could head out to the car.

***

Singer and his wife found seats near the top of the bleachers along the wall. There was a cluster of six or eight couples near the center of the stands, but most of the rest of the parents were scattered about in couples or occasionally groups of three or four. If there were three people, it was almost always two moms and one slightly uncomfortable-looking husband who looked to Singer like he wished he worked evenings. Singer's wife waved to a couple of women as they threaded their way up into the bleachers. As they sat down, Singer raised an eyebrow questioningly. Cheryl shrugged.

"Just a couple of Moms I've met helping out in Tommie's class."

Singer widened his eyes as if he were afraid and she slapped his arm.

"Don't worry. I'm not going to make you meet their husbands."

Singer looked insulted.

"Hey. What are you suggesting? I love people. Anybody who knows me knows I'm a people person."

She pushed him with both hands, so he almost tipped over.

"Most people who know you aren't sure you're even a person."

Singer sat up straight.

"Fair enough."

It was a small gym, just large enough to hold the basketball court and the bleachers along one wall. The baskets had been cranked up to the ceiling and a large, low stage covered in folding chairs had been set up in the center of the floor. A smaller stage had been erected down where Singer and his wife were sitting. Singer looked around the stands and recognized a couple of faces—a guy who had come out for hockey twice, then not returned and a woman it took him a second to place.

It was a woman he and Cheryl had been behind at parent-teacher meetings at the beginning of the year. The woman had explained to the teacher that her son only misbehaved because he was gifted, and when he wasn't challenged enough in class he got bored. The teacher had asked,

"Oh. Has Jamie been identified?"

The woman had made a scoffing noise and said,

"Those tests. They miss most truly gifted children."

The teacher had nodded and promised to try and keep the woman's son as challenged as she could. When it had been Singer and Cheryl's turn, he had said,

"Tommie only misbehaves because, as far as we can tell, he loves to torment people."

The teacher had smiled down into her fist, then looked up and over their shoulder at the woman leaving.

"Yes, well every child has different needs."

The three of them had laughed and moved on.

Singer nudged his wife and nodded at the woman. She looked and then slapped him again.

"Stop it. You're just making trouble now."

The lights dimmed so that the stands were shadowed and only the center stage was well lit. Tommie's teacher led his class of twenty-two grade one students across the parquet floor to the stage and waited for them to scramble around and find their seats. There was a smattering of applause and then the teacher motioned for them to stand. She blew into a pitch pipe, raised her hands and half the class began to sing Row, Row, Row Your Boat. She waited until they had completed the first round before starting the remaining half of the class. Tommie and a girl sitting next to him couldn't contain themselves and started early. Singer listened for a minute then leaned over to his wife and whispered in her ear.

"What do they call this event?"

She kept her eyes straight ahead and ignored him. He leaned over again.

"Hon? What do they call this event again?"

She kept her eyes straight ahead but whispered out of the side of her mouth.

"Stop it. You're not funny."

One of the women nearby took a quick glance up at them. Singer leaned over again.

"It said Talent Show out front—that can't be right."

His wife continued to stare straight ahead but Singer could see her mouth twitching. Singer leaned in again.

"Never mind, I'll ask around later."

Singer took a quick look behind to make sure nobody was sitting there and leaned back with his arms on the bench behind him and his legs sprawled out on the empty bench in front of him, grinning to himself.

***

Dougie's Grade 3 class played an instrumental version of the Theme from Rocky with Dougie on triangle. Several stanzas in Singer leaned over to his wife,

"I didn't realize that Rocky had multiple sclerosis."

Singer saw her start to go but then she caught herself. Singer leaned over again.

"Seen it three times. Hard to believe I missed that."

His wife tried to stifle it but it came out as a loud snort that she tried to disguise as a cough. Several parents turned to look at her but she just continued to look at the children playing. Singer sprawled back across the benches.

***

The grand finale was the grade six 'orchestra' playing a reasonably proficient version of Stayin' Alive. But just before that, there were two grade five saxophone players playing a duet billed as 'Summertime'. The gym fell completely dark and then a single spotlight gradually brightened to capture a boy and girl standing side by side on the small stage. There was a long pause until somewhere offstage in the darkness somebody tapped out four beats and they began to play.

When they had been playing for about forty-five seconds, Singer sat up and leaned into his wife's ear.

"Shouldn't they have taught them the same song?"

She stared straight ahead at the children but reached over in the dark and pinched his leg, hard. Singer grinned in the darkness. He waited for another thirty seconds then leaned over again.

"Or at least two songs in the same key?"

This time she snorted again and he leaned back laughing as soundlessly as he could but the shake in his body rattled the benches. Several parents looked around at them, first questioningly and then scowling. They tried to keep their faces straight and still, but it was too late, they were gone.

They scurried down from the stands after the final act, looking at nobody but feeling the stares on their back and shoulders until they were beyond the foyer and out into the parking lot. Cheryl sent Singer back in to gather up the boys who were wandering around the foyer looking for them.

***

With the kids settled into bed, Singer and his wife sat at the kitchen table, lit only by the hallway light. Cheryl took a sip of wine and looked at Singer over the lip of the glass.

"We're the worst."

Singer grinned.

"Don't look at me. You're the one who can't laugh quietly."

She reached across the slap his arm.

"I was just being kind saying 'we're'. You're the worst. Mocking eleven-year-olds! You should be ashamed."

Singer ducked his head, still grinning.

"Okay. I'm ashamed. But you laughed. If it had just been me, nobody would have even known. But then you start snorting and sputtering like you just popped a cork and it was all over."

She smiled at him again.

"Okay. I'll take some of the blame. Let's stick with 'We're' the worst."

They sat in silence for several minutes. Cheryl looked at Singer several times before speaking again.

"What did you spend the four hundred dollars on?"

Singer looked at her, deciding whether to pretend he didn't know what she was talking about.

"Christmas?"

She nodded.

"How did you know?"

She looked across the rim of her glass again, her face gentle but serious.

"The sweater was nice. And so were the earrings. But there was no way you spent four hundred on those."

Singer nodded.

"Two hundred. You know how I used the rest."

Why two hundred? Why not just admit that the sweater and earrings had only cost him $100 on eBay. But somehow it seemed important that half had gone to her.

"Are we done with it, Petey? Are you okay? Is it over?"

Singer nodded and felt something give way inside.

Chapter 14

Singer almost went down on the first step outside the warehouse. It had warmed up overnight and the snow that had been packed into a hard layer for six weeks was slush and gave under his foot like beach sand so that he had to catch himself with a hand against the wall. The sun was bright and warm. Singer shaded his eyes to look across the narrow gap between the warehouse and the new office building. He stuck to the narrow black trail that had been worn between the warehouse and the offices, only stepping off for one of the managers to pass, a young guy Singer had seen around but he couldn't put a name to. The guy looked up from his phone long enough to nod before looking back down.

Inside the door, Singer kicked the soiled snow off his shoes before crossing the granite floor to the security desk. The older woman behind the desk tapped a couple of keys and ran her finger down the screen before nodding at him and gesturing towards the single elevator on the far wall.

On the second floor, the guard buzzed Singer through the locked glass doors as if expecting him. Either the guard downstairs had messaged up to the second floor or there were cameras that Singer hadn't noticed.

"You know where you're going?"

Singer nodded.

"263."

***

The door to Watson's new office was wide open this time and Singer stood in the hallway. Watson was on the phone.

"We didn't get to where we wanted in January but we look like we're on track for this month…"

He paused as if interrupted by somebody on the other end, listened and then laughed before he looked up and spotted Singer. Watson gestured at one of the chairs against the wall to the right of his desk and Singer crossed the floor to sit down. Watson continued to talk into the phone, swiveling in his chair so that he was almost facing away from Singer.

Singer glanced around the room. It was a little larger but otherwise identical, as far as he could see. Singer noticed that he had trailed a small chunk of ice into the office, grey-white against the polished taupe beneath. It had begun to melt, the edges already sagging so that one moment they delineated the boundary of the ice fragment, the space separating ice from office floor, the place where the ice fragment existed as something separate from the place where it had been dropped and the next there was a narrow ring of melted water that belonged as much to the floor as the shrinking pellet of ice. Whatever had allowed the tiny chunk of ice to exist independently, allowed it to be a unique entity, a real object in the world was disintegrating, as ephemeral and uncertain as car exhaust. Singer watched the ice melt into a small domed pool of water and noticed a small black pebble that must have been caught up in the chunk of slush he had dragged in from the parking lot. The piece of gravel was darker than the office floor so Singer could make out the differences in shading between the floor and the pebble and then something gave—the dome of water collapsed and spread into a thin layer that shrank faster as more of the surface was exposed to the surrounding atmosphere.

"Pete?"

When Singer looked up the other man was waiting, head cocked, questioning. Singer flushed.

"Sorry, Steve. I was just thinking about some…"

Singer shrugged.

"Anyway."

The other man nodded, looked down at his hand lightly tapping a pen on the desktop, before setting the pen on the desk, moving it to the side and looking back up at Singer. Watson started to speak, the stopped himself and started over.

"So, Pete. Tell me about Monday's incident."

For a moment, "Monday's incident" meant nothing to him, like he was caught in a conversation that was really intended for two different people, and though he understood what each individual word meant, the whole was indecipherable, as devoid of coherent meaning as the sound of cars colliding. Then it came back to him.

"Sproul?"

Watson nodded.

"It wasn't a big deal, Steve. There was a problem with one of the other pickers and I was just aski—"

"Pete."

Singer looked up. Watson had picked up the pen again and was tapping the desk.

"First, it's fulfillment associates. We're asking you to make a sincere attempt to stop referring to the warehouse employees as 'pickers'. We all understand that's how you talk on the floor but we're trying to change the culture. Show more respect. Second, you were doing more than asking."

Singer nodded.

"It got a little heated, but nothing got out of hand. Sproul had been—"

Watson held up a finger to stop Singer, tapped a key on his keyboard then spun his computer screen so Singer could see it. The lack of audio created a slightly surreal quality as if they were watching some early 20th-century newsreel. The video had caught their initial exchange, the two-fingered salutes as Singer approached, and then the brief exchange, the camera angled to catch the side of Sproul's face and the back of Singer's head so that it was impossible to make out what was being said, though Singer could see Sproul's expression, placid and composed. The camera had only caught the edge of Sproul's friend, his left side and the lower half of his left profile. Singer wondered if they had chosen the position deliberately or if it had just been a lucky break. There had been little warning for what came next and Singer was startled by how sudden and violent the motion was, Sproul almost out of his seat and down the side of the forklift, the bunching in Singer's shoulders as he took the weight visible even beneath the shirt and safety vest, Sproul's face until that moment, calm and unconcerned but then wide-eyed and fearful. For the first time, Singer noticed that Sproul never reached out for him to try and find purchase or to resist, just came over the edge as if ejected and then draped down the side, powerless to do more than hang in Singer's grasp. In Singer's memory that exchange had been longer, but here on film it lasted only a few seconds, Sproul's face taut, frightened turned slightly to the side as if he anticipated being struck. At the last moment Sproul's eyes glanced up towards the camera and for the first time the video captured his full expression, the fear slid to the edges like a drawn curtain exposing a shuttered smile just as Singer tossed the other man back up into his seat.

"A little heated, Pete?"

Watson spun the screen back around.

"That's assault in anybody's court. If Sproul wanted to lay charges, he could. And that would almost certainly mean dismissal for you plus whatever penalties the courts impose."

Watson paused but it turned out he was just catching his breath.

"Steve—"

"We're just fortunate that Mr. Sproul has agreed not to press charges. I don't know what provoked your attack and he doesn't either, but he doesn't want to see you lose your job. He's assured us that all he wants is to feel that he is coming to a safe workplace, that he doesn't have to fear for his physical wellbeing when he walks into the Amazon Fulfillment Centre doors. So, Pete—"

"He was harassing one of the other employees."

There was a silence that lasted for several seconds.

"What?"

"Sproul was harassing one of the other employees."

Watson stared at him for several seconds then looked away to adjust the computer screen so he could see it better. He tapped out a series of commands on the keyboard. He examined the screen for several seconds then looked back at Singer.

"We've had no complaints from your section."

Singer flushed and shook his head.

"No, sir. Sh— They don't want to make a complaint."

Watson sat back in his chair.

"How convenient."

Singer didn't respond. Watson sat forward in his chair.

"Pete. You're a valued employee here at Amazon. We appreciate and value your service. So, we've decided that the best thing is to give you an opportunity to think about what happened and to learn from it. You'll receive an email providing you with a link to our online one-day conflict management and resolution training course. It's a series of videos with accompanying quizzes. None of it is live but there is a call center where you can get answers to any questions that might arise. And then we're asking you to stay home for two more days to digest and consider what you've learned."

Watson paused to make sure he had Singer's attention.

"None of the days will be paid."

Singer nodded.

"So, a three-day suspension?"

Watson grimaced.

"We're hoping you see this as an opportunity to get back on track. You've had a couple of bumps in the road over the last few months. This is a chance to reset and reboot."

Singer nodded again and stood up.

"Is that everything, Steve?"

Watson made a motion to stand but then changed his mind, tilting his head slightly so he could look up at Singer.

"That's it, Pete. I'm sure this is a little upsetting, but I have no doubt that six months from now you'll be looking back at this moment as a turning point, the point where you were able to get the train back on the tracks."

Singer was almost at the door when Watson spoke again.

"You might want to consider some independent counselling."

Singer stepped into the hallway, leaving the door open as it had been.

Chapter 15

Singer knew that she must have heard him come in, but she continued to sit at the kitchen table as if she were unaware that there was anybody else in the room. Her head had dropped forward like she was looking down at something in her lap, her hair draped along the side of her face as if designed to prevent anybody from peering in. The laptop was open but Singer could see that the screensaver had popped up.

"Hon? Cher?"

He spoke softly, afraid that words spoken too loudly might cause a shift, break something free that could never be put back in place. She moved one arm to tap a key so the page beneath the screen saver was revealed and used the same hand to turn the screen towards him. Singer kicked off his shoes, padded across the kitchen floor, pulled out a chair and sat next to his wife. Their legs grazed and her leg jerked away as if burned.

"I meant to tell you, Cheryl. I just didn't know how."

"You sat here. Right here. And you said you were done. It was over."

"I know, hon. I know I did. I wanted to tell you."

His wife raised her head but not towards him. Her face held nothing, like she had lost the capacity for expression—of anything, grief, pain, joy—leaving behind nothing but flesh, bone and blood. As if any of what was needed for animation, for vitality, for living, had been drained leaving rendered flesh able to move and speak but empty of any reason to. It froze Singer in his seat.

"The email came while I was at work. Insufficient funds."

Her mouth shifted as if she were imagining a smile but was unable to recall what was required.

"My first thought was. What did I do? What mistake did I make?"

Her expression remained unchanged, caught in a place she had never been.

"I was worried you wouldn't trust me anymore."

She made a sound that was intended to be a laugh.

"Imagine that. That's what I thought. Peter won't trust me."

Singer tilted his head, heard nothing then turned to the clock over the stove to reassure himself that he had the time right.

"Cheryl? Where are the boys?"

She ran a hand over her face and then through her hair.

"I took them to Mom and Dad's. I didn't want them here for this."

Singer hadn't realized he had been holding his breath until the captured air sifted out through his teeth.

"It took me two hours to even get an idea of what had happened. Then I went to the bank just to be sure I was right. Four hundred dollars every pay. How do you miss that? That's what they are thinking."

She turned to him for the first time but there was little that he recognized. It was the face she gave to strangers on a bus.

"You know how they look at you, Peter? There's pity. But still, part of it must be my fault. There must be something wrong with me. But it matters so little that they don't even have to imagine how I'm flawed, just that I am. And you did that to me. You left me there. The man I loved and who I thought loved me, let me walk into that bank and discover that I was to be pitied and discarded in the same look."

"Cher, I—"

"Don't call me that."

"Cheryl. I didn't mean to hurt you. You have to know I didn't."

She stood up, left the kitchen and Singer listened as she climbed the stairs to our bedroom. He stood to follow her then stopped, put on his shoes and left to get the boys.

***

Cheryl's father had stayed in the basement but her mom had studied his face, too polite to ask but knowing something was wrong. He had helped bundle the kids up and get them out the door. She had hugged him and held him a little longer than usual before letting him go.

In the car, Tommie talked about the Chinese food they had for dinner and why didn't we ever get egg rolls, because they were so good and they were especially good dipped in the sauce and why didn't we have that kind of sauce because anything would taste good dipped in that sauce.

It was only as Singer was tucking his sons into bed that Dougie finally asked.

"What's wrong with Mom?"

Singer leaned in and kissed his cheek.

"Daddy made a mistake, buddy, and Mom's a little bit sad. But it's going to be alright. We'll fix it, okay? You don't worry."

***

The room was dark but not full dark, the sun edged just below the lower lid but still threw light into the evening sky. They hadn't had curtains for the bedroom windows when they had moved in and they were still bare. Singer could make out the shape of his wife curled under the duvet and sat on the edge of the bed on his side. She didn't stir but he was sure she was awake.

"We have so much, Cheryl."

He sifted through the thoughts in his head trying to find the next piece.

"I always knew that but not really. I thought I knew how lucky I was, but I really didn't."

There was no sign that his wife had heard or was listening but he was sure she was.

"I had never really thought about how little was needed to save somebody's life."

"Before I met you I ate out almost every day. Did I ever tell you that?"

There was no response.

"Not expensive places. Burger, fries and a coke—ten to fifteen dollars. But I was doing it almost every day. Two of those meals could have saved a life."

Singer felt something catch in his throat.

"Can you believe that, hon? There are hundreds of people who could still be alive today if I had been willing to give up two of those meals a week. Two. But no. Imagine that. My plate of fries was more important than somebody else's life."

Singer paused, trying to find the next words.

"Do we need all of this, Cheryl? This house, with the yard? Both cars? Supper out on every birthday? Thousands of dollars at Christmas? Why not a little less?"

The words began to spill out now, held back for months, rolling around in his head but now the first word like the lead domino in a string that ran for miles.

"It wouldn't be such a big change, Cheryl. We could get a little apartment downtown. I've been looking—twelve hundred a month would give us everything we need. And the buses are fine from downtown, we wouldn't need two cars for sure but maybe we wouldn't even need one. We could free up fifteen hundred to two thousand a month. Hon, that's fifty, sixty, eighty lives, mostly kids. Kids who get to breath for another month. Or year. Or many years. I get that we would have a little less but imagine how good that would feel.

"You have to see the videos that arrive after I've contributed, Cheryl. They're unbelievable. Children who were unable to move, to swallow, with barely the strength to blink, laughing and playing. They are alive. And it is all there in their eyes, in every motion they make, in every breath they take, the pure unexpected sensation of being alive, of having received an unanticipated gift."

Her voice caught him by surprise, unaccompanied by any movement.

"Do you hear yourself, Peter? You sound like a crazy man. We've dreamed of a house like this, with a big backyard and trees and a neighborhood where the kids could play tag and hide'n'seek and ride their bikes. We both wanted this. We talked about all of this. There were times when I was sure you wanted it more than I did."

Singer sat on the edge of their bed in the dark, his shoulders curled forward over his chest, his head dipped forward as if, with gravity and enough time, his forehead would settle onto his knees and he would slip from the bed and wobble for a moment before falling on his side beside the bed. He tried to imagine the next word but the string had run out, the last domino dropped and when he searched for the word, the skein of letters that would bind them once again across the bed, there was nothing. And he was tired. He lay back on the bed above the covers, because to raise the sheet and blanket and crawl beneath so that all that separated him from his wife would be the space filled by the shared warmth of their bodies seemed like the last trespass, the final transgression.

Singer listened to his wife breathing, able to tell by the cadence and rhythm that she was awake. it was a long while before she settled into a steady meter, and when he was certain she was asleep he rose and went downstairs to his computer.

***

She was not in bed when Singer awoke the next morning and there was a moment when he was sure that she had risen early, gathered Dougie and Tommie, loaded the car and driven away. But her clothes were all still on their hangers and the kid's dresser drawers were full except for the discarded items strewn around their room, and the cereal bowls were in the sink waiting to be placed in the dishwasher when she and the boys arrived home.

Singer remembered now. She had taken the early shift. When she started at seven she got the kids up, breakfast started and lunches made and he stepped in to make sure they got out the door in time to catch the bus. But this morning he hadn't heard them and Cheryl hadn't roused him, and Dougie and Tommie had fended for themselves in those last twenty or thirty minutes after Cheryl had pulled away and before they had to leave.

Singer turned on the faucet, let the water run until he could tell by the change in the sound of the water streaming from the nozzle that it had begun to warm, then soaked the dishcloth and wrung it almost dry before mopping up the small puddle of milk that Tommie had splashed on the table. Tommie's because of where it was but also because Dougie ate too deliberately, too carefully to leave any evidence that he had been there. Rinsing and wringing the cloth again, Singer gathered the dusting of crumbs into his cupped hand and tossing them into the garbage beneath the sink. Singer started to work his way along the counter but then dropped the cloth in the sink, pulled his jacket from the hanger, put on his boots and ran out to the car.

***

They were deep enough into the year that Singer didn't have to try and discern every arriving vehicle by its headlights. He could see the buses lean into the long curve and cover the last few hundred meters before turning into the entrance of Bayside Elementary. But it wasn't bright enough to distinguish one bus from another from where Singer sat idling in the school parking lot, so when the first one made the turn he opened the door, stepped from the car and strolled towards the unloading area. Theirs wasn't the first, second, third or even the fourth to arrive, but he didn't have to wait more than ten minutes before it pulled up.

Singer had to call out to them to get their attention, neither of them looking back at the spray of three or four parents lingering in the loading area. Dougie's head came up at the first quiet call as if he hadn't really heard but sensed something in the air. The second time Singer called, Dougie turned, smiling when he saw his father but then almost in the same instance his expression tilting, worried. Singer nodded at his son and then gestured for him to catch his brother who had chased another boy off the bus, laughing. Dougie caught him just before tumbling both of them into the drift of plowed snow beside the walkway.

Singer got to his oldest son first, reached out, pulled his toque off and bent to kiss the top of his son's head.

"Don't worry, buddy, nothing's happened. I just didn't get a chance to say goodbye this morning. I didn't want you going all day without a kiss from your dad."

Singer felt his son nod beneath his lips, gave him another quick squeeze then stepped forward to catch up to Tommie, who came running once he spotted his father.

"Hey, Daddy. What are you doing here! Are you going to help in my class!"

Singer shook his head.

"Sorry, little man, not today. I just needed a kiss and didn't get one this morning."

"Okay, Daddy."

Tommie darted forward, kissed his father on the cheek then wriggled to the ground. He was already turned away, shouting at one of his friends when Singer caught him around the waist, pulled him close and kissed him again before letting him loose. Tommie sprang forward as if barely noticing that his progress had been stopped. Dougie was still standing, watching when Singer turned around. Singer nodded his head at the school and they fell into step without speaking. When they were almost at the double doors, Singer slowed and his son slowed with him. Singer pulled him into a quick embrace then let him go.

"Have a good day, buddy. I'll see you tonight."

His son nodded and smiled but there was something wary about it. Singer didn't turn away until Dougie had passed through the first set of doors. He stopped to look back once as he had made his way across the parking lot, to the still idling car and he could make out his son's small figure standing inside the doors. He couldn't tell if Dougie was facing out to where he stood or towards the interior of the school until he saw the pale flash of a raised hand. Singer waved back.

***

Singer and his wife sat at the kitchen table. She looked at her hands folded in front of her as she spoke.

"I know that nothing that you've done is because you're a bad person, Peter. I know that. But we can't go on together if we don't want the same things."

Singer started to speak but she shook her head, barely moving, her head swiveling so slightly that it seemed little more than an involuntary shudder.

"I know that you did it because you thought you were helping people."

"Singer thought there was a second when she would look over, but she didn't."

"But you don't even know who you've given our money to. You think you're helping people in need, but you don't know. You have no idea who you've been sending our money to."

Her voice had started soft and even. And though she hadn't increased the volume, if anything she spoke more quietly, something had changed. The words were sharper edged, like the space around every syllable had been shaved and honed, paring each vowel and consonant, each sibilant, fricative, explosive and approximant down to nothing more than the literal meaning contained in the sounds. She exhaled, so that her voice was taut and drawn, thin as wire stretched to the edge of visibility, to the point where what bound the pieces into a line, a single whole, threatened to disintegrate sending shards hurtling into space.

"And if the money is going to people who need it. Even if it is. You can't be responsible for saving those people. We can't. There are too many. It's too much. We get lost. And I can't go on together if we aren't imagining the same life…for each other…for Dougie and Tommie…for our family. I just can't…"

Something broke on the last word and whatever she had meant to add—and there had been something—was gone. Singer leaned forward. He wanted to touch her but wasn't sure he could.

"Cheryl. It's okay. You're right. I was wrong. I see that now. I was just trying to help. But I didn't see how much I was hurting you. The kids. Our family. I see it now. I really do. It's okay. There's nothing in the world that matters more to me than you and the kids. It's over. I'm done."

She looked over at him. Singer lingered on every part of her face, the crease where her upper lid curved above the inner edge of her eye, the narrow grooves, faint almost imperceptible, that had begun to form along the edges of her nose leading to the smoothness where her lips met and puckered even when she hinted at a smile, searching for give, yield, something other than the sadness that cloaked, soaked, drenched her face.

"I know you can't trust me. Yet. But just give me time, Cheryl. Give me time. I can show you."

Now Singer reached out and touched her hand. She didn't return the pressure but she didn't pull away. She spoke first.

"Are you going to start playing hockey again?'

There was a short pause.

"Sure. Yeah."

***

Singer woke in the dark and looked at the clock beside the bed. The kids would be awake soon. He slipped from under the covers and sat on the edge of the bed. He leaned back to slide his hand along the blanket over his wife's hip and then stood and padded down the stairs to the kitchen.

***

Singer listened to his wife moving around in their room as he shrugged into his jacket at the door, debating whether to wait until she came down so he could say goodbye but deciding against it. It was her day off and it could be a while before she made her way downstairs.

He drove around for a while before settling on the library. The mall was a little risky. He could run into somebody he knew and it could get back to Cheryl. And then he would have to explain what he was doing at the mall on a Thursday morning when he was supposed to be at work. But the library seemed safe, quiet on a weekday. It was a long shot that he would run into anybody he knew.

There were only a few cars in the small parking lot outside the west-end branch. And one or two of those probably belonged to staff. Singer and his wife often took the kids to the library on Saturday mornings, but he had never been to the west-end branch.

It was a low-slung split-level with a downstairs storage area at the back, but a single main floor open to the public. It was much smaller than the new three-story downtown branch. There was nobody at the circulation desk, but a young woman pushing a cart of books appeared as he approached the desk. She spotted him, parked the cart and slipped through a half door on the far side of the service area so she could come across to serve him.

"Can I help you?'

Singer returned her smile.

"Are there computers available for public use?"

She nodded.

"Absolutely. Are you a member?"

Singer had already pulled out his card and now slid it across the counter. The young woman shook her head.

"No need. You hang on to it. You'll just need your card number to get Internet access."

She leaned over the desk so she could point down the aisle.

"The computers are behind the bookshelves along the back wall. One of them might be in use—I don't know if Mrs. McGarrigle is still back there. She might have slipped out while I was shelving books. But it doesn't matter. Either way, there will be several free computers."

***

Singer had never used Kijiji before, so it had taken a few minutes to set up an account and then to set up a new Gmail account under a different name. He didn't want potential buyers contacting him at home. He had planned on selling his hockey gear, the skates and helmet were almost new and the rest of the gear was in pretty good shape. He figured he could have gotten three- to- four hundred for it, but he was going to need the gear now. Still. He could sell the new skates—use his old ones. And there was other stuff he could sell. He would put the baseball and hockey cards up on eBay and some of his old record albums might be collectibles.

The cross-country skis Cheryl's parents had bought him for Christmas three years ago could go, the portable battery charger, the electric sander…no way he was ever going to use that, the bread maker he had bought Cheryl that she had stored in the attic and never brought down could go.

***

Something tugged at Singer and he brushed it away, lost in the image on the screen, but it drifted back, catching his attention like fence-hung tinfoil, catching the sun and flashing at the edges of your vision as you passed. He shrugged it away again, but it had hooked and caught and pulled him back from where he was. He looked behind and the little girl was staring over his shoulder. She didn't really resemble the child on the screen except for skin color and that they were around the same age, maybe nine or ten. Somebody had taken the time to braid the watching girl's hair into tight cornrows while the child on the screen was shaved right to the skull and a faint dark bur was only beginning to show. Singer hit the button, the screen went black and it was like a spell had been broken. The little girl had stood transfixed, her expression a strange mix of fascination and horror. Even at her young age she knew that something bad was happening on the screen, knew that the image on the screen was too still, too quiet, that something was missing. When it fell black she turned from the screen to look at him. Singer had no idea how long she had been standing there nor what to do, so they just looked at each other for several seconds until a voice called out from several stacks away.

"Mitike?"

The girl spun away without answering. Singer called back the screen, closed down the window and checked the time. Shit. He was already going to be later than Cheryl expected. He shut down all the remaining windows, logged off and left.

Chapter 16

Three hard knocks. Insistent. Singer wasn't expecting anybody. Cheryl was working the early shift so there had been no need to leave the house, but there was no reason for anybody to be knocking. He waited, his fingers still on the keyboard, breath drawn and held, looking across the top of the screen at nothing. For some reason, desperate for the silence to extend so that any lingering trace of the raps at the door dissipated like smoke rings in the dark until there was no memory of being interrupted except for the air in his lungs still waiting to be exhaled. But Singer was certain of the next three, just unsure of when they would arrive. Despite knowing they were coming, he started when they did.

Singer edged to the window and parted the curtain slightly with his forefinger so that he could see the driveway and section of the porch. He recognized the two-year-old Civic and the bulky profile of Cheryl's father at the door. Singer watched through the narrow gap, waiting for Earl to turn and leave or knock again. Instead he tried the handle. Singer couldn't remember if he had locked it after the kids had left for school but closed his eyes and exhaled when the handle rattled and the door remained closed. Singer knew his father-in-law well enough to imagine that he might try the side door that led off the deck into the kitchen.

That wouldn't be a problem, they always kept the back door locked… But it had been one of the first mild mornings since December, hinting at spring, and Singer had stepped out onto the deck to get the early morning sun. And he knew he hadn't locked it when he had come back in. He let the curtain fall closed. There was time. He could make it back through the house and lock the door before Cheryl's father could get down the porch stairs around to the deck and up to the door. But he had to move quietly and get there fast enough that when the lock snicked into place, Cheryl's father wouldn't hear it.

Singer kicked out of his slippers and padded down the hall to the kitchen. There was no curtain on the door leading from the deck so he would have to stand to the side to lock it so Earl wouldn't see him as he approached. But he should have lots of time, Earl didn't move as quickly as he used to. The key in the lock froze Singer where he stood. Of course, Cheryl would have given her parents a key to their house. Singer backtracked through the kitchen to the living room and sat on the edge of the couch.

"Peter!?... You here?... Peter?"

Singer pushed off the couch and plodded out towards the kitchen, feigning a stagger as he stepped through into the kitchen, rubbing at his eyes. Acting surprised as he got around the corner.

"Earl?!"

His father-in-law had his hands up as if being held at gunpoint, the house keys dangling from one hand.

"Sorry, Pete. I got a little worried when nobody answered and thought I'd better check."

Singer rubbed at his eyes again as if trying to come awake.

"No, it's fine. It's fine, Earl. Just startled me. But why are you here? Why were you coming by?"

Cheryl's father paused then started again.

"Well, I stopped by your work and they said you weren't in today. I couldn't think of any place else you might be, so I stopped by."

Singer nodded slowly.

"Sure, Earl. I woke up feeling a little punky. Got dressed and ready to go and just wasn't up to it, decided to use a sick day. Haven't used one in three years."

His father-in-law nodded.

"No sense getting everybody sick."

Earl measured him with a long look.

"But it looks like you're feeling better."

Singer nodded.

"Yeah, nap did me good. But what's up?

Cheryl's father looked around the kitchen as if searching for something then settled back on Singer.

"You got any coffee, Peter? I just want to have a little chat and I thought maybe you and me could sit down and talk. And I could use a coffee."

Singer moved over to the counter and plugged in the kettle.

"Instant alright?"

Earl waved his hand.

"All I ever drank until your mother-in-law decided that grinding your own beans was a big deal. Can't say I notice much difference—dark, hot and bitter no matter how you make it, far as I can tell."

Singer waved at the kitchen table.

"Grab a seat, Earl, this won't take long."

Singer had to lean into the pantry and dig around in the back to find the coffee. He pulled it out, spilled a couple of spoonfuls into the cup and pointed at the fridge.

"Milk?"

Earl nodded.

"A splash and a little sugar. Not the sweetener. Don't tell Bev."

Singer leaned his back to the counter, waiting for the water to boil.

"What's on your mind, Earl?"

Singer's father-in-law looked down at the floor, ran his hands up and down his thighs as if trying to wipe something away, then set his jaw.

"Cheryl told me about what you guys are going through. The money you've been spending."

Earl looked up at him, waiting for a response but Singer only nodded. Singer's father-in-law turned his head so he could look out the door across the deck and into the yard, as if something had caught his attention, distracted him, led him off the trail.

"What are you doing, Pete?"

Singer followed Earl's gaze with his own, looking for what his father-in-law was seeing, the tree, leafless, grey, hard, waiting, the breeze gusting so that the branch tips swayed like fine hair around a sleeping child's face, then settled.

Singer remembered his grandfather's face looking up from the pillow, still, obdurate, unmoved by nerve or blood. The lines around eye and nose and lip, familiar but strange, lacquered, almost unrecognizable. They no longer shaped, guided or directed his grandfather's expressions, but were fixed as if riven in stone by an unyielding edge. Singer the boy had stayed kneeling beside the casket. Waiting. All that was needed was a gust of wind or an angled ray of sun to reanimate, to restore the angle and curl of each furrowed line that served to carry the subtle message he and his grandfather had shared. Until his mother had pulled him away so the line could continue and the two of them, Singer and his mother, were enveloped in the familiar sour mint smell.

"Peter!"

Singer shook his head.

"Sorry, Earl. I'm not quite awake yet."

"Well, you need to wake up! In more ways than one!"

"Look Earl, I'm not sure any of this is your—"

His father-in-law waved him away.

"I've spent the last couple of days trying to track down this organization you've been telling Cheryl about and I can't find anything. It doesn't exist. There is no such group. What's going on, Pete?"

Singer allowed himself a small, tired smile.

"What's so funny, Peter? What's this about? Is there somebody else?"

Singer laughed.

"What? You think I'm…?"

Singer ran a hand over his face and up through his hair.

"Look, Earl. I'm not fooling around. This is real. And it's between me and Cheryl. It's none of your—"

His father-in-law slammed his hand on the kitchen table.

"She's my daughter! And you won't tell me, what—"

Earl recoiled and closed his fists as Singer stood abruptly, but Singer waved for him to continue, walked to the sink, grabbed the dishcloth, wiped up the small puddle of coffee that had gathered around the bottom of his father-in-law's cup and tossed the cloth back into the sink before sitting down again.

"If you're not playing Cheryl, then you're getting played! These kinds of Internet scams are going on all the time. I spent twenty years doing this for a living, Pete, I know what I'm talking about."

"I'm not getting scammed, Earl."

Earl snorted.

"Nobody ever thinks they're the sucker, Peter! They believe it happens, but not to them. But this wouldn't happen if it didn't work—somebody's getting suckered. And this time it's you."

"Earl…"

"Stop, Pete. Just stop. Legitimate charities leave a footprint. They aren't trying to hide. They aren't trying to stay off the radar. These guys haven't left a single breadcrumb."

Singer started to shake his head but then stopped.

"How do you know?"

Earl flushed, shrugged and looked away.

"Cheryl forwarded one of the emails."

Singer frowned.

"Cheryl forwarded you one of my emails? From my computer?"

Earl looked over.

"You're pissed at Cheryl? Are you kidding me? Spending money you don't have without telling her? And you're pissed that she looked at your email?!"

Singer raised his hands.

"Fine."

"A buddy of mine at the old job tried to trace the email, but they're pretty savvy. The emails are coming from fake public Wi-Fi sites, and the geographic locations are fake too. My buddy 'traced' them to three different locations but he's pretty sure the locations are bogus."

His father-in-law stared at him across the table.

"Does that sound legit to you, Peter? You're not a dumb guy. Does that sound like the kind of thing legitimate charities do? You're getting played."

Singer shook his head.

"I'm not getting played, Earl. I—"

His father-in-law slammed the table with both fists.

"For chrissakes, Peter! How can you not see this!?"

They both looked up at the sound of the doorbell. Singer shrugged at his father-in-law and went to the door. The woman on the porch was young and pretty, only a few years out of high school. Singer pushed the outer door open.

"Yes?"

The woman raised her eyebrows.

"You're selling the skates? I sent a message saying I would stop by this morning. Is the timing alright?"

"Sure. Sure."

Singer looked over his shoulder.

"Earl?"

Singer gestured towards the young woman.

"Are we done here? I have to…"

Earl had shifted in his seat and was watching over his shoulder. Now, he pushed up from his chair, using both hands on the table for leverage. He crossed the floor, his face stiff and flat, looking only at his son-in-law until he reached the door before looking at the woman.

"Are you going to introduce us, Peter?"

Singer took a deep breath.

"Earl, she's here to buy skates that I put up on Kijiji."

Singer's father-in-law put his hand on the outer door and pushed so the young woman had to step back for Earl to move out onto the porch. Once on the porch, Earl let the door swing shut behind him and raised his hand to his forehead as if tipping his cap.

"Nice to meet you, young lady."

The woman nodded, puzzled, looking from Earl to Singer then back and then finally to Singer.

"If it's a bad time…?"

Singer shook his head, grabbed his jacket off the hook, pushed the door open and stepped out, forcing Earl to move down the steps.

"Thanks for stopping by, Earl. I appreciate the concern. But no need to worry. We've got this."

Singer turned back to the woman, without waiting for his father-in-law's response.

"C'mon, follow me. They're in the garage."

Singer pushed by his father-in-law. The young woman turned sideways to edge past Earl. Singer bent to slide the garage door open but had to pull hard twice to break it free of the crust of ice and it opened in a rattle of wheel, hinge, and metal track. Singer hit the overhead light and pulled the box down from a shelf running along the length of one side of the garage. When he turned around with the box, Earl had descended the stairs and was standing by the door of his car, watching. Singer stood for a moment, looking over the young woman's shoulder until his father-in-law finally opened the door and slid in behind the wheel.

The woman turned to watch and then looked back at Singer questioningly. Singer shook his head.

"Long story."

Singer crossed the space to his car placed the box on the hood of his car and opened the lid. He stepped back so the woman could see the skates.

"Almost new. Worn 'em twice. I paid four hundred and eighty-nine dollars. I'll let them go for three hundred."

They settled on two fifty.

Singer returned to their house and got online. The woman had made the transfer while they stood at the car, so he was able to send the money immediately.

Chapter 17

The schematic of his section of the warehouse flashed red in sections C and D. Singer sighed and clicked on the warning messages. Both were personnel, not technical. He sighed again, reached up for the orange emergency vest hanging on the wall over his workstation, slipped it on and stepped out into the main corridor, pausing for a moment to let one of the floor bots zip by on the way to pick up a package.

They stood almost at the very end of the aisle not far from the door leading out to loading dock C3. Three of them. Although the figures were so small at this distance that it was hard to be sure. It could have been just two or maybe even a fourth person partially blocked by one of the others.

Singer thought about going back for a Segway but then decided to walk. Twice, he had to step to the side to let a forklift by, not even needing to look back, able to judge the distance by the steady constant beep the lift emanated and time his sidestep so that the lift could rumble by without slowing. The first time, Singer recognized the woman at the wheel and raised a hand and she lifted her hand off the wheel in response. The second was driven by a new driver—or at least one he didn't recognize.

As he got closer, Singer shadowed his eyes against the fluorescent glare and could make out that there were definitely three people. Singer picked up his speed a little, not exactly sure why, just that even at this distance there was something in the lean and bend, the way the bodies were aligned, as if they were negotiating space, subtle shifts in position creating a possible lane of escape but then parried by a slide and tilt that closed the gap.

He had been sure that one of them was Clermont, the way her arms hung by her sides even before one hand reached to her face, brushing a bang to provide an explanation for hand to face. But now he was close, and she was facing him so he was certain. Sproul tuned when he heard Singer's footsteps and grinned when he saw who it was.

"Hey, Petey. What're you doing up in our neck of the woods?"

Singer ignored him.

"You alright, Hannah?"

Sproul grinned wider.

"No worries, Petey. It's all good here. We're just talking. Right, Hannah?"

Singer slowed and stopped a step from Sproul, who had now turned to face him. Singer looked over his shoulder at the young woman.

"You've got a pick-up on aisle seventeen, Hannah. It's run a little overtime, so let's get on that. I'm walking back that way anyway."

Singer motioned for her to step around Sproul.

Sproul shifted slightly to block her path.

"No need to worry, Petey. We're just having a little staff meeting here."

Sproul looked behind at his friend, who was standing just off Sproul's right shoulder.

"Right, Henry?"

Sproul shifted his gaze.

"Eh, Hannah?"

Clermont stood staring down at the floor, her hair hanging like a curtain across her face. Singer continued to ignore Sproul, looking only at Clermont. When she didn't move, Singer took a step up beside Sproul then turned and waved his arm for Clermont to pass in front of him, shielding the young woman with his body. She walked past without looking up from the floor. Singer stepped in beside her and spoke quietly out of the side of his mouth.

"Keep walking. I'll catch up."

Singer turned and walked back to the two men. Sproul grinned and raised his hands as Singer approached, as if protecting himself from attack.

'Watch out, Henry. Here he comes. Be ready. He could attack at any minute."

Singer stood for a second, looking at Sproul for the first time, then over at his friend.

"You boys should get back to work. You're falling behind."

Sproul raised a hand to his mouth as if startled and spoke in a high voice.

"Falling behind? My word. You wouldn't report lil ol' me, would you Mr. Bossman?"

Sproul's voice and face flattened.

"Don't worry about us, Petey. We'll be fine. But you better get back to work."

Singer felt the color and heat start in a place beneath his shoulder blades and rise past his collar. He spun and walked away. Behind him Sproul called out.

"Bye-bye, Hannah. See you again, soon."

Singer caught up to Clermont as she was about to turn into Aisle seventeen and took her by the arm.

"Let's take a break. It'll be fine."

***

"Not much you can do, buddy. He's got you by the short hairs."

Singer stood with Brian beside his friend's car.

"You've got a history with Sproul. He'll say you're just out to get him and they've got the video."

Singer nodded.

"So, I've just got to let him do what he wants?"

His friend made a face.

"At least, for now. But these kinds of guys always fuck up. He'll screw this up. Just wait him out."

Singer nodded. Ferris tapped him on the arm.

"It's gonna be good to have you back. The boys are all on board."

Singer looked at his friend.

"Yeah?"

"Sure. Absolutely. We tried a couple of other guys but they didn't work out. Nobody has those sweet Singer hands."

Ferris punched Singer on the shoulder.

"It's all good, buddy. It'll be like old times."

Singer forced a smile and nodded.

***

There were eleven unopened messages. It had been three weeks since the last of the items had been sold. He had been able to send almost eleven hundred dollars but there had been nothing since. Singer posed the arrow over the March 21st attachment. But there really was no point. He knew what was there. A growing list of names. And there was nothing to do. He couldn't remove even one from the list. And he could hear them. Each new name. Of course, he couldn't. The names were buried deep beneath the subject line, vaulted, voiceless, silent.

But he was hearing something. The sound of a single drop of water falling from a great height onto a smooth metal surface, the energy used to bind each water molecule to the next to create a sphere, smooth, unblemished, an accident so perfect that it seemed impossible, suddenly released as a sound wave upon collision. A noise so cold, so flat, so devoid of life as to scar and diminish the space around it. One plink upon another, unevenly spaced but with a pattern that stopped just short of being predictable so that Singer waited.

For the last three weeks, it had seemed that he was always waiting. As it appeared, it was little more than a barely discernible convexity. But it grew, building at the edges until it began to droop, the skin bound by surface tension, searching for its final shape. Finding the switch point between tear and tear, before ripping free at the edges and falling, distorted and flat as it neared the contact point. And then the sound echoing in Singer's head like shattered steel. Echoing once, twice, three times before shuddering into silence and the next drop began to build. Each name falling into place at the end of the line.

"Pete, you're going to be late for hockey."

Singer hadn't noticed his wife standing at the door to the office and started at her voice. Cheryl watched him closely but didn't say anything. He reached to rub his temple but then changed direction, picked at the corner of one eye, closed the laptop with one hand and stood up.

"Right. I wasn't paying attention to the time. I'd better get going."

Singer could feel her watching him as he walked into the kitchen.

***

Singer drove around the block twice before pulling into the rink parking lot. The money was already spent—forty-four dollars for the month. Cheryl had reminded him and stood in the door waiting for him to transfer the money. There was no way he could ask for it back now. He shut off the engine and the lights and sat with both hands gripping the steering wheel. He waited with his forehead resting just below the horn. Though he didn't know when, the building tension was as real as the cool vinyl in his hands. It took longer than he expected, building until it felt as if his skin might pull away from the flesh beneath like peeled candle wax, leaving every nerve and synapse exposed and abraded, but then it dropped and he could move. The next arrived sooner than he expected and he flinched, before pushing open the changeroom door.

***

Singer bent forward to tie his skates and his friend patted him on the shoulder.

"Good to have you back, buddy."

Singer nodded.

"Good to be back, Bri."

Ferris noticed his skates.

"What's with those pieces of shit? I thought Cheryl got you a new pair over the summer?"

Singer forced a chuckle.

"Ah, y'know. I could never get used to them. They just didn't feel right."

"Didn't feel right? What the hell are you talking about? Those were Vapor Pros, man! You loved those skates."

Singer tugged hard on the laces, pulling them tight across his foot.

"Would you leave it alone, Brian! I said they didn't feel right!"

Singer could sense his friend drawing back to look at him.

"Relax, buddy. I don't give a shit what skates you wear. Thought we were just talking here."

Singer took a deep breath and settled himself.

"Sorry. Guess I'm just a little edgy about getting back on the ice."

Ferris patted him on the shoulder.

"No worries. Like riding a bike."

One of the other guys shouted from across the room.

"Hey, Singer, you got beer money?"

Singer tilted his head up from the floor and nodded.

"Right, Phil. Sorry about that."

Singer pulled the bow tight and stood up to reach into his pants hanging from a hook behind him. He paused with his hand on one belt loop. Eleven bucks. Two weeks of beer money was almost enough to take a name off the list. He stood with his back to the room, hand on his pants and took several deep breaths, then thrust his hand into a front pocket to pull out two fives and a loonie. Singer stood facing the locker room wall, the money clutched in his hand afraid to turn around, sure that the entire room was staring at him. But when he turned, nobody was watching. He teetered across the floor on his tiptoes where he had to step off the carpet, and Phil Clevenger stuffed the money into a side pocket of his hockey bag without interrupting his conversation with Steve Ellinger, their goalie.

***

It was the third time.

Singer worried, but had found his feet quickly. Being off the ice hadn't slowed him down. Even the hands came back quickly. He had lost the puck a couple of times early, but it hadn't taken long for him to find the handle.

But it was the third time the guy had rapped him hard on the wrist.

Unable to keep up as Singer circled and wheeled in the corner and behind the net, waiting for a linemate to get open, the guy had simply resorted to hacking and slashing to slow Singer down.

This time, though, it had been hard enough to numb his hand right to the fingertips. Singer looked up and spotted Brian heading for the front of the net. He saucered the puck over a defenseman's blade, but the puck hit a little on the edge, caromed over his friend's stick and was scooped up by a backchecking winger. The other team whirled up ice.

Singer followed the play then veered to the bench for a change when he saw that the puck was tied up harmlessly in the corner. On the bench, he slipped off his glove and rubbed a spot just beyond where the radius and ulna met the bones of his hand, the slash vivid and bright, fever-red against the pallor of his unmarked skin. Singer rubbed the spot with the other hand, and for a moment the blood just beneath the surface was pushed to the sides but then flushed back into place. He put his glove back on and waited for his turn to get back on the ice.

***

Singer set up high off the boards, waiting. There were only a few minutes until the buzzer and he hoped the puck would get tied up in the corner and he could spend the last minutes on the bench. But Brian kicked it loose from the scrum, was on it and flipped the puck along the boards knowing Singer would be there. Singer couldn't help himself, he had done it too often before and his muscles knew no other way to contract. He scooped up the puck, spun away from a player trying to squeeze him along the boards, looked up for his winger, who had got caught up back in the defensive zone, but there was only one man back for the other team. Singer gave him the shoulder as if to curl right for open ice, but then cut back hard to the short side and slid between the player and the boards and took three long hard strides to pull away. The goalie moved out as Singer crossed the blue line but not far enough and he could see where the gap would be, stick side as he got to the top of the circles.

The pain was sharp and sudden enough that Singer almost dropped his stick, though he managed to hang on, but as he drew the puck back for the shot it slipped loose and drifted into the corner.

***

It took three players and the ref to pull him off. They continued to hold Singer even as he stood still, looking down at the body, prone on the ice. Somehow Singer had gotten the guy's helmet and visor off and hit him often enough that his face was a smear of blood. The guy watched him from the ice, eyes wide and wet but yielding, afraid, waiting for whatever came next. Singer jerked one arm free then the other, skated to the boards along the bench, swung himself over in a single motion and ignored the rubber runner leading from the bench to the dressing room, his skate blades ringing rough and cold against the concrete floor.

Chapter 18

"Chuckie Cheese?"

Singer's wife pulled dishes left from breakfast out of the sink and bent to place them in the dishwasher. She straightened to grab the last of the cutlery before bending forward again, and Singer noticed that her shoulder blades stood out against the thin cotton of her t-shirt.

"Hon? Cheryl?"

She spun around, a fork still clutched in her hand.

"What do you want, Peter? It's his birthday! And he gets to have a party!"

Singer nodded.

"I know. Party, sure. But what happened to Pin the Tail On The Donkey, a piñata and a piece of homemade cake?"

He wished he could take it back. Knew it had been a mistake before the words left his mouth.

"Pin The Tail On The Donkey? What are you thinking? That we all fell asleep and woke up in 1971? That is not how birthdays work anymore…"

She held up her hand to stop herself.

"I've got to get ready."

She looked at him.

"And so do you."

She turned and left the room, speaking without turning.

"We're leaving in twenty minutes. I don't want to be late."

***

There were two busgirls and they set their dish bins at opposite ends of the long table, pulled the chairs back to create a path around the table and began clearing. The table, really five tables placed end to end and draped in a plastic tablecloth covered in balloon illustrations and Happy Birthday scrawled the length of both sides in stylized cursive, looked as if the pizza and drinks had been dropped from a great height with little regard for accuracy. Singer pushed away from the table so that he wouldn't block their path as they moved around gathering up plates and cups and pushing scraps toward the center of the table. They occasionally bent to pick something from the floor and toss it into the bin or the center of the table.

Singer looked over his shoulder, his attention drawn by the shouts and laughter. The adults, Cheryl and two of the other moms, stood outside the arcade room, heads bent close so they could hear themselves above the music, the shouts and laughter of the kids, and the bells and sirens coming from the games. Cheryl said something that caused the other women to nod sympathetically and one of them looked over towards the table and Singer turned back to the girls.

"Is it always like this?"

Singer realized after he spoke that they had been talking and he had interrupted. They looked at him blankly, and he shook his head and gestured at the table.

"Sorry. I was just saying, is it always like this?"

The shorter of the two girls looked across at her friend and then back at him.

"Like what?"

Singer gestured again at the pile of food accumulating in the center of the table, mostly pizza but French fries and a few stray chicken fingers for the kids who were lactose-intolerant or didn't like pizza.

"So much food left over. It looks like the kids left more than they ate."

Both girls looked at the table as if for the first time, then the one who had spoken shrugged.

"Looks the same as always. Wouldn't you say, Sarah?"

The other girl nodded at her friend then looked at him.

"We get complaints if they run out of food."

"Nobody ever complains if there's too much."

She looked back at her friend and laughed.

"Why would they?"

Singer nodded and watched them finish. They filled their bins twice before returning to gather up the tablecloth, flipping each corner towards the center, pulling the corners together and tying them into a practiced knot. The shorter girl picked it up, but the weight of food and spilled drink was too much so she set it on the floor and dragged it across the tile to the swinging kitchen doors.

The taller girl returned to the table, draped a fresh plastic covering with the identical design over the table and pushed all the chairs back into a tight circle, all without acknowledging Singer. When she left, Singer scraped his chair in closer and looked over his shoulder again. Singer's wife and the other two moms were no longer standing at the games room door. Singer tried to stand but didn't get far before slumping back into his seat.

On the far side of the room a party was just swinging into full gear, squeals of delight from the kids as a parade of pizza stands arrived at the table. A little closer, the hostess was gathering the kids from another party together to follow her to the arcade room. She had already started across the room when she looked back and spotted one of the children still at the table, her head bent forward and resting on the plastic cloth. The hostess paused the children and waved for one of the busboys to come over and hold her place before crouching next to the little girl. She spoke to her for several seconds before the little girl stood up and followed her over the where the other children were waiting and watching. The little girl took her place at the end of the line as it started up again.

Singer gathered himself to stand again before noticing one of the helium balloons that were tied to the back of each of the children's chairs was caught in the air exchange path so that it wavered and danced a couple of feet below the ceiling. All of the balloons but one were silver with a pink border. Dougie's was blue with a large yellow '8' set in the center. But it was one of the silvers that pulled and tugged like a hooked fish at the end of its ribbon. Singer didn't understand how airflow worked. He had a vague recollection from a class he had taken in the first semester of college—probably Physics—something about laminar versus turbulent flow. One was random and unpredictable although he couldn't remember which.

The balloon seemed to get caught up in swirls and eddies, the ribbon pulled taut but then an angled stream of air sending the balloon spinning away, only to be caught again as the ribbon reached the end of its length. It stretched away from the table as if to escape, poised to flee if only it could break loose, but then drawn back directly over the chair, settling for a moment as if stepping in line with the other eight balloons. The other eight never wavered as if the ribbon was a true straight line, a single dimension connecting chair to balloon, no width or depth, no room to diverge even slightly from its position directly above where it was connected to the child's seat. When the balloon caught in the airflow and settled into place for a brief second, it still seemed apart from the others, not truly still, vibrating at some micro level so that energy continued to accumulate until it burst out of line, the impulse as unpredictable and irresistible as a Tourette's spasm.

"Dad?"

Startled, Singer looked at his son standing across the table from him, no sense of how or when Dougie had arrived at that place directly across from him.

"Dad?"

Singer could see both of them in his son's face. Already the hard planes at cheek and chin and temple that Singer had inherited from his mother beginning to emerge and set, but something of Cheryl around the eyes and mouth softened the edges, blunted the angled severity that was barely diminished even when Singer smiled.

Singer tried. Smiling at his son, trying to dim the concern in his son's eyes.

"What's up, Dougie?"

His son held out his hand, revealing the three tokens clutched in his palm.

"You want to play? I saved you some."

Singer looked at the three tokens and then up at his son's face.

"Dougie?"

Singer paused and his son waited, his hand outstretched across the table. Singer caught a flash of silver from the corner of his eye. He couldn't tell if it was real or refracted light from the fluid pooled in the corner of his eye.

"Have you had fun? It's been a good birthday?"

Dougie nodded and shrugged.

"Sure. It was fun. Logan said it was his favorite birthday yet."

Singer smiled again, nodded at the tokens and stood up.

"You hang on to those, I might lose them between here and the games room."

***

Singer listened to his wife in the kitchen. He wasn't sure what she was doing. There were no dishes in the sink. He had emptied the dishwasher and he had already put away the few groceries they had picked up on the way back from the party. So, he sat on the couch, one knee shaking up and down and waiting. And thinking,

Please go straight up to bed. Just go to bed. Everything's done. Go to bed. Don't come in here.

Singer's leg stopped and he was completely still for a moment but then his head twitched left, he blinked and his leg began to shake again. He leaned over so he could see from the living room into his dark office. He couldn't remember if he had left his computer on or not, but there was not even a hint of blue from the room. It could be on, though, and just resting. He could go in and check, turn the computer on if it wasn't yet. It would save time. But it might also draw Cheryl's attention. Singer looked down between his feet and waited.

Singer heard her step out onto the wood flooring of the hallway from the softer plastic click-tile in the kitchen but didn't hear the muffled snap of the light being switched off. He leaned forward in his seat, knowing that another step without hearing the light switch meant she was only stepping away and would be returning to the kitchen, and then it came as clear and satisfying as a popped bubble. Something loosened in his chest for a moment but then began to build again as she approached the stairs. Either she would turn and go directly up the stairs, waiting until she had removed her makeup and brushed her teeth before calling down to him, or she would come into the room. Singer bent his head and closed his eyes, barely aware that his fists were clenched.

Keep going. Keep going. Keep going. Keep going.

She was in the room. Even with his eyes closed and head bent he could sense her there. She had paused in the doorway and when he hadn't looked up, she had taken two steps into the room. He opened his eyes and looked up at her.

"That wasn't so bad was it, Pete?"

Singer shook his head, afraid of what would come out if he spoke, but then managing to grunt something that he hoped sounded like no.

"Dougie seemed to have fun."

Singer nodded again. She was right. He had seemed to have fun. Fun. He thought,

Go to bed. Go to bed. Go to bed.

"You were quiet. I didn't see you talk to any of the parents. Not even when they came to pick up their kids?"

Singer ran a hand across his face and settled back in the chair.

"Jesus Christ, Cheryl! You couldn't just leave this alone. You had to pick at it!"

Singer didn't wait for his wife's reaction.

"Did you see those kids? One bite, put it back on their plate. Forget they already had a piece sitting in front of them and take another slice. Take a bite of it, spill their drink, get it refilled, tell you there's too much pepperoni on this slice they just took and you find a piece of cheese only, even though you had already explained all the different kinds of pizza and where to find them, putting it down in front of him so he could take one more bite and then ask when the games were going to start!"

Singer stood up and began pacing around the living room.

"And who's that weaselly little blonde kid? His piece of cake touches the ice cream so he needs a fresh scoop? Was that his mom? The woman who went back into the kitchen to make sure he got a fresh scoop? There are kids out there who don't even know what ice cream is! And they never will. They can't even imagine ice cream! Do you get that?!"

Singer didn't look up until he heard her feet on the stairs. He followed her into the hallway and stood at the bottom of the stairs.

"And how much did that cost! Had to be hundreds! Hundreds! Do you know how many lives that would have been, Cheryl?! Ten? Fifteen? Twenty? So Dougie could have that freak show? That's where we're at. It's okay for people to die so that Dougie and his friends can spit cake at each other and win glow-in-the-dark plastic bracelets or fake rubber zombie fingers?"

Singer hadn't heard the door to the boys' room open and his wife had blocked his view of where Dougie stood against the wall looking down at his father. Singer's wife stopped at the top of the stairs and bent to kiss the top of her son's head before leading him back into his room. She didn't look down at him when she came out and went into the bathroom and closed the door behind her. Singer stood for several seconds looking at the bathroom door, flinched once, then turned and went into his office.

***

Singer pulled up one archived email after another, ignoring the dark black text of unopened emails that extended down below the edge of the window. He always watched them in sequence, first from *The Living List*, the images of them hanging on, holding out for help. Then the later images, sometimes smiling, sometimes solemn, but always there. He watched until the tension stopped building and he thought he would be able to sleep.

Chapter 19

"How are you doing?"

Singer shrugged across the table at his friend.

"Y'know."

Brian took a pull on his coffee. Singer looked around at the other tables, as always half-checking for the woman who had spoken to him about the emails. But she was never here. Brian followed his gaze then waited for Singer to come back to him.

"That was messed up, buddy."

Singer nodded.

"I know. But it was the fourth time!"

"You're lucky he didn't file charges. That's the kind of thing that could end up in court."

Singer scoffed.

"It looked worse than it was. Didn't break a thing."

Ferris shook his head.

"Seven stitches."

Singer, whose gaze had strayed away, looked back.

"Seven? You sure? I barely tagged him."

His friend's voice rose a little.

"Pete, would you stop acting like you remember it. I was there! I was one of the ones who pulled you off him! I'm not sure you were conscious."

Singer spun his cup on the table but didn't lift it for a drink.

"So? What now?"

"They've met already."

Singer nodded.

"What's the verdict?"

"Lifetime suspension. No appeal."

Singer tried to look upset but all he felt was relief.

"Sorry, buddy. But it's hard to argue."

Singer nodded.

"Yeah."

They sat silently for several minutes, Singer trying to stretch it out as long as he could before asking.

"What about a refund?"

His friend blew air out his nose and shifted in his seat.

"Jesus H, Pete. You punch a guy's lights out..."

Ferris held up two fingers so close that they almost touched.

"...come this close to an assault charge...and you're worried about forty-four bucks?"

Singer could feel the tension beginning to peak. He didn't know how long until the nickel dropped but he knew he couldn't sit here any longer. He pushed himself to his feet.

"Thanks for the update, Brian. I've got to go."

He started to walk away then turned.

"Do me a favor? Check into the refund, eh?"

Singer turned away but then turned back one more time.

"Brian, has Hannah been working over on your team?"

His friend looked back puzzled, trying to keep up.

"What? Who?"

"You know, the girl who had trouble with Sproul. You know the one I mean."

"The scrawny chick? Scared of her own shadow? She got let go. While you were suspended. She got caught with stuff in her bag."

"Stealing?"

Ferris nodded.

"How did they catch her? Camera?"

Ferris shook his head.

"Nah. Somebody reported her. One of the boys over in your section."

Singer looked to the side, shook his head and left. His friend just looked after him.

***

Singer spotted them standing in a tight circle at the far end of the aisle. It was too far to make out any details of their features, but he had come to recognize Sproul's slouch and the way he gestured when he spoke. He started up the aisle, skipping over a low-riding robot, not even waiting for it to glide past, then stopped and pulled in a deep breath. He spun on his heel, walked back to his workstation, took one slow breath after another, then shrugged out of his jacket and hung it on the wall hook. He stood with both hands on the narrow ledge hinged to the wall on which his computer sat.

Singer kept his eyes closed, trying to find an even pocket for his breathing, ignoring the pings as orders accumulated on his wait list waiting to be assigned to a picker. He pushed off the counter, spun on his heel, stepped into the main aisle, taking another quick hop to avoid a floor bot without even noticing he did it. The circle had drifted into a ragged line, moving from where they had gathered in the direction of a neighboring aisle. Now they paused again and drew into a small knot at the head of the aisle.

Singer slowed, able to tell by the way he was outpacing the packages moving along the conveyor belts that he was almost jogging—a long narrow box, probably an ironing board, could have been a snowboard. But it had come from the direction of household items not sporting goods, accelerated around the bend from a side aisle out into the main aisle like a dry leaf temporarily trapped in a stream eddy before breaking free into the main channel. Here, each of a half dozen or more conveyor belts widened into several lanes to accommodate the inflow from several side streams, as if the packages had begun in some distant headwater, imagined but never seen, gathering mass and momentum. As packages were plucked from shelves, scanned and deposited, the belts at the source little more than a foot or two wide, travelling at almost two feet per second, but expanding where aisles met and merged, slowing almost imperceptibly to accommodate and dissipate congestion points, so that packages occasionally collided gently, stalled and then broke loose without interrupting the flow. But the deceleration accumulating as side

streams were absorbed by yet larger and larger tributaries until by the time packages reached the main aisle they were travelling at little more than a foot per second.

Singer tried to hold his pace to around twice the package speed, but couldn't,
stepping out with long urgent strides, headed for the small cluster of men, close
enough now to make out that there were five of them before one of them stepped
away down a side aisle and left four men in a tight cluster, heads together.

The gaps between packages were too large. It was subtle but Singer could tell.
The orders waiting to be assigned were gathering at his workstation, accumulating
like sand from a sifting fist and he could see it in the way the mass of packages had
lost cohesion and direction. The clean laminar flow degraded as the intervening
spaces separating packages grew, so that a tremble or vibration passed from the belt
to a package was no longer immediately stilled by its neighbors. The subtle shocks
were now allowed to reverberate so that first one and then another bounced and
tumbled into neighbors, breaking the clean line from shelf to dock. The packages
began to tremble, still displaying a common purpose and direction but no longer
perfect synchronicity until soon they would start to shiver and sizzle like oil droplets on a hot skillet.

Singer didn't know how long he had. The flow of packages relied on the kinetic
energy of each package, the direction and speed of an individual package, being
identical to its neighbors. It wasn't possible to completely eliminate all independent motion, eliminate any jitter, wobble or flutter idiosyncratic to a particular
package, but the belt had been designed so that any such independent movement
was muted, calmed, subdued by the neighboring pressure, constant and anchoring
on all sides. As the distance among packages began to grow, there was a point, the
inflection, where the flow, laminar, smooth, layers in parallel, began to breakdown
and show early signs of turbulence. The packages tipped to one edge, nudging a
neighbor off plumb, so that they rocked for a moment, out of synchrony, before
settling back into place but slightly further apart than they had been before. When
a package tipped again it reached a more acute angle before being corrected and
the force with which it collided with a neighbor was slightly greater and it took
longer to settle. Ultimately there was an accumulating risk that the flow would
disintegrate into turbulence and random, chaotic motion, packages tumbling from
one side to the other, leapfrogging ahead or catching a corner and tumbling backwards like a man stepping onto asphalt from a moving car. Finally, the belt would

no longer contain the packages and they would drop, spin, slide and hurtle off the belt. Long before that, sensors detected random motion and stopped the belt. It had happened three times in the eight years that Singer had worked in the warehouse and each event had required an intensive investigation. He needed to hurry.

The four men were unaware of him until there was a pale flash of white as one of them looked up. He didn't know if they saw him coming but within seconds they separated and disappeared into side aisles. Singer was still a few hundred meters away and broke into a jog. Coming up on the place where they had been gathered, he slowed to a walk, eyes ahead on the aisle he thought he had seen Sproul duck into.

"What you doin' up this neck of the woods, bossman?"

The voice came from behind him. He must have miscalculated and overshot the aisle Sproul had chosen. Singer took a step backwards so he could look down the aisle the voice had come from. One of the other guys must have swung around from an adjacent aisle because there were two of them standing several strides down the aisle looking at him. Sproul grinned and raised an eyebrow.

"You down here looking for that little thing?"

Sproul turned towards the other man.

"What was her name again?"

Sproul's friend tugged at his lower lip and shrugged. Sproul turned back to Singer.

"But why am I asking Jimmy? You two seemed pretty friendly, boss. You must know her name."

Singer just stared at Sproul. He could feel the shake and rattle building on the belt behind him. It was difficult to know if the parallel layers were still stable or whether the transition was already beginning. Why had he followed Sproul down here? There was nothing to do. If he had taken a minute to think, he would have known that.

Sproul made a sad face.

"That was a real shame."

He looked at his friend then back at Singer and shrugged.

"Batteries and candy bars. Tough to figure. But you know what they say— sometimes it's just a cry for help. And Lord knows that girl needed some help."

Singer couldn't stop looking at Sproul. The way one side of his mouth curled up more than the other when he was pretending to smile but how they evened out when he was truly smiling. How there was a tooth in the top row that was either chipped or worn down by grinding. And how he had clipped one side of his moustache higher than the other so that Singer wanted to reach out and tug the long end.

"Said she didn't do it, I understand."

There was a small patch on the left side of Sproul's chin that was coming in grey already. One of his eyes was a little lower on his face than the other, but Singer couldn't tell if it was a childhood injury or just a subtle genetic misalignment.

"But it's hard to figure who would want to plant stolen goods in her locker."

Sproul grinned. Singer let his weight shift towards his back foot so that he could turn around and walk away. Singer sometimes thought about how things might have been different if Sproul had stopped there. Sproul snapped his fingers.

"Hannah. That's it. Little Hannah."

It took three of them to pull him off. And before they did, he split Sproul's cheek from lip to just below the eye. Forty-seven stitches. It was like hammering a stubborn nail. When it finally pierces, it feels just right.

***

Size must have been one of the criteria. The security guard was at least three inches taller than Singer and the suit jacket stretched tight across his shoulders, creating odd angled folds between his shoulder blades. The guard stayed a half-stride ahead of Singer from the elevator and down both hallways to Watson's office. He knocked once and waited. It took a couple of seconds but then Watson called out. The guard opened the door and took one step into the office. Singer stepped forward so he could look into the office.

"He's here, Mr. Watson. Do you want me in the room?"

Watson stood up from his desk, shaking his head.

"No. It's alright, Robert. Just wait outside the door. We shouldn't be long."

"Yessir."

The guard stepped back out without looking at Singer and took a spot beside the door, one heel back against the wall holding him up. Singer stepped into the office. Steve Watson gestured at the door then at the row of chairs.

"Close the door and grab a seat, Pete."

Singer did. Watson remained standing until Singer was seated then followed. He sighed and ran his hands over his face.

"I was hoping we wouldn't end up here, Peter. You've been with the company a long time."

The relief had lasted seconds, no more than five or six. It had happened three times on the walk from the car to the security office and then twice more from the security office to Watson's door—the sound of rapped steel echoing in his head as another name dropped into place.

"Pete?"

Singer's head jerked up.

"Did you hear me?"

"Sure, Steve. I've worked here for a long time."

Five or six seconds and the tension began to build again, not like rising water but like building water. It wasn't the height but the mass building up behind the barrier, impermeable but not unyielding, bending outwards as the pressure built, bowing until the pressure created the first small tear that expanded in a flurry of cracks and fissures, gave way and another name fell into place. Singer flinched. In the moment before it began to build again, he looked at Watson.

"…with cause, therefore, there will not be a severance package. However, because of your long service, we are offering you a fifteen-hundred-dollar settlement."

"How much?"

Watson nodded sympathetically.

"I know it's not a lot, Peter, but we're under no obligation to give you anything. Sproul has agreed not to press charges, but there is little doubt that charges could have been pressed."

Fifteen hundred dollars. Sixty. Sixty names.

"And of course, your pension contributions will be returned to you."

"Pension contributions?"

Watson nodded.

"How much?"

Watson stared at him for a moment, puzzled.

"Fifteen hundred dollars, Peter. I just—"

Singer shook him off.

"No, No, Steve. How much in pension contributions?"

Watson frowned and shook his head.

"I… I'm not sure, Peter, you would have to talk to human resources about that."

Singer jerked his head at Watson's computer.

"You can't call it up there?"

Watson watched Singer closely, took a quick look at the closed door over Singer's shoulder before answering.

"No, I don't have access to that kind of information, Peter."

"How long does it take?"

"How long does what take, Peter?"

"To get back my pension contributions, Steve. For chrissakes, stay with me. How long?"

Watson rolled his seat back from the edge of his desk and looked at the door again.

"I don't know. A week? Two?"

Singer stood up and Watson sat straighter in his chair, readying himself to stand.

"Fine. Fine. And the fifteen hundred dollars?"

Watson rolled forward so he could reach his desk again, picked a cheque off the desk and held it up for Singer to see.

"I can give it to you now…"

Singer stepped forward, but Watson held up a hand and leaned cautiously forward to push a single sheet across to Singer's side of the desk, sliding back and out of reach once it was in place.

"Before I can give you this."

He held the cheque up a little higher.

"I need you to sign that."

Singer ran his hand down the page looking for the spot. Watson rolled forward and pointed to a spot two-thirds of the way down the page, buried between blocks of text.

"Initial here. Full signature there. It's an agreement that you waive all legal rights to appeal your dismissal. If for any reason you—"

"Fine. It's fine, Steve."

Singer patted at his chest then reached out.

"You got a pen, Steve?"

Watson opened a drawer, handed Singer a pen, he initialed, signed and snatched the cheque from Watson's hand before turning and leaving the room. Robert called out, but Singer kept walking and the security guard had to hurry to catch up.

***

Singer stood outside watching people entering and leaving the building. Most never moved beyond the automated tellers in the inner foyer. There were two machines. Singer had no idea how much was in each. Five hundred? A thousand? Five thousand lives?

Was there more now, early in the day? Or more later, after people made deposits?

The cheque made things easy. Cheryl would never know anything about it. Singer could deposit it, go home and make the contributions. One hundred and twenty names from the waiting list to *The Living List*. Already Singer could feel something easing, slowing in his head. The tension was still building but it had slowed. Singer saw that one of the machines was free and crossed the street, but as he got to the bank entrance a young woman pushing a baby stroller approached the door and Singer held it open for her. She nodded gratefully, slipped in and stepped up to the empty automated teller. Singer stopped a few paces behind an older man at the other teller.

But the pension money would come in whenever it came in. If Cheryl saw it before he did, she would ask questions. He would have to watch the accounts. But there might be red flags even sooner. Once his pay cheques stopped showing up. He would need another job, but before that he had to keep this from Cheryl. It was going to be hard to understand what had happened. But she would. It would just take time.

The man in front of him held his hand near the bill dispenser, pulled the money free and took a quick look left as if checking out the sidewalk before counting the bills, folding them into his wallet and stepping away from the machine. Singer started to step forward then spun and went into the bank.

***

"So, you would like to defer a mortgage payment?"

Singer nodded.

"Right. My wife's mother can't live by herself anymore and we have to renovate the basement."

The woman behind the counter smiled at him. She had a ruddy pleasant face and her right eye wandered a little so that Singer had to concentrate not to follow its movement.

"Not everybody would be willing. Your wife's lucky to have such a supportive husband."

She tapped a few keys and looked at her screen.

"But there's other ways you could do that. You aren't at your loan limit. You could just take out a loan to cover the renovations and we could piggyback it on your mortgage. There wouldn't be any need to miss a payment."

Singer shook his head.

"No. That's okay, we've got some money set aside and if we can skip a couple of months we should be able to cover the costs without adding any more debt."

Cheryl would be more likely to notice a new loan than the fact that their mortgage wasn't being pulled out. The teller made a sympathetic face.

"Well, I can give you a one-month deferral without a problem. But if you're looking for more than one month, I'll have to talk to my manager."

Singer smiled at her.

"Do you mind?"

She looked over his shoulder at the line that had grown to five people then nodded and turned away. She took two steps then whirled back.

"It really is a formality. I know that Mr. Archambeault is going to approve. Why don't I just put it through and I'll get his approval and signature later."

Singer smiled again.

"That's great. Thanks for your help with this."

Chapter 20

Honore Owusu. She reminded Singer of his son. Tommie. It was something about the way she was unable to stay at her mother's side as they walked along the dusty cart path. Honore's mother balanced a large white basin with another smaller basin nestled inside on her head using one hand. The person filming followed thirty or forty meters behind, but neither Honore nor her mother seemed to notice.

The first time Singer had seen Honore, there had been no hint of Tommie. Like most of the children in the videos, there had been almost no flesh between skin and bone and her body would occasionally vibrate with a quick series of tremors before she fell still again. Unlike most of the videos, Honore's eyes had opened twice, suddenly and without warning as if something had startled her. Her head had remained motionless, but her eyes had slid back and forth in their sockets as if she was watching something unfolding directly in front of her even though she lay alone in a darkened hut. Her lips had parted slightly as if to speak but the result was only to change somewhat the pitch of her shallow breathing. Then her eyes had snapped shut again.

Now she gamboled alongside her mother, skipping barefoot for a stride or two then sliding to a stop, letting herself fall a stride or two behind before dashing back alongside her mother, clasping her hand for a moment. She then dropped it again so she could chase a grasshopper that had been startled into the air before settling back into the short dry grass at the side of the path. He had watched several videos, but this was the only one he had watched more than once.

Singer watched it to the end, the video freezing as Honore looked back at her mother just as she leapt away, her face open and lit from deep inside, her eyes creased by a smile her cheeks could not contain, neither foot touching the ground, her body held aloft above the ground as if suspended by invisible threads. In the background, fifty or a hundred meters beyond Honore and her mother, a muddied stream surrounded by crouching women, all with similar water basins.

***

Singer drifted just past the mouth of their driveway and pulled over so that the left side of the car settled on the verge of the street. The ground gave a little, still soft from melted snow. Singer looked over his left shoulder at the cars in the driveway. Cheryl's 2018 Mazda was pulled up almost to the garage door so that the other two cars, her father's RAV-4 and a late-model Audi Singer didn't recognize, could get in behind her in the driveway. Singer tilted the rearview mirror so he could see the side door to the house without having to twist in his seat. Nothing looked different. Singer readjusted the mirror so it pointed out the back window again, shifted a little in his seat to examine the cars in the driveway without turning, staring at them for several seconds before he straightened in his seat and turned off the engine. Singer closed his eyes and took a few seconds, searching, testing, but there was nothing, no building tension, no slow coil. It had been a good day— seventeen lives.

There had been better days over the last three weeks. His best day had been a week ago Thursday, eleven hundred and fifty dollars, forty-six videos, forty-six names that wouldn't move from *The Living List* to *The Passed List*…at least, not for a while. Some days Singer had to wait to get a computer station, killing time flipping through magazines in the periodical section, until a computer came free. Other times he got too lost in the videos, unable to pull himself away from the faces, those of the dying and those of their caregivers, pulling loose only to realize that it had been twenty-five or thirty or forty minutes since he had selected a name and arranged the twenty-five-dollar transfer payment. A couple of times Singer had run late, lost track of the time and needed an excuse for Cheryl when he got home. But today he had left in plenty of time. Cheryl shouldn't be home yet.

***

Singer stood just inside the screen door with his right hand still resting on the doorknob. Cheryl's father must have looked over at the sound of the door, because his eyes had been on Singer from the moment the inside door had opened enough for Singer to see Cheryl and her father at the kitchen table. With a man Singer had never seen before, leaning against the wall behind Cheryl's shoulder. Cheryl's father's ribbed winter jacket had slipped off the chair onto the floor and lay puddled around a chair leg, but the stranger was still wearing his coat, beige, mohair. It probably hung below his knee, but Singer couldn't be sure because Cheryl was blocking Singer's view.

Singer stepped forward so he could push the door closed behind him, then leaned down to untie his boots.

"Don't bother."

Cheryl laid a hand on her father's arm.

"Ssshh, Daddy."

Singer began speaking as he straightened.

"Cheryl, I know this seems bad. But it's going to be okay… It's actually better…"

Cheryl sat so that her forearms rested on the table and stared out the door into the backyard. Singer didn't notice the man behind her move but something shifted as he walked across the kitchen floor, something in the angle or shape of the way the man stood. Singer reached for a chair, but it wasn't there. Singer looked around and spotted them in the hallway between the kitchen and the office.

"There's no need. You're not staying."

Cheryl's voice was quiet, soothing.

"Daddy."

Singer went into the hallway and looked up the stairs, grabbing one of the chairs on the way back.

"Where are the boys?"

"Mrs. Landrigan's."

Singer set the chair down, then spun it around so he was straddling the seat, draping his arms over the back onto the kitchen table so that his hand was almost touching his wife's arm.

"Cher? I know how bad this looks. And I know I should have told you sooner. But there was just so much… The emails just kept coming… Work… And my head… It's hard to explain but I was sure I was going crazy."

Singer glanced at his father-in-law and saw that he was staring at the table, at the narrow space between Singer's fingers and his daughter's arm. Singer shifted forward so that he was sitting a little straighter.

"But I'm feeling a lot better now, Cheryl. It's going to be fine. I'll find another job. And we can figure the rest out."

She waited for him to draw a breath and when she began her voice was quiet and steady, though she didn't look over at him.

"They called me at work, Peter. Wanted to know when we thought we could begin payments again."

She tightened her lips and pushed air through her nose.

"You can probably guess what I said, eh, Peter? What payment?"

She looked down at her hands and Peter followed her gaze, noticing for the first time the unlit cigarette between her left fore and middle fingers.

"I had to ask two more times. She must not have been able to understand what I was asking. Or maybe, this is something that happens regularly…people pretend they don't know what she's talking about. And that's what she does—waits them out. But I guess when I asked the third time she was convinced I really didn't know."

"Look, Cher. I know. I know. I should have told you."

"Eleven thousand dollars. I had to go down to the bank."

She used her left hand to brush a strand of hair away from her forehead. She didn't seem to notice the cigarette she was holding. Singer had never seen her smoke, although he knew she had before he met her.

"It was like somebody had died. Can I take your coat, Mrs. Singer? Can we get you something to drink, Mrs. Singer? Coffee? Water? Mrs. Singer? But not just that. Somebody's died but I'm too stupid to really understand what's happened."

"So, they talk veerrrry slowly."

Her voice dropped.

"And softly."

"And there's always two of them in the room. Because who knows what you could do?"

"Cheryl…"

"But they walked me through everything. I don't know where the first fifteen hundred dollars came from."

She glanced at him for just a moment.

"They didn't know either. But probably some kind of severance. Then, the two mortgage payments that should have come out."

She shook her head and chuckled.

"I didn't notice. Can you believe that? After the stuff you pulled, I wasn't even watching that closely. The numbers seemed about right. I didn't notice that none of the withdrawals were for the mortgage. The numbers coming out seemed about right."

She looked over at him.

"Were you doing the math, Peter? Figuring out what withdrawal amounts would look right? Or did you just get lucky?"

Singer made a face.

"Come on, Cheryl. You know."

Singer's wife pulled her hand off her father's arm to tap her fingernails on the table.

"I know? What do I know? I don't know anything. Two ladies at the bank know more about my life than I do."

Her voice caught on the last two words and Cheryl's father covered her hand to still the tapping.

"Honey, you don't need to do this right now."

His daughter shook her head but took a few seconds before speaking. When she did, she had her voice back in place.

"You remember that night, Peter?"

She looked over at him and held his eye this time. He stared back mutely and nodded, not sure how, but knowing exactly the night she meant.

"I wished so hard to be pregnant. Seeing Tommie lying there. And Dougie wanting so much to help. I just wanted so badly to have another."

Her head dropped. Singer thought that it was to hide tears, but when she raised her chin again her eyes were dry, distant, seeing something he couldn't.

"You were asleep. And I just sat on the edge of the bed praying. Dear God, give us another baby. Please God, give us another baby."

She smiled then.

"But he knew better. He knew better."

She sat back, pulling her arms from the table and across her chest. Cheryl's father looked at the man standing behind her, who nodded and spoke for the first time.

"Mr. Singer. Peter. I think it might be best if you left now."

Singer looked at the man, then at his father-in-law then at his wife.

"Cheryl?"

She was looking away again at the backyard, but she nodded. Singer stood up. His coat had slipped off his shoulders while they talked and he shrugged back into it, padded across to the door and put on his boots without tying them. The stranger spoke.

"We'll be in touch, Peter."

Singer nodded without turning around and went out to his car.

***

Singer had been worried that his credit card might be declined but it had gone through.

"You're second from the end, Mr. Singer."

The woman leaned out across the counter so she could see through the door into the parking lot. Her glasses had slipped down her nose and she adjusted them with thick, short fingers as she stood straight again.

"You can pull right in front of your door—it doesn't look like anybody's taken that spot yet."

She pushed a smudged photocopy across the counter.

"List of amenities and house rules. Checkout's at noon and if you need to smoke, there are a couple of picnic tables out back."

Singer nodded.

***

The TV was small and bolted to the wall but it was a flat-screen and relatively new. The bed cover was a little worn, beige with a pattern that might have been meant to suggest autumn leaves but looked clean. The tub and toilet had been scrubbed.

Singer went back out to the car to get his laptop.

It had been awkward going back to the house to get it. Singer hadn't thought of it until he was back in the car and had left the engine running to go back to the house. He had stood for a moment outside, unsure of whether he should knock but finally just deciding to let himself in. The stranger must have pushed himself off the wall at the sound of the door because he was standing directly behind

Singer's wife's chair, his hands resting on the back. Cheryl's father started to stand but Singer raised his hand.

"Don't worry. I'm out. I just have to grab a couple of things."

He had thought about grabbing a change of clothes, but had settled for simply scooping up his laptop.

Now, Singer plugged it in and looked around for the Wi-Fi code while the computer booted up, finding a small card on the shelf next to the double bed with the network name and password.

***

The password to their bank accounts had been changed. But until Cheryl cancelled the credit cards there was still money. There had been no new emails since the day before, but as Singer went to open the most recent email a new one dropped in his mailbox. Always the same subject lines *The Living List* and *The Passed List*. The videos showing those who had been saved always arrived without a subject line. And there wasn't always a post-donation video. Singer was never sure what that meant.

Singer poised the arrow over the email, took a deep breath and clicked the link. He had to scroll several times to reach the bottom, but for the first time since Singer had started receiving the emails the length of the list was shorter. He was removing names faster than they were being added. But there were still too many names.

Singer started with the first three, Fernanda Barbosa, Kaikara Mbabazi, Adelina Tombe, but paused over the fourth name. Singer didn't know what the limit was on the card. He had spent almost two hundred dollars getting the room for three nights and now another seventy-five for donations. He leaned back in his chair and closed his eyes—his head was still. Despite everything that had happened, with his job, with Cheryl, even with whatever came next with Dougie and Tommie, there was nothing building in his head. He would sleep. He looked at the fourth name for a long time then slid the arrow away, stood, went into the bathroom and started the shower, letting it run and hoping for hot.

Chapter 21

Singer could hear the man's voice over the line even from where he sat several feet away from the receptionist's desk.

"Could you take Cheryl's husband down to conference room two?"

"Yes, Mr. Donovan."

He said something else that Singer couldn't make out.

"I understand."

She listened for several more seconds.

"Okay."

Then hung up, looked over smiling and stood up, smoothing her dress over her hips before catching herself.

"If you'll follow me, Mr. Singer."

She stepped through a door to the right of her desk and held it open behind her, looking over her shoulder at him. He caught the door as she let go and followed her down the hallway. They passed first a large office with the paneled mahogany door closed, but Singer could see through a side glass panel the stranger who had been with Cheryl at the house. The man seemed to glance up, but then they were past and Singer thought he might have been mistaken. They passed several smaller plain office doors, also closed, the woman glancing over her shoulder a couple of times to be sure he was following. She stopped at another door, identical to those they had passed. She stepped quickly to the side so she was facing him and raised her hand to knock on the door but stopped when she saw Singer looking at her shoes. Singer flushed and looked away. She waited as if she thought he might say something, but he had no idea what to say and she knocked then, really just a warning, opening the door without waiting for a response. The woman leaned into the doorway.

"Mr. Singer's here, Cheryl. Are you alright if I leave you two? Mr. Donovan will be here in a second."

Singer's wife smiled.

"We'll be fine, Rebecca."

Singer walked across the room and began to sit down next to his wife before noticing the large manila envelope, pad and pen on the table in front of the chair and swung around to the third chair directly across from his wife. She looked pale. Better than she had in the kitchen, but still pale.

"How are you doing, Cheryl?"

She took a minute.

"Okay. I guess. A little better."

Singer nodded then looked back at the empty doorway.

"How much do you figure her shoes cost?"

His wife closed her eyes and shook her head.

"I don't know, Peter."

Singer shook his head and started to speak but stopped as Donovan strode into the room. Singer rose, but the other man came straight to the table and sat down without a greeting, looking first at Cheryl, giving her a reassuring smile and then turning to Singer.

"You understand what we're doing here, Peter?"

Singer nodded. The other man nodded back.

"That's good. But let's cover a few things. A legal separation is an alternative when the two parties either have religious or moral reasons for not wanting to divorce or they are not yet prepared to accept that their marriage should be dissolved."

Donovan paused and Singer looked across at his wife.

"Are you sure about this, Cheryl?"

Donovan put his hand over Singer's wife's hand to stop her then turned back to Singer.

"This has already been agreed to, Peter. We're not here to rehash the decision. We simply need you to sign some documents."

Donovan picked up the envelope and slid the documents free. He picked the first sheaf off the top and slid it across the table.

"This document relinquishes any stake in the house and property you and Cheryl own. Cheryl can choose to sell or keep the house as she wishes and all proceeds from any sale of the house will go to Cheryl and Cheryl alone. You will not be responsible for payments on the mortgage except for the monthly contributions you and Cheryl have agreed upon. Take your time and read through it."

Singer flipped to the back page and found the signature line, reached across the table, picked up the pen, hefting it for a second in his hand before looking at Donavan then back down at the pen.

"Nice."

When Donovan didn't answer, Singer bent his head and scrawled his signature before pushing the papers back across the desk. The lawyer slipped them into the envelope then pushed the next stapled set of papers across to Singer.

"This is the temporary financial agreement. You're contribution to the household. It times out in a year."

Singer looked from Donovan to his wife.

"I haven't got a job yet, Cheryl. I will. But the first month could be tricky."

Singer's wife nodded.

"I know, Peter."

Donovan placed his hand over hers again, but she pulled her hand free without looking at him.

"I'm not worried, Peter. I know you'll do right by the boys."

Singer nodded, flipped to the back page, signed and slid it across the table.

***

Singer and his wife sat side by side on the couch. They had decided that sitting together was best, that sitting on opposite sides of the room with the boys between them sent the wrong message. Singer could tell that Dougie was already near tears, his eyes moving between his mother and father from the moment he sat on the floor in front of them, his hands tangled in his lap, the fingers working back and forth, looping one across the other until they were completely intertwined then uncoiling in a sudden burst like sliced rubber bands, before beginning to curl together again. Tommie crouched on his knees running a toy car down one thigh onto the rug then back up onto the other leg before reversing direction. Cheryl spoke first.

"Tommie, could you stop playing for just a minute?"

It was as if the boy hadn't heard, continuing to run the car up and down his legs now adding in quiet whirring sounds, imitating the sound of a car engine.

"Tommie, daddy and I have something important to say. Could you stop playing and listen, please."

Singer thought the boy was going to ignore his mother a second time but then he put the car down beside his leg and looked up at them. Cheryl glanced at her husband. Singer had practiced in the mirror, but he could feel himself begin to choke and paused to swallow it.

"Daddy's not going to be living here for a while."

"Why? Why can't you live here?"

The tears had already begun streaming down Dougie's face. It was only more disconcerting because you couldn't hear it in his voice. Singer shook his head and swallowed again.

"Let me finish, Dougie? Okay? Just let me finish, alright?"

Singer looked down at his hands then back up, first at Dougie then at his youngest who was now watching his older brother.

"Mommy and I have a few things to figure out. But none of it's about you guys. Nothing has changed with you guys. It's just that for a little while, it'll be better if Mommy and I live in different places."

Singer filled the gap quickly before Dougie could interrupt.

"So, I won't be here every day but you guys will come and visit me, stay with me for one day every week. And we'll do stuff together just like always. And I'll still bring you guys to hockey and then to baseball in the summer. And watch all your games."

"How long?"

Singer turned his head trying to understand.

"How long won't you be here?"

"Oh. It won't be to…"

Singer felt his wife's hand on his leg.

"It's hard to say, Dougie. We'll just take it one day at a time."

"Will you be back for Tommie's birthday?"

Singer looked down into his lap, trying to force back the pressure behind his eyes. He shook his head, not sure what he meant but not able to speak.

"Mommy's birthday? Christmas?"

"We don't know, Dougie. Your Dad and I just have to figure some stuff out. We aren't sure how long it will take. But we'll be trying."

Dougie looked back and forth between them, stricken.

"Why can't Daddy try from here?"

Singer got up and left the room, standing at the kitchen sink looking out into the backyard. He heard his wife continue to talk to the boys, but he couldn't make out what she was saying.

***

Singer put his boots on at the door. He had tucked both the boys into bed. Dougie had clung to him, crying silently into the place between his chin and shoulder until Singer had been forced to peel his son's fingers apart so he could stand. Dougie turned to the wall then and didn't turn to look even when Singer paused at the top of the stairs. Tommie looked at him over the rail of his bed and Singer blew him a kiss. Tommie grabbed it with one hand and blew it back.

Singer stood up from lacing his boots. His wife was in the door between the kitchen and dining room, watching.

"Give me a week or two—time to find a job and an apartment."

She nodded and Singer turned and left.

BOOK 2

Chapter 22

The man behind the cash was tall and slim with a salt and pepper beard. He looked like he could have been from any of the Middle Eastern countries, but when he spoke there was only a faint hint of an accent.

"I don't really need anybody right now."

Singer nodded and looked around the store and then out the window that ran the length of the store. There was a single car, something small, with a crimp in the right bumper in the lot. Under the harsh glare of the streetlight it looked black but when the headlights of a passing car washed over the lot out front of the store he saw that it was midnight blue or maybe charcoal grey. Singer watched a young man hold the door to the Pizza Pizza store across the street from the 7-Eleven for an older woman in a heavy wool sweater but no coat. She walked in without looking at the young man as she approached or as she passed. Singer wondered if she had spoken to him as she passed but there was no sign she had. The young man's hair clung damp and tight to his forehead and he brushed at it with one hand as he stepped in behind the woman and let the door fall closed behind him. Singer looked back at the man.

"I don't need guaranteed hours, I'm happy to fill in wherever you need me. And anytime. Even on short notice."

The man looked at him for several seconds then shook his head again.

"I really don't need anybody."

Singer paused and drew a deep breath.

"What happened to whoever was supposed to work the shift?"

The man straightened behind the counter.

"Excuse me?"

"You're the owner. Or the manager. Or whatever. You don't work the night shift. Somebody didn't show."

Singer was tired. He just wanted to go back to his room and sleep.

"I'll show up. Every shift."

The man looked away to push at a small pad on the counter next to the cash, then when he had it where he wanted it, he took the pencil that had rolled a little away and tucked it in along the side of the pad.

"Anytime? Midnight to seven shifts?"

Singer nodded.

"If that's what you need."

The man stared at him for several seconds before speaking.

"Okay. Tomorrow… Not tomorrow… The next night. Midnight. But be here at 11:30. I'll have to show you a few things."

Singer smiled and nodded.

"Sounds good. Any paperwork?"

The man made a small sound in his chest that might have been a chuckle.

"We'll see how things work out."

Singer nodded, turned away towards the door then spun and came back to the counter and held out his hand.

"Pete Singer. You aren't going to regret this, Mr..."

The other man looked at his hand then took it.

"Mo. Just call me Mo."

***

The dog looked up from whatever it was nosing at among the tufts of last summer's grass just exposed underneath the last of the snow as things had warmed in the last few days. It watched him as he approached on the far side of the street, turning back towards whatever it had found but then coming back up to look at him when Singer stopped on the sidewalk to look at the building. It would have been orange, almost red, but time and weather had worn away almost all capacity for reflection so that it appeared grey and streaked. The concrete steps had sunk a little on one side and the paint had chipped away except in a few stray patches to reveal the pocked porridge-white beneath. Both handrails were still in place but slat gapped.

Singer stepped off the curb and paused to let a grey truck with rust streaking the length of the lower panels like dried blood roll by. A moon-faced man with pocked cheeks and a head shaved to the wood leaned forward to look past a woman in the passenger's seat as he passed, pausing at the Stop sign at the next corner before rolling through. The dog shifted so it could watch him as he crossed the street then spun in a half circle and sidled away as Singer reached the bottom of the steps. Singer saw that it had been working on a crumpled McDonald's bag. Singer walked up the steps and paused at the door, looking for a place to buzz or ring then pushed on the door and it gave under the pressure.

Eight mailboxes lined the wall and next to each was a button. Two of the mailboxes had names stenciled on them, Weston and LaRocque, but the others only showed black streaks, the remnants of whatever stenciling had been there. There had once been a door separating the foyer from the apartments on the first floor and the stairs leading to those on the upper floors but now there was just a frame recently painted green, the color of mashed peas. But that was the only fresh paint Singer could see, as if somebody had started and then given the cause up for lost.

Singer stood looking at the two names and the buttons. The woman he had talked to had been named Gail but she hadn't mentioned a last name. He couldn't remember if she had sounded more like a Westin or a LaRocque. He looked up at the sound of the door opening. A woman stood in the doorway of the apartment at the end of the hall. She wore faded jeans and an oversized faded blue men's military dress shirt over a grey t-shirt. She pushed a strand of grey hair off her forehead and nodded at the wall.

"Don't bother. Most of them haven't worked in a couple of years. You Peter?"

"Yes, ma'am. You've got an apartment for rent?"

"Got a couple."

She turned away and reached behind her with one bare foot and stabbed it into a flip-flop left just inside the doorway. She took a second to get the other one in place, reached up to a spot on the wall inside her apartment and then turned back with a ring of keys in her hand.

"Let's start downstairs."

***

Singer followed the woman into the apartment and she stepped to the side to let him walk past, noticing him glance at the ceiling.

"Yeah. It's a little low. Eight feet."

Singer reached up over his head and trailed his fingers across the ceiling without coming off the flats of his feet.

"You think?"

The woman allowed herself a small smile.

"Maybe not quite eight."

Singer took a few steps forward into the kitchen.

"Stove. Fridge. Used to come with a microwave, but it went missing a couple of tenants ago."

She gestured at the stove.

"Back left burner doesn't work but the oven's fine. Lots of cupboard space and room for a small kitchen table if you want to eat in here."

The woman led Singer out of the kitchen and into the second room, long and narrow, running the length of the building except for a small room at the far end that Singer guessed was the bathroom. The light was a murky mix of overhead glare from the two bulbs under opaque dusted glass on the ceiling and natural light drifting in from oblique angles through the two narrow half windows set in the right-side wall. Tufts of dried grass and weeds poked up into view along the bottom of the window outside the pane. The indoor/outdoor carpet gave like damp newsprint underfoot as he walked the length of the room. The woman pointed to a curtain runner along the ceiling.

"Last tenant hung a drape down the middle—gave her an 'office' and a sitting room."

Singer nodded.

"Let's have a look upstairs."

The woman nodded.

"Sure."

***

Gail moved lightly and easily up the third flight of stairs and Singer had to take steps a couple at a time occasionally to keep up. He had pegged her for early 60s, her face deeply lined around the mouth and eyes, but he thought she was probably younger. She stopped at a door just to the right of the staircase on the top floor and fumbled with the keys, trying two before finding a third that fit the lock. She made a face as she pushed open the door and stepped aside to let him walk ahead.

"All of these top-floor apartments are the same type of key and I get them mixed up."

Singer smiled.

"Good to know that you need to find the right one."

"One way to look at it."

The apartment was cold, almost as cold as outside. The hallway from the door led to a window on the back wall of the apartment. The bottom panel of the window was broken. Not just missing but broken, small, serrated shards still embedded in the frame. Singer walked past the woman and looked out the window onto the alley running the length of the block separating the buildings on Cambridge from those on the next block over. Decades ago it might have been used as a delivery lane, ice or groceries or maybe garbage pickup, but now the narrow tracks were overgrown so the grey mottled gravel could barely be seen beneath the grass and weeds. Somebody had chained a bike to the linked fence separating the lane from a backyard down the block, but the front tire was gone and the back one was bent and twisted like it had been heated, shaped and left to harden. An old couch had been dragged onto the flat roof of the building across the way, but then left out through the winter and something, birds, rats, feral cats, had torn holes in the upholstering and stuffing leaked like seeping wounds from a dozen different places. Singer turned at the woman's voice.

"Mr. Figueuro was supposed to get that fixed. He must have forgot."

Singer could see that she was embarrassed but trying to hide it behind a shrug. He shook his head.

"No big deal. We'll get it fixed."

The kitchen was immediately to the left off the hallway, with a second entrance leading out into the other large room. It was smaller than the one in the basement apartment, but painted more recently. Gail waved an arm around.

"Again, fridge and stove…"

She smiled.

"Although here you get all four burners."

Singer moved from the kitchen into the second room, a large open space with two large windows running from almost floor to ceiling. The bathroom was tucked into the far corner. The windows looked out onto a gravel-covered roof. Singer couldn't tell if it was a connected garage or some other kind of building, but if he opened the window he could step right over the sill and onto the roof. He turned back. The woman was standing in the doorway from the kitchen, watching him. Singer rubbed with one toe at the floor.

"I like this."

She nodded.

"Could use some work but it's hard to beat hardwood."

"Should have left it downstairs."

The woman chuckled.

"No hardwood down there, that's concrete. You need something."

Singer turned a little red.

"Right. I wasn't thinking."

There was a pause while they both searched for something to say.

"How much?"

"Downstairs is two hundred seventy-six dollars a month. This one's three hundred and twelve and you pay the heat. Downstairs, the heat's covered."

Singer nodded his head at the room.

"I like this."

***

Singer sat in Gail's kitchen at a small square table made of some rich dark wood. He could see where one leg had been cracked, perhaps completely broken, then repaired and reinforced using wood that almost matched but not quite. He filled in the blanks then signed at the bottom and stood up. Gail slid the application off the table and placed it on her fridge with a magnet.

"It's just a formality. The place is yours. Mr. Figueuro leaves all the decisions about tenants to me."

Singer reached into his inside coat pocket.

"First and last?"

She nodded. Singer counted out six hundreds, a twenty, a five and three loonies and laid them on the table. He stuffed the thin sheaf of remaining bills back in his pocket. Gail had already prepared two receipts for three hundred and fourteen dollars each, and she handed them to him with a set of keys.

"The square head's for your apartment door and the smaller round key is for the storage room in the basement. There's still some space if you need it. The place isn't officially yours until Thursday but you can move your stuff in any time. They're gone and they won't be back."

"I appreciate that."

Singer stood for a moment then gestured at the door.

"I should be going. Thanks for this."

The woman slipped back into her flip-flops.

"Here, let me walk you out."

She followed him to the outer door and out onto the steps. The dog was gone.

"Thanks again, Gail."

Singer paused, smiled and shrugged.

"I guess we'll be seeing each other."

The woman nodded and Singer waited, he could tell she wasn't done.

"Peter?"

He nodded and she continued, the hard lines around her eyes softening, giving.

"What are you doing here?"

He thought about pretending he didn't know what she meant but shrugged instead.

"It's a long story."

She held his eyes for several seconds.

"Make it right, Peter. This ain't the place for you."

He shrugged again and looked away, started to answer but realized he didn't have one. She made a face.

"I'm sorry. It's none of my business."

"It's okay, Gail. You have a good day. I'll see you soon."

Chapter 23

Mo was dressed in the same worn jeans and yellow collared golf shirt that he had been wearing two nights before. But his wife wore more traditional East Indian clothes, a simple red and yellow dress with a yellow blouse beneath and a ribbon of red cloth tying her hair back behind her neck. When she walked Singer could see that she wore loose pants that tightened at the ankle beneath her dress. Mo had introduced his wife as Mrs. Laghari, she had nodded at him without speaking and returned to stocking the cigarette shelves.

"Have you ever worked a cash before, Peter?"

Singer shook his head. Mo smiled at him.

"There's not much to it."

They spent a few minutes running through how the register worked, how to work the debit and credit card machine and then the store owner led him to a slot along the back wall that fed into the office at the back of the store.

"The door to the office is always locked. Only my wife and I have a key."

Mo pointed at the slot.

"People don't use cash much anymore, but you'll get some. At the end of your shift, put the cash in an envelope along with the bundle of sales receipts and drop the envelope in the slot. That's all there is to it."

Singer nodded.

"Seems simple enough."

Mo led him back towards the cash and around the counter out into the store. Before leaving the counter, he said something over his shoulder to his wife that Singer didn't understand. She answered without turning around.

"But there are a couple more things."

He led Singer to the fridges holding soft drinks, juices and anything that needed to be cooled. He pointed at one of the fridges.

"This door doesn't catch unless you slam it."

He pointed at a note on the door and made a face.

"I've explained this in a message for customers but nobody reads it. So, keep an eye on the door and make sure it's closed. Otherwise, we use up energy like it's going out of style."

The store owner kept walking down the line of fridges.

"But sometimes people just leave them wide open. They reach in, pull something out and just leave the door open."

Mo made the face again.

"I don't understand it. Would they leave the refrigerator door open in their own home? But they do it. Kids mostly. But even some people, fully grown. So, keep your eyes open and close the doors."

Mo led Singer back to the counter pointed to the cash.

"Stand behind it."

Singer cocked his head, looked at the store owner.

"What?"

Mo pointed again.

"I want to see you stand behind the cash."

Singer smiled as if at a joke but moved behind the cash when he realized the store owner wasn't joking. The owner came behind him, grabbed him by the shoulders and shifted him around until he had Singer where he wanted him. Then he pointed at the mirrors placed around the store.

"They steal a lot. It is a big problem. And this is where you have to stand to see what everybody is doing. It gives you the best view."

Singer looked over his shoulder at the store owner.

"And what do I do if I see somebody stealing?"

Mo stepped back as if he had been slapped.

"What do you do? You stop them and you call the police!"

"Really? What if they run away?"

Mo raised a finger.

"Don't chase them. That's what they want. You chase them and their friends come in and take everything."

"Really? Has that happened?"

"Once. Before I understood what they were doing."

The store owner tapped his forehead as if remembering something.

"And no bums!"

"What?"

"The bums come in to get warm. But they stink and they scare customers so don't let them in. They won't give you trouble. They will leave if you tell them to leave."

"They just leave?"

Mo shrugged and nodded.

"Usually. They don't want trouble. They just want to get warm."

"What if they don't leave?'

Mo looked surprised.

"You call the police. Of course. They cannot stay."

The store owner looked at the cash, then back to the slot in the wall, then around the store.

"I'm sure I am forgetting to tell you something but…you will learn as you go."

He patted Singer on the back.

"You will be fine."

Then he turned to his wife.

"We're done here, Sati. Let's go home."

Her response was quick and angry in a language Singer didn't understand and she didn't turn away from what she was doing. The store owner sighed and his shoulders slumped a little.

"It is fine, Satyana. I've explained everything. He will be fine."

She spoke sharply, turned from what she was doing and walked over to where they stood. She spoke to her husband again, as if Singer wasn't there. Mo shook his head.

"No, Sati. It's fine."

She glanced at Singer then spoke to her husband again, her jaw set and angry. His shoulders slumped a little further and he spoke without looking at me.

"My wife would like to know where you worked before here."

Singer looked at Mrs. Laghari when he answered.

"I worked at the Amazon warehouse out on Bellamy Road. I was a floor supervisor."

She did not look at Singer, but spoke sharply to her husband again.

"My wife would like to know if you quit or you were fired. And if you quit, why you would quit a job such as that to take this job."

Singer smiled at her, although she still wasn't looking at him.

"I was fired."

Mo's wife spat out a few words and then waited. Her husband lowered his head and shook it.

"No."

Her eyes narrowed and she said them again. The store owner took a deep breath,

"My wife would like to know if you were fired for stealing."

Singer smiled again.

"No. Not for stealing. I punched somebody."

Mrs. Laghori tilted her head at her husband and for the first time he spoke to her in a language other than English. She looked over at Singer for a moment then walked past her husband and out the door. Mo gathered his jacket and his wife's coat from a counter beneath the cash and patted Singer on the shoulder.

"Good luck. My cell number's in the cash drawer. Call me if you need to."

Singer watched as the store owner walked to the car, unlocked and opened the door for his wife, then walked around the car and got in the driver's side. The taillights popped red, the headlights flashed on. Mo backed to the edge of the street, blocking the sidewalk, waited for a break in the traffic, backed into the road and drove away.

***

It was still dark as Singer walked back to the motel from the store, though light was beginning to gather on the western horizon. Singer cut across an empty lot to the motel. The motel office was dark but not pitch, a light was still on somewhere in the back. He walked down the row of rooms to his door and let himself in.

Singer undressed and lay on the bed, too tired to shower. He tried for several minutes but couldn't sleep, aware of his laptop across the room on the battered desk. Finally he walked to the desk, flipped it open and fired it up. He sat in the dark of the motel room staring at the screen, waiting for his email server to open. When it did, he opened a video showing a child from behind, standing straight and tall and holding the hand of a woman who might have been her mother. As Singer watched, he heard an email drop into his mailbox.

He knew what it was. He couldn't be certain. It could be Cheryl with a question. Or Brian. But it wasn't. Singer knew it was a *Living List* email. He placed his hand on the computer top to close it and his hand rested there for several seconds before he removed it and clicked the unread emails box. There were three emails, all *Living List* that had arrived in the last four or five days. He opened the most recent, scrolled and saw that the list had begun to grow again.

The first video was of a boy, Brayan, lying beneath a tree, gnarled and nearly leafless but providing some shade from a midday sun, creating narrow dark bands that striped the boy's body like burn scars. He was old enough that there was a shadow of hair along his chin, but his features were still soft and malleable, not yet set by time despite the lack of flesh cushioning his cheeks and chin.

There was still four hundred dollars in the secret account Singer had set up. He made three donations, shut down the computer, lay down and slept.

Chapter 24

Brian stood in the middle of the room and looked at the six boxes stacked against the wall in the gap between the window and the corner of the room.

"That's it?"

Singer nodded.

"Got a mattress being delivered and I saw a kitchen table and chairs at Reusables that'll do the trick. They should fit in your car."

"What about the boys?"

"What about 'em?"

"Where'll they sleep?"

"The queen was only fifty dollars more than the double—they can crawl in with me."

Brian turned and walked in a shallow circle, through the kitchenette as if taking a shortcut to the door, but then turning left and moving along the far wall of the apartment to the window, still broken. Singer's friend clasped one of the broken pieces between forefinger and thumb and tugged. It shifted but clung to the window frame. Brian wiggled and tugged as if it prying at a loose tooth and it popped free. He held it up to his eye like peering through a monocle, made a motion to throw it out into the alley then stopped himself and lay it on the window ledge.

"Might want to hang onto this. Until you can find something sharper."

Singer smiled at his friend's back.

"Good to know you've got my back, buddy."

Brian's head moved a little, following something out the window that Singer couldn't see.

"I'm barely kidding."

He tucked at another piece of glass, but it wouldn't give and he let go.

"What are you doing, Pete?"

Singer took a couple of steps over to one of the windows on the other wall and looked out in the other direction before turning and sliding down the wall beside the window. He looked across the worn hardwood at his friend, still gazing at the next block over.

"I can't tell it any different, Bri."

Singer's friend turned away from the window, came over and slid down into the gap between the two windows, rested his butt on his heels and looked over at his friend across the space created by the window between them.

"But what? You're some kind of saint? The rest of us don't give a shit? What gives you the right?"

Singer looked over but had to look down at his hands at the expression on his friend's face.

"It's not like that, Bri. I can't even get it down to that. It's just that I know something and now that I know it I can't unknow it. They're drowning and all they need is a foot of rope. One foot of rope and they can pull themselves to shore. And I've got a hundred feet of rope I'm barely using. How do I not cut off a foot and toss it to them? Eh, Bri? How?"

Singer's friend looked straight ahead, and Singer could see a muscle working along his jawline.

"And Cheryl? Tommie and Dougie?"

Singer took a deep breath through his nose, his chest rising and holding before he let it leak out through his teeth.

"They'll be alright."

Brian slapped the wall behind him with his hand.

"Alright? Alright? Are you hearing yourself?"

Brian looked over.

"I've talked to Cheryl three times and all three times she's had to hang up because she couldn't stop crying. Dougie won't go to school and she's not sure what's going on with Tommie except that the school psychologist is asking for a meeting. Does that sound alright to you, Pete?"

Singer sat still for several seconds then braced himself against the wall and pushed himself to his feet.

"Nobody's getting videos of Tommie or Dougie dying. Let's go get the table and chairs."

***

Cheryl stood in the hall just beyond the kitchenette and took in the mattress pushed against the far wall under the windows, the boombox on a green milk crate in the corner beside the door to the bathroom and the dozen or so books lined along the wall beside the mattress. She looked to her right at the window.

"When did they fix it?"

"Last week."

Tommie dashed across to one of the windows in the sidewall, spotted the lawn chair on the roof and turned to look at his father.

"Cool! Do you sit out there, Dad?"

Singer nodded.

"On the nice days."

"Mom would never let us sit out on a roof with no railing."

Singer looked over at his wife, but she didn't look back.

"Yeah. Well, that's just because Mom knows what's best."

Singer looked at Dougie still tucked in tight beside Cheryl's hip. He gestured to where Tommie stood.

"You want to have a look?"

His son shook his head. Something flashed grey and white out of the corner of his eye and Singer's younger son shouted.

"Dad! Look!"

He was pointing to something on the roof, below the sill.

"It flew right by! Now it's just sitting there!"

Singer walked over and looked out the window at the pigeon pacing along the edge of the roof.

"Yeah. That guy comes by once in a while."

Tommie looked up at his father.

"Even when you're out there?"

Singer nodded.

"Sometimes."

Singer turned and looked over his shoulder and beckoned.

"Come on over, Dougie, have a look. We should give him a name."

Dougie stood where he was for a moment before Cheryl put her arm around his shoulder and led him across to the window. Singer's wife and oldest son stood in one window looking out at the bird and he and his youngest stood in the other.

"Streak!"

Singer looked down at Tommie then over at Dougie.

"Streak. I like it. What do you think, Dougie?"

"Streak! Cause when I saw him, he was just a streak! Right across the window!"

Singer's oldest son shrugged and nodded. He looked around the room.

"Where will we sleep?"

Tommie tapped him on the leg.

"Dad? Dad?"

Singer looked from his son to his wife then back down at Dougie.

"Mommy and I thought you guys would be okay crawling in with me. Just until I get a couple of beds."

Dougie looked at the mattress and back at his father.

"I've got my own bed at home."

"I know Dougie, but I thought it might be fun to all be in the same bed. Kind of like camping out."

Dougie nodded.

"What do you think?"

Dougie nodded again.

"I guess."

"Dad? Dad?"

Singer looked down at Tommie.

"What son?"

Tommie looked all around the room.

"Where's your TV?"

Singer looked at his wife who was watching expressionless, and shrugged then looked down at his son.

"I don't have a TV, Tommie. We'll try and have fun without one."

***

"I'm hungry."

Singer stepped into the door of the bathroom. His boys stood side-by-side at the sink. Singer pointed at the toothbrush in Tommie's hand.

"You have to put it in your mouth and move it around…or it doesn't work."

Tommie looked at the glob of paste on the brush.

"Ours isn't blue."

Dougie nudged his little brother.

"It doesn't matter, Tommie."

Tommie looked over at Dougie, his eyebrows furrowed.

"I like ours."

Dougie nudged his brother harder.

"It doesn't matter."

Tommie turned and Singer stepped between them before he could do anything.

"Whoa! Whoa! Whoa! You like the white stuff with the red stripe, buddy?"

Tommie nodded.

"I'll tell you what—just for tonight, give this a try and next time I'll get the stripey stuff. Okay?"

Tommie made a face at his brother then nodded.

"Okay, you guys finish up. And no fighting."

Singer picked a spot in the middle of the bed with his back against the wall and when they trailed out of the bathroom Singer patted a spot on either side of him.

"C'mon guys. Hop in."

Tommie took several running steps, threw himself on the bed and scrambled up beside his father. Dougie walked around to the side furthest from the window and let himself down next to Singer. Singer used the bottom of his shirt to wipe the paste and foam from around Tommie's mouth.

"Did you get any inside, pal?"

Dougie scowled.

"That's what he always does."

Tommie leaned across his father and slapped at his brother.

"Do not!"

Dougie shook his head and looked up at his dad.

"Ask Mom."

"Not a big deal. I was just kidding. You guys like the library?"

Singer looked back and forth between them. Dougie nodded, but Tommie hopped up onto his knees facing his dad.

"I liked the river better. That was cool!"

Singer had taken them down to where the river ran under the bridge separating the east part of town from the west. They had watched the last of the big chunks of ice melt floating by and fed the ducks that stayed through the winter in a little pool of open water just beyond the southern edge of the bridge. Singer nodded.

"Yeah. I like it down there too."

Tommie talked for a while about the ducks and the ice and bridge and when he paused Dougie spoke.

"Are they there all winter?'

Singer looked at his son.

"The ducks?"

Dougie shook his head.

"No. Those guys."

Singer nodded.

"Yeah. I think so, Dougie."

"What do they do when it's cold?"

Singer shook his head.

"I don't know, son. Maybe if it gets really cold, they find a place to come indoors. I'm not sure."

Dougie nodded.

"Do you think maybe they ever start a fire? Just enough to keep warm?"

"Could be. City probably wouldn't like it. But they might. When it gets really cold."

Dougie nodded. Singer looked at him but couldn't figure what his son was thinking. He pointed at a book along the wall.

"Harry Potter?"

***

"Time for bed, guys, it's late. And Mom's going to be here pretty early to get you for church."

Tommie made a face.

"Ahh, church."

Singer pulled his son in close for a hug and kissed the top of his head.

"Yes. Church. Heathen boy."

Tommie pushed back so he could look up at his dad.

"What's a heathen boy?"

Singer laughed and pulled him in close.

"Don't you worry about it, Tommie. Daddy's just teasing you."

"Dad?"

Singer turned to his oldest. He was looking across the bed out the windows into the dark.

"Could somebody get in?"

"The window? Nah. No way. Nobody's getting in."

"Why? How do you know? Are they locked?"

Singer looked at the windows and then back at his son. He could feel Tommie watching them.

"No. They aren't locked. I don't think they even have locks. But they're way up off the ground."

Dougie got up out of the bed and walked over towards the windows, stopping a few feet away.

"Couldn't somebody climb up onto the roof?"

Singer looked at his son's profile.

"I guess they could. But why would they?"

Singer's son stood for several seconds looking out into the dark then shook his head.

"I don't know why."

"Dougie?"

Singer's son looked over and Singer held out his arms.

"Come here. It's going to be fine. Nobody's coming through the window. And I'm going to be right here."

Dougie came over, accepted the hug, then lay down facing away from the windows. He lay quietly for a few minutes.

"Dad?"

"Yes Dougie."

"What do you think Mommy's doing?"

Singer reached out and ran his hand in small circles on his son's back.

"I don't know, Dougie. It's pretty late—she's probably getting ready for bed. Maybe she's already in bed."

"Do you think she's afraid? All alone."

Singer took a deep breath and his chin fell on his chest. It took him a moment to speak.

"Your mom? She's not afraid of anything."

Singer's son didn't answer. Singer rubbed his back for a minute or two then pulled the blankets up around both boys and leaned across to shut off the lamp on the floor beside the mattress.

***

When Singer awoke, he didn't know how much later, his oldest son was crying quietly beside him. He lay there for a long time waiting for his son to stop but when he didn't Singer got up, gathered the boys' things, packed them into their bags, slipped shoes onto Dougie's feet because he was too big to carry, and scooped Tommie up without waking him.

He tapped lightly at Gail's door and she answered immediately.

"Can I borrow your car, Gail. I'll bring it right back."

She pushed a strand of hair from her eyes, looked at him and the boy in his arms and at Dougie, head down at his side, then nodded and walked back into the kitchen without speaking, returning with the keys.

"You know mine? The Cavalier?"

Singer nodded.

The car was across the street and a few houses up. Singer opened the front passenger door for his son and Dougie slipped in without speaking. Singer opened the back door and lay his still sleeping son across the backseat, knowing that his wife would be angry if she knew but not wanting to wake the boy. Singer got in, started the car and looked over at Dougie who sat staring down into his lap. He took a deep breath and a moment before speaking.

"It's okay, buddy. It's okay."

***

Singer had to ring three times before Cheryl came to the door. She stared at him through the panes in the door for several seconds before opening it.

"Dougie wanted to come home."

She crouched down and Dougie stepped into her arms. She hugged him for several seconds, took Tommie from Singer's arms and led the boys away without speaking. Singer reached in to close the door and went back to the still-idling car.

***

Singer sat on the edge of the mattress his knees up around his face, the computer open on a milk crate in front of him. Over his shoulder, unnoticed, through a break in the houses, a streak of cloud lit from below by the circling and almost risen sun, scarred the eastern horizon.

There was almost nothing left of his first pay cheque. The first few nights Mo had paid him directly from the till, but this had been the first official pay cheque. Singer knew what he needed to cover the rent but had made six more donations than he had budgeted for and now there was almost nothing left. And there was nothing left to sell. He needed to make more money. Singer closed the computer, crawled under the sheets and slept.

***

The first two restaurants weren't looking for help, the third needed a dishwasher but for the evening shift and Singer was worried that an evening shift could conflict with his hours at the store. Already, Mo was occasionally putting him on double shifts, working from six or seven in the evening until six or seven the next morning. The fourth restaurant needed help for the breakfast rush. And he could start the following day. It paid the same as Mo's, minimum wage but it would be enough to fill the gap.

Chapter 25

The morning broke as if the world beyond was on fire. Singer waited until the sun had edged above the horizon and it was too bright to look into the sky, then stood up and bent low to climb through the window into his apartment. There were bills and coins scattered on the small bedside table that he had found on the curb on garbage day. He counted out all the bills and a small pile of toonies and loonies and put them in an envelope.

Singer tried to be quiet on the stairs knowing that many of his neighbors were asleep. He knew because he had learned when the house grew quiet. There were voices and pacing and knocking through the evening and well into the night usually until almost dawn, when the house would begin to settle like a passing storm, leaving behind an occasional gust or squall until the last disturbance was gone. For a few hours it was still before the building began to shake itself awake. First, the faint buzz of music, recognizable as created from notes and chords but not as a particular song or even style. Then, doors opening and closing, voices in the hall and on the stairs. Finally, sounds unrecognizable, clanging and bashing and stomping, sounds Singer was unable to associate with any particular human action or behavior.

Singer removed the coins from the envelope and crouched to slide the coins under Gail's door when it opened. Gail stood looking down at him, wearing the same worn jeans and military shirt that he remembered from their first meeting. She looked from him to the envelope, the four coins on the floor and the next one poised in his hand and shook her head. Singer shrugged.

"Well, if you'd get set up for e-transfers I wouldn't have to do this."

Singer plucked the coins up one at a time, placed them all back inside the envelope then stood and held it out. Gail took it from his hand.

"It's not a great start, Peter."

"I haven't been able to catch you in."

The woman shook her head.

"Right now, I like you. Don't make me change my mind."

Singer flushed and looked at the floor.

"I'm sorry, Gail. I'll get it to you on time next month."

Singer's landlady nodded and her face softened.

"That's fine, Peter."

She stood for a moment, but neither of them thought of anything to say.

"You take care of yourself, Peter."

She stepped back and closed the door and Singer walked out into the early morning sun.

***

Singer recognized the car when it pulled into the parking lot. The store was empty and he had been standing at the door looking out at the traffic. Now, he moved back to his spot behind the cash. Brian barely glanced his way as he entered and headed to the back of the store to the milk and dairy. Singer watched him in the mirrors near the ceiling. Even if Singer hadn't seen his friend come in he would have recognized him from behind as he stood looking into the freezer—something about the way he carried himself. Singer watched as Brian reached in, rummaged around and pulled out a small tub of ice cream, then let the freezer door fall shut and headed up the aisle to the cash. He was looking in Singer's direction, but it didn't register until he was only a few paces from where Singer stood and then there was a pause, a moment of uncertainty as if there might be any other possibility than to step up to the cash and buy the ice cream. Brian let his face fall open into a wide grin.

"Buddy! How have you been?"

Singer's friend looked around the store.

"So this is it, eh? The new job? How's it going?"

Singer smiled back.

"Pretty good. Pays the bills."

Singer shook his head back and forth and smiled again.

"Well, some of them."

Brian nodded and the smile faded.

"Sorry I haven't been by. I meant to drop in and see how things were going…"

He shrugged.

"You know how it is."

Brian reached across the counter and gave Singer a gentle push on the shoulder.

"And you've got to get yourself a phone."

Singer nodded.

"Yeah, that's next. Right after I've got my rent covered."

Singer lifted the ice cream off the counter and tipped it around until he found the price and rang it in.

"$6.79."

Singer nodded at the ice cream.

"You need pickles with that?"

Brian looked at him for a second then recoiled.

"God no!"

Then paused with his pinky at the corner of his mouth.

"At least, I don't think…"

Singer laughed. It felt good.

"You'll know soon enough."

Singer's friend made a face.

"I guess I will."

"You want a bag?"

Brian scooped the ice cream off the counter.

"Nah. I'm good."

He stood holding the ice cream then reached out a fist. Singer bumped it.

"I'll be in touch, Pete. Hang in there."

Singer watched his friend leave get in his car and pull away without looking over.

***

Singer came awake when the man spoke for the second time. He had a vague awareness that somebody had spoken, but it was only the second time that he came fully awake, taking a moment to focus on the figure in front of him. The man spoke a third time.

"C'mon. What's your problem man. You fucked up?"

Singer shook his head, clearing his vision. A wool tuque pulled almost to his eyebrows though it was a warm evening, two or three t-shirts layered one over the other and something in his hand that could only be a toy handgun.

"Open it up. Give me the money."

The guy probably wasn't as old as he looked, his face worn by sun and wind more than time, nicked in spots by something hard—skin-covered bone or maybe something worse—pouched, pocked and bagged in other places. There was a patch of white high on one cheek that was probably from this past winter or the one before. His eyes were a washed-out blue, almost grey and the depressions alongside his nose were raw and red except where the skin had dried and flaked.

"What are you waiting for. Give me the fucking money."

Singer thought he was trying to sound like somebody he had heard at the movies but he couldn't think of who. Singer nodded at the gun.

"Is that real?"

The man looked down at the gun then back up at Singer then backed up a step and waved it.

"You wanna find out, buddy?"

Singer raised one hand to cover his face.

"What do you want the money for?"

The man took several quick frantic steps, needing to move but unsure of what to do and then waved the gun again.

"Just give me the fucking money, fuckface!"

Singer hit the buttons to open the cash. There were six twenties a ten and a five, more cash than usual. Singer looked up from the till at the man across the counter then down at his position behind the counter and shifted his feet so that he was angled a little more towards the door.

"What the fuck! Give me the money!"

Singer peeled three twenties off the top and pushed them across the counter. The guy was dancing on the spot a couple of paces from the counter now and he waved at the money.

"What the fuck do you think you're doing? Give me all the fucking money!"

Singer reached out and pushed the bills with one finger, right to the edge of the counter. They balanced on the edge for a second, then tipped and fluttered to the floor. The guy looked back and forth from Singer to the money on the floor several times before he crouched and disappeared below the edge of the counter. Singer felt the open cash drawer against his hip, reached across his body with his left hand, slipped the remaining bills from the till and let his hand drop back to his side. The man stood without looking at Singer spun and ran for the door. Singer turned to follow the man's departure keeping his arm tight along his side.

Singer stood for a moment, thinking, still looking in the direction of the door, then came out from behind the counter as if to go through the door before he turned down the aisle to the cereal, reached to straighten one of the boxes but knocked it to the floor. He palmed the bills behind the box as he placed it back on the shelf, returned to the counter and called the police.

***

The cop looked up at the camera over Singer's right shoulder.

"Can we have a look at the tape?"

Singer shook his head.

"I don't have a key to the office."

She nodded and looked over his other shoulder at the office door.

"Have you contacted the owner?"

"Yeah. He should be here any minute."

***

"You alright?"

Mo brushed a hand through his hair then absently patted at a tuft sticking out at almost right angles from his head and let his chair tip forward so that all four legs rested on the floor again. Mo nodded at the chair on the other side of the desk.

"Sit down, Peter. Have a seat. You must be a little shaky."

Singer shouldered off the door frame to stand straight and took a quick look back into the store. The store owner slapped both hands lightly on the desk.

"Relax, Peter. I've locked the door. Take a minute here."

Singer shrugged.

"I'm fine, Mo. No big deal. I'm just sorry about the money."

The store owner waved a hand.

"We're covered. It's about time I get a little back on what I've been paying those crooks."

Singer took another quick peek over his shoulder then back.

"You think they'll get him?"

Mo nodded.

"The tape caught him pretty good. And he's been around before. The cop said she recognized him. They might get this one. Doesn't matter, though. The money's gone. And he didn't get much."

Singer looked over his shoulder again.

"We can open up, Mo. You don't have to keep it closed. I'm okay."

Mo smiled and shook his head.

"You sure? I could take over. You go home, get some sleep."

"I'm fine, Mo. Randy's going to be along in a couple of hours. You go home. I'll be fine."

The store owner stood up from behind the desk and leaned forward to shift some papers on the desk and to move the stapler over beside the invoice tray before looking up and holding Singer's gaze. The silence drew out for several seconds.

"Next time, Peter, just give the money. No hesitation."

Mo looked down at his hands still resting on the desk.

"If something ever happened, one of you got hurt…"

Something caught in the other man's throat and he made a small murmuring noise to clear it.

"If…. I would have to sell the store. I couldn't keep…"

When he looked up this time his eyes were fierce, almost angry.

"Just give them the money, Peter."

Singer looked at the floor and nodded, feeling the flush across his chest and rising up his neck.

"Okay, Mo. I froze a little. I'll be quicker next time."

Mo came around the desk.

"Okay then. Let's open up before somebody decides to break in."

Singer stepped back to let Mo pass and gestured back into the office.

"You going to load in another tape?"

The store owner waved dismissively.

"That was my last tape. I'll pick a couple up today but we're good for now."

***

Singer watched until Mo had backed into the street and pulled away, then turned and walked to the cereal shelf and pulled the money from behind the box.

***

Singer sat staring at the computer screen. Behind him out the window, the clouds glowed fever red on the horizon just above a band of porcelain blue sky, but he didn't notice. He couldn't decide. No matter how he scrimped and cut corners, the list kept growing. At first, he had convinced himself that he was making progress, that he was keeping ahead of the bodies, that names were coming off the list faster than they were going on. But it wasn't true. He had to scroll further and further to reach the bottom of the list with each new message. And that changed everything. Now, who he chose was so important.

Singer watched the videos over and over searching for some sign, some mark, some signal, some foreshadowing of what was to come. And they were there. Moisture gathered at the corner of her eye, not quite a tear. It reflected a shape hovering just below the low ceiling, little more than a subtle shift from grey to pewter, revealing something winged and watching, that disappeared as the camera angle shifted. Or a mark upon his cheek, subtle as the sliver of an early morning moon, pale, translucent, holding its place as faint and ephemeral as breath condensed on cool glass. Until the fever broke and the sun washed the sky clean and Singer couldn't be certain he hadn't imagined the signature of God. Or there was nothing, the skin rough, smooth, slack or taut, beige or bronzed or dark as asphalt, black drawing heat like water down a drain, rarely cream, bone or smoky white, but always the bones unmoored, loosed and rising too near the surface, the whole less than the sum of every part, as unremarkable as a blade of grass bent by any careless foot. And then what? When there was no sign? With only three bets to place, who to choose? Because it was so easy to miss the sign.

***

Singer and the police officer watched as he pushed the bills to the edge of the counter and then waited for them to drop. She looked over at him.

"What were you doing there?"

Singer shrugged.

"I don't know."

Singer could feel her eyes on him as he watched the screen.

"Were you thinking you could get at him while he was bent down?"

Singer shook his head.

"No."

She continued to watch him as, on the screen, Singer knocked the cereal box to the floor.

"Always let them have the money. Don't be a hero."

Singer didn't answer and she hit the stop button and the screen went black. She pushed off the wall where she had been leaning and Singer stood up from the chair in front of the screen.

"We'll bring you in the room and you simply tell us if you see the man who robbed your store."

It was the same police officer who had taken Singer's statement and left from the store with the tape. She misunderstood his silence. She pointed at the television mounted on the wall of the room.

"Do you want to see it again?"

Singer shook his head.

Again, she misunderstood.

"Don't worry. He won't be able to see you."

Singer nodded.

"I'm fine."

She led him out of the room and down a short hallway to a narrow room that jutted out into the corridor and looked like it had been added as an afterthought. She opened the door and stood aside for him to lead her in. A cop in uniform leaned against the back wall and another man in a jacket and jeans was near the window running the length of the room.

"Okay. They'll be led in. You'll be given a head-on view followed by both profiles and we'll ask each of them to say the words 'Open it up.' Then we'll ask you if you see the man who held up your store. Do you understand?"

Singer nodded. She looked at him for several seconds, then nodded at the uniformed police officer. He stepped into the hall, knocked on the door leading into the connected room, then stepped back in and closed the door behind him.

Singer watched as they were led in.

Singer's guy was the fifth of the six men. One of the other five was black. Singer wondered how that worked. He had been definitive that the man was white. But they included a black man in the lineup. Maybe it was hard to find five people willing to stand in a lineup so you simply took what you could get.

Only one of the other men looked even a little like the man who had robbed the store. Two of the others were much bigger and fleshier, the third had something wrong with his face. If he had been older, Singer would have thought stroke, but he was only in his 20s. Maybe Bell's palsy or an injury. Even the one who resembled his guy was thinner and buck-toothed, so there was little danger of making a mistake. His guy was wearing the same clothing and clutched his toque in a misshapen bunch in his right hand.

Singer thought he might have been able to pick him out even if he had been blindfolded during the robbery. The way he shifted his feet no matter which way he was facing, as if it took all of his self-control to contain himself from throwing himself into the window or against the door. His hands fidgeted along his sides, clutching for something he had dropped or lost. He never stopped staring at the window. But his eyes and head moved like they were disconnected so that his chin would twitch backwards, forwards then to the side. His eyes, startled by the unexpected motion would pull quickly back to the window, trying to see beyond the shadowed glass.

He reminded Singer of somebody he had seen before. Not one of the dying. He was too old to resemble one of the dying. A relative maybe. Although Singer wasn't always certain who sat with the dying. Sometimes you could tell by the curve and line at eye and lip and nose, something shared that could only be shaped by gene and time, a resemblance beyond random chance…but often he couldn't tell. It came to him then, though nothing about the woman Singer remembered resembled the man he watched through the window, except that as she had crouched by the child's side there had been the same shudder and snap, back and forth, from shoulder to shoulder. The same broken line between her gaze and the dying child's face, restored immediately as her eyes adjusted to their new location in space. And the gaze was the same, searching to see beyond the shadowed veil to what lay beneath.

"Do you see the man who robbed you?"

Singer waited, letting his eyes trail along the line of men, aware that he had been staring at the one who had robbed the store. He let his eyes rest on the black man.

"It's definitely not him."

Singer continued, his eyes sliding up and down the line several times before he stepped back.

"No. He's not there."

The cop frowned.

"You don't see him?"

Singer shook his head.

"No."

Singer continued to look at the men, but he could feel her eyes on him. He caught a flash of motion out of the corner of his eye, but couldn't tell if it was hands on hips or crossed arms.

"You don't see the man who robbed Mr. Laghari's store?"

Singer could hear the disbelief in her voice.

"No. I don't"

"Mr. Singer, are you sure? We could go back down the hall and have another look at the video."

The other man who hadn't spoken before now stepped off the wall.

"Officer Rowsey? I think we're done here."

Singer turned to her.

"Sorry about that. Can I go now?"

She gave him a curt nod and waved her hand at the door. Singer left.

Chapter 26

Cheryl stood in the doorway and Singer stepped back so Tommie could scoot into the apartment. Dougie stayed with his mother. Singer waved her in.

"You want a coffee, Cheryl. I just put the kettle on—it won't be long."

She tried a smile, barely made it, but took a step forward so she was inside the door.

"Instant?"

Singer made a face and nodded. She tried again and did a little better.

"I'll pass. I guess I'm spoiled."

She looked down at her oldest son who was still tucked in against her side.

"Could you go see how Tommie's doing, Dougie? I want to talk to your dad."

He looked up at her for a moment then nodded and went to walk past his father. Singer held out one arm and Dougie allowed himself to be folded into it and held close, then Singer let him join his brother. Singer turned, couldn't see them beyond the corner of the wall but shouted after them.

"It's nice out there. You can go out on the roof."

He started to turn back but stopped.

"Tommie? Stay away from the edge!"

Singer took a step and leaned so he was beyond the wall and could see the boys. Tommie was already out on the roof.

"Keep an eye on your brother, Dougie."

Singer turned back to his wife, reading the expression on her face he waved towards the other room.

"They're fine, Cher. They've been out there lots of times."

She nodded. Singer waited. Cheryl looked at the floor and then back at him then down again. Singer tilted his head.

"How are you doing, Cheryl?"

"I'm okay. I guess."

She looked up.

"How are you, Peter?"

"Getting by."

"School starts up in a week."

Singer nodded.

"That means hockey tryouts soon. The boys still want to play?"

Cheryl nodded.

"Yeah."

She looked down at her hands then back up at him.

"That's probably not a bad place to start."

She took a breath.

"Dougie needs new skates. He's up almost two shoe sizes since last year. Tommie's okay for now but I don't think he'll get by Christmas with the ones he's got. And they both need clothes for September."

Singer let his head drop before bringing it back up again.

"I know, Cher."

They were quiet for a minute.

"You said you'd help, Peter. I know you're not making a lot of money. But you said you'd help. They're your boys too. "

Singer nodded.

"I know I did."

"I know they are."

Singer's wife looked to the side and scratched at a fleck of dried paint on the door jamb.

"Don't make me do this, Peter. I never thought you'd make me do this."

Singer nodded.

"I'm not some bitter ex-wife, just trying to get a bunch of money out of her ex-husband. I know things are hard for you, Peter. But they're your boys too."

Singer nodded again.

"I know."

He waited for several seconds.

"I can't right now, Cheryl. You know I want to."

Singer searched for the words in the spaces between the hardwood planks.

"If I could, I would, Cheryl. You know that. But right now I'm not even keeping up. It just keeps getting worse, the list just keeps getting longer."

They stood like that for several seconds. His wife looked over to the sounds of the boys shouting.

"Are they okay?"

Singer took a step and leaned so he could see them again then turned back.

"They're fine."

"Are you getting help, Peter?"

Singer looked at her.

"Help?"

"Are you seeing somebody, Peter. You should be talking to somebody. Getting help."

Singer shook his head.

"Help? What do I need help for? How is what I'm doing a problem?"

Singer's wife waved beyond him at his apartment and the piece of cardboard taped over the window, broken again and then waved it back and forth between the two of them. And then in the direction of the two boys on the roof.

"How is it a problem, Peter? How is it a problem?"

Singer could feel it building inside him and bit it down.

"Yeah. Alright, Cheryl. Give me a week or two. I'll get something to you."

His wife reached out as if to touch his arm but then pulled back.

"Peter. It's not about that. You need to talk to somebody. Get some help."

Singer held up his hand.

"Don't worry, Cheryl. I've got this. But I promised the boys we'd go to the library. And we'd better get going."

He turned away from the door without looking at her again and heard his wife shut the door behind her when she left.

***

Singer and his boys sat on the stone steps leading up to the library entrance, over to the side so they didn't block people coming and going from the library. They ate the cheese and crackers that he had prepared before they left. The stone was still cool beneath his hand though the sun had braised the early morning chill. Singer tugged at his oldest son's jacket sleeve.

"Aren't you getting hot?"

Dougie pulled the sleeve from between his father's fingers and shook his head. Singer looked over to see Tommie hold a piece of cheese up to his nose and wrinkle his face.

"I don't like orange cheese."

Singer smiled and acted surprised.

"Don't like orange cheese?! Since when don't you like orange cheese?"

Singer's youngest put the cheese back in the baggie and bit into a Ritz cracker.

"Mommy's friend brings over white cheese. I like it better."

Dougie's head came up but Singer didn't notice.

"Mommy's friend brings white cheese, eh? So, she's spoiling you guys?"

Tommie looked over at his father, his turn to be surprised.

"She?"

Dougie stuck out his leg and rapped his brother on the shin with the toe of his shoe.

"What?"

Tommie looked over at his brother then up at his Singer.

"Dad? Dougie just kicked me for no reason!"

Tommie stood and took a step to kick his brother and Singer put a hand on both of them.

"Whoa. Whoa, whoa. Settle down. I'm sure Dougie didn't mean anything. Did you, Dougie?"

Dougie shook his head but watched his father. Singer reached out, unsure what to do, but then let his hand fall on his son's shoulder and squeeze.

"It's okay, buddy. Mommy's allowed to have a friend. It doesn't need to be a secret."

Tommie, still angry, leaned across his father sticking out his tongue.

"Yeah, Dougie. Mom can have a friend. Anybody can have a friend."

Singer put a hand on his youngest son's head and stood up.

"C'mon guys. Let's go down to the river and see if anybody's fishing."

***

Singer lay on his back looking up at the sky. He shifted to relieve the pressure where the sharp edge of a stone dug in just beneath his shoulder blade.

"Daddy, why are there more stars at our house than here?"

"There aren't more stars, dummy."

Singer put his hands on his oldest son's chest to still him.

"It's true, Tommie, there aren't more stars. You can just see them better at our… your house because there's less light."

"Do you know the names, Daddy. Mommy's friend knows the names."

Dougie sat up on his elbows.

"Who cares if Ken knows."

Singer put his hand on his son again.

"It's okay, Dougie. It's okay."

Singer turned to his youngest son.

"I don't know the names, Tommie. So, maybe you can learn them and teach them to me. Yeah?"

Singer clapped his hands.

"But it's getting late. Time for bed. Let's go."

Singer ignored the groans of complaint and stood up, pulling the boys to their feet and moving across the roof to the window. Singer helped them over the window ledge into the room, then followed and turned on the lamp beside the bed so there was a little light in the apartment.

"Okay, let's go guys. It's late. If your mom knew how late you were up, we'd all be in trouble. So, brush your teeth and then into bed."

"I'm hungry."

Singer pursed his lips.

"Tommie, we ate already."

"That was a long time ago. And I don't like beans."

"Beans are perfectly good, Tommie. There are lots of people in the world who would be thrilled to have beans."

"I don't like them. And Mommy doesn't make us eat them."

Singer stood up from the windowsill.

"Enough, Tommie. We're not having a big talk about this. You've had your supper and now it's time for bed."

"I'm hungry, too."

Singer looked over at his oldest son.

"Dougie, don't make things worse."

Singer's son's chin set hard.

"I'm not making things worse. You are. We're hungry."

Singer walked to the edge of the bed and stood over them.

"There's nothing else to eat. Now go brush your teeth and get in bed."

Tommie shook his head and moved over closer to his brother at the edge of the bed.

"No. I'm hungry. Sometimes Mommy lets us order pizza when we're hungry."

Dougie had pulled himself to the edge of the bed, pulled his knees up, wrapped his arms around them and rested his chin on top and stared across the room as if trying to see into the next apartment. Tommie looked at him and then did the same.

Singer ground his teeth, closed his eyes, took a deep breath and relaxed his jaw, forcing himself to stop grinding.

"Boys, it's late…"

Tommie looked up at him, waiting but Dougie continued to stare across the room.

"I don't have any milk in the fridge but there's a little juice left…and some crackers."

"I want pizza."

Tommie looked at his brother for support. Dougie didn't respond so Tommie pulled in closer and looked at the same spot on the facing wall.

"Tommie, I can't afford to order pizza. Let's have some crackers."

Singer's oldest son's head swiveled sharply to look at Singer, the boy's eyes narrowed and furious.

"You're just saying that! Who doesn't have money for a pizza?"

His son held his eye, refusing to look away and Singer felt something give, shear, an ablation as abrupt and cold as calved ice. He pushed himself up from the mattress, the rising causing his head to spin so that he had to pause and set himself before walking across to where his laptop sat on an overturned milk carton. He picked it up, returned to his spot beside his sons and booted it up. It took a few seconds, and while it flashed to life Singer leaned across to turn off the lamp on the floor beside the bed so there was only the light from the computer screen and the faint wash of city lights through the apartment windows.

Two new emails had arrived and remained unopened because he had no money and there was no sense looking at a list of names he could do nothing about. Singer could tell by the size of the files that the list was growing. He clicked on the most recent email and then on the name at the top of the list. A window opened and Singer tilted the screen on his lap so both of the boys could see. The camera began on her face, eyes open but unfocused, gleaming and luminous like the last embers in a pile of ash and stone, as if what was left of her had gathered and flared in a single spot just behind her eyes, the skin of her face shaved so thin and stretched so tight that it must come apart in a final burst of muted light. The camera trailed down her body, her neck as narrow and taut as bunched wire, the soiled shift covering her from shoulder to knee, the fold and line uninterrupted by joint, muscle or movement so that it was as if whoever had worn it had stepped free and walked away so it lay loose and abandoned where it had fallen to the ground. The camera settled on her feet, tilted towards each other in an inverted V, the soles still worn and rough showing where the friction and pressure of living had thickened the skin. When the screen faded to black, Singer and the boys continued to stare at the place where she had been.

"They had no money for pizza."

Singer clicked the next name and they watched to the end.

"They had no money for pizza."

Then the next name.

"He had no money for pizza."

Singer clicked through a dozen or more names, not counting, simply watching, until he was able to stop and close the computer. He placed it back where it had been on the overturned carton and lay down in the bed. His boys watched him, Tommie confused, looking from his father to his brother and back, Dougie pale with two spots of red high on his cheeks. After a while the boys lay down on each side of him. Singer couldn't think of what he should say.

Chapter 27

Singer pulled the pancake mix down from the cupboard along with the syrup and the bread, reached into the fridge for the milk, butter and eggs, forgetting the bacon and reached back in to pull it from the crisper. Most had come from the food bank, but he had spent money on the eggs and bacon. Singer stood back from the counter looking at what was there, his eyes running back and forth until he was sure he had everything. It was all there.

Singer barely heard the first knock and paused to be sure it hadn't been somebody walking by and brushing against the door but the second tap was stronger. At the door, Singer looked past his wife for his sons but her father stood one step down, his arms folded and resting on the chipped balustrade. Singer looked back at his wife, seeing her face now, dark beyond the space just beneath her eyes as if the fatigue could no longer be contained by the usual boundaries, the lines that had only hinted at the corners of her eyes and mouth now bold scoured statements under the and residual puffiness in her lids. Singer nodded over her shoulder.

"Hi, Earl."

Cheryl's father nodded but didn't speak. Singer looked at his wife again.

"What's going on, Cheryl? Where are the boys?"

Cheryl looked at him and then at the floor.

"What were you thinking?"

Singer sighed, turned a little as if to move back into the apartment but then caught himself and swung back.

"I don't know."

Singer waved his hand as if to take in everything around him.

"They need to understand that it's different for a lot of people. Most people can't even dream of what we have. Because if they do, it's too hard to be awake."

"Peter..."

"Do you understand what I'm saying, Cheryl? They won't even dream of this. They can only dream of something much less than this. Or living their actual life is unbearable!"

Cheryl's father straightened and he stepped up on the landing as Singer's voice rose. Singer raised a placating hand.

"It's fine. I'm alright, Earl."

Singer turned back to his wife.

"I shouldn't have done it, Cheryl. I won't do it again. But you can't—"

Singer's wife was shaking her head before he had finished.

"Three times last week Dougie started crying in class."

Singer's wife stared at him.

"He wouldn't say why. No reason. He wouldn't say anything."

Singer closed his eyes, remembered standing to get the laptop and experienced for a moment the same vertigo he had then.

"— told us about the videos."

Singer shook his head.

"I don't know, Cheryl. But it's happening. Shouldn't they know that?"

"Peter, they're little boys!"

"And if you know it? How could you not cry? How could anybody not cry?"

Singer's wife held up her hand.

"We're not having this discussion, Peter. They are children. I can't let you do this to them."

Singer's wife paused and her father reached out to pat her back then withdrew his hand.

"The school psychologist talked to Dougie for a long time. She said he's very troubled. And it may take some time for him to process and work through what he's seen."

She stopped, looked at the floor then looked at him again, her face twisted and clenched.

"Do you know what she talked about, Peter? Do you know...?"

Singer shook his head.

"PTSD! That's what she said! She made reference to PTSD!"

Singer winced, then looked to his left at the sound of a door opening then closing again. He looked back at his wife.

"C'mon Cheryl. PTSD?"

Singer's wife's mouth worked but no sound came out for several seconds. She raised her hand as if to hit him but stopped, let it fall to her side and that allowed her to speak.

"What, Peter!? You know better!? She doesn't know what she's talking about!?"

"I didn't say that, Cheryl. I'm just saying..."

Singer's wife took a deep breath and spoke more quietly.

"The boys won't be coming here anymore."

"Cheryl, c'mon.... You can't..."

She nodded firmly.

"We talked to our lawyer, showed him the psychologist's report. He said there won't be any problem getting a court order. Of course, you can contest it, but our lawyer says you'll lose."

She paused.

"You'll spend the money...and lose."

"Cheryl, I need to see the boys. They need to see me."

Singer's wife nodded.

"You can see them. Supervised visits. But you will have to arrange for the supervision and cover the costs."

Singer's wife turned and walked past her father and down the stairs.

"Cheryl..."

Singer stepped forward, but Cheryl's father slid over to block his way. They were almost nose to nose. Singer took a step back.

"Really, Earl?"

The older man shrugged but didn't answer then turned and followed his daughter. Singer spoke to his back.

"You get orders not to open your mouth, Earl?"

Singer stood at the top of the stairs and watched until his wife was out the door with her father trailing behind.

***

Singer stood on the corner looking through the chain link fence at the empty school playground. Singer kept walking up to the next block, turned right then right again, and then once more until he was back where he started. Just as he arrived the bell went, and in seconds a door flew open and kids poured out onto the playground. Singer saw Tommie, one of the first out of the building racing a couple of other boys for one of the empty swings. Tommie arrived first, skidding into one of the curved leather seats and pushing off, rocking back hard so his body was almost parallel to the ground then leaning forward and pulling hard with his legs. Dougie was one of the last and he straggled over to a spot against the fence and slid down with his back to the street running alongside the school.

There had been two supervised visits. During the first, the boys had barely spoken to him, unsure what to do in the presence of a stranger, a middle-aged woman, who read the paper through the meeting. Singer had tried but had felt as awkward as the boys. For the second visit, Singer had brought a deck of cards and they had played War and Go Fish, but both boys had been eager to leave long before the hour was up. And it had cost him eighty bucks.

Singer watched until the bell rang for the students to go back in, wandering away once when a woman glanced at him once and then again as she entered a dry cleaner's near the corner, but returning to his spot when she had left with a garment bag over her shoulder. Tommie never stopped, growing tired of the swings after a few minutes before moving to the slide structure, then getting caught up in a chaotic game that looked like tag although Singer was never sure who was 'it' before getting in a wrestling match with a girl a head taller than him, which had to be broken up by a teacher. Dougie never left his spot along the fence. Twice, boys came over and tried to coax him into a game of road hockey they played in a corner of the playground. Both times, he shook his head and the boys shrugged and left.

Singer watched until both his sons went inside. Tommie among the first lined up at the door to re-enter and Dougie not getting up from the fence until the line at the door had dwindled to almost nothing.

Chapter 28

Gail stood in Singer's doorway, arms crossed without speaking. Singer raised his hand as if to interrupt.

"I know. I know. I'll have it for you today. Some expenses I wasn't expecting came up."

She shook her head.

"We talked about this, Peter. I can't carry you."

Singer nodded and stepped back from the door, padding back into the main room to scoop up a t-shirt he had dropped beside the mattress and slip it over his head before returning to the door. Gail had stepped inside and stood just inside the door.

"I know, Gail. I'll have the rest for you today."

"Peter. It was due a week ago. And the rest? You gave me a hundred bucks...the rest is almost everything."

Singer nodded again.

"I promise, Gail. Today. If I don't have it today, I'll move out today. You won't even have to ask."

Singer's landlady smiled despite herself.

"Peter. I don't want you to move out. You're a good tenant. You don't make much noise. I'm pretty sure you're not doing anything illegal. And you and Murray in 208 are the only ones I can have a decent conversation with. But you gotta' pay your rent."

Singer nodded.

"Today. I promise."

Gail backed out of the door, turned to leave but stopped at the top of the stairs.

"Everything alright, Peter? Haven't seen the boys in a while."

"All good, Gail. Everybody's doing fine."

Singer shut the door with his landlady still looking at him from the top of the stairs.

***

She looked the same as she had on the loading dock, her hair governed by gravity and indifference, her features small, vague, indistinct. Singer had lost her name.

"Yes?"

She looked up from the floor, but showed no sign of recognition.

"I'm here about the computer."

It took Singer a moment.

"Right. The computer."

He stood in the door then stepped back.

"Come on in. You can have a look."

She hesitated but then stepped through the doorway. Singer moved back to give her room and went for the computer from the other room calling over his shoulder.

"You can leave the door open if you'd like."

But when he turned back, she was in the room just behind him so he put the computer back on the carton, stepped back and gestured at it.

"Go ahead. Fire it up. I've got rid of my files."

She looked at the computer, then at him.

"I thought it was you. Same name and all."

Singer nodded.

"There's a few of us out there. But not many."

"Do you remember me?"

"Sure. Just not your name."

She looked away from him to the computer.

"Hannah."

"Right. It's been a while. But I remember now."

She looked up from the computer and around the room.

"What happened?"

Singer shrugged.

"Y'know. Shit happens. They canned me."

"Cause a' me?"

Singer chuckled.

"I wish."

She stared at him without speaking.

"It was around the same time. But it had been coming for a while. They were glad to have an excuse."

She looked at him for several seconds then at the computer again.

"How much you asking?"

Singer shrugged.

"I was thinking three hundred. But all I really need is two-fifty."

Hannah shook her head.

"Nah, three hundred's good."

She pushed her hand into the front pocket of her jeans, twisting a little sideways to make room and pulled out a thin sheaf of bills.

She counted out two fifties and ten twenties, started to shove the last couple of twenties back into her pocket then folded them back into the pile in her hand and held it out. Singer put his hands up.

"No. Three hundred's good. More than fair."

The young woman stood with her hand out, waiting for him to take the money. Singer did, peeled the extra forty off and started to hand it back, but she had already turned and was in the hallway at the door. Singer hurried after her and almost bumped into her, where she had stopped to put on her boots.

"You didn't have to worry about that."

She finished tying the second boot, scooped the laptop up from the floor where she had set it and stood up, ignoring the bills in Singer's outstretched hand.

"You have anything I can carry it in?"

Singer went to the drawer beside the sink and pulled out one of a handful of crumpled plastic bags. He held one up.

"This do?"

She nodded.

"Maybe double it up."

Singer did and handed the bags to her with the same hand still holding the bills. She took the bags, fit the computer carefully inside, opened the door and stepped out onto the landing at the top of the stairs. She paused at the top and looked over her shoulder.

"I thought it was you. Same name and all."

Singer watched Hannah until she was down the stairs and out of the building.

***

The young librarian looked over Singer's shoulder.

"Where are your boys?"

Singer returned her smile.

"Just me today. Are any of the computers free?"

She pulled a binder out from under the ledge, opened it and placed it in front of him, pointing at a spot on the page.

"All of them. You picked a good time. Just print your name here and sign here."

Singer was able to take three names off the list. He was glad he had dropped the rest of the rent off with Gail before coming to the library. He wasn't sure he would have been able to stop at three.

Chapter 29

The school bell would ring soon. Singer had acquired a feel for the lunch hour, how the urgency built

Over the last several minutes, everything vibrating at a slightly higher frequency, the kids moving faster, shouting louder, sensing the last, fading notes of the carousel. Dougie sat, his narrow shoulders yielding beneath the wire, waiting for the bell. Other kids rarely approached, sure of the answer, although occasionally one of them would give it another try but Dougie always refused. Today there had been nobody. Singer strolled across the street, bent to tie his shoe right behind his son's back and spoke through the fence.

"Hey buddy. How you doing?"

His son turned to look at him. Then looked over his shoulder at the yard.

"Dad?"

Singer smiled at his son.

"How have you been, Dougie?"

Singer's son looked over his shoulder again then back at Singer.

"I don't think you're supposed to be here. Mom says we aren't supposed to talk to you unless somebody is with us."

Singer smiled at his son again.

"It's okay, Dougie. We're just talking. How have you been?"

Singer's son shrugged.

"Okay I guess."

Singer spotted a teacher scanning the yard.

"You should probably turn around, Dougie. You don't need to look at me while we talk."

Obediently, Dougie spun around.

"How's hockey going?"

"I quit."

"Quit? What do you mean? You love hockey."

Singer saw his son's shoulders shift against the fence.

"I don't know. It wasn't fun."

Singer tapped his son between the shoulder blades, let his fingers rest against the boy's back, where the vertebrae rose to ripple his skin, then scraped his fingers back and forth. Dougie leaned into Singer's fingers, his narrow shoulders bunching and relaxing, as familiar to Singer as the sensation of his own breath entering and leaving his body.

"What's going on, Dougie?"

His son didn't respond.

"Dougie?"

"It's stupid."

"What's stupid? Hockey?"

While he waited, Singer scanned the playground. He spotted his youngest, racing for one of the swings that had just come free, getting there just after one of the other kids had dropped into the seat but hurling himself on top of the other boy so that they both fell backwards onto the sand. A teacher, who had been drifting over towards where Dougie sat, turned and hurried back to separate the two boys.

"Dad?"

"Yeah, Dougie."

"Were those kids real?"

The teacher had the two boys apart and spoke to both, her head swiveling back and forth from one to the other. Tommie was already distracted by something he had spotted across the yard.

"I think so."

"Mom says they might not be. That maybe they're just pretending."

Singer continued to scratch his son's back with three bunched fingers through the narrow space created by the steel tie wires.

"Your Mom's pretty smart. She might be right."

The young teacher who had separated Tommie and the other boy paused near the entrance to the school, talking with a second woman, older, whose eyes moved to look over the younger woman's shoulders, studying the yard while her lips moved, a question or comment, then shifting her focus to the fence line.

"But I'm pretty sure they're real, Dougie. I'm pretty sure."

"Why?"

Singer walked away, back straight, eyes ahead, his breath congealed high and tight in his chest until he was several steps beyond the corner of the building and beyond the sightlines of the playground. He held his breath for a moment longer, reluctant to exhale the air he had shared with his son but then let it hiss out between his teeth.

***

"Were you at the school, Peter?"

Singer stood back from the door and gestured towards the kitchen.

"You wanna' come in, Cheryl? I've got some instant?"

Singer's wife shook her head.

"Peter! Were you at the school!?"

Singer turned away from the door into the kitchen, twisted the tap and ran his fingers under the water, waiting for it to cool.

"Peter!"

Singer could tell by the sound that she had stepped into the hall so she could look in at him standing by the sink. Singer opened the cupboard door over his head, pulled out a worn yellow cup frayed along the rim where somebody had chewed the plastic into strands but waited, hoping the water would cool a little more.

"They're my sons, Cheryl. And I have to pay to see them. Pay. Like a movie."

"And whose fault is that!"

Singer filled the glass, shut off the water and watched the last of the flow gather and coalesce before disappearing down the drain. But not all. The last molecules of water, the fragments that had splashed to the edges while the water ran, gathered, drawn by gravity and the weak pull of hydrogen to oxygen into a few domed droplets, building, growing, until the forces that bound them to the scratched aluminum of the sink gave way to the forces drawing them towards the drain and they released in a thin, clear sudden line like a tear down an infant's cheek. Singer emptied the glass in a single swallow and turned from the sink.

"They think everybody gets to eat pizza, Cheryl."

"They're just little kids, Peter!"

"People die every day, Cheryl. Children."

Singer's wife closed her eyes and looked to the side as if there might be somebody there who could help, before she turned back to Singer.

"I know, Peter. I know that. But little kids shouldn't see that."

Singer pulled one of the chairs away from the table and sat down.

"So, who should see it? Children are starving to death every day and that knowledge…that children are dying every day…is extremely traumatic for our kids. That's what we believe."

Singer looked at his hands then reached across with his left to still the tapping of the index finger on his right.

"And what's our solution?"

Singer looked at his wife.

"Don't let them know."

Singer held her eye.

"This thing that is so horrible, that if our kids know about it, it causes them deep psychological damage, this terrible fact, the only thing about it that matters…is that our kids don't know about it."

Singer shook his head.

"And I've got a problem."

"Leave the kids alone, Peter."

Singer heard the door close behind her, but didn't look up.

***

The library would close in a few minutes. They had already announced it. Singer stared at the screen.

Three hundred dollars. All that was left in the account. His next pay cheque wouldn't come for a week and the rent was due. Past due.

The tension began to build. It was so subtle at the beginning that he hadn't been sure it was there, as uncertain and liminal as the hour before dawn, but it was happening so often now that his detection threshold was honed, keened, so fine that he could no longer deny what he knew, even in the earliest moments. It grew until it felt as if his eyes were being pulled back into his sockets, stretched taut as a drawn bow.

The number wavered for a moment in front of Singer's eyes as if flashing, but he blinked twice and it was still there. Three hundred. The tension gave and the harsh metallic clink as another name fell in place echoed for a moment. Singer changed screens, refreshed, reopened the email and scrolled to the bottom.

Mi-Sun Gye.

Her name had arrived in the last few seconds. There was no way that he would ever get down to this place on the list. Singer scrolled back to the top of the list. Clicked through three names in succession, glancing over his shoulder twice for the librarian coming to shoo him away. His hand poised over a fourth for a moment, then moved quickly to the top right of the page and shut it down. He switched screens again, closed down his banking screen without refreshing, not wanting to see the new balance, logged off, stood up and left the library.

***

Singer watched them walk to the back of the store. They stood in front of the drink cooler and she pointed to something a little above her head but he looked down at her, smiled and shook his head and she pointed again. This time he nodded, let go of her hand to open the door, reach in, pull out the bottle of juice and hand it to her.

At the cash, he pulled a twenty from his pocket and handed it to the little girl, looked up at Singer then back down at his daughter.

"You can pay the man, honey."

The little girl looked at the money in her hand, up at Singer then back to her father. He smiled at her and then at Singer.

"It's okay, Kyesha. Just give the man the money."

She looked at the bill in her hand then up at Singer again, her eyes wide, luminous so that Singer could see himself, wavering and distorted in the reflected light. She held out the money, reaching up to get it to the edge of the counter and Singer took it from her hand, pressed the button to release the till and counted out her change. She reached up and Singer bent across the counter to place the two bills and the scattering of coins into her hands, cupped as if to capture poured water. She turned, smiling to her father and held out the money. He took it, shoved it carelessly into his pocket, grabbed the bottle of juice from the counter, smiled and nodded at Singer.

"Have a good night, sir."

Singer nodded back.

"You too."

Singer watched them until they disappeared beyond the corner of the neighboring building. He looked down at the cash tray still open in front of him. It had been a busy night. And more people paying with cash than he could remember on any other night. Singer lifted the sheaf of bills from the twenties drawer slot and rearranged them so that all the faces were pointing in the same direction. Two hundred and twenty dollars. Singer pressed his thumb into the bills in the drawer for the tens—the pile was at least as thick. Probably four hundred dollars in the till. Singer looked into the open cash drawer for several seconds then pushed it closed.

Chapter 30

Singer stood back from the corner of the street, partially blocked by the streetlight post and watched the playground. Dougie sat in his usual spot against the fence away from the other kids. He was playing with something in his hands and occasionally glancing quickly over one shoulder or the other to the street beyond the fence. Singer scanned the yard and saw the two teachers monitoring the yard were absorbed in breaking up a scuffle on the other side of the playground. He walked across the street and crouched at a spot along the fence a few feet from his son, where a small clump of weeds had struggled up through the brick-hard soil and cracks in the playground asphalt, partially obscuring the view of the sidewalk from the playground.

"Hey buddy."

Dougie's head swung around.

"Hi Dad."

"Eyes front, pal. You know the drill."

Singer's son turned back to the yard.

"How have you been?"

"Good, I guess."

"How's Tommie?"

"Terrible. Like always."

Singer smiled as he untied and retied the shoelace on his left sneaker.

"But he's alright?"

"He's fine. Why didn't you come yesterday?"

"Something came up. I'm sorry, Dougie. I couldn't help it."

Singer raised his head and saw that both teachers were still involved in settling the dispute across the yard.

"Mom told me you're back in hockey. How's that going?"

Singer's son shrugged.

"Fine."

There was a short pause.

"Mom says you're sick."

Singer closed his eyes and took a deep breath.

"Sick, eh?"

"Yeah. She says you can't help yourself."

"She said that to you?"

Dougie glanced over then looked down at what he held in his hands.

"No. She was talking on the phone."

"Uh-huh."

"Are you sick?"

Singer smiled again.

"I don't feel sick."

"Mom says it's crazy for you to give all your money away for people you don't even know."

"On the phone?"

Dougie nodded.

"What do you think, Dougie? Do I seem sick?"

Singer's son shrugged then shook his head.

"Are you sending them all your money, Dad?"

Singer watched an ant dragging a tiny scrap of something across the hardpack dirt. It stopped for a moment then started again at a slightly different angle.

"Well…quite a bit."

"So somebody can help them?"

Singer nodded, although he knew his son couldn't see it.

"Yeah."

"Why does Mom think that makes you sick?"

Singer looked across the playground again and saw that both teachers were looking in their direction. There was a moment before they moved that Singer thought they might look away, but then the male teacher who Singer had only seen monitoring the playground twice before directed the woman he was with towards the door and started striding across the yard towards the fence.

"I'm not sure, son. I gotta go. I love you, buddy. You give your brother a hug for me."

Singer kissed the tips of his fingers, touched his son's cheeks through the gap in the linked chain, stood up and took a step away from the fence.

"Dad?"

Singer stopped and looked back at his son, who was holding something through the fence.

"Give them this."

Singer leaned down and Dougie dropped the coins in his hand. Singer stood and walked away, ignoring the voice shouting at him through the fence.

***

Gail sat on the front steps of the apartment. She was bent forward, tapping the ash loose in the space between her feet, then brushing it away with her hand. Singer kept walking across the street and out of her line of vision, hoping that she wouldn't look his way. He ducked down the alley behind the apartments along his street, climbed the fire escape to the roof and crawled through the open window into his apartment. He slipped his shoes off before setting his feet on the floor and padding over to the fridge.

The knock came before he could open the fridge door. Singer stood still.

"Give it up, Peter, I know you're in there!"

Singer opened the door. Gail stood arms crossed on her chest, a cigarette trailing smoke in one of her fists.

"You saw me."

"What do you think I was sitting out there for?"

"You know there's a bylaw, eh?

His landlady looked down at the smoke and gave a heavy-lidded blink.

"Oops. Busted."

She raised the cigarette to her mouth, took a long drag before letting the smoke out in an even stream.

"You're a week late."

"I know Gail. I just…"

"We're on month five and there hasn't been a month you've paid on time."

"I know. I know. But I've always paid, right? You know I'm good for it."

She made a face.

"That's not the point, Peter. You know why you haven't heard from the owner? Because I pay it. If he knew this was the fifth straight month you were late, you'd be out. I mean out. Furniture on the street."

"You pay?"

She nodded.

"That's right, Peter. I like you. I don't want you out. But I can't keep covering for you. You need to pay on time. Just like everybody else."

Singer nodded.

"You're right, Gail. I've got it. Gimme' a day. I'll have this sorted out…and it won't happen again. Alright? Okay?"

She looked at him for a long time, then nodded.

"I'm gonna tell him you're late this month. He lets me handle the first month. But if I tell him the same thing next month, I guarantee you'll be looking for a new apartment."

"That's fair. That's fair. I appreciate that, Gail. I promise we're done with this."

***

Singer pushed up out of the sway-backed lawn chair he had pulled from the trash three apartments down. He put a hand on the windowsill to hop back into his room. Maybe Gail had forgotten something. But this knock wasn't Gail—too loud, too insistent.

There were two of them, a man and a woman. It seemed when Singer saw cops these days it was rarely two guys or two women—almost always a mixed pair.

"Mr. Singer?"

It was the woman who spoke. The male officer, taller and thicker, stood a little behind her shoulder, hands loose by his sides. Singer nodded.

"That's me."

"Peter Singer?"

Singer nodded again.

"We'd like you to come down to the station. We have a few questions."

Singer looked from one to the other then back into his apartment.

"Right now? Questions about what?"

"Yessir, now."

"I don't understand. You want me to come with you to the police station?"

The female police officer nodded.

"Yessir."

Singer frowned.

"And if I refuse?'

Something subtle changed in the male officer, some shift in muscle tension, though he didn't move in any discernible way.

"Refusing isn't an option, Mr. Singer."

***

"You comfortable, Mr. Singer? Coffee? Water?"

Singer shook his head. The room had probably been for storage. Singer could see where shelves had been clamped to the wall along the three sides without a door. Now, the room contained a table, scarred by a dozen or more cigarette burns and two plastic chairs. The detective in the chair across from him wore a short-sleeved yellow shirt and beige dress pants, frayed at the hem that had been a little snug several pizzas ago. He looked at something on his phone, scrolled through several pages then tapped the screen, placed it upside down on the table and looked at Singer.

"Okay then. Let's start with an easy one. Where were you today at approximately two o'clock this afternoon?"

"Two? I'm not sure. That sounds like about the time I went out for a walk."

The detective nodded.

"And where did you go, Mr. Singer?"

Singer took a moment.

"I usually just stroll. No particular destination. Just a chance to get a little fresh air and clear my mind."

The detective looked at him and smiled.

"Your mind need clearing often, Mr. Singer?"

Singer looked back.

"It's just a turn of phrase, detective."

The other man nodded.

"Could you be a little more specific about where you went today?"

Singer shook his head.

"Not really, I just wander. I couldn't even tell you where I've been most of the time. I'm usually on autopilot, lost in my thoughts."

The detective smiled again but there was a harder edge.

"Let me put my cards on the table, Peter. We have a report that you were at your sons' school, talking to your oldest through the fence."

Singer just looked back at him. The detective waited for a few seconds then sighed.

"Peter. There is a restraining order on you. You are only able to see and communicate with your children in a supervised context. You cannot approach or talk to them anywhere. If you do, you can be arrested. Do you understand that?"

Singer nodded.

"Good. But this is the third report we've got. And this time…"

He gestured at the phone on the table.

"…we have photographs."

He reached for the phone.

"Would you like to see them?"

"No need."

The detective nodded.

"If your wife was willing to press charges, you'd likely be in cuffs right now. But she's not, Peter."

The detective shook his head.

"It always amazes me how often they're willing to get the order but won't enforce it. What good's a gun if you won't pull the trigger? You know what I'm saying?"

The detective stood up.

"But I have a pretty good feel for these, Peter. She's almost there. One more, maybe two and I think she'll be ready. And then what? How is that good for your sons? You in jail, and their mom put you there. Is that really what you want?"

He looked at Singer who remained in his chair, then nodded his head at the door.

"You can go, Mr. Singer."

Singer scraped the chair across the cement floor, stood up, moved to the door that the detective held open for him walked through, turned right and headed for the stairwell leading down to the lobby. When Singer was almost at the end of the hall, the detective's voice stopped him.

"Mr. Singer?"

Singer turned. The detective stood outside the door, unsmiling but with something gentler in his face.

"Don't ignore this. You're not helping your boys."

Singer turned and opened the door into the stairwell.

Chapter 31

Singer hadn't heard this knock before. He knew his wife's…and Gail's… this was loud but lacking the explicit threat he had heard when the police had arrived to take him downtown. Singer lay on his mattress, waiting, his eyes raised to the ceiling but closed, counting off seconds, deciding how long was long enough. If he got to twenty, did it mean they would give up? Or thirty? Maybe fifty? Or perhaps it didn't matter at all. It didn't matter how long he waited. Maybe whoever was there was prepared to wait until time and rot and the blowing wind brought down roof and wall, until all that stood was the knocking man, the door and Singer in the empty space behind.

Singer lay still, his breath drawn and held, and strained against the pre-drawn grey of his room - to hear, to detect a sound, any sound from beyond his door. He searched for the faintest wave curling through the gap between the floor and the door, some hint of what moved in the hallway - the tips of fingers brushing across worn denim or the regular tap of a soled foot on the streaked stained linoleum at the top of the stairs. Or perhaps inspiration, as the diaphragm contracted, so pressure is released around the lungs and air drawn across the pharynx and the larynx into the lungs. Then expiration, as the diaphragm relaxed and air is expelled almost without resistance, but not quite, the frequency of the sound within the range of human hearing. But the amplitude depending on the shape of the mouth and whether stress, fear or anger had quickened the contractions.

But no sound came to him. Singer exhaled and let his muscles relax. The second knock was louder yet.

Singer eased the blanket to the side and swung in a tight circle so that his feet were flat on the hardwood floor and pushed off into a crouch before he stood. His left knee cracked as he rose and sounded loud in the room like a cracked shell. Singer paused in mid-rise, but there was no indication he had been heard and went to the window. The sun crouched just beyond the eastern horizon so that Singer could make out the silhouettes of the buildings, extending down the alley to the cross street, all of them stooped, rounded, bent against the first glow on the skyline, like aging soldiers unable to square shoulders to full attention but giving what they had. Singer turned from the window, stepped across his mattress, padded across the room, kitty cornered through the kitchenette to the door and stood listening. He stood for several seconds, sure that somebody was on the other side, their head as close to the door frame on their side as the few inches that separated Singers from the worn white paint on his side, unsure how he knew, but knowing nonetheless that, despite the stillness, the quiet, they had not turned and left. And then Singer heard the rub of one material on another, soft and sibilant as brushing silk—and opened the door. It caught Cheryl's father with his arm raised to knock again. The two men stood for a moment, staring at each other before the older man's arm fell to his side.

"You're here kinda early, Earl."

The other man reddened a little but didn't look away.

"I wanted to be sure I didn't miss you."

Singer paused and resigned, opened the door wide and gestured towards the kitchenette.

"You wanna come in, Earl? Grab a seat?"

Singer turned and walked past the kitchen table, pulling out a plastic chair for his guest but not checking to see if Cheryl's father followed him in.

"Lemme just get some pants on."

When Singer returned, his father-in-law was standing behind the chair. Singer nodded at it and went by to the chair facing the sink, pulled it out and sat down. Earl waited until he was seated then sat down. They sat in silence for several seconds. Earl opened his mouth several times to speak but couldn't start. Singer waited.

"How have you been, Peter?"

Singer gestured around the apartment.

"Well, as could be expected, I guess. You want some coffee?"

Cheryl's father nodded.

"Yeah."

And then, as if just catching up to the second part.

"No. No coffee."

Singer allowed a trace of a smile.

"Probably best. All I've got is instant...and you love your coffee."

His father-in-law nodded, looked down at the tabletop, scratched at something there that was burnt in or buried under the enamel.

"Look, Peter. I don't think I ever told you…"

Earl looked up at Peter, shook his head and smiled.

"Although you probably knew, I've never been very good at hiding my feelings."

He paused and looked back down at the table, scratching at the spot again as if forgetting that he had tried already.

"I didn't like you for Cheryl. Not at the beginning. I didn't think you were right for her. I don't know why. I'm not sure what it was."

He looked up to see if Singer was paying attention and then back down.

"Just that you weren't always there. We would all be talking and laughing, me, Cheryl, her mother, and I would look at you and you were somewhere else. I wasn't sure you even knew we were still there. And then you would drift back in. Not snap back in, startled, like most of us do when our minds wander. You would just gradually bring your attention back to the room, as if you had been away, a place you meant to go, and were now returning. No explanation needed."

Earl looked up again, but this time held Singer's eye."

"But that changed."

Earl leaned forward, letting his elbows and forearms rest on the table.

"How you were with the boys…with Cheryl. For them, you were always there—every minute. And the job."

He raised an eyebrow and nodded at Singer.

"I know it's not an easy job. And nine years. Every day. Never missing. Moving up. Getting to where you could afford the house."

Earl grinned at Singer.

"With a little help, mind you."

Singer stood up, took a glass down from above the sink and ran the water for a second. Cheryl's father twisted a little in his chair so he could see Singer. Singer filled the glass, started to turn back but then stopped, pulled a second glass down and filled it as well. Singer set the second glass down beside Earl's elbow then took a sip from his own as he settled back into his chair. If Earl sensed Singer's irritation he didn't show it. He shrugged.

"I didn't know you. Neither of us thought we did—Cheryl's mother and me. But you were good to Cheryl, and to Tommie and Dougie. So we loved you. We were happy that Cheryl had found somebody."

Singer was tired. He just wanted to sleep. He could feel the first couple of turns as the tension started to rise. It was hard to tell how fast the torque would accelerate and how quickly the next name would drop. He raised a hand to rub his eyes, but then let it drop back to the table.

"But..."

Earl tilted his head, his brow furrowed, waiting for Singer to explain.

"Earl. Everything so far has been leading to 'But'. You're here for the 'but'. So..."

Singer made a circular motion with his finger. His father-in-law's face darkened and there was a moment where Singer wasn't sure what would happen next but then he released a sigh allowed himself to deflate a little.

"Alright. If that's how you want it."

Earl looked at the glass beside him as if seeing it for the first time, picked it up and took a sip before setting it down. He touched a thumb to his upper lip to catch a drop that had caught there.

"I don't know what's wrong with you, Peter. I only know what Cheryl tells me... And I don't think that's everything. I'm not sure what you're into. What Cheryl tells me - the money for the kids? It doesn't sound right. I think you're hiding something. I think there's something else going on."

It was like a rollercoaster train approaching the highest point on the track, slowing so that it seemed unlikely the wheels could make the final revolution and reach the pinnacle, it seemed that they would stop just before the drop. But it never did stop. It always made that final revolution and the name fell into place at the bottom of the list. Waiting.

Corine Nkuru.

"Peter?"

"There's nothing else, Earl."

Earl shrugged.

"It hardly matters though, does it, Peter? Whatever the reason, you've done this."

Singer nodded.

"It was a relief when Cheryl threw you out."

Singer's father-in-law waved his hand in front of his face as if to wipe the words away.

"We weren't happy. Cheryl was miserable. And the boys… Dougie…?"

"But we thought it was the bottom. And now she could work her way back up."

Earl's voice hardened.

"But it wasn't the bottom. Was it, Peter? Now there's this. You showing the kids pictures…"

Earl settled back in his chair arms folded across his chest.

"You know Dougie has to take something to sleep? Did you know that?"

Singer straightened in his chair.

"What?"

Earl nodded.

"That's right. Eight years old and he needs a pill to get to sleep."

"Who…"

"Who do you think, Peter. The doctor. Do you think Cheryl would just decide to dope him up!? He wasn't sleeping, Peter! Kids need to sleep! And now you're not abiding by the restraining order. Supervised visits only. You're visiting Dougie at school! Lurking outside the fence! Getting hauled in by the cops!? What the fuck are you doing!?"

Earl closed his eyes, raised a hand to his face and then back through his hair.

"Sorry, Peter. I really didn't want to do that. I'm sorry. I'm not here to shout at you."

Singer looked at him and smiled.

"Really, Earl?"

"Really, Peter."

His father-in-law held Singer's gaze without breaking for several seconds before looking down. When he began to speak, Singer had to lean forward a little to make out the words.

"You're tearing this family up, Peter. I really don't think that's what you want, but it's happening anyway. I don't think you can help it. And it's just going to get worse. And then Cheryl is going to have to ask the police to enforce the restraining order. And then they will arrest you and put you in jail. And she will blame herself. She will be the one who put you there. That's how she will see it. But she will have to do it to protect her sons. Do you get that, Peter? That's what you will have done. And I don't know if she can make it through tha…"

His words caught in his throat, thick and strangled, as if caught up in a slurry of mud and sludge. Singer stared at the streak in the tabletop. It took a long time for Earl to speak again.

"Here's the deal, Peter. Ten thousand dollars."

Singer's father-in-law glanced up and then down again at his hands folded in front of him on the table.

"You need the money. It's clear you need the money. But you move away. Out of the city. Out of the province. And you leave Cheryl alone. And the boys. I don't care where you go. It just has to be far away."

Singer knew he should be angry, but he could already feel the ratchet beginning to turn again. Earl waited for a moment then continued.

"You give me your banking info. When I get something postmarked… A postcard. A letter. Whatever. Something showing you've left, I'll transfer the money to your account."

Singer looked at his own hands laid flat on the table in front of him. He didn't remember taking them from his lap.

"I could just come back."

Singer could hear the smile in his father-in-law's voice.

"I know almost nothing about you, Peter. But the strange thing is I'm sure I can trust your word. That I don't doubt. Plus, you know this is the right thing. You can see what you're doing."

"How would I get there? I've got no money. Nothing to sell."

His father-in-law shifted in his chair so he could get at his pocket and pulled out a sheaf of bills, laying them on the table.

"Eight hundred dollars. Should be able to get you a pretty long ways. I don't care how. Bus, train, plane."

Singer stared at the money. His father-in-law reached out and used two fingers to spread the twenties so they fanned out in a long line.

"You were pretty sure."

"You know it's the right thing, Peter."

Singer continued to look at the money.

"I'm not sure I know anything anymore."

They sat for a long time, before his father-in-law stood up, took his glass to the sink, emptied and rinsed it, placed it in the cupboard above the sink, and walked by him out the door. The door didn't catch. Singer thought he heard Earl pause then step back and pull the door shut tight.

Junior Ettienne.

***

Singer stood across from the school and watched the boys. Tommie struggling to be first in line and Dougie leaning against the chain link, waiting for the last minute before standing. He turned to look behind him and then scanned up and down the street, taking in both intersections that he could see from where he stood. Singer stood well back from the corner, out of his son's line of vision unless he turned in almost a full circle. A teacher called and Dougie looked towards the door, gave a final look over his shoulder then turned and took his place at the end of the line.

Singer swung the pack off the ground, around onto his back and turned away. His last stop was the library.

***

Singer stood in front of the ATM, holding the envelope in his hand. There were three dollars left in the account. He reached into his pocket and took out the remaining bills. Two hundred dollars. Singer had to be sure to keep enough money to get him as far as he needed to go. Singer hadn't decided where that was, but it had to be far enough that Earl would send the remaining money. That meant more than a day's drive. He would need to eat and a place to stay for at least one night.

Singer heard a cough and turned. The line waiting for the machine had grown to three people. Singer stuffed another hundred dollars into the envelope, sealed it, placed it in the slot and took his receipt. He didn't look at anybody in the line behind him. A hundred bucks should be enough.

***

Singer stared at the back of the old man's head, the hint of a scar through the thinning grey hair over the occipital bone, just above the spot where the skull tapered into the neck. It was jagged and irregular, not a surgical scar. It looked old, faded to the same color as the surrounding skin, only apparent because of the raised creased edges. It could have been anything. A childhood accident. A bad beating. Or losing his balance on a drunken bender. He looked the kind. The skin loose and sagging around his neck, cheeks sunken but with high-red blotches splashed just beneath his eyes and his nose almost purple but veined like a map of Ontario roadways.

The old man sensed something and looked over his shoulder, away from the computer screen to where Singer sat pretending to read a magazine he had pulled from the periodicals rack. Singer was looking down at the open magazine by the time the man swiveled enough to see him. The second time he looked, Singer allowed himself to be caught staring, impatient for the man to leave. But it was the boy two computers down who left first and Singer slipped into his seat.

The list was long but not quite as long as it had been on the last email. Singer had not been able to make any donations in a week, so he knew why the list was a little shorter. The only thing worse than hearing another name fall onto the end of the list was knowing that names were disappearing from the top of the list when he wasn't able to donate.

Singer made twenty-eight donations. It only took a few seconds for each, he was sure he could have done it in his sleep, muscle memory leading him from one screen tap to the next. He didn't store any passwords or account numbers, but they came to him now as easily and fluidly as blinking or swallowing. He felt the tension ease in his head until by the last of the donations his mind felt as clear and clean as it had in months. He exited from his account, stood and went to the check-out counter. She was facing her computer but she looked up when Singer cleared his throat. Singer realized then that he wasn't sure what he intended to say. He hesitated and she waited.

"I just wanted to thank you. You've been very kind. To me."

She blushed. Singer had noticed she did that often.

"You're welcome. It was a pleasure."

Singer stood for a moment then turned and left the library.

Chapter 32

Singer hadn't had to wait long. Maybe twenty minutes. The first ride had got him as far as Chalk River. The driver, a security guard at the nuclear research lab, happy to talk about his team, the Dallas Cowboys. He had never been south of Boston or west of Detroit, but somehow he loved the Cowboys.

The second ride took longer and it was getting near dark. But he was all the way up the Trans-Canada to North Bay. The two sisters, middle-aged and returning from a high school reunion in Perth, apparently past worrying about being kidnapped and assaulted by a man they picked up by the side of the road, dropped him off just west of North Bay, a town called Yellek. It was almost midnight when Singer got out of the car and they offered to put him up so he could continue fresh in the morning, but Singer sensed they were relieved when he turned them down.

Singer watched the sister's taillights disappear, opened his pack and drained the last of the water from the bottle he had filled at the Chalk River gas station and tucked the empty bottle pack into the front pocket of his pack. A sign just before he had gotten out had said the next rest stop was three kilometers up the road so he began to walk, out in the middle of the westbound lane, feeling what was left of the day's sun seep up through the soles of his sneakers. He checked over his shoulder often as he walked, knowing that in his jeans and blue windbreaker he would be almost invisible. Only three cars passed in the hour it took him to walk to the rest stop. When he saw car lights appear in the distance he moved to the gravel verge. As the car approached and the curtain of diffuse light condensed to two bright cones. Singer stepped off the gravel into the grass and weeds and stood still, facing the vehicle until it passed, the parallel beams streaming out of the night, inhaling the darkness as if bred for it. Then there was nothing left but the glare, as harsh and cold as polished ice, washing up and over leaving him light-scalded and blind until the vehicle flared past and the night fell back into place like a big, blued curtain. Twice he caught a glimpse of a pale round face, eyes wide and startled by the apparition at the roadside, right arm held out straight from its side like a one-armed scarecrow pulled loose of the hanging stake. None of the three cars slowed, although the third swerved across the line into the eastbound lane as if the driver had only seen him at the last second and pulled to the left before correcting and drifting back into their lane.

***

Singer took a last look over his shoulder but the black of road top and sky rolled out behind him smooth and even as if made by a single brush stroke so that there was no place where the thin line of asphalt met the sky on the horizon, no first blush of headlights ploughing out of the night gathering the darkness and then sliding it to the side. He had to imagine the place where the highway met the sky, imagine that the darkness flowing out behind him still contained the gentle curve of tarmac back to the wide verge where the sisters had slowed, then stopped to let him out, imagine that the darkness hadn't crept up behind him with each following step so that he was always but a slight backwards stumble from falling away into the pitched black. Singer turned away from the highway following the off-ramp leading to the rest stop.

There was an unlit building to Singer's left, its bulk creating a slightly different shade of charcoal than the backing sky. At the end of the lane about 200 yards off the highway, it widened into a parking area with about a dozen empty spots. Singer caught his foot on the curb of the sidewalk that ringed the parking area and almost went down, taking three quick steps before catching himself. Just beyond the sidewalk was a cleared area on the grass containing four picnic tables, vague grey shapes crouched in the darkness. Singer slumped onto the bench of the nearest table, glad to sit even though most of the day had been spent in the back of a car. He had eaten the last of the dry cereal before leaving his apartment and nothing since, though he wasn't hungry, just weak and unwilling to move from where he sat.

The breeze came up a little and Singer snapped a couple of buttons on his windbreaker. He sat for several minutes then let himself to the ground and slid under the table, pulling his knapsack in behind him. He pulled the water bottle free, shook it, uncapped it and emptied the last few drops into his mouth before returning it to the side pocket. He unzipped the main section and pulled free the balled sheet he had taken from his bed. He had thought about buying a sleeping bag, but the cheapest had been twenty-two dollars and he had been unable to bring himself to buy it.

The day had been pleasant but the warm air had almost completely seeped away and the ground felt chilled through Singer's shirt and pants. Singer pulled the sheet tight around his shoulders and shifted the pack around to cushion his head. It felt clear and still and he fell asleep thinking of his boys.

The rain began a couple of hours before dawn and, though the table provided some shelter at first, the water puddled then drizzled down between the slats. Singer shifted, trying to find a spot protected from seeping rainwater but the rain continued, sometimes heavy, pounding the surface above his head and sometimes fading to little more than a dusting, but never stopping so that before long Singer, sheet and clothes were soaked. He crawled out from under the table, sat on the bench and waited for morning to come.

Chapter 33

Singer stepped down out of the truck and turned back to the driver.

"Thanks, Sue."

The woman nodded and then gestured to her left.

"Just up the street. Sea-Vue's probably the cheapest. It's a shithole but it'll be a bed."

"I'm not looking for luxurious."

The woman smiled.

"Good thing. It's Thunder Bay."

She put the truck back in gear then paused and looked at Singer.

"You take care of yourself, Peter."

Singer nodded, caught, choked for a second by the woman's concern, then found his voice.

"Thanks, Sue. You too."

***

It was the gap-toothed end of town, body-shops, do-it-yourself car wash, budget van rental, empty lots where buildings had come down and not been replaced, a sprinkling of residential homes, probably built when this had been 'outside of town' now mostly hanging on, a sudden hailstorm from needing emergency roof repair, driveways heaved and cracked the last of the summer weeds still hanging on, reluctant stragglers after the party's broken up.

Singer paused to let a short line of cars and a single eighteen-wheeler roll by before he crossed the four lanes to the opposite sidewalk. The motel had parking spaces for maybe a dozen vehicles in a tight asymmetrical horseshoe in front of the fourteen rooms, six along the east arm, six along the top furthest from where Singer stood and a couple more on the shorter west arm. There was a grey Toyota Corolla with mud-spattered fenders parked in front of the room in the far elbow and a black RAV4 in front of the office. A fence, grey and weather-beaten except where two slats had been replaced, the fresh white lumber standing out like pearls on a candy heart necklace, separated the rooms from the office building. Beyond the fence was a single-story bungalow.

The man behind the counter looked up from whatever he was reading—Singer couldn't see what it was—and smiled.

"Can I help you?"

The man flipped the book over to hold his place and used both hands to flatten the tufts of hair sticking from the narrow fringe over his ears, then felt the collar of his faded yellow gold shirt to make sure it was in place.

"I'm looking for a room."

The man looked over Singer's shoulder.

"Just you?"

Singer nodded.

"Just me."

The man smiled again.

"We've got one just opened up. It's a bargain, seeing how we're already into the off-season. Thirty-six bucks a night."

Singer felt the bills in his pocket. He hadn't spent any yet. He wasn't hungry but he would have to eat soon. The man misunderstood his hesitation.

"But we can give an even better rate if you're staying three or more nights."

"Can I have a look?"

The man stood up and disappeared into a side room, returned almost immediately with a key in his hand. He came around the desk and held the door open for Singer before following him through. He skipped a couple of steps so he was leading the way and gestured to the room closest to the street.

There was one double bed set against the far wall, a small flatscreen installed in the left corner of the room near the ceiling and a table with two plastic outdoor chairs along the wall just inside the door. There was a narrow strip of mint-green indoor/outdoor carpet covering the faux-wood click-lock flooring to the bathroom at the back of the room. The bed was covered in a worn beige duvet. The manager made a clicking noise, stepped to the bed and tugged on the duvet so the near corner came off the floor where it had been resting and the bottom ran straight along the edge of the bed. He stood back and looked at Singer.

"It looks fine."

"Just the one night?"

Singer nodded.

"For now."

***

Singer felt the first ratchet like the first slow turn on a watch spring, something that had been lying loose and relaxed at the base of his skull pulled straight like stretched fence wire. Not yet tight. Not tuning-fork taut so that if plucked, it would shimmer and vibrate for several seconds, pitched to a frequency beyond human hearing. But it was no longer slack.

"Visa? Mastercard?"

Singer took a second and the man waited.

"No. Cash."

The man looked puzzled.

"Cash?"

He paused.

"Nobody pays with cash anymore. I'm not even sure…"

The manager pulled out a side drawer and rummaged inside. Singer held the two twenties between his fingers, feeling the build.

"Do you have a library in town?"

The man didn't look up from where he was leaning, peering into the drawer.

"I think I've got…"

"Is there a library nearby?"

The manager looked up now.

"Library? Sure. I guess."

He looked out through the window.

"You almost passed it coming into town. It's just off the main drag."

Singer stuffed the bills back into his pocket.

"Thanks. Thanks for your help."

***

The motel manager stood outside the motel office and watched Singer stride away.

***

"Yessir. We have our computer room just beyond the reading area."

The librarian pointed to an open door just beyond a reading area with several large, padded chairs set in a semicircle around a low circular table covered in magazines.

"Do you have a library card?"

Singer made a face.

"No, I don't."

The woman smiled and leaned to reach for something under the counter.

"No problem. It's free. You just have to fill out this form."

"I just arrived in town. I don't have an address yet."

The woman paused and frowned.

"Oh."

She raised her figure.

"Just let me…"

She started to come around the counter but then spotted a stoop-shouldered man shelving books towards the back of the room.

"Jason! There's a young man here who wants to use the computers but he doesn't have a library card or a permanent address."

An older woman sitting in one of the padded chairs looked up when the woman called out then looked at Singer. Singer shrugged. The man pushed the cart of books to the side and came over to the desk. He went right to the computer screen without looking at the woman or Singer, felt around on the top of his head for his glasses, slid them down, peered at the screen, tapped several keys, wrote something on a slip of paper then paused with his fingers over the keys.

"Your name?"

"Peter Singer."

He tapped several more keys then wrote something else on the slip before sliding it across the counter. He slid the glasses back up onto his head and looked at Singer.

"It's not a problem. I've signed you up as a guest. That's your username and password. They'll work for the rest of the day but if you want to use it tomorrow, we would have to set you up again."

"Thanks."

The man nodded, slipped around the counter and walked back to where he had been shelving books. The woman looked after him, then back at Singer and smiled brightly.

"There you go."

Singer held the slip of paper up between his fingers and nodded.

***

"WHERE ARE YOU?"

"THUNDER BAY."

It took several seconds for the next email to arrive.

"I THOUGHT YOU WERE GOING FURTHER WEST."

"THIS IS AS FAR AS I GOT."

Singer watched a young father crouched with his daughter flipping through a picture book, but she shook her head after the first few pages and he returned it to the shelf and removed another. The bell of an arriving email brought Singer back to the screen.

"HOW DO I KNOW YOU'RE REALLY THERE?"

"WHY WOULD I LIE ABOUT THUNDER BAY?"

The reply was quick.

"TO GET THE MONEY."

Singer returned to the library home page, memorized the number.

"PHONE 807-345-8275. ASK FOR ME."

"OKAY."

Singer stood up from the computer, slipped out of his windbreaker and draped it over the chair then walked to the desk. The phone rang just as he arrived at the counter. The woman raised one finger and picked up the phone, listened for a moment than glanced over at Singer.

"Yes."

She listened for several more seconds, then looked at Singer again.

"Yes."

She listened again then held the phone out towards Singer.

"He would like to speak to you."

Singer took the phone.

"Hey Earl."

"I'll send it as soon as I'm off the phone. Good luck, Peter. Don't come back."

"Earl—"

But his father-in-law had already hung up. Singer handed the phone back to the woman. She took it and stood with it in her outstretched arm, waiting. Singer started to speak, then stopped, started again then just shrugged.

"Thanks."

***

Singer pushed the packet of fries to the side, a single fry spilling free before he placed it back on the pile, and pulled the hamburger still wrapped in the cheap yellow wax paper over in front of him. He reached down to pull the water bottle from the pocket on the front of his knapsack, unscrewed the cap and took a long swig. It was lukewarm. He had let the water run for a long while in the bathroom but it had never run any colder. The ratchet wheel in his head shifted and the catch clicked into place on the next tooth, the sound as sharp and loud as two clapped stones, the wire drawn fiber-thin to the point of breaking.

Singer placed the bottle beside the hamburger then shifted so he could get at the money in his pocket. He pulled it out and laid it on the table—four twenties, a ten, three toonies and a penny. Singer looked at the burger and the French fries— would they take them back? Refund his money? He rose from his seat but then sat down again. Of course, they wouldn't.

Singer reached for the burger but his hand caught on the water bottle, tipping it forward so that a few drops splashed onto the burger before he caught and righted the bottle. The droplets maintained their shape and form and slid from the wrapping onto the table before pooling on the table. Singer ran his finger across where the water had landed on the wrapping but couldn't detect any remaining moisture. He unwrapped the burger and took a bite, chewing slowly until it was a fine moist paste but he still had to swallow twice to get it beyond some esophageal narrowing. He followed with a sip of water. Singer filled the bottle twice before finishing his meal.

***

Singer looked through the front window at the man behind the counter. He could only see the top of his head to just above his eyebrows because of the way he was bent forward reading. The tufts of hair had come loose and jutted from the sides as they had when Singer had first entered the office. He wondered if they came loose after being plastered down or if the man toyed with them, unaware of what he was doing. Singer turned away and headed back towards downtown Thunder Bay. He had been sure he wouldn't be able to spend the money on a room, but he had thought he better check.

***

Singer stuffed the twenties, the ten, and the five he had exchanged for the toonies into the envelope and inserted it into the slot. It didn't really make sense to put all of the bills in because there was only enough for three donations. But he didn't like the feel of the money in his pocket, as if there, it could lure him into spending it on trinkets and baubles. In his account, it was beyond spending.

***

Ninety-five dollars. The money from Earl had not arrived yet. Singer stared at the screen, willing the numbers to change but they did not. Earl had said he would send the money immediately. But it hadn't arrived. Singer closed his eyes and took several deep breaths, fighting down the panic in his chest, but the sound of the email dropping into his inbox pulled him out. The subject line never changed. He opened the email. It had been almost two days since he had removed twenty-eight names from the list but it had begun to grow again. Singer could tell just by scrolling through. Not an additional twenty-eight but maybe a dozen new names. And there would have been some names removed from the list because they could no longer be saved. Singer made three donations.

Salma Rahman

Anjali Ghimire

Michael Persaud

Singer rotated his neck on his shoulders. It felt good, like his brain could now be contained by his skull. But the money needed to arrive.

"I'm afraid we're closing in five minutes, sir."

Singer minimized the screen and looked over his shoulder. It was the librarian who had set up his guest pass, but he showed no sign of recognizing Singer.

"Yessir. I'm almost done."

The man was already turning away towards the other occupied computer.

Singer brought the screen back up and unpaused the video. A young boy, hands held on both sides by two women of similar age. Singer couldn't tell if they were sisters or maybe just friends. But they smiled at each other over the child's head as they swung him forward in the air. Six weeks before, Singer had watched the same child drawing breath like it was thick as porridge, barely able to get it across his lips and down into his lungs, and when it arrived it was as if he was able to extract almost nothing of what he needed from what he had inhaled. In the second video, he spent each breath as carelessly as if there was no end to breathing, so that he could use each inhalation, each inspiration, as he chose, to laugh, to shout, even to be held until it could be held no longer. Singer heard the approaching steps, closed his screen, stood and took his jacket from the back of the chair. Singer clapped the man on the shoulder as he passed, the librarian shying away as if he thought he might be struck.

"Thanks for everything, sir."

Chapter 34

Shelter House was tucked down a side street on a block gapped by empty lots and makeshift parking lots so that what was left were a couple of commercial offices, a single bent home clinging to the street like a loose tooth and the two Shelter House buildings in the middle of the block, a two story red and white building at the corner and a low slung building painted out of the same can. A young man with straight black hair past his shoulders in just a red t-shirt and worn jeans and a woman wearing a misshapen wool sweater and cap and missing one front tooth shared a joint on the sidewalk across the street. Singer set his pack down against the chain link fence and sat. His back settled into a subtle curl in the fence like he wasn't the first to have used the spot. He pulled his jacket a little tighter around his shoulders and looked across the street at the building then over at the young man and woman. The woman, holding the last of the roach out to her friend, looked him over then away.

Singer was tired. Shelter House had been a longer walk than he expected. He closed his eyes, heard the first faint click buried somewhere deep in his head. It had started already. The second nudge against his boot opened his eyes. The young man stood directly in front of him, leaning slightly forward so that he was almost overtop of Singer.

"Haven't seen you around."

Singer shifted back against the fence and tilted his head back to get a better look.

"Yeah. Just got into town."

The young man looked at Singer's pack and back again.

"You got any money?"

Singer put his hands behind him against the fence and edged to his feet. The man's face was pouched beneath the eyes and chin and Singer realized he wasn't as young as he had first thought. Singer shook his head.

"Nothing?"

Singer shook his head again.

"Fuck off, Stevie. Leave the guy alone."

The man looked over at the woman.

"What? We're just talkin'."

"Leave him alone."

She held the last of the joint in the air.

"Yours?"

He wandered back over, slipped it from her fingers, held it at the very end of his fingernails and drew it down until there was almost nothing to flick away. The woman caught Singer's eye and gestured at the door. When Singer continued to look at her, she frowned and gestured with her head again. Go on.

***

The man at the desk was bald with a ponytail that trailed down his back between his shoulder blades. He spun face forward from the file cabinet when he heard Singer at the counter. He had been expecting somebody else, Singer could see it in the moment it took for him to recover.

"Can I help you?"

Singer looked at the wall behind the man, searched the surface of the counter then looked at the man.

"I… I need a…"

"Never been here before?"

Singer shook his head. The man spun away, plucked a sheet from a table behind him then spun back and slapped the sheet in front of him.

"House rules."

Singer read through the list then looked up at the guy.

"You really have to worry about this stuff?"

The guy smiled and shrugged.

"Not usually. Our folks are pretty good."

He nodded at the sheet.

"Anything there you can't live with?"

Singer shook his head and the man nodded.

"Good."

He spun away and back again with another sheet.

"First time we just ask for a little medical history. The doctor'll be by in the morning to give the newbies a quick check-up. Are you working?"

Singer shook my head.

"Just got here. But I'll be looking."

The man nodded.

"Good. You looking for long-term or just the night?"

"I may need a couple of nights. Once I've got a job, I'll find an apartment."

The man leaned across the counter to look Singer over.

"You need anything? Boots? Clothes?"

Singer pointed at his pack propped on the counter.

"I think I'm okay for now."

He nodded and stood up.

"Might as well show you 'round."

He started to come around the counter then turned back and shouted towards a door that led back into a space behind the reception desk.

"Che-Che, I'm gone for a minute. You listen for the desk?"

A young woman, straight black hair, blunt-cut to a place just above the collar of her t-shirt with a ring through one eyebrow, stepped into the doorway.

"Sure, Paul."

She nodded at Singer then disappeared back into the room. The man grabbed a set of keys and stepped around the counter, checking his watch.

"Everybody has to clear out until five so you won't be able to stay. But I can show you the layout and where you'll bed down."

***

Singer shuffled along with the line, accepted a towel from a small man with a narrow fringe of white hair and watery eyes and a rolled mat from a young man with a snake tattoo poking above his shirt collar and followed the men through the front room with the dozen or so bunk beds and into the room, just off the cafeteria that Paul had showed him earlier. A man inside the door shouted as they funneled in.

"Shower first!"

But everybody seemed to know the drill and continued down a short hall at the far end of the room to the shower stalls. A few of the men in the line talked to each other or themselves. Singer spotted the young man in the red t-shirt near the front of the line.

Singer and several of the others stood just outside the shower room, trailing in one at a time as somebody left, freeing up a shower. Singer stood under the shower for a long time, the hot water feeling good on his scalp and shoulders. The man under the shower next to him said something but when Singer looked over the man was looking down, just making noises at the grey-tiled floor, guttural expirations that burst from his lips at odd intervals, as involuntary and unintentional as a synaptic leap.

***

Singer found a spot near the front wall, unrolled his bed mat and let himself down. A big man in a sleeveless corduroy shirt and thick canvas pants that stopped several inches above his sockless ankles stopped and stared down at Singer's mat. His arms were thick and undefined and the muscles in his jaw roiled just beneath the surface. A man about halfway along the wall to Singer's right watched, but the others were either settling their mats or already lying or sitting in their spots. The man pointed at Singer's mat.

"'At's my spot."

Singer nodded, rolled his mat, grabbed his pack and moved to a spot along the back wall where there was still room for several mats, unrolled his and settled onto it again. He lay back with his head on his pack and one arm crooked across his eyes. He let his arm drop away when he felt the nudge against his boot. It was the man who had watched the earlier encounter standing at the foot of Singer's mat, looking at him, unblinking. He reached behind his neck and tugged at the ragged rattail then rubbed the corner of his eye. The skin around his eyes crinkled as if at something funny that only he could hear and his lips drew back from his teeth. His eyes didn't leave Singer's face, but he jerked his chin at the pack behind Singer's head.

"What's in the bag?"

Singer pushed himself to a sitting position then looked behind to the man's spot along the wall then back at the man.

"You should go lie down."

The man looked at him for several seconds, his eyes lost in some internal calculation, then he nodded and walked back to his spot and sat down. Singer lay back, arm across his eyes. Every time he looked from under his arm, the man was watching.

Chapter 35

The man looked at the application then pushed it back across the counter.

"You forgot your address."

Singer looked at the application then up at the man.

"I'm new in town. No address yet."

"Where are you staying?"

"Shelter House."

The man across the desk made a face.

"We need a permanent address."

Singer nodded.

"I'll have one soon. I'm looking at a couple of places this afternoon."

The man kept two fingers on the application as if Singer might snatch it back from him and start filling in imaginary addresses.

"Come back then."

Singer nodded and left.

***

The money was in. All ten thousand. Singer stared at the number on the screen. The money from Earl and the twenty-dollar leftover after he had made the donations for Salma, Anjali and Michael. A new email, the subject line still black and bold, had dropped since the previous day. But the growing tension was still manageable. Names were dropping into place at the bottom of the list, he had heard them through the night, roused by the dull clack but lacking the volume, the echo and the pull weight that could prevent him from returning to sleep. It was coming—the tension, the torque as each name pulled against the one before until it seemed they couldn't hold and would fly apart as lost as grains of sand in a desert storm. And whatever held Singer together, whatever bound each synaptic link would go with them. But he wasn't there yet. He could wait. He opened the email.

Singer watched each of the first forty videos and donated to each one.

***

At the first place, Singer sat on the stoop picking at the flaking paint on the wooden steps and dropping the pieces down between the narrow slats until forty minutes after the scheduled meeting time. He thought about going back to the library and sending a reminder email but decided against it.

The second place had a bedroom with the door missing in a shared apartment. The linoleum on the kitchen floor was worn down to the stickum and the doughy-faced young woman in the shapeless shift who showed him the room didn't comment on the fat man in a Flintstones t-shirt that didn't cover his genitals, snoring on the cushionless couch, the TV muted but showing a rerun of a mid-seventies game show. Singer had a vivid memory of the long, thin, wand-like microphone but not the host's name.

The third place was better. A single large room with a hot plate stand in the corner and a shared washroom across the hall with a door that locked. They stood, Singer and the landlord, outside on the sidewalk in front of the house.

"So what do you think?"

Singer nodded.

"It would be fine."

The landlord touched his head with one hand, paused to rearrange one of the strands flattened across his head, ran a forefinger across his moustache and nodded.

"It's two hundred forty a month plus heat. I need first and last. So, four hundred eighty."

Singer played with the bills in his pocket, working through them one at a time with his thumb and forefinger. Twenty. Twenty lives. So he could sleep on a mattress instead of a bed mat. The man tilted his head to the side, touched his scalp again and wet his lips, waiting. Singer winced and shook his head.

"I've got a couple more places to look at. I'll be in touch."

***

Singer spotted the guy from Shelter House watching from across the street. He would have recognized him even without the way he fingered the rattail at the back of his neck. The woman at the ATM completed her transaction and smiled at Singer when she turned and slipped by. He nodded to her as she passed and took another look. The guy had shifted but was still watching. Singer angled his body so his hands couldn't be seen from where the guy stood, placed the five hundred dollars in an envelope and deposited the money back into his account. It was a relief to get it out of his pocket.

The guy followed Singer for a few blocks, but by the time Singer had crossed the railroad tracks and made his way down to the Port Authority he was gone. The wind blew up hard from the lake, whipped away the last whisper of summer and Singer broke into a jog following a path along the shoreline until he was forced to head west to find a way across the floodway and back to Shelter House.

Chapter 36

Singer lay with his arm draped across his face but watched them across the room—rattail guy and the guy he had met out front on his first day at Shelter House—red shirt. Singer had spotted them talking on his third night at Shelter House and then noticed them come together several times to exchange a few quick words and move on. They had taken to eating together at suppertime.

***

"How's the job hunt going, Peter?"

"Not so good, Paul. They always want a permanent address."

Singer had arrived early to avoid the crowd, as he almost always did, and stood leaning against the counter waiting for Paul to sign him in before killing time until five. Paul made a face.

"Yeah. And who can afford a permanent address without a job? Catch-22."

Paul looked up from the sign-in sheet.

"But that reminds me—it looks like one of our long-term bunks is opening up. You want it? It's not a permanent address but better than a mat on the hard floor."

"You sure, Paul? There must be guys ahead of me."

Paul smiled and shook his head.

"Jesus Christ, Pete. Would you take a break when you get one?"

Singer shrugged, embarrassed.

"I know. I know. I just don't want to jump the line, Paul."

Paul shook his head.

"It's not first-come, first-serve for those beds, Pete. You guys might be together for a while and we want to make sure it's a good fit. No hotheads, no scumbags, just the good guys."

Singer raised an eyebrow.

"I'm one of the good guys?"

Paul shook his head, impatient now.

"Jesus Christ, Pete—you want it or not?"

Singer took a second.

"Sure. Sure, Paul. Thanks. I really appreciate it."

Paul had turned away and was filing something in one of the cabinets.

"Not a problem, Pete. You're on the mats tonight but you'll have a bunk to-morrow."

***

The man standing at the end of the bunk tucking socks together was slim but stooped as if his neck, shoulders and head were almost more weight than he could hold aloft. If the jacket and pants he was wearing had been new he might have been able to pass for low-level white collar, a small-office manager or night man-ager at a retail chain, but the seat was worn shiny and the cuffs past frayed to shredded. He turned when he heard Singer approach. His face was patrician, eyes wide-set in a narrow face, nose straight and even, lips not full but not thin either, and when he removed the narrow-brimmed fedora and placed it on the bed behind him, a thick strand of hair fell loose and white across his forehead and he brushed it back, the gesture of a much younger man used to admiring looks. But when Singer looked closer, the wear and neglect was apparent, in the tangle of veins that ran from the tip along both ridges to the cavity where nose seeped to cheek like stray threads tugged free by time and drink's anxious hand, in the skin gone slack at lid and lip and at the neck where it slumped around the hyoid. But the smile rested easy and natural on his face.

"You must be Peter. Paul told me to be expecting you."

He held out a hand and Singer took it, light and dry as an autumn leaf, in his.

"I'm a Peter, as well. McGarrigle. I'm not sure what's to be done with two Peters."

McGarrigle grinned.

"But we'll make it work."

Singer nodded.

"Yessir. I'm sure we will."

McGarrigle turned back to his socks.

"Here, let me get these off your bed."

He turned back to Singer.

"I'm the lower, if you don't mind. If I ever fell off the top, there'd be not much more than eggshells left."

***

"I usually set up outside the McDonald's or across the street…"

McGarrigle gestured across the four lanes of Central Avenue.

"…at the Royal Bank."

He looked at Singer.

"There's lots of foot traffic and you've a little shelter from the wind."

He looked at Singer's windbreaker then tugged at the ragged parka he had thrown over his suit.

"You may need to find something a little warmer soon. There can be some cold days out here."

He flipped his thumb back and forth between the McD's and the bank.

"So, which do you want?"

"I'll walk over to the bank."

McGarrigle nodded.

"Good enough then. Here's your cup and your sign. If you get bored or cold, come on over and we can grab a coffee."

***

They walked up Memorial for a block or two before McGarrigle turned east.

"Jaysus, let's get off the busy streets, Pete. The noise and the fumes are a bit much, no?"

They walked in silence for several blocks. Singer spoke first.

"How did you do?"

McGarrigle readjusted his hat, pushed it back on his head.

"Never count your money when you're sitting at the table."

Singer looked around.

"But we're done."

The other man shook his head.

"I never count until I get home. Bad days, it makes the walk seem longer. Good days, I might be tempted to do something unwise. But…"

He pulled back his unzipped parka, lifted his suit jacket pocket and it fell back with a thick jangling sound.

"I think it was a pretty good day. Lots of toonies and loonies in the mix."

Singer felt at his own jacket pockets weighted down on both sides by coin. The sun was low in the sky so that he had to shade his eyes to look up the street and he kept a hand across his forehead when he turned to McGarrigle.

How often do you do this?"

The other man shrugged.

"Most days. When I can."

Singer looked over.

"When you can?"

McGarrigle ignored the question and they walked in silence for another block. Singer tapped his pockets again then slowed and stopped. The other man took another step or two before he noticed and stopped to look at Singer with a raised eyebrow.

"I want to get this into the bank."

McGarrigle smiled.

"What good'll it do you in the bank?"

Singer allowed a trace of a smile and shrugged.

"I'd just feel better…"

He gestured back the way they had come, already half-turned.

"Sure. Sure, laddie. I understand. You want some company?"

Singer shook his head.

"No, Mr. McGarrigle. You head back. I won't be long."

McGarrigle gave him a long, measuring look.

"It'd be there in the morning, eh? You know that? Yeah? It's been a long step down…but not that far."

Singer's eyes widened.

"No. No, Mr. McGarrigle. It's not that. Not at all. I don't… I wouldn't think that."

McGarrigle took a couple of steps back to where Singer stood and put a hand on his shoulder.

"Alright then. I'll see you back at the house."

He turned away and took a couple of steps before turning back.

"And call me Peter, laddie. It's just Peter."

Singer watched him silhouetted against the last glittering sun splash on the horizon, until he reached the end of the block and crossed the street, bent, curled and hunched as if each step pulled him forward but also down into the ground. Singer had the thought that if he watched long enough the old man would gradually disappear from the soles up until there was just the fedora, left on the sidewalk like an abandoned child, unable to follow the old man down. But instead he grew a little smaller step by step, just like anybody walking away.

***

Seven thousand, one hundred and fifty-seven dollars. Singer watched the numbers, white font stark against charcoal background. The teller had waited patiently as Singer stacked the coins, a few toonies but mostly loonies and quarters, then tapped a few keys before nodding at Singer and looking over his shoulder for the next customer.

Singer had used a thousand dollars on the second day. Avoided the library on the third day, but gone back on the fourth and spent another one thousand dollars. One hundred and twenty names in four days. The list was still long, but so much shorter. He could tell by how few swipes it took to reach the bottom.

The bell sounded as an email arrived. It had been three days since Singer had donated. The list would be longer. But for now, his head was clear, quiet, no sense that something was waiting to drop. Usually, immediately after a donation, there was relief but even as the tension receded leaving a gap momentary refuge where Singer could draw a breath, he could sense it building again preparing to crest and crash, but now it was as if, whatever was gathering, building, it was beyond Singer's ability to perceive and there was no sense that there was anything to resist, no gathering energy that need be opposed—and he could rest.

Singer opened a video and watched two young girls walk away from the camera, their arms around each other, one a head taller than the other. They followed a rutted road, designed for goat- or cattle-drawn carts, walking uphill towards the crest of the road, low green hills in the background. They turned and the shorter of the two pulled free to wave wildly at the person holding the camera, her lips moved in a soundless joyful shout. Singer recognized her from an earlier video where she lay still, beneath a ripped sheet strung between two shrubs to provide shade. Now the video stopped, the young girl captured as she raised on one foot to pirouette back in the direction they had been walking, as if without instruction or training, by chance and physical fortune she had captured the joy and grace of a practiced arabesque, her arm towards the rising sun, her leg 90 degrees from the ground on the toe of her supporting leg, not quite perfect, bent slightly at the knee but the subtle flaw and in that pose, that captured moment, Singer could see her, what she was. He stared for a long time then changed screens.

There was nothing on the subject line of the email that had just arrived. It had an attachment but it was not a *Living List*. He didn't recognize the sender. There was no message. Just a single link. Singer pressed it and the video began to play. The camera caught Tommie standing on the lower bough of the remaining tree in their backyard, facing the camera, both hands reaching up to grab a branch above so that he stood, eight feet off the ground as loose and easy as if on the ground. He had not been able to quite reach the branch above his head in the spring and now he held it easily. Singer's son allowed himself to drop forward, leaning towards the ground but anchored by his arms holding the branch above and his feet on the bottom bough, so that his body bowed. An arm appeared for a moment, the motion causing the sleeve of the sweater—red with faint grey threaded lines, a gift Singer had given her two, maybe three Christmases before—to pull up revealing her wrist, narrow and fine and strong as leaded glass and a flash of warning fingers, then it was gone again, pulled back behind the camera. Tommie laughed and held, swaying for a moment before standing straight then he turned and began clambering higher into the tree. The camera followed Tommie for several seconds then shifted to Dougie on the ground watching his mother. Her arm appeared again as she gestured towards the tree, and Dougie let his gaze shift for a moment with the camera as it swung towards Tommie, now high in the tree, but when she came back to Dougie, he was watching the camera again. Slowly, the camera pulled in tight on Dougie's face, narrowing, beyond the place raw and sore on his lower lip where he pulled and bit without knowing, past where the skin pulled tight, bone-stretched across his cheek, by the places just beneath brow and eyes shadowed by fatigue, until Dougie's eyes filled the screen, more grey than green, unblinking as if he had forgotten how or why and then the screen went black. She had changed her email but still had his. Singer swiped at his eyes, stood and without realizing it, brushed against the woman waiting for the computer as he left.

Chapter 37

Singer stood in line behind two other customers waiting for a teller to come free, happy to let the warmth seep back into his bones. Winter came early in Thunder Bay and it was rarely a false start—when it arrived, it stayed until the days had got long enough to notice.

Singer pushed his hands out from where he had pulled them back into the sleeves of his ragged parka, waiting for the feeling to come back into the tips. It came in a rush, leaving them stung and buzzing. He tugged off the wool mittens, squeezed his hands into tight fists and rubbed them together hard. The young woman in front glanced quickly over her shoulder at the motion and then back around, shifting slightly so that she was directly between Singer and her stroller. He stamped his feet. The boots were too big for him but that had been the plan, so Singer could wear several layers of socks and still get them on.

Paul had found him the parka among the castoffs, green, faded to almost grey, the fake fur around the hood pressed flat, a tear along the seam at the shoulder so that when he raised his arms you could see the felt lining beneath, but it was warm. The mittens were new, donated just before Christmas by the ladies' auxiliary from the Westfort Baptist, hand-knitted, a bundle of fifty or a hundred that they had worked on through the summer and fall. The mittens were warm, but a full day crouched or standing against the wall of the bank and the cold found its way through, starting at the edges but digging in a little deeper each day, so that it always seemed he was a little colder than the day before.

Singer heard the scrape of the snowplow beyond the bank window even before it was visible ,so that when he looked to the window that ran almost the length of the bank it was a second before the leading edge crept into view, pushing the greyed slush to the curb and then up onto the sidewalk. He watched as it passed, the driver up high in the seat, in a way that reminded him of the forklift operators in the warehouse, the same practiced, relaxed alertness, aware but unconcerned, one hand on the wheel as he took a long draw, almost to the filter and flicked the butt out the open side window without looking away from the cutting edge of the plow.

They stood across the street shuffling in place, crossing their arms back and forth in front of their bodies, almost in unison as if they had practiced but not enough. Red shirt and rattail. Singer wouldn't have noticed them if he hadn't been following the plow. There was no visible red shirt or rat tail, but it was them. The sun had slid beyond the corner, but even in the near-dark he could make them out. The long, lank black hair hanging beyond the toque pulled down around his ears and the face pouched like marbles against a cloth bag and the other, face pinched even narrower by the cold, eyes pulled in tight around his nose as if seeking refuge from what was beyond the edges of his face.

Singer heard the man clear his throat but it didn't penetrate and he had to tap Singer's elbow to get his attention. Singer looked back at the man, who nodded at the counter running in front of the teller's stations—Singer swung back towards the teller who was beckoning him forward impatiently, looked back at the man behind him and made a face.

"Sorry."

The man nodded. The teller didn't change expression as he approached but there was something in the way she held her head. Or hands. Or looked past him that made him want to explain his distraction. Instead he pulled the coins from his pockets, three fistfuls, then the last few straggler coins, clinging to the inside corners and the one bill, a ten. The coins clattered against the counter in a way that brought the other teller's head around, before she returned her attention to her customer. Singer's teller waited while he piled the coins, and when he was done she counted them and swept them into her drawer with a practiced hand. She tapped several keys, looked at the screen.

"One thousand, two hundred and forty-four dollars."

Shit. Singer had thought the money would last longer. He was down to about a week between donations. After that first week, it had been ten days before he had even noticed a change, a drawing at the base of his skull, so faint that it could have been imagined. Except that it was so familiar, as visceral as held breath or infection fever, that he knew he wasn't mistaken. It had taken four more days before he began to hear the names falling into place, sudden and sharp as a cracked knuckle, and then another day before he had gone to the library and sent the next one thousand dollars. But the clear, quiet intervals were shrinking—he was losing twenty-four or twenty-six hours every cycle. And now he was down to a week.

"Still no receipt. Sir?"

Singer looked up, once again snapped out of a reverie. It took a moment but then what she had said came to him.

"No. No receipt. Thanks."

Nobody was at either of the ATM's or waiting for one so Singer stood in the alcove, soaking up the last of the warmth before he stepped out into the cold. He peered across the street for red shirt and rattail but it was full dark and the overhead light reflected off the glass so that Singer couldn't see more than headlights and vague grey shapes. He leaned in close to the window and shaded his eyes, waiting for a couple of cars to pass. They were gone. Or had shifted positions so that Singer couldn't see them from where he stood. Maybe it was a coincidence. There was no reason for them to watch him. Except he was at a bank.

Singer pulled back from the window, relieved and took a step away from the door as the man who had been behind him came through the inner door across the alcove and pushed through the outer door without looking at Singer. The blast of cold air reminded Singer why he was waiting. One thousand, two hundred and forty-four dollars. The panhandling helped, had stretched the money further than he had anticipated. But it wasn't nearly enough. Singer wasn't sure what he would do when it was gone.

***

Singer paused outside the entrance to Shelter House, stepped back into the shadows beyond the small pool of light. It was cold but the building blocked most of the wind rolling in from the north. It was going to get colder over the next few days. They stepped around the corner two blocks down, swiveling their heads back and forth searching for him and Singer stepped out into the light. They froze where they stood and rattail's head shifted. They were too far away for Singer to hear but he knew rattail said something. They started walking again, heads down, but turning occasionally to the other as if talking casually. Singer watched them for a second then turned, opened the door and stepped into the intake area. The bell sounded and Paul stepped out from the back room.

"Paul? Shouldn't you be gone by now?"

The other man nodded and smiled.

"Yeah."

He gestured back over his shoulder without looking.

"Wendy's here but I wanted to catch you before I left."

"Me? What's up?"

Paul gathered his coat up from the back of the chair, a newer, cleaner, thicker version of the one Singer had on and started shrugging into it, struggling with the far sleeve. Singer leaned over the counter and reached to tug the parka over so Paul could get at the sleeve.

"Arm still bothering you?"

The other man grimaced.

"Yeah. Nothing heals as fast once you hit fifty."

Paul looked at Singer.

"I think I might have something for you."

Singer forced his face to brighten.

"Oh yeah?"

"My buddy's the night manager over at Walmart. They need somebody in the warehouse. I remember you saying you did that kind of work. It might be good for you. Give you a chance to get out of here."

Paul looked up from the counter, a little shy but smiling, pleased.

"What do you think?"

"Yeah. Yeah. That sounds great, Paul. I really appreciate you thinking of me. That sounds like something that could work out."

Paul had already turned back to his desk to grab a scrap of paper and a pen, holding his phone in his other hand and scrolling through phone numbers.

"Here it is."

He put the phone down so he could hold the paper still with one hand and write with the other, scrawling down the number, pausing to make sure, draw over a couple of the numbers so that they were legible, then holding the slip out to Singer.

"Here you go."

Paul gestured for Singer to come around the counter.

"You can use the phone on the other desk there. He started fifteen minutes ago and he said you could call anytime."

Singer took the slip, holding it up.

"This great, Paul. I really appreciate it. But I'm wet and cold and really need a hot shower."

Singer started to turn away, still holding up the slip.

"But once I'm cleaned up I'll come back down."

Singer nodded at the phone on the far desk.

"Wendy'll let me….?"

"Sure, Peter…but it's not a job interview. You don't have to—"

Singer had already turned away, had the door to the stairwell open and held up the slip again.

"Thanks, Paul. You're a good man."

Paul started to step around the counter to follow.

"Sure, Peter. But—"

The bell rang as red shirt and rattail stepped in. Paul looked after Singer then over at the two men, then stepped back behind the counter to sign them in.

***

A job wasn't going to work. A decent job meant an apartment. Shelter House wasn't for people who had jobs. Shelter House was where you went when you had drifted out into the badlands beyond the edges of decent functioning society. An apartment meant rent…and that meant the first month of missed rent, then the second…and then the third…and then Singer standing out on the sidewalk looking up at the rain-streaked window of the latest place he had called home, trying to figure out where to sleep that night. There was no other way it could go. Because even now, with the money almost gone, facing something uncertain, but sure that it was going to be bad, he couldn't stop donating. Singer knew rent past due wasn't going to stop him. So, nope. A job wasn't going to work.

***

The old man's breathing had changed. Singer could tell he was awake.

"More traffic out there than usual."

Singer stared up at the ceiling, the room dark but not pitch, a little light bleeding from the watch room.

"Yeah."

"McMartin and Bendo."

Singer could tell by the drawn-out 'o' on the last word that McGarrigle had been drinking. It wasn't often. But regular.

"Yeah."

"What are they up to?"

"Not sure. But they were watching me at the bank. Then they followed me home."

Home. Shelter House. Home. Singer closed his eyes and shook his head. There was a long pause before the old man spoke again.

"They're bad'uns."

"Yeah."

Another long pause.

"Don't hesitate. If things go sideways."

Singer couldn't think of an answer.

"How are you doing, Mr. McG?"

"Still? No, Peter? Will you never call me by my Christian name?"

Singer smiled up into the dark.

"Give it time, Mr. McG. Maybe when we know each other a little better. How are you doing?"

The old man snorted.

"Know each other a little better! If I was a younger man I'd crawl up there and thrash you bloody. But seeing's how I can barely catch my breath after a long yawn, I'll probably just lay here and think poorly of ya'."

There was another long pause.

"Alright I guess. Probably shouldn't have had the third…or however many came after that."

Singer poked around the edges, searching the perimeter for building tension, the sense that whatever held him in place, anchored him to his body had not yet begun to tighten…but it was there just beyond the lit place, out where things grew thick and shadowed, where the binding ties disappeared like abandoned train tracks into a caved in tunnel. Out there, Singer could sense the first slow twist, drawing slack a little tauter, spooled wire drawn straight until each would shiver like a tapped tuning fork. Two days and it had already started.

"Huh?"

"I said, are you sleeping? But it sounds like you were almost there. Sorry, lad."

"Nah, Mr. McG. Not even close. Just thinking."

The old man chuckled.

"There's a habit you want to avoid. You'd be better off taking up smoking. Or the drink."

Singer listened as the old man shifted in the bunk below.

"I've not seen you take a drink, Peter?"

"Nah. Never much of a drinker."

"Wish I could say the same."

Singer nodded in the dark.

"Yeah."

"You married, Peter?"

"Yeah. I am. I'm not sure if she'd say so."

"Kids?"

"Two boys."

"Uh-huh. I thought you might. They okay?"

Singer thought of Dougie looking at him through his wife's camera.

"Hard to say. I expect they'll be alright."

"Why?"

Singer shuffled the word around in his head, looking from different angles, but couldn't find a hold.

"Why what?"

"Why do you expect they'll be okay?"

"I guess I meant, hope."

Singer looked towards the door as somebody passed the door leading into the bunk room, heard them pause just beyond the edge of the door then keep walking. The old man was quiet for a long time but Singer could tell he was still awake.

"She didn't throw me out until she woke up with the couch on fire. Looked like I was resting the cigarette on the arm of the couch—too drunk to find an ashtray. And way too drunk to stay awake."

The old man paused.

"You ever seen a couch on fire, Peter? The stuffing catches like shredded paper. Took three pails to douse it. And I didn't wake up until the third. Melody and the boys, Eddie maybe three, and Jamie just turned four, standing around me, the couch scorched and still smoking. It was a mess."

"That's when she said I had to go."

"Harsh."

McGarrigle made a sound that Singer couldn't decipher.

"No. She probably waited too long. I'd drunk myself off the job and was drinking away what little we had saved."

Singer lay looking up at the ceiling, eyes open because closing his eyes drew himself back into his head.

"You ever try…? Do you ever see…?"

"No. She'd had enough. Didn't wait long. Remarried within a year—the guy who'd fixed our stove."

Singer could tell he wasn't done.

"He seemed alright. But Gail never was much of a judge… Turned out he liked the wee ones. Probably had his eye on Eddie and Jamie from the drop."

Singer listened for the catch, but the words came out in a hard, cold line.

"Went on for years. That kind a thing doesn't set the couch on fire."

"Never knew until we read the notes. They had their own apartments by that time, but they were both at Eddie's when we found them."

"They were good friends, Eddie and Jamie. More like twins than brothers. So, at least they were together."

Singer lay awake for a long time waiting, but the old man didn't say anymore.

***

The sound of a name dropping into place at the end of the list woke Singer. The hard clack as the name fell provided momentary respite, as always, but was followed by the steady ratchet pull that restored the tension then stepped a tooth beyond. Singer swung his legs over the side and leaned down to look into the lower bunk but the old man was already gone.

***

Singer placed his plate on the long table, swung a leg over the bench and slipped in beside the old man. McGarrigle caught the last scrap of toast between fingers and thumb and mopped up the last of the syrup before looking over.

"You ready?"

Singer shook his head.

"I'm going to get a late start. I've got something to do."

McGarrigle nodded.

"Just remember—time is money."

The old man used a hand on Singer's shoulder to push himself up from the table and Singer had to catch an arm and steady him when he stepped back over the bench. McGarrigle gave a small, embarrassed smile.

"Never quite as steady on the day after."

Singer reached across to pat McGarrigle's hand still on his shoulder.

"I shouldn't be too long. I'll stop by to see how you're making out."

The old man smiled but it seemed forced, held in place by spit and grit.

"Don't you worry. I'll be making out same as always—like a bandit."

***

Singer stared at the screen for a second longer but then let his head drop forward and closed his eyes, feeling it build, the thin cold clack as a name fell into place preceded by a dissonant hum, the guidewires, the holdfasts pulled so tight that the faintest turn of his head set vibrations in motion, a plucked string. Usually the videos of those he had moved off the list provided relief. But today it gave little. The hum and rattle was cycling too fast, one name seeming to follow upon the next in the time it took to breathe.

Singer opened the latest *Living List*, selected the first name, watched the video and contributed twenty-five dollars before moving to the next name. By the time he had selected the first ten names, it had slowed, already leaving spaces where the tension was almost imperceptible for a few seconds. When he was done there was five hundred and thirty-four dollars left in the account. Singer logged out and left the library. He felt good.

***

Singer shifted to the other corner of the bank, leaning his hand-printed sign against the wall, crouching with the red brick against his back and settling the cup in front of his feet. There was less traffic here but a little more protection from the wind. Singer watched the old man shuffle across the intersection, the last of the sun scuttling for cover against the cold, the few lingering rays leaving the old man backlit, the curve of his head, neck and back as stark and black as etched charcoal on scritta, the curl as brittle and final as dried meat. He was too deliberate to make it across all four lanes on a single light, waiting on the island for the next chance to cross. The sidewalk had been cleared since the storm the evening before, but the trailing wind had drifted snow into shifting dunes and McGarrigle walked with his eyes on the ground placing each step carefully, before crossing the parking area to where Singer crouched.

"How are you doing?"

"Slow day, Mr. McG. But it'll pick up."

The old man tapped his wrist where a watch would have been.

"It's past four. Let's pack it in."

Singer shook his head.

"You go ahead, Mr. McG. The bank's open until nine and things will pick up when people get off work."

The old man leaned in to look closer and pointed at a spot on Singer's cheek.

"You've got a little white there, Peter. Probably best to quit while your ahead."

Singer forced a smile.

"I'm fine, Mr. McG. I'll see you back there. I'll be fine."

McGarrigle looked at him for several seconds then nodded and turned away. Singer watched him walk back across the lot and looked up at a woman who leaned to drop some coins into his cup.

"Thank you, ma'am."

But she was already by. A second woman, younger, handed some coins to the little girl holding her hand and the child dropped the coins in his cup. Singer had a flash of his mother turning in the pew to hand him coins to be placed in the collection plate. Singer smiled at the girl and she ducked her head, turning so that it was almost against her mother's leg. The woman paused.

"Are you warm enough?"

Singer looked at her and then away, embarrassed by the tears that caught, just short of spilling, at the corners of his eyes.

"I'm okay. I'm fine, ma'am."

It didn't feel enough.

"Thank you for asking. I… Thank you for asking."

The young woman stood, caught, frozen, then reached out as if to touch Singer's head and he felt himself leaning in. For what? Blessing? Divine help? Guidance? But then she drew back her hand as if suddenly aware again. She nodded at Singer, took her daughter's hand and walked away towards the bank. Singer followed her and then looked beyond for the old man. There was a shadow on the island between the lanes, a shape shaded somewhat darker than the surrounding gloom but Singer couldn't be sure it was him. Or if it was anything at all.

Chapter 38

The words the old man spoke drifted up like the smoke from a dying fire, without form or shape so that Singer knew the other man spoke but sensed none of the meaning. There was a little over a hundred dollars left in his account. Singer had donated another two hundred and fifty dollars earlier but the relief had been subtle and temporary. He had almost spent the last hundred, but the thought of having nothing, no way to still the noise, had stopped him.

The inside of his head hummed and rattled like the last moments before the gathering wind ripped the house free from what held it together and to the ground, the layered concrete, the fitted timber, the anchoring beams, before what held it together lost to what pulled it apart. And behind it all, the names falling into place at the end of the list, one after another.

"Peter?"

Singer wasn't sure how this single word had made it through, but the old man was out of his bunk, leaning on the bed frame, his lips close to Singer's ear.

"Are you alright, Peter? Should I get help?"

Singer would have laughed if he remembered how. What would help look like? Unmarked bills in a large leather satchel? Singer shook his head and raised his hand from the thin mattress before letting it drop back into place.

"It's okay, Mr. McG."

Singer looked for more. Words with more weight, more reassurance. But.

"It's okay."

***

Singer stood across the street from the bank waiting for it to open. The noise steadied in the morning, took on a rhythm, an order that allowed him to think. So, he was able to formulate an idea, figure out what he needed to do.

The vicious cold had broken for a day, the temperature almost reaching the melting point, but now it was back with ill intentions. Singer pulled at the edges of his toque, but the wool was stretched and worn and wouldn't cling to his head so he cupped a hand around each ear and tried to stamp warmth back into his feet.

Singer didn't recognize the first woman, who used the keys to open the door, but the woman who followed her had served him several times. The windows, dark when he had arrived, flickered bright and Singer caught a glimpse of both women turning the corner into the back office. Singer shifted so he could see the counter through the window and waited until the younger woman took her place at one of the computers. Singer hesitated before crossing the street. Every movie he had ever seen, they had hit the bank when it would have lots of cash. Singer had no idea how much money would be on hand at a small Thunder Bay branch on a Wednesday morning. Whatever she had would have to do.

Singer took a step into the street but had to pause to let a car go by. There wasn't much traffic, but it was beginning to build. He jogged the last couple of steps to the far side so a car didn't have to slow for him and pushed through the outer door. Singer paused at the ATM to pick up a deposit envelope. He dug in his pocket, around the crumpled plastic bag, for the pencil he had remembered to bring. Only at the last minute, as he had passed the sign-in counter at Shelter House. Nobody had been on duty and he had been able to lean across the counter and grab one of the short yellow pencils that were always lying around.

Singer looked at the blank side of the envelope, unsure of what to write. He could feel the noise and tension beginning to rise, feel what little clarity he had starting to dissipate. Singer wrote two words then scratched them out and began again before crumpling the envelope and grabbing a new one. He decided to keep it simple.

GIVE ME ALL YOUR MONEY.

LOVE PETER

It was always Cheryl he left messages for. It was automatic. He crumpled the envelope and wrote the first five words again, slipped the envelope into his coat pocket and pushed through the inner door. The woman looked up when she heard the door and smiled at Singer before returning to her computer, eager to get something finished before her first customer. Singer started through the roped aisle, but as he did the older woman came out of the back office and stood beside the teller, flipping open a manila folder to show her a document then pointing at the screen. The young woman looked up, noticed him waiting and held up a finger then turned back to her boss.

Her fingers were long and slim, and she had a ring on the hand that she held up. Engaged or married. Or maybe it was simply decorative. Maybe she was still waiting for the person she could love and who could love her. Singer had been lucky. He had loved Cheryl first and then no other woman.

The older woman motioned for the other woman to hit some keys, nodded at what popped up on the screen, said a few words to the teller, nodded again, gathered up the manila folder and walked back to her office. The young woman said something over her shoulder then turned and beckoned Singer forward. He stood for several seconds before he could make his feet move him to the counter. Singer faced the teller without speaking and she waited for him. Her expression shifted slightly from placid, waiting, to slightly puzzled as Singer continued to stand without speaking.

"Sir."

The sound of her voice shook Singer loose and he reached into his pocket, took out the deposit envelope and placed it face down on the counter with his hand still covering it. The teller looked at the envelope, then at him, then reached for the envelope expecting Singer to slide it across, but he pressed it tight against the counter. When she looked back at him she must have seen something, because her eyes widened. In the moment that her eyes widened, her hand still stretched towards the envelope, Singer recognized her. She had a daughter. And perhaps a husband. A facial expression related to the one he had seen in front of the bank, awareness caught in the frozen moment between conscious and subconscious, but here, as dread becomes more than just raised hackles and dimpled flesh and what you feel becomes what you know. Something let go, the lines of her face had been clean and smooth and even as a snapped sheet but now the skin loosened, rippling at the mouth and eyes and Singer wanted to reach out as she had, to smooth and calm, but he couldn't. He knew that he couldn't. Knew that he would never be able to do that for her. Singer pulled the envelope from the counter, stuffed it into his pocket and walked away. As he pushed the door into the ATM alcove open, Singer looked over his shoulder and she was standing still, one hand to her mouth, the other still stretched to where Singer had held the note against the counter.

The second door, out to the street, caught and Singer had a moment where he thought that she had hit a button that could lock down the building and he would be stuck inside waiting for the police to arrive, but he leaned into the door, it popped open and he was on the sidewalk. Singer paused at the curb waiting for the glare to pass, little more than a splash of light trailed by a hunched shadow, the car only coming into relief as it passed, the face that turned his way before shifting back to the road ahead, flashing pale and featureless, a burrowed animal chancing a glimpse then pulling back again.

Singer broke into a jog as he crossed the street up onto the opposite sidewalk and turned away towards home. The first couple of steps took him away from the pool of light beneath the streetlight and into the rising shadows. The first shot hit Singer high on the cheekbone just beneath his right eye. He had a moment where he thought that something had snapped loose in his head, the tension had stretched beyond the point that it could hold and the recoil had staggered him. But the second punch smashed his lips back into his teeth and he tasted the blood in his mouth as he went down. One of them bent close, booze- and sweat-soured, cut by stale cigarette smoke and the faint odor of cheap shampoo, tugged roughly at his jacket, found the pocket and pulled the envelope free.

"Fuck. It's empty!"

"Empty?"

"Fucking empty!"

"You said he had money."

"He's got money. He comes here all the time."

The cold of the sidewalk seeped up through Singer's coat and he curled to the side and pushed with his elbow, trying to find purchase to sit up.

"Where's the fucking money!"

Singer paused, waiting for his head, for the shimmer to settle. The smaller of them crouched so he could look directly into Singer's face, his eyes, small and almost perfectly round, set close, crowding his nose into the center of his face so that there seemed too much empty space at the edges.

"Where's the money?"

"The… The… no money."

His mouth felt too thick, like the pieces didn't fit the way they had and his memory of how to form words was failing him. The man slapped him twice, hard. Palm then back of hand.

"What's your PIN?"

Singer shook his head.

"What's your fucking PIN?"

Singer shook his head again. There were still three lives left. It wasn't much. But it was something. The guy tapped his cheek, shook his head and stood up. Singer pushed with his elbow so he tipped over onto all fours. The boot caught Singer in the middle of his body between his hip and chest and lifted him off the ground, driving the wind from his body but incongruously, landing him almost where he started. Singer's head hung down between his shoulders and he watched as a thin, dark line of blood-creased drool stretched towards the sidewalk, building momentum as it lost surface tension with his lips and teeth. Singer's arms shook and he wasn't sure how long they would hold him up.

"What's the PIN?"

Singer shook his head. It was enough to break the spittle free and it slumped against the snow and concrete. The sidewalk felt rough and cold against his hands and beneath his knees. Singer raised his head, looked for help, for somebody on the street who might see and call out. The sidewalk stretched away, a series of lit pools separated by long stretches of darkness until the streetlights gave out several blocks away. But it was empty. This time it exploded against his ribs. Bone, tendon and ligament broke and gave to allow his body a position and shape unfamiliar and unimaginable. Singer thought his heart had stopped. As if the force of the blow had thrown a breaker, freezing every bodily function exactly at the point it had been when the steel toe of the leather boot had struck his body. Except for the sound of a name falling into place, echoing like a dropped coin in an empty marbled room. A car passed on the street, the headlamps throwing light ahead, the two men stepped back into the shadows until it passed, and the light washed up and across Singer's body.

It began at the tips of his toes and the tips of his fingers, working from the edges to the center, feeling traveling through his hands and arms, feet and legs, from his cheeks across his neck and shoulders, drawing together at his core, a first false start of his heart, then a series of sputtered beats, a hesitation before it settled back into a steady rhythm and Singer could draw a chest-deep breath that released a new wave of pain where his diaphragm torqued a broken rib.

"Gimme the PIN, asshole!"

The names just kept coming, one after the other—what did another three matter? Singer shook his head. The boot came out of the dark and nudged his side. It was as if touching that single spot set off a pipe bomb, shrapnel hurtling to every edge of his body, every screw, nail, nut, bolt, tearing, piercing. But somehow completely contained by his body, stretching his skin to the place just before it would split and release some of the pain to a place beyond where Singer could sense. Singer rode it out, let it pull back, leaving him weak and panting. The smaller man crouched down again, the toe of his frayed sneaker almost against Singer's chin, saying nothing.

"7728."

Singer turned his head so he could watch them enter the bank and use the machine. The smaller man pulled the money from the slot. They stood for a moment near the door, arguing before the man holding the money peeled bills and handed them to the other guy. He was still wearing the red t-shirt beneath his parka. They left the bank, crossed the street, walked past not far from where Singer lay. Both men looked over and then away before they walked around the corner. Singer struggled to his feet and followed.

***

Singer looked up at the bottom of his bunk. The old man would be back soon. He should move up to his own bed. It had taken him a long time to walk back, much longer than it had taken him to get to the bank. He had been forced to stop often. By then the foot traffic had increased and when Singer stopped to lean against a wall or let himself down to the ground, it had drawn the occasional glance but no comment.

The old man had already been gone for the day when Singer had managed to make it to his bunk, and he had stood at the side leaning against the frame, imagining a way to get up to his bed before finally giving up and dropping into the bottom bunk. He had been in and out. Only able to sleep for minutes at a time, because any small movement could leave him shocked and breathless. Once, the need to relieve himself had been so great that he had managed to hobble to the toilet, the stream of urine, more than just pink if not crimson. There was a moment as he crossed the floor from the bathroom to his bed that he thought he would have to let himself down and crawl to the bunk. But the thought of having to rise again kept Singer on his feet. He collapsed into the lower bunk, bathed in sweat. The line drew tighter in his head, the tension building. Another name would drop soon.

He had given them the last of the money, convinced himself that there were only three lives to give—that it didn't matter. That avoiding the pain was more important than three lives. He raised his hand in the air then stopped himself from driving it down into the spot where he had been kicked. That would help nothing.

He would just have to get it back. Earn it back. No days off. Out there every day, until it was dark. He could make back what they had taken and more. That's what he would do.

***

"What happened to you, laddie?"

Singer shook himself awake, forced his eyes wide, reached to rub them but the movement forced him still. He turned his head to look at the old man, the red flush beneath his eyes and across his cheeks showing that he had stopped on the way back. McGarrigle frowned.

"Looks like a bad one. Not just a couple of wee shots?"

Singer shook his head.

"I'm fine. I'll be alright."

The old man snorted.

"So fine that you couldn't get up into your own bed?"

Singer nodded and tried to shift to swing his legs onto the floor, but the pain stopped him. The old man held both hands out.

"Whoa. Whoa, Peter. It's fine. I can take the top bunk until you're feeling better."

Singer tried again but only got a foot over the edge of the mattress before having to stop. McGarrigle placed a hand on Singer's foot and let himself down at the end of the bed.

"McMartin and Bendo?"

Singer nodded.

"They must have followed me to the bank. Jumped me when I came out."

"Bastards."

Quiet but acid. McGarrigle nodded at Singer's face.

"That's the least of it, eh?"

Singer laid a hand near his hip and winced.

"Yeah."

The old man leaned forward to look up and down the aisle that fronted the row of bunks.

"They let you stay here all day?"

Singer shook his head.

"I waited outside until Sharon went into the back office, then slipped by. Freddie's been by once, but he would have had to really be looking to see me."

McGarrigle nodded.

"What did they get?"

Singer looked up at the bottom of his mattress, then drew a long shuddering breath.

"I gave them my PIN."

The old man shrugged.

"You can change it."

"They emptied the account. Seventy-five dollars."

The old man shrugged again.

"It's just money."

Singer nodded.

"Yeah."

"Just money."

***

Singer woke with the old man's hand on his forehead. His eyes opened as if they had been greased with a mixture of spit and sand. McGarrigle drew it away when he saw Singer's eyes open.

"You were mumbling. And you're hot."

"I'm fine. Just need a little rest."

The old man reached into his jacket pocket, pulled out a thin battered flask, took a swig and held it out. Singer shook his head.

"If they catch you, they'll toss you."

McGarrigle took another short sip, screwed the top on and tucked it back into his pocket as if he hadn't heard.

"You don't look good, son. I'm not sure you'll sleep this one off."

"I'm all right, Mr. McG. I'll be better in the morning."

The old man looked at him, doubt in his eyes, then nodded and patted the bed beside his hip.

"You sleep. I'll be right here."

***

Singer woke early, the old man's low sputtering snore drifting down from above. Sometime during the night, the old man had managed to get into the top bunk. Singer wasn't sure how. He lay with his eyes closed, his lids heavy and aching. The tension in his head was higher but now it was fevered as if the line wasn't just drawn tight but spooling fast so the friction made it glow. But he needed to get up, start early and go to late, make the money back.

It took several minutes for Singer to shift and sit with his feet on the floor and it took all he had not to cry out several times. He sat at the edge of the bed recovering, draped in sweat, his eyes still closed.

***

Singer stood at the toilet waiting. He had been forced to open his eyes for the trip from bed to bathroom and though he wanted badly to let them drop closed again he forced them open. It had felt as if his bladder was ready to burst but now it took several seconds for the stream to begin and when it did it was crimson now, thicker than the day before. Singer stared down into the toilet as the water turned from clear to pink and then to red, before flushing and watching it spin away, leaving the water clear again, against the scarred greyed enamel beneath.

***

Singer closed his eyes waiting for the light to turn, somebody brushed against his side and he had to steady himself against somebody's shoulder who pulled away as soon as Singer made contact. It took a moment for Singer to find his balance, and when he opened his eyes the light was red again and so he waited. When he opened his eyes again, the light was still red. He looked to both sides, a young woman and an older man stood to his right and two teenagers waited on his left. He looked across the street, working hard to bring it into focus. A cop stood at the edge of the curb, watching. Singer straightened his shoulders, forced his eyes to stay open, but still missed the light when it turned green only moving forward when he saw the two teenagers step in front of him. Singer concentrated on getting one foot in front of the other, eyes ahead and focused far down the street, aiming for a spot far ahead rather than watching the asphalt at his feet. The cop drew alongside him slowed, head turning and Singer could feel the cop's eyes for several seconds, even after he had made it to the other side of the street.

***

Something was broken. Inside. Singer could feel it. He leaned against the side of the building, waiting for the flashbang to subside. They hit him every couple of blocks. He wasn't sure if it was a movement he made or just that the injury flared at regular intervals. This wasn't going to be better in a day. Or maybe even in a week. He was just going to have to tough this one out.

When he came out of it, he was still leaning against a building. He looked at the wall he was propped against, red brick, worn almost orange, the mortar flaking so that there were narrow, dark crevices where nothing bound adjacent bricks. Singer tilted his head to look up, four stories with a faded white eavestrough come loose and hanging almost to the window below. He couldn't remember if this was the same building or if he had moved on. Looking up caused Singer's head to spin and he turned so he could get both hands on the wall to steady himself. Somebody spoke behind him, but he couldn't make out what they said. Singer looked up the street to get his bearings and saw that it wasn't far now, only a few more blocks to the intersection by his bank. He looked down and saw that the small hand-printed sign and his coin can were still clutched in his fingers.

***

Singer put out his hand to touch the bank wall, to be sure that it was real and it felt rough and cold under his fingers. He stared at his hand for several seconds, confused. Where was his mitten? He turned to look back the way he had come, hoping it might be lying where he could see it but there was nothing, a blur of buildings and cars and people entering and emerging from one or the other. He turned his back to the wall and let himself down until he was sitting on the walkway leading to the bank entrance.

The coin can had tipped over and rolled a couple of feet away and the sign lay between Singer and the can. He leaned forward to grab it but the wind kicked up, caught and spun it away. Singer watched it settle several feet away, one corner caught up against where the snow, fresh, hard and fine as dust had gathered. It flipped loose several feet into the air before dropping again just beyond the walkway. It skittered and burled across the parking lot until he lost it beyond the edge of a parked car. He caught a last glimpse as it got tossed above the cars for a moment, framed against the haze of blowing snow and then it was gone. Singer watched for a long while but it never reappeared. He looked down again for the can, where he had seen it last, but it had rolled several feet further away. Singer considered going after it but changed his mind.

***

Singer heard her voice first, then felt her hand, then saw her face.

"Pull the van in close—you and David can get him in the side door. I doubt he'll be able to walk on his own."

When she had approached his table in Tim Horton's, Singer hadn't made note of her voice, but it had stuck with him, how each word seemed sure, unwavering, like a held note. It was unmistakably hers. Her fingers, long and slender, the back of her hand faintly scarred, found where the blowing snow had melted and then froze again at the edges of his lids and worked it free until Singer could open his eyes. She was crouched, one knee on the ground and pressed up against his shin, the other bent and turned towards a van pulling into the curb. Her face had changed little, still unlined except at the edges of her eyes and mouth, the skin greying, beginning to ash with age, but the black, deep, glowing rich and bright, just beneath the surface. Her eyes, deeper than even Singer had remembered, drew him in, gathered him close though her hands rested at her sides. Her braids peeked out from beneath a bulky wool cap and Singer tried to reach to touch her face, but his hand fell back into his lap. She lay her fingers on his cheek.

"Hello, Peter. We've come for you."

When Singer exhaled, his head emptied into the blowing winter wind.

BOOK 3

Chapter 39

Singer noticed the stillness first. The thrum and buzz was gone, the spill of static discharge drawn, so that the flow was steady silent and laminar. He reached out from the quiet place, exploring, testing for where the tension built, the place where the ratchet began to turn, but couldn't find it. Singer shifted and pain caught the breath in his chest.

"It'll hurt for a while."

Singer moved his head cautiously until he could see her. She no longer wore the wool cap, her hair braided and beaded tight to her scalp. She gestured to the man sitting just off her right shoulder and then to the man leaning in the door frame.

"This is my son, David. And that's Bobby. He's the one who operated on you."

Singer's eyes drifted to the tree just beyond the facing window. The blooms were thick as roosting monarchs, obscuring leaf and branch, each pink flower cupped like a beckoning hand.

"Where am I?"

The woman stood.

"You should rest."

The young man stepped to the side so she could pass and then followed her to the door.

"Who are you?"

The woman paused at the door and looked over her shoulder.

"We'll talk, Peter. You rest for now."

***

"We almost lost you."

Singer sat in a plush easy chair the younger of the two nurses had pulled up to the window before helping him from the bed. It had only been a few days but already petals were flaking from some of the blooms, dappling the grass in a flurry of petals like pink snow.

"Almost lost me?"

The woman nodded, her face grave.

"They ruptured your spleen. We didn't realize until the evening of the first day. By then you had been bleeding for more than 24 hours. Bobby had to operate in transit."

"In transit? In the van?"

The woman's mouth curved slightly—the intention of a smile.

"No. Not in the van. We have friends along the way. They helped us out."

Singer looked away out the window.

"Look. I appreciate what you've done for me. I don't want to seem ungrateful but who are you? And where am I?"

"My name is Angella Carter. You're in Mississippi."

She pointed at Singer.

"And this is what we do."

Singer shook his head.

"I don't understand."

She paused.

"Peter. How are you feeling?"

Singer touched his side.

"Better. It's a little sore. But better."

Angella shook her head and tapped her temple.

"Here."

Singer looked at her for a long time.

"How did you know?"

She shrugged without looking away.

"It affects people differently. Some hear voices. Some see things, visions. For others, it's a feeling, like their drowning, or trapped in a tight space."

Singer placed a hand on his thigh to stop his foot from tapping. He shook his head.

"A ratchet."

Singer put a finger to the corner of one eye then pulled at his eyelid. Angella waited.

"Always turning. Always drawing the band a little tighter, coiling the spring, until it felt as if my head would come off my shoulders."

Singer looked up from his lap.

"Ma'am?"

She nodded.

"When you were a kid? In springtime? You ever pull dandelions? Hold the stem with your fingers and curl your thumb under the flower? Then 'Momma had a baby and its head popped off'."

She nodded again.

"Yeah. I thought about that a lot."

He was quiet for a few seconds.

"Then another name would drop. It made a sound. Like two stones colliding with something small and soft caught between."

Angella looked down at her hands in her lap.

"I'm sorry."

Singer watched her, waiting. She toyed with the index finger of her left hand for several seconds before looking up then reached out to touch the place where the edge of his eye creased.

"It was sealed shut. Felt like it might never open again if we couldn't get it open now."

She stood up.

"I'm sorry, Peter. We'll talk again."

***

Angella walked beside Singer, allowing him to set the pace. She pointed at a bench between two of the pillars supporting the gabled roof of the three-story house, but he shook his head.

"I've been sitting enough."

The grounds were large and well kept, the grass mowed tight and even, the shrubs ringing the house shaped and symmetrical, the small gardens beneath each of the half dozen magnolias weeded and the perennials evenly spaced. Even the falling magnolia petals looked as if they had been layered and placed by hand. She circled the house, crossed the circular driveway in front of the double-doored front entrance and started the second circuit before she began to speak.

"We started this mission thirty-five years ago. My husband and I. Archie was a lawyer. Got his degree from Hampton University in 1974 and we were married in 1975. Had our first son, Michell, in 1978 and David two years later."

Singer looked over.

"David's forty-four years old?"

She smiled at him.

"We Carters have always aged well."

She took a moment to start again.

"Archie…he was always restless, determined, trying to make a difference. Especially for black folks. Felt like he had been blessed and needed to find a way to pass along the blessing. But when Michell died…"

She took several steps without speaking.

"…something changed."

She looked over, noticed the questioning glance.

"Leukemia. It took eighteen months from the first diagnosis and he was gone."

"Archie took on every cause. Death-row inmates, missing persons, access to education… It was like Michell's death was a warning—he hadn't done enough. And Michell was the first installment on what he owed."

She looked over at Singer.

"He never said that out loud. But I could tell it was what he was thinking. He wasn't eating, barely sleeping, He was spending almost no time with David, wouldn't touch me. Like, if he could keep 'their' attention off of us, we wouldn't be in danger. I couldn't see a way out."

We had circled the house again and Bobby stood on the front porch, arms crossed, looking out past the dirt road in front of the house to the even leafy green rows of soybeans on the other side. We nodded as we passed but didn't speak.

"Archie got invited to travel with a delegation of US citizens to Zimbabwe. We had just appointed our first ambassador to Zimbabwe and committed more than 200 million dollars and we were trying to create links between our people and theirs."

Angella made a face.

"It didn't take long for that to go south. But Archie came back different. No more settled, still restless but focused. It took him three weeks to tell me what he had planned."

She didn't ask this time but just went and sat on the bench, patting the seat beside her.

"He had seen things in Zimbabwe that he could not shake, people dying for lack of a dollar. A single dollar. To buy food. Or water. Or medicine. And he was tired of helping from a distance. That it was individuals who needed help. If the world was to survive, we had to reach out, one hand to the next, feel skin on skin."

She patted my leg without looking over.

"That's what he said. 'If the world was to survive…' But I think what he really meant was 'If he was to survive…' And he explained his plan to me. That he would become A Seeker."

Singer looked over.

"A Seeker?"

She nodded.

"That's what he called it."

The wind stirred and she watched a petal shake free of a blossom and spin to the ground beneath before starting again.

"He would quit his job and travel back to Zimbabwe. He would travel around the country seeking out people in need. And help them. That's all. He would help them. And he was very clear—the difference between living and dying was almost always money and almost always a few dollars."

She paused.

"And he did it. He knew…we both knew that David and I couldn't come with him. We would stay and do what we could from here. We had some savings, but we went through most of it in the first year. It sounds crazy but I think it saved him. Saved us. I don't know how much longer he could have continued that way he had after Michell's death. Each day had shaved him a little finer and I woke each morning fearing that there would be nothing left."

She looked over.

"Have you heard enough for one day?"

Singer shook his head.

"He came back twice that first year. To raise more money. First talking to his law cronies, but then reaching wider, universities, black organizations, usually being refused but occasionally finding a sympathetic ear and a few more dollars before returning to Zimbabwe."

"Just walking around?"

She nodded.

"It was hard in those days because Archie had to carry the money with him. He was robbed and beaten twice in the first year. When I sent cash, it had to be wired. He wouldn't carry all of it, he used a bank in Harare. But when he came back the first time, a scar over one eye and missing one front tooth, he was whole. The man I had married and who had fathered our children. It was like fearing the night would never end and then seeing the sun break across the horizon. I cried. He thought I was crying about the marks on his face and body and held me as he had not in years."

"Word began to get out and by our fifth year we had raised enough money to buy this place—we needed a place for David and me to live and to run the organization—and there were three more Seekers."

"Three more?"

Angella nodded.

"Two of them didn't work out. Well-meaning but not prepared to make the sacrifices. Archie had to travel to Ghana and then the Sierra Leone to bring them back. We realized then that we had to select Seekers more carefully. That there weren't many who could do the work.

But Archie learned a lot in those years. About what it took to be a Seeker but also how to raise money. Early on, he realized that pictures worked better than words. That if he could show a dying child, people would donate more. He brought a camera—a Polaroid—in his fourth year. It wasn't long before he figured out that it was not just seeing the lost that brought in the most money—it was the lost and the found—the saved. And that became the pitch. Archie and Rebecca, the other Seeker, would send the polaroids back and I would use them to find donations. And that was my pitch, that you were looking at the face of a child who had been saved by a few dollars just like the ones in your pocket."

"How many are there? Seekers?"

She looked up and to her right as if seeing something in the sky, tapping her fingers one after the other and soundlessly shaping their names as she counted.

"Eleven. We have had as many as seventeen over the thirty-five years. But we're down to eleven. It's hard. People get tired. And they die. It's thirty-five years now. Sometimes they die.

"But it's easier now. No more big bulky camera and having to keep care of the photographs. Now we have photos and video uploaded and available within seconds. Easier for us, David and I, too. Because our pitch is no longer 'You can save a child *like* this child.' It's that you can save this child and see them brought back from the edge."

She looked over.

"I guess I don't need to tell you."

"And your husband?"

She passed a hand across her eyes.

"We haven't heard from him for three years. But I believe he's still working. I'm almost certain I still see his work. He has a gift for it."

They were silent for a long while before Singer looked over.

"Why am I here?"

Angella stood up. For the first time, Singer could see the years and the loss in her face and shoulders, in the way skin slouched against cheek, jaw and brow.

"We'll talk again tomorrow."

Singer watched her walk across the grass and around the corner then stood and followed.

***

They sat together, David and Angella, on the far side of the four-person dining table. David gestured at the single chair across from them. Singer sat and pulled in a little closer to the table. He smiled, first at David then Angella.

"Job interview?"

David smiled. He had his mother's features but blunted in places where Angella was fine, almost sharp—a murmur of his father.

"Of a sort."

"What sort?"

David Carter nodded.

"Twice you've asked my mother why we brought you here."

He paused as if waiting for confirmation and Singer nodded.

"Why do you think we brought you here?"

Singer looked at Angella then back to her son.

"Because if you hadn't, I would have died."

Carter frowned.

"Yes. You probably would have. But that's not why we brought you."

Singer knew but waited.

"We wish to invite you to become a Seeker."

Singer nodded.

"Why me?"

Angella spoke.

"Selecting Seekers is not an exact science. But we've got better at it over the years. You have the mark of a Seeker."

"The mark of…?"

Angella paused.

"An extraordinary willingness to sacrifice for others. A compulsive need to help others."

Singer could feel the anger building in his chest.

"I'm the right guy for the job because I was willing to blow up my whole life for this crazy shit!? Lose my family, my job, every friend I ever had, my fucking sanity!"

Angella and David sat watching him. Singer looked down at his hands.

"You send out those videos. And you know what it's going to do. You know you are destroying people's lives."

Singer held up his hands to stop them from speaking though neither had moved.

"I know. It's for a good cause. I know. But still. You know when you click 'send' you are ruining somebody's life."

Angella shook her head.

"The emails are only intended to get donors. We send out millions of them each year. Most people ignore them—they have the same impact as Viagra spam. A few choose to give money. Most give once. A handful give several times. A tiny fraction never stop giving."

Singer closed his eyes took a deep breath then opened them again.

"So, I'm one of those suckers."

Angella smiled and shrugged.

"If that's how you want to look at it, Peter. But we don't see a deep concern for others as a character flaw."

Singer held her gaze for several seconds.

"How many people do you visit in person?"

"Very few. Maybe a half dozen a year."

"Why me?"

It was Angella's turn to take a deep breath.

"We have become much more sophisticated over the years, Peter. It's amazing what we can learn from how people interact with the emails. The first video you open puts code onto your machine that lets us track your behavior, how much you watch of a video, where you stop watching, how often you watch it, even how often you hover your mouse over the link before deciding not to press it. This allows us to identify which recipients will become long-term donors—*if* they make the first donation. If they are able to see the first life they save. You showed all the signs."

She gestured at the three of them, herself, her son and Singer.

"We weren't thinking of this. We were just seeing you as a potential long-term donor."

"So, somebody who's willing to screw up their life but not quite as terminally as I did."

David shook his head.

"A few of our donors are affluent. They make significant contributions for many, many years without creating a wrinkle in their lives. Their spouses know and approve, their friends may or may not know. But what does it matter? They save lives every year without disrupting their own."

Singer looked to his left out the window.

"But some end up like me?"

Angella and her son nodded but only Angella spoke.

"Yes."

Singer looked back at them.

"And you're okay with that?"

Angella nodded again.

"Under the circumstances, perfectly okay with it."

Singer sat for several seconds before speaking.

"What if I refuse?"

"We provide bus fare home. Wherever you decide that is."

Singer smiled, the angle not quite right like he was searching for a different expression and couldn't quite find it.

"And what happens to me?"

Angella's face softened.

"I'm not sure, Peter. We can't reverse this. The changes this has made, for better or worse, are yours to deal with. What I can assure you is that you will receive no more emails. You have done enough."

Singer tapped his temples with both hands.

"And my head?"

Angella shrugged.

"I don't know, Peter. I don't know."

Singer nodded. It was still there. He was sure. Buried. Waiting.

"I'm in. What choice do I have?'

He knew he had been from the moment they asked.

***

David waited for his mother to leave the room and then pulled his chair closer.

"I'm sure you have a lot of questions, but let me go through my little spiel here and then you can ask any questions you still have. Alright?"

Singer nodded.

"We assign you a territory. Yours will be India/Bangladesh. It's been fifteen years since a Seeker has been seen in India or Bangladesh. Many will have heard of Seekers but be unsure if they are real.

The organization provides a modest income—modest even by Indian and Bangladeshi standards—not enough to rent a long-term apartment or feed yourself indefinitely. So, to some extent you will rely on the kindness of strangers."

Carter held up his hand.

"Let me finish. Then ask all of your questions."

Singer nodded.

"You will be provided with a phone for taking pictures and videos. If you lose it or it is stolen, we'll replace it. But try not to lose it. It will be loaded with all the apps required to transfer money to you from donors. That said, relatively few of the people you will be dealing with have bank accounts, so they will need cash. We will set you up with accounts at several of the banks in India. Many of those banks are also established in Bangladesh. In addition, you'll have a Western Union account. It may take some work to get donated money to the people who need it, but you'll get better at this as you get more familiar with the country. Because so much money is transferred to India from families abroad, even relatively small towns usually have ways to access cash from banks or Western Union.

There is no itinerary or schedule. There are no quotas. You move around as you see fit. You decide who to help. We don't have rules for this. You're the Seeker. It's your job to find those most in need. We will not question your decisions. Except donated money can never be used for anything or anybody but the person intended.

Practice with your phone. Remember, it's the videos and photos that do the work. Get good at them. Think about angles, lighting, the aspects of videos that hooked you and try to mimic those."

Carter started to move on then stopped himself.

"Oh yeah. Remember that when money is donated, you need the 'after' shot. So, you either have to stick around until you can get the shot you need or make sure you circle back within a couple of weeks to get the shot. No exceptions. Every donation earns an 'after' shot. Our experience is that donors track this very closely."

Singer raised his hand. Carter made a face.

"You're already starting to bug me, Peter."

"How often do people donate? How often do we save them?"

Carter looked down at his hands then back up.

"Hard to say."

Singer cocked his head.

"Based on what you just told me, it should be easy. How many of the total number of videos end up with associated 'saved' videos. How can you not know the number?"

Carter looked across the table.

"I didn't say we didn't know the number. It's just hard to say. Between two and three percent."

Singer rocked back in his chair.

"So, for every hundred people I choose, ninety-seven or ninety-eight will die?"

Carter nodded.

"I know. You can't think about it that way."

Singer thought back to the names he had meant to watch but had dropped off the bottom of the list before he could. Singer nodded for Carter to continue.

"There are two unbreakable rules. We call them Seeker's Laws. First, you can never eat unshared food. If you buy, find or are given food, no matter how little, you must always find somebody to share it with. And you must learn to accept shared food when it is offered. It will be difficult at times because people will have so little. But when people offer to help, you should accept. You will become known for giving, people will be looking for opportunities to help in return. Don't deny them. And you will likely need the help. Second, you may never sleep under an unshared roof. If for some reason you must rent a room for the night, you must find somebody who needs shelter. And if you are offered shelter, accept it. That's it. You leave in three days."

"Three days?"

Carter nodded.

"Any reason to wait?"

Singer made a face and shook his head.

"I guess not. Do I land in Mumbai?"

Carter smiled.

"Land in Mumbai? That's funny. We run this thing on a budget, Peter. You'll ship out from Miami, thirty-two days to Chennai if the weather's good. You'll be helping in the kitchen. Any more questions?"

He had a thousand but none that weren't just a version of 'what the hell are you talking about?'

***

Singer watched the crane winch one of the last of the cargo containers off the dock then slide it out across the ship and lower it into place like the last block in a rusted Lego tower. Singer tilted his head back and shaded his eyes from the sun, still high enough in the sky that it peeked over the shoulder of the shipping container tower. The container settled slightly askew on the stack, eleven high, and the crane operator lifted, swiveled and dropped the container neatly into place, like readjusting a spoon in the utensil drawer. A gull disturbed by the metallic clang lifted off a few feet into the air then settled back at the edge of a container, glancing down to Singer then away. The winch and hook released and then slid back along the rail and descended swiftly to where the next container had been dropped into place. The crane operator inside the glassed cage leaned forward to watch the hook and winch settle above the next container, operating the levers without watching his hands.

Singer turned back to the rail, looking across a short strip of water then a busy expanse of concrete to where David and Angella had parked near a low one-story grey building. Angella stood with her hands resting on a low fence that separated the parking lot from the loading dock and David stood by the back of the van, looking at something he held in both hands, maybe a map. A forklift skimmed by and she was gone for a second but then popped back into view in the same position as before he had lost sight of her. He couldn't see the expression on her face, but it would be as it always was, calm, still, worn, sculpted and shaped by sorrow and determination.

The ship rocked almost imperceptibly and Singer shifted his feet to recover. He looked out past the crane, beyond Angella and her son, able to see a thin strip of ocean and the edge of the Florida coastline from where he stood. If he followed that line almost due north to West Palm Beach, angled right and followed the coast, past Virginia Beach, Washington, Philadelphia, New York, by Bar Harbor, bear right, skirt the northern tip of Nova Scotia, Cape Breton island, through the Cabot Strait around the northeastern thumb of New Brunswick and into the mouth of the St. Lawrence he would only be a few hours away, a straight shot upriver to Brockville and a forty-five-minute drive to see the boys. Not even to hold them. Just to stand across the street in the shadow of the big maple near where they waited for the school bus and watch them play in the driveway, hammering shots at the net but missing, punching shallow depressions in the garage door behind.

The sound of metal on metal as the crane began to move, sliding down the tracks to the next stack of crates waiting to be loaded, pulled Singer back. He watched the crane glide by. The operator noticing him and raised a hand, Singer was afraid she would be gone but once the crane had passed she was still standing at the rail. She had waited. She raised a hand and held it in the air. Singer raised his in return and they stood for a moment, each with an arm in the air. Then Angella lowered hers, turned and walked back towards o the van, crossing behind and around to the passenger side. Singer could tell she spoke to her son by the way his head came up and his eyes followed her as she stepped beyond the van and out of sight. He seemed to reply, then pause as if waiting for a response, then folded the map—it was a map—and got in the driver's side. The taillights flashed on, David backed out of the spot, pulled onto the road leading from the port and into Miami. Singer watched until what he could see of the van blended in with other vehicles and he was no longer sure he was watching Angella and David. Singer stood on the rail until the Margarethe M edged out of berth, swiveled east for Chunnai and the dock and Miami skyline dissipated into the evening gloom.

Chapter 40

Singer stood on the dusty dirt road at the base of the hill. From what he could see, the town had changed little in the four years since he had been here last. He removed his hat and ran his hand through his hair, almost to his shoulders, blunt and uneven at the tips as if chopped with a dull blade, before reaching for the pack at his feet and shifting it across one shoulder, trying not to think of the kati roll tucked in the bottom. He had bought two in Krishnanagar, the day before last and shared the first with the driver of the truck—a Tata Ace held together by baling wire, spit and char magaz—who had let him out near Hatra on the evening before last. Singer had been walking since then.

Singer leaned into the hill, fatigued in his feet and shoulders. Incongruously, the dirt path turned to asphalt for the last and steepest two hundred meters. Singer reached the crest of the hill and looked down at the village. It was as he remembered it—a cluster of small round huts, thatched wall and roof, ragged as if constructed from scraps discarded by wind and rain, except even here, where there was rarely enough for food, somebody had tagged three of the huts. Faded black letters that Singer couldn't make out. Two roofs were covered in shredded tarpaulin. The monsoons were still a few weeks away, but they had likely been installed during the last rainy season when the roofs began to leak.

A middle-aged woman crouched by the single water pump, filling a crumpled plastic water bottle. She wore a simple white sari and the mud around the pump had soiled the hem while she crouched to get water. She finished filling the bottle then remained crouched as she watched Singer draw closer.

"Nomoskar."

She nodded.

"Hello."

"Amar nam Peter."

She nodded again.

"I remember you."

Singer nodded. The woman gathered up her water and stood.

"You weren't able to help."

Singer nodded again.

"Are you hungry?"

She looked at him, but Singer wasn't exactly sure what she saw. It had been more than a year since he had seen a mirror, only catching his reflection in panes of glass or puddled water. He tugged self-consciously with the stub of his left pinky, wiping the dust free where it had gathered in the lines at the edge of his eye. It took several seconds for her to reply.

"How long since you've eaten?"

Singer shook his head, waving the question away.

"I have food. Will you share it with me?"

She looked at him then at his backpack. Her face had slackened at cheek and chin where flesh once gathered beneath holding it smooth and taut had melted away so that there was little but tendon and bone and the skin draped in subtle folds. She didn't answer and Singer gave a small shrug so that the strap slid down his arm and he could lower the pack to the ground, slowly as if trying not to disturb a wary animal. Singer crouched beside the bag, flipped open the top flap and dug into the main pocket, feeling around until he found it, wrapped in a scrap of old newsprint. Singer pulled it from the bag and showed her. Her eyes left his face and settled on the food. He held it towards her.

"Will you join me?"

She looked from the sandwich to him and then back.

"And my son?"

Singer nodded.

"Of course."

She gestured at the food.

"Put it away. Follow me."

She spun on her heel and Singer followed. Hers was the fourth hut in the line. Word had spread, a man stood in the doorless entrance to the second hut, two small children peering out around his legs. He held a crude hand-carved unlit pipe between his teeth. The man watched him but ignored the woman. She hurried by, head down, and led Singer to the back of her hut, barely space for a single person to pass between the huts on either side. Her son, a young man in his early twenties, sat on a rickety wooden crate cleaning a small fish.

"Aamod?"

The young man looked up and tilted his head so that he could see out of his good eye.

"We have a visitor. The Seeker."

The man looked at Singer for several seconds, nodded then returned to the fish, scraping at the insides with a small metal kitchen blade missing a handle.

"He wishes to share food. Could you please get plates? And the water? I left it by the door."

The young man rose, was gone for a few seconds and returned with three chipped porcelain plates and three small plastic cups, blue, green and yellow, each frayed at the sipping edge and containing water. The plates might have once been orange, but now they were the color of baked mud. Aamod crouched and placed the plates on the crate, though there was barely space to hold them. Singer pulled the kati from his pack, lay it on one of the plates and peeled back the newsprint. The scent of curried mutton rose sweet and pungent as flowering jasmine. Singer pointed at the roll.

"It has been two days."

The woman shook her head.

"Egg? Maybe not. But mutton? It's fine."

The young man held out the blade he had been using to clean the fish without looking away from the food. Singer nodded for the woman to take it, she bowed her head in thanks.

She held the blade for several seconds, examining the kati, then drew a thin shallow line before pausing again. She examined the kati, nodded then drew a second shallow line and inspected once more. When she was satisfied, she cut through the kati, placed one piece on each of the two empty plates then looked at Singer. He shook his head.

"I am in your home."

She examined the pieces carefully, chose what might have been the largest piece and handed it to her son. He raised the food to his mouth but she stopped him, slid a plate towards Singer then spoke a few words in Bengali he didn't understand, then nodded for them to begin.

***

"I am looking for a family."

The woman had stacked the plates and returned them to her house. She, Singer and her son sat in a circle around the wooden crate.

"The name I was given is—"

The woman shook her head again.

"I know the family."

She gestured to her left.

"They live in another village."

Singer frowned.

"I was told they were here."

The woman shook her head.

"Whoever spoke to you was wrong. They live in another village."

Something about the way she ended her sentence told Singer she wasn't done.

"They have nothing. Her husband was struck by an illness. He cannot move and but he doesn't die. And she must care for him. She has a young daughter. Before the illness, they were poor but they could eat. Since…"

The woman shrugged. Singer nodded. It might be the same family of which he had been told. But it didn't matter.

"How far?"

"Three maybe four hours."

Singer nodded and began to stand up.

"Thank you. I should go then."

The woman put her hand on his arm and shook her head.

"You should stay with us. It will be dark soon. And you will need help finding them. I can take you in the morning."

Singer shook his head.

"No. I've troubled you enough."

She patted his hand again.

"It is no trouble. Tomorrow, Aamod will catch another fish and I will show you the way."

Singer nodded and sat down again.

"Thank you. For your kindness."

The woman nodded, pleased.

***

Aalia pointed at the shack. It might have been thatched at one time but now it was scraps of broken, discarded plywood held standing by the weight of corrugated metal serving as a roof. The roof gapped in spots where the metal had been flayed back, leaving ragged edges. It would provide some shelter from the rain but the inhabitants would not remain dry once the heavy rains arrived.

"She is inside."

It had taken most of the morning and Singer was tired. He wasn't hungry. For breakfast, they had shared the fish, roasted in a small terracotta oven still half-covered in glazed ceramic, and three small potatoes, which Aamod had peeled as carefully as he might have shelled an egg, buried in the coals to bake. But his eyes felt gritty and sore and his head ached. The hat helped, but the sun seemed to find a way to burrow through the thick, coarse fabric. Aalia looked as she had when Singer had seen her crouched by the pump, alert and watching. Singer paused.

"Will you come in?"

Aalia shook her head.

"We have never met."

Singer nodded, relieved. It was best with just the family.

"Thank you, Aalia."

The woman looked back the way they had come.

"You will be able to find your way?"

Singer smiled and nodded. The woman smiled back at him.

"Okay then."

She turned away and took three steps before coming back and standing in front of him.

"Thank you for the kati."

"Thank you for the fish."

She looked at the hut, then back at Singer and patted his arm.

"I will pray for her."

Singer watched her walk away until she rounded a bend in the path and he could no longer see her.

***

The child lay in a small hollow in the dirt floor of the shack. Singer couldn't tell if the hollow had been shaped deliberately for comfort or simply worn to its present shape. She wore a grey shift that came almost to her ankles, but her feet were streaked with dirt where she must have scraped against the floor. She looked about five or six years old, but Singer knew that the malnutrition could stunt growth in a way that was deceptive. Her mother, her face pinched as if at the very beginning of a drying process that would leave her desiccated and inanimate, looked at him in the doorway then back to her daughter. The woman remained crouched at her side, soaking a small scrap of cloth in a tiny clay bowl before she wrung it out and wiped her daughter's cheeks and forehead. A man lay behind her against the back wall. He didn't move, but Singer could make out the wet gleam of his eyes in the dimness of the shack.

"You know who I am?"

The girl's mother looked at him without comprehension. Singer tried again with the few words in Bengali that he had. It took a moment, but she nodded without looking away from her daughter.

"Hy, Anbesi."

The Seeker.

He nodded.

"Hy."

Singer looked at the child.

"What is her name?

The woman looked up, confused. Singer tried again.

"Tara nama ki?"

The woman looked at her daughter than at Singer. For a moment he thought she still did not understand.

"Aaheli."

Singer set the pack at his feet, dug inside and pulled out the cell phone. He had charged it in Krishnanagar and not used it since, so it would be fine. It gurgled musically as it fired up. Singer stepped in closer, circled the place where the child lay, identifying where the best angle would be, where he could capture her face, still and brown, but also the hut and where she lay and her mother crouched beside her, the last quivering guywire between her daughter and whatever came next. Singer found his spot and the woman looked up at him for a second time. He gestured at the phone and then at the child.

"May I?"

She seemed to understand, nodded then returned to her daughter. Before Singer could begin, she spoke, a flurry of words that Singer didn't understand. Singer stared back at her, unsure, and she repeated the same words again. He shook his head.

"Will it help?"

The voice came from the man in the corner, the accent thick but the words discernible.

"She asks if this will help our daughter."

Singer shook his head.

"I don't know."

The man translated for his wife and she spoke again.

"She wants to know if it ever helps."

"Sometimes."

The woman's husband translated again and his wife's response was short.

"Often?"

Singer shook his head.

"Not often."

The woman looked up, her eyes weary, near empty, almost dry, the last moment before the rain seeps into the sand and there is nothing but a dark stain. She held his for several seconds before nodding. Singer started the video. He began at her face. He no longer shook. In the early days, it had been difficult to keep the camera still, but it had been a long time since his hand had been anything but steady. Her face held the same fevered glow most of them carried in their last days, the last spark of vitality leaking free, so that her skin wasn't simply brown or even golden brown but a sort of burnished topaz, lit from beneath so one couldn't deny what was about to be lost. What energy remained in her body could no longer be used to do anything she needed, move, think, talk, pray—it was simply burning up so that for a while there was light…and then only heat. He held on her face for a minute or more, shifting the angle of the phone slightly so that the shading shifted on her face as if her face was somehow completely still but changing expression. After that, he let the camera trail down her body, the shift nearly flat along the ground, the child's body wasted so that it left almost no impression, as if the shift had been laid out for somebody but they had chosen not to wear it. Singer allowed the camera to trace the inside of the hut, what little there was of it, settling on the dim form of the man at the back, then to the woman crouched beside her daughter. Singer clucked his tongue and she looked up and he could see that he had captured her expression, empty but waiting to be filled. Then he returned the camera to the child's face.

"Wendy. Twenty-five dollars can save Aaheli's life. Just follow the instructions in the email."

Singer hit the 'Stop Recording' button and saved to his Videos folder. The woman did not look up from her daughter. Singer turned, ducked even lower to stoop through the gap that served as a door. He tapped for Wi-Fi and saw that there were two bars. It would be enough. Singer scrolled through his contacts list, found Angella's email, attached the video and sent it. He waited for the 'ping' of the return email. It took a couple of minutes.

GOT IT.

Now, he waited.

***

Singer had stayed through the night. There had been no shelter, no place to sleep, but it didn't really matter—he could never really sleep while he waited. Even after all this time, he wasn't able to sleep until he knew if the money was arriving.

Singer had still held out hope when the first hint of morning, a faint exhalation of grey, more threat than promise, had shadowed the eastern horizon. If the money arrived, he would have to make his way to Chapra, the nearest town, to buy food, perhaps blankets.

But it was late afternoon now. More than twenty-four hours. The money never arrived after twenty-four hours had passed. Singer stood from the roadside, one knee cracking as it unfolded. He looked at the hut, silent and grey under the cold steel of the overcast sky. The child's mother was still awake. She didn't look up when Singer ducked into the tent. He had missed the child's last breath but only by moments—the woman's hands rested on her daughter's body, trying to hold in the last of her warmth. This video was shorter and the girl was barely visible on the screen against the grey of the dirt floor. Singer stopped recording and let himself out.

He took a moment to send the video, grabbed his pack from beside the path, shrugged into it and walked back the way he had come.

***

The sun had set by the time Singer reached Ailia's village. He passed through quietly and without notice. The night was dark, silent and empty. The road out of town wound away to the western horizon and he walked slow and steady, grey against the night, a single tear trailing down a still black cheek.

Other fine books available from Histria Fiction:

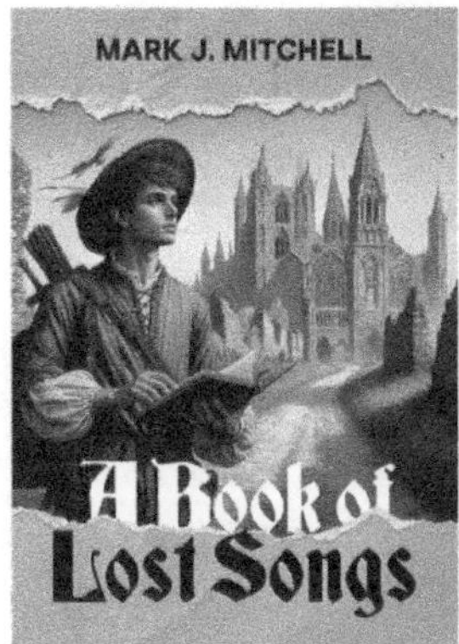

For these and many other great books visit

HistriaBooks.com